THE VICTOR OF DAY AND NIGHT

The Victor of Day and Night

Copyright © 2023 by Malina Dahl

All rights reserved.

This novel is entirely a work of fiction. The names, characters, and incidents portrayed in it are the work of the author's imagination. Any resemblance to actual persons, living or dead, events or localities is entirely coincidental.

No part of this book may be reproduced in any form or by any electronic or mechanical means, including information storage and retrieval systems, without written permission from the author, except for the use of brief quotations in a book review.

First Edition published December 2023

Published by Malina Dahl

Map Design © 2023 by Abigail Hair

Cover Design and Illustration © 2023 by Malina Dahl

Identifiers

ISBN: 978-82-693407-1-6 (paperback)

ISBN: 978-82-693407-0-9 (hardback)

ISBN: 978-82-693407-2-3 (ebook)

Til Lille M

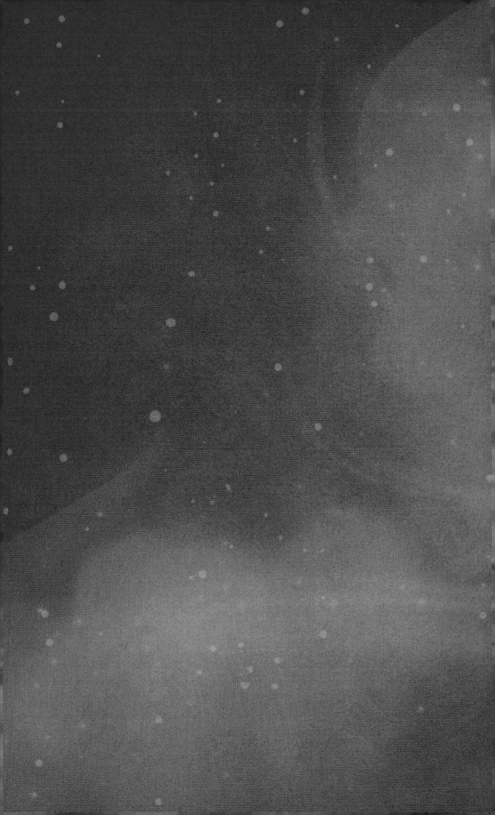

PART 1

RISING SUN

CHAPTER ONE

The dead man's pewter eyes are unseeing as my dagger carves swirling lines into his skin. His head is tipped back toward the sky, his soul ready to depart for the Shadow Realm. Drops of crimson prickle from his pale skin, and the memorized words pour from my lips.

"From the earth and the sky were you gifted and made, in the earth and the sky will you stay, from the earth and the sky will you rise again. By the sky above and the earth below, may your life essence only be borrowed instead of gone as I connect your end to my beginning."

A chill prickles over my skin as I rip away the sleeve of my dress and repeat the motions on my skin, the tip of my dagger still dripping with the man's blood.

There is no pain when I break the skin on my forearm, only the trickle of my blood, the crimson liquid mixed with traces of gold so faint I'm not sure if I'm only imagining it.

"From the Sun came the light and life, and the dark and shadows from the Moon. By the sky above and the earth below, attach one's beginning to another one's end."

A wind blows through the clearing, the breeze too cold and eerie to be a part of the bright summer day. The magic is tangible in the air as it settles on my skin, and shudders rock through me until my whole body is trembling.

The wind starts to roar. It blows my white hair around my face like a wave of ice crashing toward me. The sun disappears behind a graying cloud, and a coldness settles within me.

An image of a sky so dark it's almost black shining with an endless sea of stars fills my mind, silver eyes brighter than the stars peering at me from the darkness.

The eyes of the redirected soul or the eyes of the god or goddess gifting me this magic?

The silver eyes blink at me and a string of silver satiny rope shoots from the darkness, the magic wrapping it around my heart and soul before pulling it taut and yanking me forward so hard and fast my palms scrape against the forest ground.

The tangy taste of magic fills my mouth as it surges through me, the life I've taken merging with my own. Just as the first time I encountered magic years ago, I feel my heartbeat slow to the point of no return before it quickly speeds up again.

Something shatters inside me and blinding pain erupts in every part of my body. A piercing scream rocks through the clearing, and I don't know if it's coming from me or the roaring wind.

Something is wrong, it has to be. It shouldn't feel as if my very soul is being cleaved in two, should it? As if by taking a life, I'm also relinquishing a part of mine.

Whatever it takes, Asteria.

The silver eyes narrow into a scowl as if the god granting me the magic regrets it and is already plotting its revenge.

Or maybe the revenge has already started.

"Magic always comes with a price. Especially for someone like you. You've already been marked. Doing it again may come with a cost too high even for a princess," the witch warned me when I purchased just enough magical ink to carve the forbidden mark on my skin.

"That's not any of your business, is it? Unless you want me to tell the king about your little establishment."

The witch only pursed her lips, her long braids slapping against her neck as she shooed me away from her cave in the forest.

Perhaps the price for the magic is a part of my life, a part of my heart, or even a part of my soul.

The wind rustles the leaves of the trees around me and I suck in a sharp breath as I'm brought back to the present moment, the pain vanishing as fast as it came.

With shaking hands, I light a match and drop it onto the cooling body in front of me.

A bird screeches in a nearby tree before leaping away from the rising smoke. The gray smoke bleeds into the thick fog in the ominous forest, blocking out every trace of sunlight should the sun choose to reappear in the pale sky.

Flames lick at the ornately tailored clothes on the dead lord, the golden fabric transforming into a blazing inferno. I reach forward to remove his sword from the scabbard at his side before the flames reach higher on his body.

There's no point in letting a perfectly good sword go to waste.

I consider reaching forward again to close his eyes, but I'm afraid it might tamper with the magic and a part of me enjoys seeing that his disgusted look is no longer evident in his eyes.

And what is the morning sky if not a beautiful last glimpse of this world?

The man's mouth is slightly agape, his shocked expression now permanently etched onto his face. It's the look of someone not expecting danger, the look of someone not even considering that I could be dangerous.

He was wrong.

Lord Byrin took one look at me and realized I wasn't one of the golden princesses before deciding I at least had to be good for something.

Wrong move.

Before I even had a chance to threaten or take him on a stroll near one of the inhabited beast lairs like I usually do with the endless line of suitors shoved my way, he was upon me. My dagger practically flew into his chest.

A sneer forms on my lips as I remember the feel of his clammy hands around my throat, transforming to a smirk when I think of his confusion and shock when I pulled out the dagger hidden in the bodice of my dress.

I never expected my first kill to happen before the Tournament had even started.

Perhaps taking his life will be a big enough price for the magic.

It doesn't matter that he probably would have killed me after he was done with me or that I only defended myself. I couldn't tell anyone.

No one would believe the cursed princess.

The people in Soria are always looking for excuses to get rid of me, never even considering that I could be something more, just like the lord now disintegrating into nothing but ashes.

The feel of his blood coating my hands as I dragged him into the thick forest surrounding the Sun Palace is still lingering on my skin, my nails and hands stained with dried blood. The crashing waves of nausea have calmed, the contents of my stomach already emptied on the way to the forest.

"That filthy battleground is no place for a princess."

I flinch at the words echoing in my mind, the words I heard

this morning when I uttered the most important question of my life, desperately hoping this would finally be the year he would say yes. When Father refused me once again, the words fueled my anger and forced me to take a life and use forbidden magic.

The words have been screamed at me so many times it's a wonder they're not permanently etched onto my forehead, and oh, how the gossiping people of this kingdom would love that.

Every year, when I was forced to sit dutifully next to my sisters and cast longing looks at the warrior women allowed to beat men to the ground, I would hear them.

Every time another Victor was crowned, I would hear them.

And this morning, the words were once again screamed by the Sun King, accompanied by a shove in the direction of the chosen lord forced to endure my company for the day.

The smell of burning flesh fills my nostrils as I trace my fingertips over the bleeding mark on my arm, the cracking of bones and wood echoing in my ears.

Soon, there will be another mark on my body, no matter what the king says.

I move my fingers to the side of my neck, brushing away the long strands of hair as I wonder how this year's binding mark will look and how it will feel to have it carved onto my skin.

I've been training for the deadly competition for as long as I can remember. It is my only chance to prove I'm worthy of something more than the life I'm bound to.

I know the gods will welcome my sacrifice, and I'm ready to give them my life and soul.

In the middle of the thick forest, surrounded by gray smoke seeping up from my first kill, I look like the cursed princess they all believe me to be. My dress is ruined—the yellow and golden fabric is dirty from struggling through the forest, the skirt is shredded and torn, one of the sleeves is ripped away to carve my skin, the other soaked with blood. Leaves and branches are tangled in my hair, my hands are covered in ash and blood, and the smell of smoke is clinging to my entire body.

If only the kingdom could see me now.

No one ever believed I could be queen. As the youngest of seven sisters, it's not that strange I'm considered the most unlikely heir, but that's not the reason the people would riot if I were to sit on the throne.

Now, with magic coursing through my veins, I feel it more than ever.

There's something different about me, an unsettling feeling I've always been unable to understand.

Maybe it's my yearning for the Tournament, for a life so different than the one I was born into.

Or maybe it's the forbidden magic that is now a part of me.

I know playing with magic is dangerous, but I will take every advantage I can get in the upcoming competition.

I didn't plan to murder the man who is now nothing but ashes, but isn't it better that his death will be useful?

This year, I'm competing in the Tournament of Day and Night. And I'll do whatever it takes to win.

CHAPTER TWO

There is a crowd gathered outside of the palace gates—a myriad of colors swirled together in an intangible mess, the gilded hues of my kingdom always the brightest. Moria—the capital city of the royal court—gleams in the distance, the sunlight warming the cobblestoned streets and lighting up the first day of the Tournament of Day and Night.

Inside the palace gates, in front of the peering eyes, the Royal Guard is preparing the procession headed for the city. Their polished uniforms are blinding in the sun, the line of ornate carriages and decorated horses even brighter.

The royal procession will be cleaved in two—one part will be led by the Sun King, the other by the Moon King from the opposite direction. The processions are always planned to arrive at the same time in Moria—when the sun sets and numerous warriors have already bound their lives to the Tournament.

This year, the Sorian procession will have one less princess.

With my hood securely tucked over my head, I skirt around the main path in the palace courtyard, finding one of the spots in the gates worn from the harsh winter storms yet to be repaired before darting into the crowd. I maneuver through it, passing children barely able to walk, elders with canes to support them, and other people from all over the two Kingdoms of the Sky.

Some of the people in the crowd give me strange and curious looks as I hurriedly press my way forward and I can't blame them. I'm wearing my usual fighting leathers, the dark fabric worn and molded to my body. I stole them from a group of Lunan warriors one year, their leathers more suited for sneaking around in the shadows than the light fabric reserved for the Sorian warriors.

During the Tournament Times, people from both kingdoms mingle together and it wouldn't surprise me if parts of this crowd are from the enemy kingdom, but someone clad in warrior clothes with enemy colors outside of the palace will raise questions. I would be dragged into the dungeons buried deep underneath the palace if the guards were to notice me, before realizing who I am of course, then I would be dragged into Father's study to await my punishment.

It's a good thing I don't plan to reveal my identity yet. I do enjoy causing some trouble after all.

When I make it to the city, the market square is already bustling. People clad in all colors of the rainbow crowd the streets, warriors in both light and dark leathers mingling between them, several of them proudly displaying the raw binding marks on their necks.

Vendors filled with goods ranging from fruit, fabrics, jewelry, and weapons are scattered throughout the place, the chain of border mountains–the Diamond Mountains–separating the two kingdoms peeking up in the far distance.

In the very center of the city, there is a large open-space circle, the cobblestones picturing the sun and her light with ancient gilded carvings that sparkle in the sunlight. During the opening festival, this is where the fighting rounds will happen, including anything from hand-to-hand combat to sword fighting and other bloody methods. Practice for the games, and also a way for the warriors to catch the attention of nobility willing to bet generous amounts of coins both gold and silver.

Racks of various weapons are placed to the side, groups of warriors hungrily eying them as they plan how to fight their opponents. Others are already deep in battle, the sounds of the fights echoing through the market, their blood seeping onto the streets.

My fingers are itching to grab one of the weapons and join the battling warriors, but I force myself to keep walking.

Not yet. There is something else I need to do first.

The bindings are the first part of the Tournament of Day and Night. This year, as it is a Summer Solstice Tournament, the bindings will take place here in the Sun Court, the royal court of my kingdom, where people will venture from all over both kingdoms to gift their lives to the magical games. Tonight, the sun will set for the first time since last year's Tournament, temporarily relinquishing her place to the moon, and the binding ceremonies will continue throughout the dark night until the sun rises again.

It doesn't matter that it happens every year. Every time the sky above me transforms from the familiar light to darkness, it takes my breath away. Only the magic of the Tournament allows for it to happen. For the rest of the year, the Diamond Mountains block out both the light and the dark, casting one side in everlasting light and the other in never-ending darkness.

There is no break from the light in the Sun Kingdom. The sun may disappear behind a cloud or a tree, and the light may dim a little during the harshest winters, but when the sun has traveled from one side of the sky to the other, she will rise again and make her way back in an endless circle of light.

The silver and gold ceremonial knife used for the magical

bargains is lying on a pale limestone shrine in the ancient temple in the very center of the fighting ring. The temple has open walls to allow the fresh summer breeze to blow freely throughout the market and the wide pillars are carved with pictures of the gods. The flower-scented wind carries magic that sends shivers down my skin, the hidden mark on my arm pulsing in rhythm with my heavy heartbeats.

The temple is heavily guarded with soldiers surrounding the entire area. Their eyes are glued to the sacred knife glinting in the sunlight, their gazes only briefly moving to the pair of warriors walking up to the shrine–a woman and a man clad in leathers as dark as mine.

The woman's fingers curl around the knife–not the handle, but the blade. The blade of the sacred knife is so sharp it spills her blood without effort, the drops dripping onto the shrine mixing with the blood of the countless warriors before her.

I expect her to trace her bloody fingers over the side of her neck, but she only looks up at the man next to her, waiting.

A secretive smile plays at his lips as he grabs her hand, his fingers closing around the blade of the knife, his blood joining hers.

Hands still clasped, the woman dips her fingers in the man's blood and traces the darkened red mark already present on his neck–a sign that he participated in another Tournament and didn't win.

The man bows his head, and when the woman retreats, he looks to the sky before dipping his fingers in her blood and repeating the action of drawing a binding mark on her skin, the blood glistening in the setting sun.

I've seen countless bindings before, but never have I seen anyone do it together like this. The act seems so intimate, so powerful, and I'm standing so close to the temple I can almost feel the rush of magic in the air as the Tournament and the gods accept the bargains, binding the warriors' lives to the games.

A clattering sound resounds from the temple as the knife is placed back onto the shrine and the warriors walk away.

Pulling the hood a little more tightly over my head, I step away from the shadows and into the temple.

An eerie feeling creeps into my body as my feet step onto the ancient limestone. There is a prickling sensation at the back of my neck and it feels as if a beast is watching me from the shadows, daring me to take another step forward, ready to pounce if I do.

A roaring sound erupts in my ears as the tips of my fingers touch the handle of the knife, something deep inside of me screaming to step away from the bargain that can never be undone.

Whatever it takes, Asteria.

I catch sight of movement to my side, a shadow approaching from the market.

The guards of the palace can't have found me already, can they? There's no doubt the king has realized I'm gone, but the procession shouldn't be anywhere near the market at this time. Perhaps the king has sent some of his spies.

Rushed on, I pick up the knife and slice the blade across my palm. The sting is somehow a relief and blood easily pours from my skin.

I quickly dip my fingers in the warm liquid, tracing the memorized lines on the side of my neck, my head still concealed by the hood of my leathers.

"You will give me my victory or I will give you my death."

My breath catches in my throat as magic surges through me in a violent rush. The power seeps into my body and settles on my skin, in my bones, becoming a part of my soul. It's like a string being tied, promising my future to the Tournament as much as promising my soul to the Shadow Realm.

The approaching shadow halts as I finish drawing the mark, my blood boiling as it creates the permanent lines of the binding mark. The mark will be as red as my blood, a clear sign that my life now belongs to the gods and the Tournament.

The guards around the temple are frozen still, their eyes glued to the knife in my hand.

I allow myself to study the intricate pictures and patterns carved onto the handle for a few seconds. The moon and all its phases in silver on one side, the gilded sun and her light shining around the metal on the other–two opposite sides of the sky destined to fight for dominion. And at the top–a crescent moon intertwined with the sun–the symbol for the Tournament of Day and Night.

One of the guards makes an impatient sound, startling me out of my trance. A line has formed outside of the temple, warriors all waiting to bind their lives.

The knife clatters against the stone of the shrine and I hurry out of the temple and back into the bustling market. There's a small tremble to my steps as I maneuver through the crowd, the skin on my neck tingling and aching, the magic now a part of me unfamiliar.

The opening festival is held once a year, either at summer or winter solstice. And just like every trial in the Tournament, it starts during sunset or sunrise to honor both the sun and the moon.

Anyone can compete in the Tournament, and if you make an appearance at the opening festival you're bound to participate.

It doesn't matter if you step into the fighting ring without a bleeding mark. Once your feet cross the invisible line drawn on the ground, your life no longer belongs to you, but to the gods.

Over the centuries, a lot of people have made that grave mistake either by chance or the hand of another.

Those strict rules around the Tournament are exactly what I need. Being the King of the Sun, lawfully bound by rules and regulations, Father wouldn't dare refuse me in front of both kingdoms.

It was surprisingly easy to bind myself, now all that's left is to make an impression so everyone will know about it. Something that shouldn't be too difficult as I'm known as the cursed princess.

The pair of warriors binding themselves only moments ago are already deep into battle, fighting each other as if they're true enemies. Their movements are sharp and precise, proof of many hours spent honing their skills.

A shiver runs through me as I study the warriors that will be my opponents.

It's not as if I haven't seen skilled warriors before. I'm as prepared as I can for the brutality of the games. Perhaps it's just the reality of it all that makes all my nerves stand on edge.

This is the moment I'm finally going to start my destined journey.

Whatever it takes, Asteria.

I'm so wrapped up in the scenes before me with the clashing of swords and warriors from all over both kingdoms dancing around each other, that I don't notice the man in front of me before my head bumps against his broad chest.

"Watch it," he growls, his dark husky voice sending a shiver down my back. He is wearing the same dark fighting leathers as me, a dark hood concealing everything but his sharp chin and sneering lips.

A warrior from the enemy kingdom.

"Watch it yourself," I sneer back, firmly pushing his chest, refusing to take a step back. A heady smell of citrus mixed with something I can't place embraces me, so different from his rough exterior it momentarily startles me.

The man doesn't budge, he only crosses his arms and refuses to move out of the way. Even though I can't see his eyes, it's as if I can feel them scorching me through the darkness of his hood. "You have to do better than that if you're going to survive. You shouldn't even be here."

"We'll see about that," I croon, lowering my head to show off my best alluring smile.

Arrogant men are nothing I'm not familiar with.

"Go ahead. Underestimate me. It'll be fun–" I turn around and pick up a sword from the racks lined around the training ground, "–for me. When I beat you to the ground."

The man snorts and I can practically feel the way he's rolling his eyes, but the corners of his lips tug with amusement and he reaches around me to pick up a sword of his own. "Fine. Let's see if you can back up all that venom you spit."

The moon soldier gestures with his hands, a challenge and an invitation to back out. The weight of his hidden gaze is as tangible as the steel he holds in his hands.

A wicked thrill shoots through me at the challenge. Making sure my hood is still in place, I lift my chin and clear a way through onlookers and warriors getting ready to fight, ignoring the sour protests and shoving hands.

The man is poised when I turn around, casually leaning on his sword, the tip embedded into the ground. As if he has all the time in the world, as if he doesn't believe for a second that I will be a valuable opponent.

It's a good thing his face is hidden, or I would be highly tempted to wipe the arrogant smirk off his face with my fists instead of honorably fighting him with the sword I've chosen.

The tip of my sword is aimed at his throat in a heartbeat. To my surprise, he meets the blow effortlessly, the man transforming into what can only be the true warrior lurking underneath the surface.

"Cute," he remarks as his sword sweeps away mine, his feet expertly moving with his strikes.

"You won't find me cute in a few moments," I retort back, sword clashing against his. The unfamiliar sword feels wrong in my palm, the hilt digging into the raw skin from tripling up the practice lately and I curse the gods for not reminding me to bring my own weapon.

"I was talking about your moves. I never said I find *you* cute." The words make me falter for a fraction of a second, and a dark chuckle escapes him as the tip of his sword slices the inside of my forearm, exposing a red line in my skin.

A roar of applause bursts out behind us and I grind my teeth together.

"Ah, don't worry, I'm sure you can't be that hideous underneath your hood."

"Speak for yourself," I spit and aim my sword at his feet.

He chuckles again as he moves away from me. It's like we've made our own personal dance in the way we move against each other, the sounds of our swords clashing and clanging seeming to echo all the way to the Diamond Mountains.

His sword slices across my thigh, another line of skin exposed to the sky above. And then another slice to my other thigh before I have the time to move away.

"You really need some more practice before the Tournament. I'm almost falling asleep over here."

"You must be a really bad warrior if taunting is your best tactic."

"I will never deny my mouth being my best feature. I've been told it can be quite persuasive."

He chuckles darkly as he slashes a cut on my other arm, blood dripping to the ground. The thin strip in the fabric is enough to reveal a sliver of the raw mark hidden underneath. The man seems to falter for a fraction of a second, as if the mark on my skin somehow offended him.

I use it to my advantage, darting forward with my sword aimed at his chest.

The warrior quickly recovers by effortlessly taking a step to the side. "I must say I already enjoy this little game of ours, but I wonder how long you will hold out in the real competition."

"You'll see," I mutter, my strikes growing more deliberate and vicious. To my rising frustration, he meets every one of them.

"Unfortunately, yes. I don't particularly feel like ending you just yet. And it seems we both have made a bargain to compete." He grits his teeth so hard I'm sure it must make his head pound.

A glance around us and I realize the other duels have ended, every single pair of eyes glued to our performance. In the distance, the sounds of the royal procession from the Sun Palace are getting closer, the king no doubt angrily searching the crowds for me.

I only need to prolong the duel a little longer so there is no question that I've thoroughly bound myself to the Tournament. The royal procession from Luna has to be due to arrive any second now as well.

The man is suddenly in front of me, startling me enough to make me fumble backward. He reaches forward and grabs my arm, his hand landing on the exposed skin from one of his cuts, his fingers dragging the fabric back to reveal even more of the wound. "Although it seems you've already been marked."

The warrior is standing so close that I catch a glimpse of his dark eyes glowering at me. With the darkness from his hood, I can't tell if his eyes are black or another very dark color, but there is a faint trace of silver around his irises unlike anything I've ever seen before.

"Tell me how you got this," he demands, his grip on my arm tightening to the point of pain.

I yank away from his grip, taking a step away to put some much-needed distance between us. "No. The only mark that matters is the one we now share."

I can't stop a grin from spreading across my lips as I tilt my head to the side to reveal my new mark. "I look forward to thoroughly beating you in every trial."

The warrior's lips pull into an angry sneer. "That makes two of us, princess."

Before I realize what he is planning, the warrior reaches forward and removes the hood of my leathers, revealing my identity for all to see. My snowy hair has come undone, some of the strands blowing in front of my face.

He tucks a loose strand of hair behind my ear, his fingers briefly stroking against my cheek. His skin is cold against mine, the touch featherlight and startling.

And then he bows, letting his sword drop to the ground before casually stalking away, the cheering crowd gone silent parting to let him through. The man disappears in the shadows, the only sign that he was ever here the blood dripping from my wounds and the lingering feel of his fingers on my skin.

The eyes of the crowd bore into me as I quickly straighten my posture before raising my sword above my head.

My gesture of victory doesn't result in cheering and applause. The city square is so silent I can practically hear the heartbeats of the people around me, or maybe that is an effect of the magic carved into my skin.

The wind flying through the city increases, rattling the jewelry hanging in a nearby vendor. When it stills, the first sound that renders the silence sends a jolt of fear through my heart.

"Asteria."

Ignoring the way the king's warning tone slithers across my skin, the scars on my back aching, I take a deep breath and turn around.

The Sun King looks regal and almost godlike in the setting sun. The golden armor of his uniform is blinding in the fading sunlight, his long hair blowing freely in the wind. Gilded light emanates from his body, his eyes sparkling gold.

"You did not tell me one of your girls was competing. I must say it pleases me that you envy the princes winning so much you decide to let one of your own compete. Although this one does not quite look like the others," a deep voice croons behind the Sun King.

Father's face hardens, his jaw locking and his golden eyes raging. "The Tournament is no place for the royals, but the sun is making an exception this year," he says through gritted teeth, giving me a look that screams I'm going to regret this later.

"Yes. The magic of Night and Day is exceptionally binding." The Moon King chuckles before stepping forward.

He is the complete opposite of the glowing king beside him. His dark armor seems to block away the dimming sunlight, not allowing any trace of light to reach the king of darkness. His raven hair clings to his sharp features, and his eyes lack any sort of color. It's like staring into a void of shadows threatening to swallow me whole any second and yet I can't look away.

'I do not think our ancestors considered the possibility of reckless royals when they formed the deal between our kingdoms. Let alone a *cursed* princess," the Moon King continues, ignoring the seething king beside him.

Cursing the gods for making me so reckless, I take a step

forward. "If I were you, I would pray to the gods that your sons make it out alive of the Tournament now that a reckless cursed princess is competing."

And then I walk away, ignoring the glowering looks from the wrathful rulers of the Kingdoms of the Sky as the binding mark on my neck throbs with the reminder that my life is no longer mine.

CHAPTER THREE

The Kingdoms of the Sky always strive for balance. Light and darkness–two opposing sides of the sky, two kingdoms meant to balance each other.

The Tournament always makes sure of that.

The opening festival signals the start of this year's Summer Solstice Tournament, starting with the bindings and ending with a masquerade ball held at the Sun Palace. And at the end of the Tournament, the final ball will be held at the royal palace in Luna.

The masquerade ball is an illusion of two kingdoms coming together as equals for one night before the competition begins and we kill each other, and the same will apply for the final ball when the supposed peace for the rest of the year is accomplished.

Lies, all of it.

The masquerade balls held in the royal court are the only gatherings I actually want to attend. They are the only occasions I'm not forced to play a role not suited for me. I don't get a single sour look for not wearing fabric spun from sunlight or for my hair not being dusted with gold. It's one of the few moments of freedom where I don't have to be anyone other than myself. Of course, that is only after I've fulfilled my royal duties and I'm able to sneak away to put on another costume.

Tonight, I should be wearing a royal costume with my sisters. Second, I should participate in the ceremonial dance with my sisters. Third, I should be observing the ball from a distance with my sisters. And lastly, I should be covered in raw wounds as a courtesy from the king.

But not tonight.

By some miracle from the gods, I have managed to stay out of sight since I bound myself to the Tournament and defied orders from the king. It was easy enough to stay out of his grasp the remainder of the binding rounds when he couldn't do anything in front of the enemy kingdom, and after that, I've mostly hidden deep in the forests surrounding Moria, my training fueled by imagining the rage Father will be in when he finally gets his hands on me. Hands which I plan on staying far away from until I've won the Tournament and finally proven myself worthy of a title better than the cursed princess.

The evening of the ball is a time when everything and everyone is allowed, and tonight I'm not a princess of the sun. I'm a frozen sun, a storm of ice, winter incarnate.

The pale alabaster and pearl fabric of my dress makes my snowy hair stand out even more, the strands cascading down my back like streaks of pale light. The silver details on the ivory mask reflect my eyes to the point of making them glow. My lips are a stark contrast to my skin, the crimson color making it look as if I've just taken a bite out of one of my opponents.

One of the ballrooms on the lower levels of the palace is decorated with banners in the colors of the sun crested with the symbols of the five courts of Soria. A bright sun for the royal court, a pink flower for Verbena, lilac and lavender flowers for Lavendula, a bright sunflower for Helianthus, and a swirling line ending in a circle for the court of Light that represents the sunlight. The large pieces flutter in the slight breeze coming in from the high-ceiled windows and open doors at the back of the room.

The courtyard garden outside is brimming with flowers in every shade of the rainbow, the fresh flowery scent carried inside by the wind. The light from the setting sun mingles with the lights from the lit candles and the king's magic–the kinglights–and the combined light is too bright and on the brink of blinding.

Of course, there's no such thing as too much light for the Kingdom of the Sun.

The palace is too crowded tonight, people clad in sparkling gowns and tailored suits milling about, their masks ranging from beautifully crafted jewelry to pictures straight out of a nightmare.

Magic is stirring in the air, coating my skin and seeping into my bones, the mark on my neck and arm beating in rhythm with the music. The magic is as much a glittering light as an approaching darkness, haunting yet alluring.

"May I have this dance?" A deep voice croons behind me, an involuntary shiver running down my back at the sound of it.

A very good-looking man is standing behind me, a hand held out in invitation. Lush black locks of hair curl down to a pair of twinkling blue eyes, the blue so dark it looks black in the few shadows of the ballroom, and the silver mask adorning his face is doing nothing to conceal his rough beauty with his sharp jaw and high cheekbones. An arrogant smirk plays on his lips, giving me the impression that he's not usually the one to ask anyone to dance.

There's something vaguely familiar about him.

I've met countless lords and other men of nobility throughout the years, but somehow I know this man is not one of them. I just know I would've remembered someone like him.

I hate the way I'm drawn to him. It has to be because of the mark on his neck and not his beauty.

The magic of the Tournament is always working to push together warriors with the binding mark, urging them to a battle of death both during and in between the eight trials. I've felt it ever since I drew the life-binding mark with my blood, but not quite like this.

This is dangerous.

I'm about to roll my eyes and quickly dismiss him when he suddenly sweeps me into his arms and out onto the dance floor, his strong arms pressing me against his broad body.

"I didn't say yes, did I?" My nails dig into his shoulders, the fabric of his dark suit making little resistance.

The man chuckles, his breath tickling my face. "I just couldn't help myself. That dress does wicked things to me."

A shiver runs down my spine at the huskiness of his voice and the closeness of his body.

It has been too long since someone held me like this but I'm not going to let the first good-looking man I meet distract me. And especially not someone from the enemy kingdom.

I roll my eyes with a snort. "You won't be saying that when my dagger is deep in your chest, moon boy."

He raises a dark eyebrow, amusement flickering in his gaze. "Why are you so eager to paint me as the enemy?"

I let my eyes wander over him, from his silver mask to the dark details on his suit in the shape of faint stars. His costume can't be inspired by anything else than the dark glittering sky. A sky that Soria is only blessed with during the weeks of the Tournament.

A warm finger brushes against my cheek before trailing over the silver stitching on my mask. "Perhaps it's just a part of my disguise. Silver is not the favored color of Soria, as it's clear you're also aware of," he drawls, the corners of his lips tugging with amusement.

I slap his finger away before resting my hands back on his shoulders. "Who says I'm from Soria?"

Another arrogant smile appears on his lips and the stranger looks at me in the same manner I looked at him, his gaze trailing from the top of my head down to the flat slippers hidden underneath my long gown. "Lucky guess," he says with a shrug.

My fingers curl around his shoulders as sparks of fury flicker inside me. "No matter where you come from, you will still be my enemy in the games," I sneer, ready to step away from him.

The man's grip on me tightens, a hard edge slipping over his features. "You're competing in the Tournament?" His tone is casual and bored as one of his fingers reaches forward to trace the mark on my neck, yet again sending shivers down my spine.

As if he already doesn't know the answer to his question.

With a glare, I shake him off, waiting for the inevitable remark that I won't stand a chance.

"Scouting the competition, are we? Well then, what have you gathered so far?

I blink in surprise. Deciding to entertain myself a little longer, I glance around the room, delivering remarks in a low tone.

"Him over there." I nod toward a man leaning against the wall, sword on display and arms crossed with a cocky smirk. "Easy. His pride will be his undoing. And her?" I nod to a woman with a sharp jaw and a murderous look in her eyes. "She has her eyes on him. She thinks he will be hard to beat." I snort. "But–"

"But you'll be the one the hardest to beat?" The man croons, his eyes twinkling as his gaze rakes over me.

I shift my hip against him, the hilt of my hidden dagger pressing against his thigh. "Actually, yes," I retort back in the same purring tone.

The man's sensuous lips pull into an amused smirk, his hands on my waist tightening. "I look forward to meeting you on the battleground then. Perhaps we'll even realize we can help each other."

I stand on my toes to whisper in his ear and a muscle ticks in his jaw. "I look forward to seeing your blood ruining that pretty suit of yours. There are no allies in the games."

The man chuckles, the sound reverberating in my bones. "This pretty suit will be nowhere near your claws unless it involves taking it off. I'll be seeing you, princess. And I do urge you to carefully think over my words until next time–" his lips snag on the bottom of my ear, a flare of heat igniting within me at the sensation, "I'll only keep your secret safe if you make a bargain with me. A bargain that will be in both our favor." And then he abruptly releases me and walks away.

I stand frozen, blinking at his disappearing form, reeling with a chaos of emotions and a storm of churning thoughts.

What did he just call me? It can't be the man from the opening market, can it? But the odd familiarity of him and his arrogant smirk tells an entirely different story.

And my secret? There are no rules in the Tournament of Day and Night, so using magic to steal the life essence of a suitor is not technically forbidden, although the Sun King undoubtedly would have his own punishment for such a crime. Magic is reserved for the Tournament and the royals, giving any warrior the ability to attempt to use it, and I am a royal, but–

When the stranger has almost disappeared in the crowd, I gather the hem of my dress in my hands and swiftly maneuver through the crowd.

We move up the long trek of stairs out of the magical ballroom and into the long hallways winding through the palace. The halls are cold and eerily silent compared to the packed ballroom. The last of the sunlight has faded, leaving the palace in shadowed darkness, the king's magic lights reserved for only parts of the palace tonight.

"Wait!"

The man disappears around a corner, the darkness making it seem as if the shadows cling to him.

My shoes click against the marble tiles, the fabric of my long dress dragging behind me like a pool of liquid ice.

The palace grows darker and colder the longer we walk and a heavy stone of dread sinks in my stomach when I realize which direction we're going, an ache running through the scars along my back.

We're nearing the king's study, his favored room when it comes to handing out punishments.

"Where do you think you're going?" I try to keep my voice low, but the empty hallways make my voice echo throughout the palace.

I'm starting to imagine Father bribing the beautiful stranger to lure me to his study, and I'm not entirely certain that thought is completely ridiculous.

The man briefly turns around, just long enough for me to notice the smirk on his face and the mischief glinting in his eyes. "I don't think that's any of your business, is it?"

"It is when you're sneaking around in my palace."

"Oh, your palace is it? So you do admit to being the princess?"

I ball my fists at my sides, my nails digging into the scars in my palms. "Since you somehow seem to know who I am, it is only fair you tell me your name."

"Why? So you'll have a name to put your dreams to? You know, one of my kingdom's tricks during the Tournament is visiting people in their dreams–or even better, nightmares," he purrs and actually has the audacity to wink at me.

"No, I–"

The man is in front of me in a heartbeat, the speed startling me so much I stumble against the wall.

One of his hands moves to the wall beside my head, caging me against him. He leans down so close our lips are only inches apart, his breath hot on my face. "How much trouble would a princess be in if she were to be noticed with someone from the enemy kingdom in a position such as this?"

My heart beats rapidly as his gaze lowers to my lips. "Let's just say it wouldn't be good for either of them," I say, hating the breathlessness of my voice.

"Then it's a good thing we're both disguised." He moves to the side, his nose grazing my neck. "And how much trouble do you think two guests of the starting ball suspiciously sneaking through the palace would be in?"

"That wouldn't be good either."

"Hmm." His other hand moves to my hair, his fingers moving through the pale strands. "And how about two guests of the ball sneaking away for a private moment?"

I don't get the chance to answer the question.

His lips crash onto mine, taking my breath away and erasing every thought from my mind. The kiss is gentle for a fraction of a second before it turns desperate, as if he is struggling to breathe and I am the air he needs to survive.

I'm so stunned I don't pull away and I can't help the gasp that escapes me and allows his tongue to dance with mine. My hands are suddenly in his hair, my fingers gliding through the silky locks as his hands land on my hips, pulling me against the hardness of his body.

A desire and need unlike anything I've ever felt before washes over me, fire igniting in my core at the feel of him against me.

A small growl escapes him as I bite his bottom lip and his lips leave mine to trail kisses along my neck, each scorching touch igniting something deeply buried inside of me.

"Who are you?" I manage to mutter between gasps, his presence everywhere and not enough. My hands fumble with the lapels of his jacket, my entire soul screaming to get closer and feel more of him.

"No one important," he says, his lips moving up to nibble at my exposed collarbone.

"Tell me your name." I shove him off only to mimic his actions, my lips finding what appears to be a very sensitive spot on his neck from the sounds reverberating from his throat.

"Cael," he gasps before moving my face up to his, his lips once again crashing onto mine.

Fire erupts where his skin touches mine, flames heating the ice in my veins. My instincts are screaming to just claim him right here right now, the feel of him through the fabric of our clothes not nearly enough.

My fingers tug at his shirt, the first button flying off and hitting the floor with a small clank. His hands are on my thighs, his fingers finding the split in my skirt to caress my bare skin. I glide my hand across his chest, down his stomach, my fingers reaching for the button on his pants–

"Get out of here!" The sharp voice breaks through the trance, my mind fumbling to figure out a single reason to stop what I'm currently doing.

Cael presses his forehead against mine, ignoring my small whine as his lips leave mine. His whole body is heaving, his eyes as dark as the shadows surrounding us.

"I said get out of here!" The voice is more insistent now, and some of the haze clears from my mind.

A low growl reverberates from Cael's chest as the source of

the voice lets out an impatient sound, my whole body tensing as recognition dawns on me.

The Sun King is fuming behind us, the Moon King leaning against the wall beside him, a pleased expression on his face. Both of their masks are missing, but the ornate clothing leaves no doubt that both of them are honorary guests of the ball.

"Apologies, Your Majesties," Cael says, his voice calm and sincere, but from the glowering look now in his eyes I know it's all an act. His hands pull me behind him, shielding me from the kings.

"Get out of here before you find yourself unable to fulfill the bargain you have made with the gods," Father snarls, the Moon King chuckling behind him.

"You are lucky the king in charge of this palace is so pathetic–"

I don't hear the rest of the Moon King's insults as the warrior grabs my hand and hauls me away from them, his skin cool and soothing against my clammy hands.

My heart is beating so hard I'm half afraid it's going to burst out of my chest.

What are the chances Father didn't just pretend to not recognize me, saving his punishment for a later time when the king of the enemy kingdom is not watching his every move?

When we're almost outside of the ballroom again, I drag Cael into the shadows before abruptly letting go of his hand. "How dare you–"

"I believe a thank you is more in order," the warrior says before readjusting his silver mask and smoothing down his dark hair, my face heating from the evidence of our unexpected salacious moment.

I try to repress the way my body is still blazing with flames and the way the feel of him still hovers on my skin. "That wouldn't have been necessary if you weren't sneaking around in the first place! What are you up to? Taunting the princess definitely won't give you any advantages in the Tournament. And if you think I don't recognize you, you're wrong–"

"I never said that. How could you not recognize the person who thoroughly beat you with the shabby swords–"

"You didn't beat me–"

"Cut you then. Does it really matter how, starlight?"

"What?"

"Whether I beat you or cut you–"

"No." I cross my arms to keep out the cold suddenly seeping into my body. "What did you call me?"

He purses his lips, an emotion I can't decipher flickering across his features. "Never mind, princess. I'll see you around."

"No." I grab his wrist and he halts with a raised eyebrow that makes me quickly release him.

"No," he says, dragging out the word as if it's unfamiliar. "So you've already found a way out of the bargain and I won't be seeing you in the first game?"

"Yes. I mean no." I make an exasperated sound, causing the corner of his lips to tug upward. "That's not what I mean. I will compete in the Tournament and I will–"

"Good." He turns to leave again.

"Why do you even care?"

Another emotion flares across his face so fast I can't place that one either. "It would certainly be a waste for the gods to claim your life before I've had a chance to do so myself. I only want to make sure you're aware of the consequences should you decide not to show up to the first trial."

"Of course I'm aware," I snap, "I will be there and–"

"Good."

"Stop interrupting me." I take a step forward and instantly

regret it when his dark presence envelops me. "You're a warrior from the enemy kingdom. I don't know what you're up to, but I'm going to find out. And I'm going to make us even–No, I'm going to beat you so well in each game you won't even remember your name."

The dark warrior leans down so his eyes are aligned with mine, his midnight eyes like a storm of stars with the silver specks. "I know what you're up to, princess. And sadly, it's not going to work. And as for my name–" he licks his bottom lip, starry eyes flickering to my throbbing lips. "When we're done with each other, I might not remember it, but I'm going to make sure you will."

"Stop that."

He raises an eyebrow again, his dark eyes swallowed by the glittering silver of his mask.

"Stop whatever it is you're doing that makes me unable to think clearly–"

"I guess you could say it's my good looks and unnaturally good charm." He moves to walk away, his fists balled at his sides as If he has to hold himself back from grabbing me and finishing what we started outside of the king's study.

"Cael, wait."

He halts, the shifting muscles on his back visible through the fabric of his shirt, his jacket still discarded where I only moments ago tore it off.

"What about my...secret? And the bargain you were threatening me with?"

I don't know if it was all a ruse, but I won't take any chances with a warrior from the enemy kingdom. I need to figure out what he thinks he might know and make sure he never spills so much as a word.

"I'm confident we'll meet again. Let's discuss it then."

"Cael–" The murderous look that crosses his face when he finally turns around to look at me makes me snap my mouth shut.

"There will be plenty of time for us to discuss our bargain," he practically spits before sauntering away and disappearing in the shadows, leaving no trace of the beautiful strange warrior behind.

CHAPTER FOUR

"One." The Royal Sword's sharpened blade leaves a torturous pain on my back, sparks shooting along my spine and down the length of my body.

"Two."

The sound of the blade digging through my skin.

"Three."

The feel of blood trickling down my back.

"Four."

A low hiss escapes through my gritted teeth.

The movements halt at the sound and I close my eyes, praying to the gods he will let this one go.

"The least you could have done was wear something else than the enemy kingdom's leathers!" The king's voice is possibly even sharper than the blade slicing across my back.

"And then you did not even bother showing up at the ball," he spits, increasing the pressure in the pointed tip of the blade. The blade of the sword that has embedded itself in my back as a cruel punishment and a reminder of his power for as long as I can remember.

It seems the gods are not in the mood to answer any prayers today.

At least he doesn't order me to continue counting. The counting has always been the most humiliating part of his punishments. Not only because I'm still ordered around by my father in my twentieth year, but because of my forced participation in the act. Count the cuts or we will start all over again, utter the words perfectly or more lines will be added.

At least he is not using his magic today.

Whenever the Sun King gets in one of his moods and I'm forced to endure his *company*, I envision myself just leaving everything, distancing myself from the present and the pain of the blade against my skin.

One would think a princess of the sun would prefer one of the places permanently gilded with sun and warmth, but I think I would enjoy living in a place where I don't have to be reminded of my past every time the sun shines and where my icy exterior would blend in instead of being a stark contrast.

If it weren't for my deeply rooted hatred for the Kingdom of the Moon, I might even consider hiding in the darkness. Maybe it would do me good to spend some time away from the sunlight and under the starlight instead.

Starlight.

The word rings through me in a deep husky voice accompanied by an image of dark eyes filled with silver, for a second replacing the cold pain in my body with a burning warmth as I'm reminded of his skin against mine.

"I said– do you understand?" The sharp blade rips open some of the scar tissue on my back and I have to grit my teeth and dig my nails into the skin of my palms to keep from crying out as I'm brought back to the present moment.

"Yes, Your Majesty."

Majesty. King. Never father. Especially not when I'm being punished like this.

I was only two years old the first time he struck me. An open slap with his palm right across my cheek, punishment for playing with my mother's things still hidden in the queen's quarters. The Royal Sword was added years later.

"Good." He moves away as I place my shirt back on my body, carefully arranging the fabric and willing myself not to flinch when it touches the raw wounds. Protesting, however silent it may be, always makes it worse. Sometimes it even makes him start up again.

"Let this be a reminder in the first game. No matter how much you may fight it, you will never escape who you are, *Asteria*." My name is like an insult coming from his mouth, as if the combined letters are the worst thing he could possibly call anyone. And I suppose it is. I was the one who stole the life of his queen, my name her only dying wish.

The king wipes the Royal Sword with a handkerchief, coloring the white fabric. "Now, get out of here before I change my mind and lock you in so you are completely unable to participate."

I close the shirt, thankful I chose one that locks from the front, and with as much dignity as I can muster, I wobbly get to my feet. "I'm legally and magically bound–"

"I am a king, *Asteria*. I can do whatever I want. I do not care about the magic." Warning laces every word along with the storm in his eyes, the pure gold only showing a fraction of the magic lurking underneath his skin.

"You made a choice. Now you have to deal with the consequences. I expect you to not humiliate this kingdom any further. I am running out of patience. Maybe that is why the gods granted me so many daughters. If one goes missing, there are still six left."

MY BACK IS BLEEDING. I feel the drops slide along my skin, the raw wounds so painful every small movement sends a sharp ache through my body.

I reach for my glass, welcoming the bitter taste of liquor burning down my throat. Anything to numb the pain.

I put my glass down a little too forcefully, the movement making the plates on the long table rattle, some of my sisters reaching forward to steady their glasses.

My sisters are all wearing beautifully made dresses with expensive fabric in shades of yellow and gold, all made to accentuate the best side of the sky.

Solina, my oldest sister, gives me a scolding look, her eyes the same shade of honey as the king's when they are not pure gold from his magic. She is seated next to the empty seat of the late queen, her golden blonde hair braided into a crown atop her head.

My perfect sister and the one expected to inherit the throne.

The twins Arina and Erina are seated next to Solina, both of them shaking their heads as they cast wary looks in the direction of the king. With their amber eyes and copper hair, they are so identical even I struggle to pick them apart, a trait they've used to their advantage numerous times.

The triplets Davina, Deya, and Delia are seated on the other side of the table. They are as different from each other as the two sides of the sky, but they all share the same warm brown eyes speckled with gold.

I'm left at the end of the table, the farthest away from the king. Always the odd one out.

I had no choice but to follow the king, still wearing my white shirt dirty from training in the forest, the back soaked with blood. With my white hair and pale skin, I might've been translucent were it not for the blue in my eyes and the mud on my shirt. And the blood coloring my back.

The Sun King sends me occasional warning looks, challenging me to reveal that I'm in pain. I try to ignore him, knowing that if I so much as flinch, he will gladly drag me back to his study.

He is wearing one of his usual golden suits embroidered with endless small suns, the swirling lines like small snakes ready to strike anyone who dares look at him too long. His blond hair is tied at the back of his neck, a few short strands framing his face, and the brightness of it reminds me of the glowing halos surrounding some of the deities portrayed in the temples.

King Helios might've belonged with the beautiful and elegant beings, were it not for his sharpness and cold demeanor. The angles of his face are sharp and harsh, too brutal and cold for a king of the bright and warm sun. Beautiful yes, but cunning and conceiving in front of his people. The honey eyes do nothing to warm him, neither does the pure gold brightening them whenever he uses the royal magic descendant from the gods. If anything, Helios is more a king of winter and ice than the sun, and maybe that is where my appearance comes from.

There's a tangible tension in the air, as it always is when all of us are gathered like this. Again, I feel that otherness at the back of my mind. The unsettling feeling that has my sisters looking at me warily and occasionally flinching when I get too close.

Today, they are rattled for an entirely different reason.

I don't bother hiding the mark on my neck. The entirety of the two kingdoms probably knows about my bargain to the gods by now.

"What did you think of Byrin, Asteria?" Solina asks, always trying to ease every situation like the perfect queenly candidate she thinks she is. "The High Lady was very pleased to send one of her sons our way."

"Not my type," I murmur with a glare in her direction, the hidden mark on my arm pulsing in reminder of the life I was forced to take.

No one in my family knows what I've been doing to my suitors. They only know I'm doing *something* to scare them off, and they are too unbothered or horrified to confront me about it. All of them but the king that is.

Davina sighs. "Asteria, I don't understand why you insist on acting this way. You're running out of options." My sister lowers her voice at the last part, casting a wary glance at Father who only grunts in agreement.

"If you will not pick one, I will pick one for you," the king says, using the same empty threat he has for years, thankfully too busy to act on it.

Stabbing my fork into the meat on my plate, I picture how it will feel to stick my sword into one of the moon brutes in the Tournament and hopefully one of the princes.

"I won't have time to entertain any more suitors," I snap, ignoring the pounding pain threatening to make me pass out. "I'm destined for the Tournament now."

Silence descends in the room, my sisters visibly paling. Even the servants stationed against the walls seem to bristle at the renewed tension.

The door to the dining room opens before Father has time to say anything, and I heave out a relieved breath.

A general walks straight up to the king and starts speaking in a voice too low for me to hear. The words make the king's knuckles around the knife whiten and I'm half afraid he is going to stick the knife in the general's throat.

"So," Delia says, a little more relaxed now that the king's attention is diverted elsewhere, "do you think Elio will compete again this year?" The dreamy look crossing her face makes me grind my teeth together.

"No," Solina says, patting a handkerchief at the corner of her lips. "He is already a Victor, so why would he?"

"He's so handsome and skilled and–"

I rake my knife across my plate to silence my sister. Elio has always gotten a lot of attention from both women and men, something he very much enjoys, but I'm not willing to let my sisters snatch him away from me.

"You really need to work on your manners, Asteria," Erina snaps, wrinkling her nose in my direction, the glimmer in her eyes telling me the dutiful princess role is all an act.

As always.

Perfectly poised in public and within the palace walls, but behind the king's back, my sisters can be just as brutal and cunning as any warrior. It's not as if I'm the only one sneaking out of the palace.

We all have our secrets, theirs are just more hidden.

"Yes, definitely," Arina echoes while eagerly bobbing her head in agreement, always backing up her twin, lies or no.

"In fact," Erina continues, her posture straightening even more against the golden chair at her back, her mouth dropping into a ridiculous pout that would make our old tutors proud, "you've missed quite a few lessons lately. And is that dirt underneath your fingernails?"

I give her my best glowering glare. "My bleeding has arrived. I'm not feeling well," I murmur, slumping a little in my chair as I quickly hide my hands underneath the table.

Arina rolls her eyes and then quickly glances at the king to make sure he didn't notice. He is still deep in conversation with his general, oblivious to his daughters.

The king thinks we are nothing but weak pathetic women, incapable of anything worth mentioning. I could bleed out of every hole in my body and still take over this kingdom and beat every warrior in the Tournament. Being a woman has never been a weakness, but I'll sure confirm his beliefs if it gives me an excuse to sneak away.

My sisters taught me that trick a long time ago, and it might be the only secret we share. It's an unspoken agreement between us, a silent protest against our ruthless father. If one of us claims to bleed, we back it up without question.

I've never dared ask them if I'm the only one bleeding from the king's punishments. Their backs might not be scarred like mine, the many dresses with open backs proof of that, but perhaps in places more easily concealed.

Not all scars are visible.

As if he can feel my glance, Father's eyes lift to look at me, flashes of gold sparking in his gaze. I take that as my cue to leave, feeling his glare on my back all the way out of the palace.

ELIO FINDS me face down in the dirt, the thick trees shielding me from the prying eyes of the palace guards.

I hear him suck in a breath and I firmly shut my eyes against the wave of shame washing over me. The last thing I want is for him to regard me with even a small ounce of disgust, or even worse, pity.

"Asteria–"

"No," I murmur, my voice muffled by the ground.

He lets out a heavy sigh before I feel him sit down next to me. "Let me help you, at least. I had this…feeling. So I have something that might help."

Three heartbeats pass before I answer him. "Fine."

Elio is the only one still breathing who knows about the punishments, and even with the title of Victor, he might not be if the king finds out he knows.

Elio found me once after. When I was about thirteen and too wounded to make it into my room. We never spoke of it, and years later, when my naked body was tangled with his, we didn't speak of it either.

"I'm hoping you're not too fond of this shirt," Elio says before ripping the fabric on my back. I feel him tense, another rough exhale escaping him.

Something cold touches my skin and my back arches from the pain. Elio rubs the ointment over my back, the creamy texture both soothing and stinging.

I feel the silent words churning in his mind, the forbidden words he's never dared speak to me.

He won't say them today either.

Some things are better left in the dark, no matter which kingdom we're in.

"So," he says, his fingers soft against my skin, "you bound yourself."

"Yes," I hiss through gritted teeth, trying to suppress the rising screams in my throat.

"Hmm."

"That's it? You're not going to scold me?"

His fingers stop moving. "Of course not. Do I wish you would've told me? Yes. There was a time when you would involve me in your scheming plans."

"A lot has changed since then."

"Yes, it has." His fingers start to move again, trailing over a particularly painful wound.

We were supposed to compete in the Tournament together. That was always the plan. That was what we had been training for. We would've thrived in the games together until the very end when only one of us could be crowned Victor.

There's a part of me that's still bitter that he robbed me of that chance. It wasn't his fault I was unable to bind myself last year, but there is still a deeply buried part of me that wants to scream at him for not trying. For not waiting.

We'll never get another chance to fight in the Tournament together. It's impossible for him to join me now.

"The Tournament isn't going to be like you think. It's entirely different to live through it than to observe it with the crowd or on the dais with the other royals. By the sun, there's a lot the crowd don't even get to see." He swallows, and even though I can't see him, I feel the haunted look in his eyes. "There's so much the people don't know about, and even you can't imagine how many terrible things happened last year. I would hate for you to get in the middle of it."

I bite my bottom lip to keep from crying out from the pain on my back as I ponder his words.

There are no rules in the Tournament, everyone knows that. And that also means that a lot of people don't make it out alive, which is the whole point. Of course, I've heard the rumors about the warriors going insane after the competition–of their haunted eyes and traumatized souls and bodies, but Elio wasn't like that when he won last year. He only seems more confident and strong, even though I can't deny that a lot has changed between us in the past year.

I can't even imagine how different our lives will be in just a couple of months after my participation in the Tournament.

What else will change between us?

"Out of everyone in the two kingdoms, I would at least expect you to support me. I had hoped that after all these years you didn't see me as a princess more suited for gowns and balls than the battleground," I say through gritted teeth as he finishes rubbing my back.

"I didn't mean it like that, Ria. I'm only trying to prepare you. No one can stop you now. Not the king, not me, no one. You're marked and if you don't compete–"

"My life will be claimed by the gods," I finish as I carefully roll myself up on my feet, holding the ruined shirt to my chest.

My heart aches at the sight of him when I turn around to face him.

His familiar hazel eyes flicker with concern for only a second before being replaced by the usual mirth evident in his eyes when his lips pull into a small smile, the sight making me want to leap forward to taste it and see if I can steal some of his warmth.

His tan skin has darkened from our outside training sessions the last few weeks underneath the summer sun, and combined with the shadow of a beard, it makes him even more handsome than usual. And then there is his victory mark, pure glittering gold in the sunlight, enhancing the warmth in his eyes.

When a warrior wins the Tournament and becomes a Victor, the binding mark will be gold or silver the following year, depending on the origin of the competitor. If not, the mark will continue to stay as red as the warrior's blood, serving as a reminder and sign of your loss and failure. Forever.

I still get startled by my own mark every time I look in the mirror and sweep my hair away from my neck, and the thought of someday seeing it golden like Elio's, of sharing something special with him, sends a dizzying thrill straight through my heart.

Elio shrugs out of his jacket and drapes it over my shoulders before carefully guiding my arms into the sleeves. The jacket smells like him—a warm earthy aroma mixed with a faint trace of the Helianthus flowers.

If sunshine had a scent, it would be Elio.

"You need to be very careful, Asteria," he says as he fastens the buttons on the jacket. "I'm serious." He sends me a stern look when I only roll my eyes in reply.

"It's not only the gods who may claim your life. You may not like it, but you're a princess and you're going to be a prize of your own in the games. If there's any truth to the rumors I've already heard, that prize just keeps growing as more people weigh in on the bets."

He finishes buttoning the jacket and takes a step away from me, hazel eyes boring into mine. "Not only do you need to survive the games, you need to survive everyone else. More than the others. The Tournament always turns into war, but with you on the battleground—" a shudder rocks through him.

"And what do you bet for?"

My heart beats rapidly as I await his reply, praying to the gods his concern is not a sign of doubt. After the last couple of days, I need to know at least one person would miss me, and Elio has always been the only one who mattered.

Elio's forehead creases, his mouth pulling into a thin line as he closes the distance between us. "Asteria," he sighs, his hand tipping my chin up to look at him.

"Haven't you been listening to anything I've been saying for the last minutes? I care about you and I don't want to see you hurt, let alone see your life end when there's nothing I can do about it." He cups my cheek with his hand before tangling his fingers in my hair.

My eyes flutter at the touch, my whole body aware of his warm skin against mine.

It has been too long since he touched me like this.

"There is something you can do," I say, a bit breathless.

"Anything, Ria."

"Train with me. More than we've done lately." Hope blooms in my chest, its roots sprouting out through my limbs.

We've barely trained together since last year's Tournament and Elio's crowning. With a new title comes new responsibilities and I rarely get to see him anymore.

I miss him.

We used to train together for hours and hours, day and night, both inside and outside of Moria. It started years ago, when we were only children and he caught me sneaking around to observe the soldiers and follow their training in the shadows. I tried joining them once, but the king banned me from ever setting foot near them again, so we found other ways to train.

Elio's hand lingers in my hair for a moment longer before letting go, his gaze locked with mine. "Of course we'll train. And I'll help you in the games too. I don't care about the rules or lack of. I'm going to make sure you have an advantage over the others. I mean, not everyone will have a Victor as a trainer," he says with a wink and smug smile that erases the creases in his face and some of the tension in his body.

"Fine," I say and cross my arms, not able to stop a smile from spreading across my lips. "Even though I don't actually need your help. You know, since I beat you every time we fight."

Elio tips his head back and laughs, the sound stirring the butterflies in my stomach. "Whatever you say, princess."

As we walk back toward the palace, I can't keep out the memories of another man calling me princess. Not in a soft teasing way like Elio, but as a taunt and a challenge. Like he can't wait to rip the title off me along with the invisible crown atop my head.

CHAPTER FIVE

The summer breeze is scented by the fruity aroma from the verbena fields in the distance, the flowers ranging in shades from pale pink to deep purple. Above the ocean of flowers, the sun is hanging low in the sky, as if she too is eagerly awaiting the first trial of the Tournament.

Kylo–the highest peak on the Sorian side of the range of mountains separating the two kingdoms of the sky–is towering amongst the colored fields, thousands of warriors scouting the rocky ground beneath it.

There's a static in the air, an invisible blanket of magic wrapped over the kingdom, the promise of the brutal Tournament on the horizon where the sun is slowly starting to settle.

The news of a princess of the Sun binding herself to the Tournament traveled fast, outnumbering the usual ruckus about the Moon Princes' participation and the rebellious groups opposed to the games.

Imagining the grumbling looks on their faces gives me a small piece of smug satisfaction, but not enough to block out the hungry looks around me.

There are twelve Lunan princes and several of them appear in the Tournament each year, wearing ornate royal uniforms and an assortment of weapons in an attempt to put the other warriors to shame.

As if the princes need any more armor than their arrogant smiles and wicked tricks.

I can't remember any of the princes actually becoming a Victor. Royals don't usually bother fighting for titles less prized than the ones they already own.

Until now.

Cursed princess to Victor.

This year, the warrior princes are yet to be seen, but there is no doubt they're going to be here. They are just waiting to make one of their grand entrances.

The crowd of people and warriors search the crowd for the cursed princess, hoping I'm going to join the princes in their extravagant shows.

Never before has a princess of the Sun bound herself to the Tournament. If any of my sisters were going to participate, the Sun King would parade them around like the princes, but he would never even think of praising me in the same manner.

I'm a walking target.

A package was delivered to my room before the procession left for Verbena. White fighting leathers stitched with yellow. No note, but the message was clear just the same.

Wear the colors of *his* kingdom or face a wrath worse than the Royal Sword.

As if the Tournament isn't going to be brutal enough.

The white leather is blinding in the sun, marking me as a very visible target for the horde of warriors around me. The clothes are stiff and unfamiliar against my body, so different from the usual leathers as familiar as my skin.

This is nothing but another trial and I can only assume that was the point behind the order—a punishment and an attempt to quickly end my humiliating participation.

It wouldn't surprise me if Father has put a prize on me too.

The wind tears at my leathers as I scan my surroundings. My eyes have unwillingly been searching through the crowds of warriors all day, looking for a pair of midnight eyes and an arrogant smirk, the memories of our last encounter resurfacing in my mind like a churning sea.

A wave of anticipation rocks through me, and I grit my teeth and press my nails into the scars of my palms.

I can't afford any distractions today, especially not one in the form of a beautiful warrior from the enemy kingdom claiming to know my darkest secret.

I continue moving through the assembled crowd, pulling my hood more tightly over my head.

There are so many competitors this year–too many. Thousands of hopeful and bloodthirsty warriors ready to sink their teeth into the lone princess.

Perhaps a bargain with an ally wouldn't be so bad after all, if only the one offering it weren't from the opposing kingdom.

The dais reserved for the royals to observe the Tournament is raised in the distance behind the crowd of warriors. Made of ancient white limestone and enormous pillars, the dais stretches wide and big enough for at least fifty people, the spacious stairs gleaming in the sunlight. With carvings of the sun and Soria on one side, and Luna and the moon on the other, it's perfectly clear which side belongs to whom.

The magic of the Tournament allows the dais to magically appear and disappear around the kingdoms during the

Tournament, the dais too mighty for any number of servants to even attempt to move it, too powerful for any warrior to destroy it.

It's the way of the gods.

I can almost feel Father's glowering look from where he is standing at the front of the dais, my sisters all standing poised around him.

On the other side of the dais, the Moon King is a towering shadow even in the sun. Behind him stands half a dozen princes clad in silver with various weapons, their arms raised to the sky as they receive applause and praise from the people below.

There is the grand entrance the crowd was waiting for.

The rest of the princes are nowhere in sight. The ones who don't compete usually don't bother showing up for the Sorian half of the Tournamant.

After all, someone needs to stay back and guard the kingdom.

A chorus of chanted prayers is drowning in the roar of the crowd, but the wind carries the voices of the priestesses toward me, their chanted words following the rhythm of my heavy heartbeats.

A temple of the Sun is located at the bottom of the mountain, tucked into the mountainside, the gilded limestone basking in the sunlight. And as with everything in this world, its opposite part–a temple of the Moon–is located on the other side of the border.

The priestesses' prayers send shivers down my back and I pat my hand on the dagger strapped to my thigh, absentmindedly making sure it's still there.

Elio found me the moment the procession arrived in Verbena. He pulled me away from the crowd and into the shadows of the forest, embracing me so hard I struggled to breathe.

"Promise me you'll be careful. The first trial is the worst in many ways. There will be so much chaos it's easy to be completely overwhelmed. Don't rush it. Slow and steady wins the race. Take this," he whispered and pressed a dagger into my hand along with a quick kiss to my cheek that grazed the side of my mouth.

It was only after he disappeared and I strapped the dagger to my thigh I realized what it was.

His Victory Dagger.

Along with the victory mark on his neck, the Victory Dagger is proof of Elio's status as Victor when the crown passes to the next Victor. He is supposed to carry the dagger at his side today when he opens the first trial–the job reserved for the latest Victor.

Elio gifting me his Victory Dagger is the only proof I need of his support.

The sound of a sword hitting the crest with the symbol for the Tournament–the sun entwined with the crescent moon–on the dais clings through the clearing, silencing everyone and everything. Even the chirping of the birds in the trees and the cricketing of the grasshoppers seem to quiet as Elio steps forward on the dais.

"The Tournament of Day and Night was created by the gods. Now, it is a means to an end, a way to keep the peace between our two kingdoms and a balance in our world," Elio's voice rings out, magnified by the magic surrounding the dais, allowing everyone in the Kingdoms of the Sky to hear his words no matter where they are.

"Today, we honor the gods and the sun and the moon which created us as we once again come together and begin this year's Tournament of Day and Night!"

A thundering sound of applause and cheers descends in the clearing, so loud it feels as if the very earth is shaking. The people stomp their feet and beat their fists against their chests, arms raised to the sky as they shout for the gods.

"Our magnificent, glorious, divine, and ever victorious gods and goddesses gift us some of their magic each year so we may create enthralling and breathtaking games in their honor, the details of which will be revealed as it begins, not before," Elio continues, and I can practically hear the small smile in his voice as he looks to the sky.

As Elio speaks, it is as if I can feel the gods peering down at us from the sky, their power and magic ready to strike out should anyone displease them.

I've always wondered what would happen if the kingdoms failed to host the Tournament, to fulfill their ancient bargain. Would the gods let the land sink into the ocean or would their magic strike from the sky and disintegrate everything until the kingdoms were nothing but dust on the wind?

I pray I will not live to find out.

"Eight trials for the eight courts of the two kingdoms, the royal courts reserved for the binding rounds and the finale followed by the crowning. Eight games, a week-long break between each, except the halfway mark where the month-long reprieve will allow for the long journey to Luna, all ending in a spectacular finale. One half in each kingdom, the time and place rotating with each year. Starting at summer or winter solstice, ending in the dark or the light."

Elio takes a step forward so he's standing at the very front of the dais. The setting sun is glowing behind him, the rays reflecting his bronzed gold armor and sending cascading bright light throughout the clearing.

If I ever thought the Sun King looked godlike, that is nothing compared to how the Victor looks now.

"And remember, there are no rules in the Tournament of Day and Night but one; survive. May the best Victor win!"

The finality of the words sends a shiver down my back. I've

heard countless speeches about the Tournament, but never have I been about to venture into it myself.

Stay alive.

I can do that. I've managed to do it all my life despite being the cursed princess.

This is just another day.

"In this first trial, making it out alive of the Tournament entails getting to the top of the holy Kylo before our beautiful sun goes to sleep with her last rays of light and the day is covered by the darkness of the moon," Elio says before clapping his hands together, his victory mark glowing in the setting sun before a surge of magic escapes it, blowing through the clearing in a strong gust of wind.

"The first trial has begun!" the Sun King shouts, his magnified voice rattling the leaves on the trees, sending another flurry of chirping birds flying across the sky.

I duck behind one of the pillars of the Sun Temple as the crowd surges forward, several of the warriors already taken out by the stomping of the crowd.

While Elio was giving his speech, I slowly crept away from the crowd toward the temple, deciding to scout the competition and make a strategy before tackling the first game.

Yes, the warrior who completes the trial first will bring honor to their kingdom and settle the score in countless waging bets, but I'll follow Elio's advice and just make it through this first game.

Showing off will come later.

"Is the princess already so scared she finds herself incapable of acting?" The voice slithers along my skin as I turn around to find a large man standing behind me.

It seems I'm not the only one that decided to not rush into it. Or maybe he has his eyes set on another prize.

The warrior is wearing the black signature leathers of Luna

and I can't help wondering if the Moon King himself has put a prize on my head, or maybe even one of the princes.

"Demon princess, that's what I heard. Cursed her mother and killed the queen." The man starts pacing, a predator circling its prey, speaking as if he is talking to someone I can't see. And maybe he is.

"Look at her. So different from the rest of them. White hair without a trace of light, paler skin, frosty eyes," he continues, spitting on the ground.

I can't deny that one. I was early scolded into averting my eyes in the presence of the king, the sapphire ring around my irises reminding him too much of a sky too dark to be a part of his kingdom.

"It's probably because she sucked away the life of the queen like the leech she is."

That one hurts. But it's also true. I am the princess who wasn't supposed to be born, the princess who stole the life of the Sun Queen, a curse to the kingdom.

"Are we even sure she is a real princess?"

"Probably not."

"You are nothing but a curse to this world."

My fingers curl around the Victory Dagger, my feet slipping into a fighting stance.

"I heard she curses everyone she touches. So I would stay far away if I were you. Lucky for me, I don't mind being cursed," another voice purrs, and before I even have the time to register what happens the man falls to the ground.

"Hello, starlight."

The warrior from the binding rounds and masquerade ball emerges from the shadows with a wicked grin, blood dripping from the dagger in his hand.

His face without a mask or hood is even more beautiful than

I've imagined. The shadows make his sharp cheekbones and perfectly sculpted nose even more striking, the silver in his eyes practically glowing. His hair is a little shorter than the last time I saw him, but the dark locks are still silky and tempting.

He is wearing the same black leather as the dead man lying at his feet.

No one is spared in the Tournament, not even the warriors from your own kingdom.

"What in the sky do you think you're doing?" I hiss, willing my raging heart to steady.

The warrior snorts and wipes the blade of his dagger on the dead man's sleeve. "And once again I don't get a thank you."

"How did you find me?" I cross my arms, trying to shield myself against the cool wind blowing through my leathers. "Cael," I add, remembering the name that may or may not be a lie.

"The shadows betray you because they serve me," he says through gritted teeth, his eyes darkening at the sound of his name.

I'm about to snarl something more when a group of warriors emerge around the corner of the temple, swords already raised in their hands.

"Hold that thought," Cael mutters before throwing his dagger.

The blade flies through the air and hits the first warrior in the throat. The man tumbles to the ground and the rest of the warriors scatter, unbothered by the blood seeping into the ground.

A woman in Sorian leathers runs straight for me, teeth bared and sword raised. In a blink, she's on the ground, another dagger protruding from her chest, her white fighting leathers soaked with blood.

Cael moves and strikes at a speed that shouldn't be possible.

One after one, the half dozen warriors hit the ground, their deaths inflicted by the most skilled warrior I've ever seen, his honed body the deadliest weapon of them all.

Less than a minute has passed before Cael is once again standing in front of me, blood coating his hands and parts of his face. "You were saying?"

I can only stare at him, my mind racing with what I just saw.

There's no way in the entire realm I will be able to beat him in a fight, no matter how many suitors I kill and how much magic I gain. Perhaps if I were to fully access the royal magic–

"If you've got something to say, princess, you better spit it out before more of them come lurking," Cael mutters before wiping his hands on his thighs.

"Who are you?"

The warrior studies me for a moment, his eyes nothing but pure darkness. "Are you afraid?"

My heart is a thundering storm against my chest as he takes a step forward, and something I can't place stirs deep inside me. Not fear, but something carnal and unfamiliar.

"No. I'm not afraid of you."

Cael raises an eyebrow but doesn't say anything else, his eyes boring into mine.

There's something hypnotizing about him, like an unseeable power is pulling me toward him so hard I'm struggling to breathe.

The gods haven't spared any of their magic this year.

I can almost hear their screams from the sky urging the two kingdoms to slay each other and keep the balance in the world. It's an instinct in my very essence, a call for blood that needs to be fulfilled.

Whatever it takes, Asteria.

"I would've thought you'd be on your way to the top already," I snap, needing to put some distance between us to stall the persisting magic.

THE VICTOR OF DAY AND NIGHT   57

If I can't beat him in a fight, I have to beat him another way.

Cael raises his eyebrows and gestures to the mountain in the distance. "As much as I would love to slaughter my way through that, I'm just not in the mood."

As if he didn't just slaughter more people than I hope I ever will. But he's right.

Kylo is lethal in the setting sun, the towering mountain a battleground drawn from the worst nightmares.

A chaos of weapons is flying in a sea of red bodies—swords, daggers, knives, clubs, arrows, shoes. Dead bodies cover the ground, their blood coloring the grass and rocky ground with splatters of crimson and black.

Countless warriors are already climbing, but finding a clear path seems almost impossible. There simply isn't enough room for all of us despite the enormity of the mountain.

A woman kicks a man down, causing him to fall into the chaos below. Another warrior uses his sword to chop the head off another, the bloody mass taking down three climbers on its way down.

Archers are standing on the ground, shooting for the climbing warriors, desperately trying to lessen some of the competition. Others don't bother climbing at all, instead battling on the ground, their souls already halfway to the Shadow Realm.

"Not going into that is probably the smartest thing you've done, princess."

Cael's breath against my ear sends a shiver down my spine and I realize he has stepped close while I was distracted watching the mountain.

With a muttered curse, I suck in a breath and take a step away.

I can't allow myself to get distracted. He may not have done anything to harm me in the past, but we're in the middle of the Tournament now, and there are no longer any rules.

"Let me guess. Your king has put a prize on my head and you've come to collect it yourself." My hand fumbles for the dagger on my thigh, but his hand clamps down on my wrist.

"If anyone is taking your life, it's going to be me. But not today. I'll see you on the top." His nose brushes against the skin at the back of my neck, reminding me of all sorts of emotions I've been trying to forget. "And by the way, I liked you better in black."

When I turn around, he's gone, and I think that maybe he didn't lie when he said the shadows serve him.

THE PRIESTESSES in the Sun Temple of Verbena are not pleased with me.

"The temple is not part of the Tournament. You can't do this, Your Highness."

Their whispered voices follow me as I assess my possibilities, their long white ropes snaking across the limestone floor. The ones unable to speak are only glowering at me from the few shadows in the temple, their lips sewn shut as an offering to the gods.

"There are no rules, remember?"

"But the gods–"

"The gods will be pleased they are helping a princess win," I snap, narrowing my eyes.

"The Tournament was created as a gift to the royals, isn't that what you're all blabbering about at the coronations? I'm sure you don't want me to disturb the king during the most exciting trial of the Tournament, the bargain and gift from the gods, but if you insist–"

Those words finally make them stop pestering me and retreat

into the shadows of the temple, their lips pursed as they undoubtedly chant silent prayers to the gods.

At least my princess status is useful for something else than being a prize in the games.

Some of the roaring chaos outside has subsided. There is no longer a clambering crowd at the bottom of the mountain—at least not a moving one. Countless bodies are lying strewn throughout the clearing, some bloody and missing limbs, others still left with a slight movement in their bodies.

The holy mountain is still nothing but a battleground, warriors climbing and fighting each other for both space and victory.

The sounds of battle are consuming and enthralling. Steel is clanking against steel, swords and daggers are flying through the air, and piercing screams echo as warrior after warrior tumbles to the ground. And then there's the roaring of the crowd—the combined sounds so loud it feels as if the very mountain is shaking.

Using the columns as momentum, I heave myself up on the roof of the temple.

The white limestone is cracked and ancient, the cracks allowing the sunlight to cast an eerie light in the rest of the temple. I carefully maneuver around the worst parts, each step light and deliberate.

As I'm about to start the climb, I notice a lone figure above me.

Cael is almost at the top of the connecting mountain to Kylo, high above everyone else climbing directly on the large mountain, his movements fast and efficient.

That shouldn't be possible.

He has to be an exceptionally good climber to outrace the

competitors who started right as the game opened, but he doesn't have to fight anyone off like the rest of the warriors.

No one else seems to think about taking another route.

No one else but him and me.

The wall of the mountain is sharp, the rocks cutting and scraping the skin of my palms as I climb. My feet are fighting to find secure spots in the cracks and crevices, my heart dropping each time my foot slips.

Climbing the holy mountain is very different from climbing the trees outside of the palace to hide from the guards–a talent I've been perfecting ever since I managed to sneak out of the palace as a little girl. Kylo is so tall and jagged that it's absolutely crazy to even think about climbing it, but of course, nothing is deadly enough when it comes to the Tournament.

It doesn't matter what the trial is. My body is used to hard work and it will take a while before my muscles start to ache and scream from the effort.

I can do this.

Whatever it takes, Asteria.

I try to ignore the pummeling drop underneath me along with the shrieks of other warriors, the sounds of their screams swallowed by the roaring wind as the clearing claims their lives. With deep breaths, I count each new grip of my hands and feet, willing my heart to steady enough to keep me somewhat calm.

Two more grips and I finally reach the top of the temple mountain.

I collapse on the ground, my whole body shaking–my soul vibrating from the adrenaline coursing through me and the magic screaming in the air.

The top of Kylo is still far away, its crown gilded by the disappearing sunlight, the cluster of clouds gliding above making me wonder if the gods have finally descended from the sky.

I only allow myself to breathe for a moment before crawling to the edge of the mountain, instantly regretting it when I see the ocean of warriors hurrying toward me.

"You're not on the top yet! And here I was thinking I would have some real competition!" Cael's shouts echo in the mountain range. He's nearing the top of Kylo, still way ahead of the other warriors that are soon going to catch up with me.

The moon warrior's taunting is highly effective.

My blood thrums with the challenge, some deeply buried instinct screaming to catch up with him, the magic a string pulled taut between us. I can almost hear the most bloodthirsty of the gods urging me on, their magic seeping into my limbs and giving me the strength I need.

Whatever it takes, Asteria.

I heave myself off the mountain ground, desperate to not lose the advantage over the other warriors. When they reach the same height as me, it's going to be a much harder climb.

My body is stiff and sore as I align myself with Kylo, the holy mountain seeming endlessly tall as I again crane my neck to look at the top.

Cael is sitting on an outcrop in the mountain, legs dangling over the edge with an insufferable grin on his face as he looks down at me. He waves his fingers in my direction, and I grit my teeth as I increase my tempo.

"Hurry, princess, or I might start thinking you don't care about beating me like you promised–what is it now? Four times?"

The sun is almost gone on the horizon, her rays of light desperately lighting the path for the warriors. Silver glittering stars blink into existence, reminding every warrior that the Tournament is also for the night and the moon.

Time is running out.

I have to reach the top before the last trace of sunlight disappears and darkness envelops the world.

"If you've trained as much as you claim, this shouldn't be that difficult for you, starlight. Or maybe your trainer didn't think long enough to even consider the holy mountain to be a crucial part of the Tournament. What was that? No one supports your participation? Pity. Maybe you're simply playing for the wrong team."

His taunting voice is closer now, and if I strain my arm enough, I might be able to reach his feet to drag him down.

"Careful, moon boy, or I might drag you off this mountain myself," I say through gritted teeth, hating how breathless I sound and how much my body aches.

The warrior laughs, the sound echoing throughout the chain of mountains, and if I turn around I'm almost certain I could glimpse Father glaring in our direction.

"Careful what you wish for, darling. You know what?" He leans forward, hand outstretched. "Why won't you just let me help you? We wouldn't want you to lose already, princess. Maybe this is a good time to make that bargain."

My foot slips on a loose rock and for a second, I'm almost tempted to actually take his hand.

"It's clear you're new to the reality of the Tournament despite your royal status, but bargains are a big part of the games," he says, a muscle ticking in his jaw, the blue in his eyes darkening. "There can only be one Victor, but there are ways to make sure you'll live long enough to see the finale. A bargain is an excellent way to do that."

"Did you learn your ramblings from the witches? I'm never going to make a bargain with someone from the enemy kingdom, that I can promise the gods. Now move before I shove you off."

Silver sparks in his eyes, the sight more magical than anything

I've ever witnessed. "It seems I'm not the only one conversing with witches, and you should be careful what you promise the gods, starlight—"

"Call me that again and you'll find my steel somewhere uncomfortable."

A slight tug of his lips is his only reply to my threat. "Don't interrupt me again unless it involves the same method I used the last time we were together."

He gives me a wink before all playfulness is replaced by a glowering look that sends a shiver down my spine. "As I was saying—You've already made another bargain than the one on your neck."

My heartbeat quickens at his words, my hands pressing against the rocky mountain so hard it hurts. "I don't know what you're talking about. And I'm warning you for the last time—"

"I guess I'll see you on the top, then," he says with another wink. And then he hauls himself up the mountain as if it's the easiest thing in the world.

Stirred on by his taunting, I hurry after him.

The climb grows more steep and jagged, the rocks continuing to cut and slice my skin. My long braid slaps against my cheek, the pale loose strands blowing in front of my eyes remind me of harsh winter storms. And with all the sounds and chaos roaring around me—there is no doubt the Tournament is the most raging tempest of them all.

The sun disappears on the horizon. Kylo is cast in the shadows of the night, its crown a beacon of light with the last traces of sunlight.

That is where I need to be. That is where the goal is.

Whatever it takes, Asteria.

Cael has vanished, his dark form nowhere in sight.

I curse the gods. If it weren't for the man attacking me—

Silver light erupts in the sky above like a storm of lightning before swirls of silver dance across the sky in a beautiful cascading pattern. The thunderous sounds of the magic reverberate through the kingdoms, so loud it threatens to take down the entire world.

Silver for Luna.

The first victory goes to the enemy kingdom, and with it, a surge of magic is added to the kingdom's life essence–an essence which the royals draw their power from.

My fingers reach for the top of Kylo–the crown and sacred ground, and I feel the rush of magic in the air. It's as if the binding mark on my neck has come alive, the lines thrumming in rhythm with the dancing silver lights.

Just as my fingers grasp the ground of the mountain, something tugs at my foot, yanking me back.

A woman with short-cropped blonde hair is the first in a line of warriors that seems to have appeared out of nowhere. Her face is contorted in a sneer and blood runs down her face from a gash on her forehead. One of her hands is braced on the mountain wall, the other has a strong hold around my leg.

Always be aware of who and what's around you.

The most important rule Elio made me repeat during our last training session, a rule that seems to have slipped from my mind as my body grew tired and the trial more brutal.

I kick the air with my foot, trying to wriggle out of the woman's grasp. Her sharp nails dig into the leather at my ankles, sending small sparks of pain shooting up my leg.

"I'm not letting you win this, princess," she spits, her grip hardening as she continues trying to drag me down.

"Someone already won–"

The silver light is still visible in the sky, the color a mirror image of the silver in the eyes of the first winner of this year's Tournament.

The woman spits again and mutters a string of curses. "Winning is not only about being the first to complete the trial. Winning means surviving. And you're not going to survive. I'm here to claim another prize." She gives another hard tug, and I try to dig my fingers into the soil of the mountaintop.

Whatever it takes, Asteria.

"You went after the wrong princess," I snarl and finally manage to kick her in the face, but not hard enough for her grip to falter.

I fumble to unsheathe the Victory Dagger, the carvings on the handle digging into my skin as I ready myself to use it as a last effort to shake her off.

I'm too late.

The warrior lets out a hollering scream and plunges her dagger into the back of my thigh, her hand still wrapped around my other leg.

The pain of the blade startles me and my leg slips from the frail rock, debris flying as the rock comes loose.

The Victory Dagger slips from my hand, barely missing the raging warrior beneath me, and my heart cracks as the dagger is lost to the wind.

The only thing keeping me from plummeting to the ground is my fingertips.

A wave of fear slams into me, my heart beating so hard I'm afraid that will be my undoing.

I try to heave myself to the top, my fingers grasping for anything more stable than the strands of grass currently between them.

My chin grazes the top of the mountain and my eyes land on a dark form in the distance, a shadow in the last light of the sun.

The dagger is yanked out of my thigh only to be slammed into other places on my leg again and again, the woman still trying to drag me away by practically hanging from my ankle.

I vaguely wonder if she even cares that she is risking falling with me.

My whole body is shaking and I don't know how much longer I can hang on.

Whatever it takes, Asteria!

Arrows puncture my back, a victorious cry from the shooter sounding in the distance.

A piercing scream echoes off the mountains, blood roaring in my ears, the pain in my body blinding and all-consuming.

A pair of glowing silver eyes as bright as the stars of the night sky is the last thing I see before my grip on the mountain falters and I slip away.

I fall through the air, straight for the roof of the temple down below.

CHAPTER SIX

The world is nothing but darkness and everything hurts. My limbs are too heavy, my blood a rushing river threatening to topple over any second. My skin is burning, scorched by flames, and hot red sparks shoot through my body. And then there's the cold. An icy wind is blowing through me, chips of ice hitting me as if I were standing in the middle of a harsh winter storm, my soul as cold as the depths of the ocean.

"Asteria?"

The voice is distant and too far away for me to grasp.

Is it the voice of the gods fighting to drag me deeper into the Shadow Realm? Or maybe–

My eyes flutter as a wet cloth is pressed against my forehead. A white limestone ceiling with carved symbols of the sun flickers across my vision.

Something or someone is prodding my leg.

"Asteria?"

The world fades back into darkness and I don't know how much time passes before I hear the voice again.

"Asteria? Are you awake?"

A warm hand strokes my cheek, the feeling of something other than pain a relief.

"Asteria–"

My eyes blink open, and the light of the world is too bright and blinding.

After a few seconds of rapidly blinking, my eyes adjust to the light, revealing an unfamiliar room.

The sun is shining through large open windows, the breeze fluttering the purple and pink tinted drapes scented by lemon and something sweet. An assortment of herbs, plants, potions, and other healing remedies are stacked on the walls, the room reminding me of the healing rooms at the Sun Palace where I've been forced to sneak into when the wounds on my back wouldn't stop bleeding on their own.

"Asteria?"

My attention snaps to the person sitting at the edge of my bed, to the warm hand still pressed against my cheek.

"Thank the sun. I almost thought–" Elio's voice breaks off, but the unfinished sentence lingers in the air.

I almost thought the Tournament claimed your life. I almost thought you were dead.

"Still alive," I croak, the words ending in a cough.

"Here."

Elio carefully pours a glass of water into my mouth, the cool liquid a relief to my burning throat. He helps me sit up in the bed, my body protesting each small movement.

"Did I make it? My fingers touched the crown but I can't remember if I managed to get on top or not–"

"Asteria–" Elio sighs heavily and drags a hand through his short-cropped hair.

There's a tiredness to him that wasn't there the last time I saw him. His bronzed skin looks paler than usual, and there are lines etched underneath his hazel eyes. Even his victory mark seems dimmer, the sparkling gold reduced to only a faint yellow tinge.

"What?"

My mind is racing as I try to remember the events of the first trial. The bloodbath before I even started climbing, the moon warrior, the woman trying to cut me down, the Victory Dagger–

"No, Ria. I'm sorry, but–"

"Don't say it," I mutter through gritted teeth, firmly closing my eyes as the back of my head bangs against the wall.

"By the sun, Asteria–" Elio mutters a low curse and I feel his hands reach forward to move my head away from the wall.

A humorless chuckle escapes me as I mutter a curse of my own. "I bet the king is thrilled I'm out of the Tournament, and perhaps a little annoyed that the gods didn't claim my life."

A sharp intake of breath is Elio's only reply and I open my eyes to see him looking up at the ceiling as if he's searching for the gods.

"Spit it out, Elio."

Another heavy sigh escapes him, but this time he meets my eyes.

"I haven't left your side since I carried you in. The king–" he purses his lips and a shudder rocks through him, his gaze flickering to my shoulders and the scars hidden behind them.

I can't help flinching at his words.

"It shouldn't surprise me. Failing just before the finish line is humiliating enough, but for a princess of the sun finally able to participate–"

"That's not it," Elio interrupts, shifting in his seat. "Your participation in the games is not the only thing that has him in a mood."

Rubbing my aching temples, I give him an exasperated look

before reaching for the glass of water left on the table next to my bed. "Spit it out, Elio," I repeat, more slowly this time.

"The Sun Temple of Verbena is ruined."

"What?" I choke on the water and spit it out onto the mattress.

"You fell right through the roof."

I blow out a breath, trying to suppress the laughter bubbling in my throat. Imagining the look on their faces as I fell from the sky like some sort of goddess–

"I'm sure the priestesses were very pleased with that."

Elio gives me a stern look and drags a hand through his hair, a gesture I realize has turned into a nervous habit. "Asteria, you shouldn't even be alive right now."

The smile disappears from my lips.

I shouldn't be alive right now.

My fingers trail over the bare skin on my forearm underneath the sheets. Where there only weeks ago was a raw wound, only faint scrapes remain–a mark now void of magic.

It should be impossible to survive a fall from Kylo and see the light of the next day.

I'm only alive thanks to the stolen life essence.

"I'm afraid to ask how," Elio whispers. "I don't want to know what kind of trouble you got into to get an advantage like that. I'm only happy you're alive." He rests his hand on top of mine, the warmth of his skin seeping into me.

I give him a weak smile.

Right now, being alive does not feel like the great gift it should be.

Elio's eyes bore into mine, an urgent expression on his face as he opens his mouth to say something. "Asteria–"

The door to the room crashes open, revealing the last person in the world I want to see right now.

"You are alive." The Sun King's glare throws invisible daggers at me, the pain in my body intensifying in reply.

"Are you displeased by that?"

"I would not want your ending ceremony to take the attention away from the Tournament. But you have already managed to bring the attention away from the trials." He shoots a look at Elio, silently ordering him to leave before scowling at our touching hands.

Elio doesn't move from his position on the bed, his grip on my hand tightening.

Anger flares in the king's eyes, the gilded sparks of his magic lighting up his face. His mouth pulls into a sneer, his fingers twitching in the direction of the Royal Sword strapped to his side.

Magic crackles in the air, raising the hairs on my arms and clenching my heart.

I brace for the storm of his fury.

"I'll see you later, Elio," I say, willing the gods to keep my voice steady and my body from trembling.

Elio only locks his jaw, his head giving a slight shake as his eyes continue to bore into mine.

"Do we have a problem, *Victor*?"

"No," I say, squeezing Elio's hand with as much strength I can–a silent plea and order.

The Sun King's hand is now firmly closed over the handle of the Royal Sword, the gold in his eyes brighter than the sunlight seeping in from the windows.

I don't know why, but at that moment, I hear the awed rumors whispered throughout the kingdom.

"They say he can talk flowers into opening their petals during the dark nights, as though his face is the sun. And that when he walks through gardens, all flowers bend to his will."

If only they knew the truth about him.

Elio might be the latest Victor, but the title doesn't grant him immunity when it comes to the wrath of the king. No matter how much I dread the inevitable punishments, I won't risk the life of the only friend I may ever have.

"I'll see you later, Elio," I repeat, giving him another squeeze. And then, a little lower, "Leave. Now."

The Victor's eyes stare into mine for a little longer, his teeth grinding together so hard I can only imagine the pounding in his head.

I give him my best encouraging look, straightening my posture and lifting my chin with as much dignity as I can while still lying in the bed.

Please leave. It will be so much worse if you stay. I can take whatever he throws at me, but I can't bear the thought of him hurting you too.

Elio holds my gaze for a second longer before reluctantly letting go of my hand. The Victor bows his head toward the king and silently exits the room without looking back.

I hate that there's a small part of me that's hoping he will come back and save me from this mess, that I will see his glimmering hazel eyes and mischievous smile as he emerges through the door.

But of course, he doesn't come back.

I learned a long time ago that no one will save me from anything, and I'm starting to doubt that I can save myself.

I slowly move my gaze away from the empty doorway to the gilded tips of the king's boots.

Alone with the king, my breath is too heavy, my chest constricted and my heart hammering so hard it feels as if it's threatening to break out of my skin. The scars on my back tremble and I brace myself for the pain that will come.

I can only imagine the punishment for destroying a sacred

temple, let alone the humiliation of failing in the very first trial of the Tournament.

"You are lucky your body is so beaten it cannot take anymore," the king growls, the words so unexpected I almost think I heard him wrong.

I don't answer, spotting the challenge and threat for what it is. If I keep my gaze averted and stay silent, I might be able to escape the worst of his fury.

"And we would not want you to look like this when we present you to your betrothed," he drawls, voice dripping with disgust.

"What?" My head snaps up, the abrupt motion causing the muscles along my neck to start throbbing.

A grin that can't mean anything good spreads across his lips as he trails his fingers over the carvings on the handle of his sword "We do not want you looking like that when we present you to your betrothed," he says, as if repeating the words will somehow make it more final.

"I have made a deal with the bastard. I am giving you to one of his sons."

"No-"

"You are in no position to argue, *daughter*," he snaps, moving to stand in front of my bed as a roving mountain even more intimidating than Kylo.

My whole body stiffens when he unsheathes the sword from his side, and I once again brace for the pain, praying to the gods it will be quick.

The long blade glimmers in the sunlight, and I'm reminded of all the times I was forced to polish it until the blade was nothing but gilded perfection, blood from his enemies as often as my own staining it.

A low chuckle escapes Father when he notices my expression.

"Oh, do not worry. The knowledge of your future should be enough punishment—" he slides the tip of the blade over the sheets covering my body, the blade brushing over the places another pierced my skin only hours or perhaps even days ago, "—for now. But perhaps I will give him some pointers on how to discipline you later."

"You can't be serious," I blurt, unable to stop myself despite the brightening of his eyes and the closeness of the Royal Sword.

"They're the enemy. A marriage between the sun and moon is unheard of! By the sky, you enjoy punishing those who break those rules. You can't give me to them. I refuse—"

"You refuse?" The king is practically screaming now, the tip of the blade pressing into the mattress right next to my ankle. Feathers spring out of the fabric, the small pieces fluttering away on the slight breeze blowing through the open windows "Just like you refused to even consider the countless suitors sent your way?"

"That's not the same! They were never going to accept me anyway. They were either too friendly or terrified—"

He lets out a laugh that sends shivers down my arms. "Do you really want to talk about the suitors? Fine. How about the time you purposely chose a hike through the hydra lairs or the time when—"

"I get it," I mutter through gritted teeth, carefully moving my foot away from the blade he is twisting into the mattress. "But the Moon Princes are the enemy. Either one of them will do me worse than a hike through the woods."

A cruel smirk pulls at the king's lips, his eyes glinting from the promise of future punishment. "I am sure you will be well-behaved for them. And if not—" he pushes the Royal Sword all the way through the mattress, the clinking sound of steel meeting marble echoing across the walls.

"I'm not leaving," I say, voice barely a whisper.

Father yanks the blade out of the bed and aims it straight at my neck.

The blood in my veins freeze and I hold my breath, the sound of my beating heart too loud in the quiet room.

The tip of the Royal Sword presses against the side of my neck, and just as I'm sure he's finally going to end me, he moves my hair away with the blade to reveal the binding mark of the Tournament.

"I warned you not to humiliate my kingdom. And since you failed, you are no longer worthy of the sun. So, I am making you someone else's problem," he growls as he traces the blade over the pulsing lines on my neck, each line a little harder than the last.

"No," he continues, dragging out the word. "You will not be a problem any longer. For anyone. No more destruction, no more humiliation, no more rumors, and certainly no more trouble. You know where that will get you."

I swallow against the lump in my throat, trying to ignore the way the blade presses a little harder against my skin at the gesture. I lock my gaze on the wall behind him, the gold in his eyes too bright to look at.

It wouldn't be the first time he blinded someone with his light.

"Do not look so sad, *daughter*. You always knew the day would come. If only you would have stayed out of trouble and taken the chance when you had it." He lets out a dramatic sigh. "And now you will even get to cross the border for real."

I resist the urge to close my eyes against the memories flooding my mind of the last and only time I attempted to cross the border.

"Make sure you paint over this when I present you to your betrothed or I will personally see it removed. There is no need to display your failure," he spits, pressing the blade so hard I feel a few drops of blood trail down my neck.

"Oh, and the Tournament? You are out. Forever. You have humiliated this realm enough. I told you the battleground was no place for a princess and now you have proven it yourself. Do not bother praying to the gods for a second chance. They will not grant you one, and neither will I."

The Sun King wipes the blade of the Royal Sword on my cheek before sheathing it back at his side—the gilded blade always an extension of his being.

With a last cruel smirk in my direction, he turns around without another word.

When I'm sure he's nowhere near the room and my body has gained some movement back, I take a deep breath and open my mouth.

My shattering screams echo off the marble tiles, startling the sleeping birds in the trees outside of the open window, and it wouldn't surprise me if even the gods stirred in their deep slumber at my utter despair and rage.

CHAPTER SEVEN

Hiding in the shadows outside of the tavern, I peek in through the window. The small space is already crowded with warriors, the liquid in their glasses spilling onto the wooden tables.

The border market in Verbena is bustling and thriving in the weeks of the Tournament with its taverns and vendors that's closed off the rest of the year, and after the court game is finished it's so crowded it's difficult to find an available spot.

Making sure the hood of my dark cloak is still in place, I slip in through the door, choosing a seat in a dark corner.

It will still be a few days before the remains of the magical mark have done all the healing it can do, and the dark clothes conceal my healing bruises and tender skin as much as my identity.

It's easy to blend into the crowd. Tonight, I'm just one of many thirsty warriors celebrating their first completed trial or drowning their sorrows of not making it.

I've barely taken a sip of my glass when someone slides in on the bench next to me.

The man is also concealed in a dark cloak, only the lower half of his face visible in the candlelight.

His disguise doesn't matter.

"I'm not interested," I hiss, taking a sip of the watered-out drink.

"Really? And here I was, thinking that was exactly why you were here, lurking in the shadows. I would've thought you preferred the light, princess." His deep voice slithers through my skin and rattles my bones.

Slamming my glass down onto the table, I sneer at him, "Keep your voice down, moon boy."

Cael reaches forward and lifts my glass, observing it in the dim light. As he leans forward, I catch a glimpse of his frowning expression. "Is this the best your kingdom has to offer?"

I snatch the glass from his hands, my fingers grazing his. "Definitely not. This is surely something from your kingdom."

He snorts. "I was almost afraid the Shadow Realm had claimed you already, but it seems I wasn't that lucky after all," he purrs and leans forward to rest his elbows on the table.

"Don't say that. I'm out. It seems the gods may have blessed you after all. A perk of winning the first game, maybe?" The meek liquid burns my throat as I chug it down, the taste sour on my tongue as I try to drown my bitter jealousy.

A crease forms between his perfectly sculpted eyebrows. "I didn't take you for one to give up. And–" his hand reaches forward to trail his fingers along my binding mark before I can stop him, "you're bound to the Tournament. I don't think you have a choice, starlight.

His fingers linger on my skin for a moment, stroking against the sensitive skin on my neck before retreating into his dark cloak.

"Didn't you hear me? I'm out. I'm sure seeing me fall through

THE VICTOR OF DAY AND NIGHT 79

the temple roof was entertaining enough," I sneer, slamming my now-empty glass back onto the wooden table.

"My bargain with the gods is over." I make an exasperated sound as I reach for the other glass with the same dull brown liquid. Deciding against it, I put the glass back on the table and push it away.

I should've raided the king's storage instead. The townhouse in Verbena has a very interesting assortment hidden away.

Cael studies me for a moment, the lit candles in the tavern reflecting the silver specks in his eyes. "It doesn't have to be over."

I roll my eyes before snapping my fingers for a server to refill my glass with something better. "I told you I'm not in the mood. Leave before I drag you out of here myself."

"Your threats aren't very good at the moment, princess. But there is a way for you to prove yourself."

Cael raises his eyebrows in challenge, intently studying me while the server fills my glass with a red liquid, the sight reminding me too much of the blood dripping from his hands when he slayed the warriors outside of the Sun Temple.

I hand a heap of golden coins to the server, ignoring her confused looks. I wave a dismissive hand, lowering my head so she won't realize who I am.

"I'm not in the mood."

"I thought winning the Tournament was the most important thing in your life."

Whatever it takes, Asteria.

The red liquid leaves a sweet tangy taste in my mouth. I pour it all down my throat before throwing a few more coins onto the table.

"Goodbye, Cael."

His hand shoots out to grab my wrist. "Didn't you hear what

I said? I know how you can continue competing in the Tournament."

"And let me guess, the only way you'll tell me is if I make a bargain with you?" I try to wriggle free from him, but his grip is as solid as iron.

"Yes. A bargain that will be in both of our favor."

'Like I said–" I lean close to him, ignoring his heady scent and the way the magic of the Tournament still has a grip on me despite my humiliating exit, "I'm not interested."

A low growl reverberates from his chest, but his grip slackens enough for me to shove him away and walk out of the tavern.

The cool air is a relief compared to the hot air inside, the summer breeze carrying with it the sweet smell from the fields of verbena flowers. Countless kinglights are floating through the city, lighting up the darkness and displaying Soria's greatness.

People of all ages are strolling through the market, numerous guards and soldiers mixed into the crowds, silver and gold armor clanking as they patrol the streets. Cheers and applause echo through the city, victorious cries bleeding into desperate pleas to the gods for a second chance.

I keep to the shadows, ignoring the light footsteps trailing behind me until I'm out of the bustling market, the only lights the glittering stars and moon overhead.

"What will it take for you to leave me alone?" I shout, cursing the moon for shining light on my dark future.

"Make a bargain with me."

Cael is suddenly in front of me, the darkness seeming to cling to him as he crosses his arms. There's a subtle pulsing energy that rolls off him in the moonlight, as if he draws his power from the night itself, and perhaps he does.

It wouldn't surprise me if he is out bargaining with other people than a lonely princess and has stumbled upon ways to borrow magic. I'm too unfamiliar with the ways of the Lunan people to exclude that possibility.

I easily found forbidden magic, and so could others.

An exasperated sound escapes me before I let out a frustrated scream. "Damn you insufferable men who won't take no for an answer and damn the king from selling me to one of you. My future is already spoken for. It doesn't belong to me anymore. It's over."

I move past him, my eyes glued to the white ruins in the distance.

The once magnificent Sun Temple of Verbena is a mess of shattered limestone, the beautiful carvings of the gods gone in a heap of debris. Kylo is a towering giant behind the ruins, its crown hidden by dark clouds, its mighty height so intimidating it sends a shiver down my spine.

No one should be able to survive a fall like that.

I defied the gods and used forbidden magic all for nothing and I've yet to pay the price.

"And now you're just going to be a perfect bride for the prince?" Cael is in front of me again, blocking my path with a hard expression on his face.

"I never said I was going to marry a prince," I say, wariness creeping into my voice.

From the first time I laid my eyes upon him, I've known he's not simply another warrior in the Tournament. There's something different about him—something dangerous I'm afraid to learn the truth about.

Cael shrugs. "I don't expect the king to promise one of his princesses to anyone but a prince. And I didn't think you took orders from anyone but yourself. Are you going to let a stupid prince stop you?"

"Why do you even care?"

"I don't," he says with another shrug, "but you should." He waves his fingers in the same taunting manner he did on Kylo before moving away to let me pass.

"Well, I don't care either," I snap, shoving my shoulder into his side as I pass.

"And I don't believe you. You sacrificed a lot to bind yourself, and now you're just going to give up? I'm telling you, there is a way."

"I'm out! It's done." I turn on my heels, pressing a finger into his broad chest. "That won't change no matter what bargain you offer me–"

"Oh, but it's not over. I'll tell you how you can get back in the games if you do something for me in return."

A dark chuckle escapes me. "You're a warrior of the enemy kingdom bent on taunting a princess. Why should I believe anything you say? There's no way I'm trusting you enough to make a bargain. You're just a warrior in the games, how could you possibly know anything of value–"

I'm silenced by a finger on my lips, his other hand removing my finger from his chest before pulling down one of his sleeves.

Seven scarred lines are etched onto the skin just below his wrist–the count of how many times a warrior has participated in the Tournament. His pale skin is glowing in the moonlight, the lines a red so dark it's almost black–just like the binding mark peeking up from the collar of his shirt.

"Well?" Cael's thumb briefly strokes along my bottom lip, and when he retreats his finger, my skin is frozen cold.

"Who are you?"

Instinct has me reaching for one of my hidden daggers, and I silently curse myself for forgetting them in my cloud of despair and rage.

Cael shrugs and walks past me toward the ruins. "Someone

willing to make a bargain with the most interesting princess of the sun."

"You're a Victor."

I can't help hurrying after him, the invisible string of magic more tangible than ever.

And then there is the voice in my head that will never quiet, reminding me of a lifelong promise I can't break.

Whatever it takes, Asteria.

"Yes." His voice is hollow and so very different from the bragging tone of the other Victors I've met who are always ready to shout their achievements to the sky.

"Then why haven't I seen you before?"

The previous Victors always make a grand point out of their title, and if they're unable to–their families are always there to make sure they're not forgotten.

"It has been a while since my last victory," Cael says simply and squats down in the middle of the ruins to dig through the wreckage.

"So, do we have a bargain? I'll tell you how you can continue playing the game in exchange for a favor." He gets back to his feet, dusting off his hands before tucking them into the pockets of his pants.

"A favor?"

"A favor." A wicked smile pulls at his lips, mischief glimmering in his eyes as his gaze rakes over me.

I don't like the knowing look in his eyes.

Using magic is not technically forbidden in the Tournament. He could be lying about the whole thing, but the marks on his body speak otherwise.

And after all, there are no rules in the Tournament of Day and Night.

But magical bargains–they can be even more dangerous than the forbidden magic I used.

He only wants a favor. How bad could it be? I'm already doomed to live out my days in the enemy kingdom and nothing could be worse than that.

Whatever it takes, Asteria. Whatever it takes!

"Fine," I say through gritted teeth, praying to the gods I'm not making another mistake.

"What's the favor?"

"I'll tell you what it is when I need it."

His lips are pressed against mine before I even have the time to blink, the kiss rough and branding.

"What a tragic way to spend a favor," I mutter, shoving away from him before wiping my hand over my mouth in a dramatic gesture.

"That was not the favor. For someone claiming to be well acquainted with magic you sure know little about it. I'm the one doing you a favor by sealing our bargain that way. You know, considering you're still beat up by the first trial I thought a kiss was better than blood." The corners of his lips tug upward in amusement, his eyes pure darkness now.

"Speaking of the Tournament–spill," I snarl, ignoring the way my heart sped up at his closeness and the way it now refuses to steady.

Cael's hand reaches forward to pull my hair away from my neck, his fingers tracing the lines of the binding mark. "You are in the Tournament. You made it through, princess. Didn't you feel the magic?"

"What?" I slap his hand away, stumbling back only to be caught by his arms before I tumble to the ground.

His breath tickles my neck when he speaks, his hands snaking around my waist to cradle my back to his chest. "That day in

Moria during the bindings, you bound yourself to the Tournament. So unless you want your life claimed for good, you don't have any other choice than to continue. Your feet may not have touched the crown of Kylo, but as long as parts of you did—" one of his hands moves to my hand, his fingers featherlight against the tips of my fingers.

My mind is racing from his words, images of the trial and the mountain flickering across my vision.

I remember feeling the power in the air when the sky sparked silver, how it slithered across my skin and made the marks on my body pulse in reply, but that was only because of the Tournament magic–

"You're lying. I don't believe you."

It's too good to be true. If there's one thing that has been certain these last few days, it is that I failed.

Cael shrugs, his head coming to rest on my shoulder. "I guess you don't have to believe me. Go ahead. Take the chance. Don't compete and see if you survive. I would've thought you knew the risks of playing with magic. You might be a princess, but the magic is binding for that exact reason. There are no perks for the royals, not in the Tournament of Night and Day. We had so much fun the last time we played together, why should I lie to you now?"

His breath sends shivers down my neck, the invisible string between us pulled taut, and I vaguely wonder if the Tournament will have a grip on me until my soul departs for the Shadow Realm, active binding mark or not.

"And besides, we have a bargain. I promised to tell you how you could continue in the Tournament. If I was lying, my life would have already been claimed by the gods. Do I feel dead to you?" His lips graze the sensitive skin on the spot between my neck and shoulder, his touch igniting sparks all over my body.

"No, but–"An involuntary sigh leaves my lips as his fingers start stroking idle circles on my hands, his lips leaving a scorching trail down to my collarbone.

"Wait, that's it?!" I push away from his grasp only to fall down in the middle of the ruins scattered on the ground.

Cael's arms are outstretched in the air, as if he is considering reaching for me again.

"You can't be serious. That was the piece of information I bargained for?"

His hands curl into fists at his side, something I can't place flickering across his features. "You got what you wanted. I'll see you at the next trial," he practically spits, every last bit of teasing and taunting suddenly gone.

"There has to be something more! The king will kill me if he sees me in the next trial–"

"Then wear a disguise. We're done here," Cael growls before reaching into his pockets to throw something into the ruins behind him.

"We are not done!" I jump back on my feet, cursing myself for the large amount of liquor I consumed as I sway unsteadily. "You tricked me!"

"There are no rules in the Tournament, remember?" He stalks past me, the gentle wind blowing through the night embracing me with his heady scent.

"This is not the Tournament."

Cael halts and turns around enough to give me an indignant look. "The Tournament doesn't end between the trials, princess. If it did, your kingdom wouldn't currently be blessed with this beautiful night. I'm sure I'll see you around. You owe me a favor after all."

And then he's gone, disappeared in the shadows as if he was never here at all.

I scream and curse him, daring him to come back and finish what he started, screaming that I'll do him a favor and send him to the shadows for good.

He doesn't come back.

One last scream and my eyes land on the spot in the ruins where the warrior was standing only moments ago.

Something glimmers in the moonlight, drawing my attention forward.

The Victory Dagger is lying in the middle of the ruins.

The sign from the gods couldn't have been any clearer.

My participation in the Tournament is not over. It has only just begun.

Father has promised me to the enemy kingdom, diminishing my light–a light that will extinguish and then cease to exist altogether.

He thinks I'm disposable, just one of many daughters of light, never even considering that my light might be the one of a queen. I was the child that wasn't supposed to be born, an inconvenient accident and deadly mistake for the late queen.

The Sun King is wrong.

Not only am I going to win the Tournament, I will kill the prince of night and destroy his kingdom. My light will outshine all their darkness, leaving our land in never-ending light forever.

The prince thinks he's getting a submissive daughter of the sun, a loyal bride, but he is about to meet his worst nightmare.

Whatever it takes.

CHAPTER EIGHT

"You're so lucky with that beautiful hair. You can choose any color you want," a voice rings out behind me, startling me, my fingers halting their exploration of the exquisite fabric on the vendor's table in front of me.

In the midst of the bustling market, no longer an obvious target for the other warriors in the Tournament, I let my guard drop enough not to notice someone sneaking up on me.

I mutter a curse before turning around, my fingers itching to grab the dagger hidden underneath my shirt.

"Oh, I'm sorry, princess. I didn't mean to scare you. Although I did expect it took a little more to scare someone like you."

The woman is wearing fighting leathers in a deep shade of cobalt blue, the stripes in her hair the same shade of blue. Her eyes are a mix of light blue and green, the sunlight making the colors swirl together like the water of a tide pool.

She tilts her head to the side, exposing the mark on her neck–the binding mark of this year's Summer Solstice Tournament glistening in the sunlight. "That was some stunt you pulled. You should've seen the look on those priestesses' faces."

The warrior chuckles, holding out her hand. "You can call me Skye. And yes, the irony is not lost on me."

When I don't take it, she only shrugs before tucking her hands into the pockets at her sides.

"How did you recognize me?"

Ever since I snuck out of the palace this morning, I've made sure the hood is tightly secured over my head, but I don't bother denying it now. That often draws even more attention.

Skye waves her hands dismissively. "How could I not?"

"Where are you from?"

The color of her fighting leathers doesn't give it away. The cobalt blue could represent anything from the ocean basking in the daylight or the night sky as it is rumored to be right next to the Diamond Mountains in Luna.

It wouldn't be the first time a warrior chose to wear the colors of the enemy kingdom.

Skye shrugs again. "I guess you could say a little bit of both kingdoms and a whole lot of other places too." Her lips pull into a mischievous smile, giving me the impression she has a lot of tricks hidden up her sleeves. And why wouldn't she when she is a part of the deadly games?

"And what do you want?"

I realize I've placed my feet in a fighting stance, ready to defend myself if this strange woman decides to suddenly pounce on me.

The killing is usually reserved for the games, but forgetting the Tournament is still very much a presence outside of the games is a mistake I won't ever make again.

"You're a princess. Surely you must be used to people just wanting to talk to you." She frowns before briefly closing her eyes. "Right, the cursed princess and all that. That was a bad joke. I take it back. I guess I forgot about all the rumors for a second. I don't usually believe any."

I don't answer. I only blink at her, trying to read the puzzle in front of me.

From the way she holds herself, I can tell she must be a skilled warrior. The playfulness in her features is not fooling me.

"What do you want?" I repeat, letting a hard edge slice through my words so she knows I'm not in the mood for more games than the ones I'm already playing.

"I want to be friends."

The earnesty in her gaze surprises me, but I'm not one to easily fall for kind smiles and pretty eyes.

I've perfected a few masks of my own.

"I don't have friends," I say, trying to dismiss her and be done with my errands.

"Really? What about that handsome Victor carrying you away from the ruins?"

I wonder if I would've been left to die if I didn't have Elio. I can vividly imagine the king pretending the Tournament claimed my life and leaving me to rot alone in the middle of the ancient ruins.

"Allies then," Skye says with a sigh when I don't reply. "Temporary allies? For the Tournament?" Some of the earlier mischief creeps back onto her features, a secretive smile playing at her lips.

"I'm no longer in the Tournament. Like you said, it was some stunt I pulled. Now leave me alone." I retreat from my fighting stance, leaning my hip against the table as I cross my arms.

My body is still sore from the fall, but the days spent resting in bed have done me good. Only a few bruises and scrapes remain, thanks to the healing of the magic. Without it, there wouldn't be much of me left.

Her smile widens. "Yes, it was definitely a moment worthy of the gods. The most spectacular win I've seen in quite a while."

"It was nothing but a loss–"

Skye takes a step forward and lowers her voice, "I saw you touch the crown with my own eyes, princess. You're still in the competition and you would be a fool to think otherwise."

She moves to the side to trail her fingers over a piece of black leather lying on the table. "But it's obvious the fall didn't take all your wit seeing as you're here searching for new leathers. I would go for something a little less inconspicuous this time," she says with a wink in my direction.

I grind my teeth together, my nails digging into the scars in my palms.

If only I had met this warrior before the one who fooled me into promising a favor for a piece of information I should've been able to figure out for myself.

"Why?"

"Why not?" Skye gives me another secretive smile, seemingly pleased by my lack of refusal. "It's a smart move. You never know what the next trial might be."

"There can only be one Victor," I say through gritted teeth, hating that this stranger holds something over me.

All it would take for the king to doubt me is one person claiming I'm still bound.

"You'll have to survive the games first. And from what I hear, you'll need all the allies you can get." She glances down at my body, and it's almost as if I can feel her gaze on my hidden bruises —the evidence of my failure.

"What's in it for you?"

I don't want to think about another trial with the same outcome as the first one, but it would be useful to have someone on my side just in case it should happen.

But I can't trust anyone, especially not someone seeking out a royal with a very exploitable secret. Every warrior in the Tournament fights to win, and the stranger in front of me might be searching for another prize than a Victor's glory.

"I already told you what's in it for me. Having someone on your side is a smart move." Skye strokes her hand over the dark fabric on the table. "Go with the black. There is just something funny about a princess of the sun in the dark, don't you think?" She tilts her head to the side with a smirk.

She speaks again before I have the time to answer, "And get that dress. You're going to need it." She nods to a dress hanging on a rack to the side of the table. "I'll see you around." And then she winks again before walking away into the crowd.

There's just something funny about a princess of the sun in the dark, don't you think?

The words echo in my mind as I trail my fingers over the fabric of the dress.

It has a tight bodice with loose arms and ends in a long billowing skirt. Made of a silky fabric a blue so dark it's almost black with silver threads—the dress is crafted for Luna, the kingdom of darkness. Small silver pearls are scattered across the dress, representing the countless stars in the night sky, the darkening fabric underneath a perfect replica of the night sky during the Tournament Times.

It's absolutely beautiful and definitely something a Sorian princess shouldn't wear. But a princess betrothed to a prince of darkness—

How could a stranger possibly know about the new arrangements involving my destiny?

I HATE THE COLOR YELLOW. For me, it has never been the color of the sun.

It is the color of tight corsets and stiff fabric. It is the color of the Sun King's eyes right before they turn golden. It is the color of my oldest sister's decorations in her hair as I'm forced to stand behind her.

Yellow is the dreadful color of many things, but it is not the color of the dress I put on tonight.

The dress from the market fits perfectly, the silky fabric clinging to every curve of my body. The form-fitted bodice still leaves room to hide the Victory Dagger I refuse to part with after finding it in ruins, and the long sleeves hide the mark on my arm. The billowing skirt of tulle and silk is long but not long enough to hinder any movement should I need to run away from my betrothed.

If it weren't for the inspiration taken from the wrong kingdom, this dress could've been made solely for me.

Yellow is not the color of my hair or skin tonight either. The heaps of golden powder used for dusting my hair and skin stays untouched by my vanity mirror. My snowy hair is left loose, a line of silver painted over my eyelids to bring out the sapphire of my eyes and the pale color that is so different from the rest of my family. And the binding mark on my neck is painted with silver, not gold.

There is not a trace of the yellow and golden shades of my kingdom tonight. A silent protest hidden behind the act of honoring my betrothed's kingdom.

I haven't forgotten how enraged Father was the last time I wore the colors of the enemy kingdom, but tonight, he won't disgrace me, not when I'm wearing the colors of the kingdom he has decided is to be my new home.

I need Father to believe he has finally broken me, but I can't be quiet. He wouldn't expect me to. It was as easy to hide the dress on the journey back to Moria from Verbena as it is to pretend I'm still drowning in misery.

There's barely any sunlight left when I find my way to one of the many large balconies of the palace, the outdoor space decorated with countless swirls of golden light from the king to keep away the approaching darkness. A large table has been brought out in the middle, elaborately decked with gilded silverware and countless bright flowers.

I've always been excluded from important events such as this and I half expect the guards to escort me away from it all, but they only send me a few curious glances.

My gaze is instantly drawn to the Lunan Royalty standing in the darkest parts of the balcony.

The Moon King is a towering shadow in the dim sunlight. There is not a single trace of color to be found on him, his dark suit blending in with the shadows of the palace. Even his eyes are pure black, and when his gaze briefly moves to mine, it feels as if he can see through my clothes and into my very soul. It's as if the night itself has seeped into him. Or maybe the Moon King is carved from the night.

I don't know much about Luna's magic, and from the looks of the king—I'm afraid to find out what he can do.

Two princes are standing next to their king, both beautiful and brutal. The bare skin peeking through their immaculate clothing is painted with silver swirls and symbols, the paint shining in the darkening light.

The oldest of the princes is standing closest to the king, his posture one of practiced elegance. Prince Axton, the one most likely to be crowned the next Moon King.

He shares the same sharp features as the king, but the deep green shade of his eyes softens him enough that I can stand to look at him. Brown hair so dark it borders on black hangs loosely down to his shoulders, some of the locks swept behind his ear to reveal a silver crescent pendulum.

The other prince is one I don't recognize. He seems younger than Axton, and I can't help wondering if he is one of the princes who usually participate in the Tournament and if he too was forbidden from it this year. Fiery red hair curls down to just below his ears and his scowling eyes are a mahogany brown. His balled fists and stiff shoulders give me the impression he is not particularly pleased to be here.

My betrothed. But not for long.

Solina and the twins are standing next to Father a good distance away from our guests, heads bobbing and well-practiced smiles on their lips. They are all wearing dresses in different shades of yellow and gold, Solina's dress shining with the brightest colors.

I repress a pleased smile from not suffocating in yet another matching outfit.

"Ah, there she is," Father says as he puts his hand on my arm, his grip hard despite the smile on his face—a silent warning.

"And you're wearing a new dress." His golden eyes are a scorching storm as he studies me, trailing from the silver clips in my hair to the silver details on my shoes, twitching when they land on the silver paint shining on my neck.

I can only imagine how I must look in the approaching night. The silver adornments make my white hair luminescent in the darkening light, the dark blue fabric perfectly bringing out the color of my eyes.

Solina sends a pleading look in my direction and I conjure up my most dazzling smile. "Yes, in honor of my betrothed, of course."

"Of course." Father's grip on my arm tightens and I fight the urge to shove him off.

"Well then. Asteria, this is Prince Castor, your betrothed. The seventh son of the Moon." Father gestures to the prince with fiery hair. "Prince Castor, this is Princess Asteria, ironically the seventh daughter of the Sun."

Prince Castor's dark eyes briefly lock with mine before he gives me a discontent look, as if I'm just another peasant not worthy of a single second of his attention.

Of course, he doesn't want me.

He has probably heard every foul rumor about me, and possibly even saw me crashing through the temple roof.

I understand his hatred because it's burning through me too, and it's hard to stop the urge to tackle him to the ground and wipe the look off his face.

"Yes, I guess she will have to suffice," the Moon King says, giving me a look of disapproval, his soulless eyes sending an involuntary shudder down my back.

I'm about to scream at both of them, but a sharp pinch on my arm stops me.

Playing along might not be easy after all.

"I can assure you my Asteria will be a most excellent bride for your son," Father says curtly, leaving no room for argument.

"If she is a better bride than a climber I am sure it will be fine," the Moon King says with a dark chuckle.

"She will be."

I have to grind my teeth together and press my nails into the palms of my hands to keep myself from pouncing on either of the kings.

"Destroying the ancient temple." The Moon King clicks his tongue as he shakes his head, his dark eyes still boring into me. "What a tragic incident, indeed. Soria losing such a treasure. What a shame." His lips pull into a smirk that says he's not sorry at all.

No, he seems pleased with me, and perhaps a little indignant that he didn't get to destroy the temple himself.

"I'm only lucky to be alive," I say, slightly bowing my head, hoping my eyes don't reveal the truth I'm dying to scream at them all.

I will destroy every last one of you and then I will take the throne. Whatever it takes.

My insides are bubbling with giddy amusement thinking about what I'm going to destroy next, this time something in his kingdom, and I fight the smile tugging at my lips.

"Yes. It would be a shame to lose a princess such as yourself. Especially now that you are promised to one of mine. My kingdom looks forward to welcoming you." The smirk on the Moon King's lips widens, as if he can't wait to give me a proper welcome, a welcome I'm sure he doesn't plan for me to survive.

"I am not even sure Castor can wait as long as the halfway point. Maybe we will get the honor of seeing you in our palace sooner," he says, gesturing between me and the prince.

The prince looks eager indeed. Eager to skin me alive or burn my flesh from my bones.

It's a good thing I plan on beating him to it.

"We will discuss that further at a later time, I am sure," Father cuts in, his hand finally releasing my arm, no doubt leaving a mark that will later bruise my skin.

"Solina dear, will you escort Prince Axton and Prince Castor to the table? And make sure to seat Prince Castor next to his betrothed."

"Of course, my king." Solina is all smiles and sunshine as she leads the princes to the decked table in the middle of the balcony, Erina and Arina trailing after them with equally blinding smiles on their faces.

Father impatiently nods his head toward the table. "Go ahead, Asteria."

I give a quick curtsey to the Moon King before walking toward the table, dread filling me with each step.

The kings exchange some low words before walking to the table when everyone is seated. Two honorary seats looking very much like thrones are placed at the head of the table, not a single inch separating them in size–one gold, the other silver.

After the kings are seated, I notice there's an empty chair across from me.

I cast a confused glance at Erina seated beside me. "Are we expecting anyone else?"

Erina leans forward to whisper in my ear. "Prince Star. And he's even more late than you. I can't imagine his king being pleased with that. I've heard the princes suffer cruel punishments from their king."

My heartbeats quicken at her words.

If the punishments in Luna are anything like what I've suffered from the Sun King, I might have to work quicker than anticipated. And considering the stories I've heard about their courts–my future doesn't look very promising.

We are quiet as we wait, the palace patio eerily quiet. More and more stars make their appearance in the evening sky, each one a reminder of my new future. Both of the kings are getting more impatient by the second, their mouths pulled into a thin line and eyes set on the open doors of the palace.

My hands trail along the fabric of my skirt, my fingers absentmindedly stroking over the silver strands.

"Forgive me, Your Majesties."

I snap my head up at the sound of the familiar deep voice, my breath catching in my throat at the sight in front of me.

The warrior with the midnight eyes is casually strolling

toward the table, his gaze locked on me. He is wearing a tailored dark suit stitched with silver stars, his dark hair perfectly combed, the binding mark on his neck gleaming in the moonlight.

The warrior, Cael, Prince Star, takes the seat in front of me, eyes twinkling as if the stars themselves have taken place in them. A wicked grin pulls at his lips as his eyes rake over me, over the dress that perfectly matches his clothing.

"You," I breathe.

The wicked smile expands fully on his lips.

It's the same smile he had when he cut my leathers in the market square, the same smile he had only seconds before devouring me at the masquerade ball, the same smile as he looked down on me from the outcropping in Kylo.

And it is the same wicked smile he had when I foolishly bargained away a favor to a prince of the enemy kingdom who knows my darkest secrets.

"Me."

CHAPTER NINE

"Is there something on your mind, princess?" Prince Star says before taking a sip of his wine. In the dark night, the silver in his eyes is twinkling as bright as the stars above and he looks so regal it's a wonder I didn't notice before. It's as if the magic running through his blood became more evident the second he revealed his true identity.

The others are politely chatting around us, Arina and Erina thankfully questioning my betrothed so I won't have to look at the hungry gleam in his scowling gaze.

"Star? That's the name of the mysterious warrior?" My hand is firmly closed around the golden knife and I'm strongly resisting the urge to throw it at the prince in front of me.

"You think I'm mysterious?" Star bares his teeth as he takes a bite of the elaborate meal we've been served. "A name is a very powerful thing. Make sure you just don't give yours away to anyone."

"And that's what you're doing? Star is not your real name?"

"Of course not. And neither is the one I presented you with

during our previous encounters." He lowers his voice at the last part, a hard expression crossing his features.

"And what poor soul did you kill to gain that name?" My grip on my glass hardens, and I can practically feel it on the brink of shattering in my hand.

Star only shrugs as he raises his glass to his lips, his knuckles white. "As I said, a name is a very powerful thing and I make sure to never reveal mine. You didn't think the king's true name was Moon, did you?"

Castor snorts beside me. "He is only trying to distract you from the fact that his mother didn't bother to name him properly," he says, seemingly bored of answering the twin's long list of questions about Luna.

Star winks at his brother across the table. "And you're only jealous that you didn't think of an alias before it was too late. King Castor doesn't really have a ring to it." He tilts his head to the side, a cruel smirk on his lips.

Castor opens his mouth to say something, only to be silenced by Star raising his hand. "Perhaps you should tell your fiancé a little bit of your story. Or maybe I should continue elaborating on the subject of Moon politics?"

"Careful, *brother*," Castor mutters, his fingers curling around the handle of his knife. "Or you might reveal all of our kingdom's secrets." He shoots a look in the Moon King's direction who, fortunately for his princes, is far enough away to be out of earshot.

"Asteria is going to be a part of our kingdom soon enough."

The sound of my name on Star's lips sends an unfamiliar sensation through me and I press my nails into the scars of my palms, cursing the magic of the Tournament.

It will be dangerous to stay in a palace filled with Tournament-bound princes urged to kill me by ancient magic. If the magic is this strong in the presence of only one competitor, I can only imagine what it will be like once I travel to Luna.

"Yes, Asteria will be claimed by the moon and brought into the darkness," Castor purrs, the hungry gleam back in his eyes.

Disgust is the only thing I feel at the sound of my betrothed's voice.

If only he knew that he is going to be scorched by the sun until there is nothing left but ashes.

"This will be fun, huh?" Castor leans toward me, his breath smelling of wine. "That fall from the mountain will practically be painless compared to what's waiting for you."

"There's not a binding mark on you, dear betrothed. Afraid you'll lose? And I don't see any other marks on your skin besides the paint. I think I'll have to change that." I lean closer and give him a look that I know will make him rage before leaning back in my chair as far away from him as possible.

This is not my first time dealing with an unwanted suitor.

"Careful, *brother*," Star practically spits. "I think this one is more than just a pretty side piece. Or have you forgotten what happened to the last poor soul promised to you?"

Castor picks up his knife, his eyes a dark storm of rage.

It seems I'm not the only one who wants to throw a knife at *Prince* Star and the only one with a bad reputation.

"Interesting," I purr, swirling around the liquid in my glass. "What happened to the last one?" I direct the question at Star, ignoring the glowering prince beside me.

Star shrugs, the corners of his lips tugging with amusement. "She threw herself off one of the palace balconies. Couldn't stand being with this one a second longer," he says, gesturing to Castor with a nod.

That seems to break the last of the prince's control.

"She fell," Castor snarls and throws the knife at Star, his lips pulled into a grimace that transforms his face from brutally handsome to dangerous.

The sound of the knife flying through the air silences the low chatter around the table.

Star effortlessly catches the knife in his hand but it doesn't stop a few drops of blood from running down his wrist. He sighs heavily and drops the knife onto the table before reaching for a folded handkerchief.

"You're lucky you didn't ruin my suit," Star says, voice low but laced with venom as he wipes the blood from his hand. "And saying that she fell doesn't quite capture the truth."

"Enough," the Moon King snaps from across the table. "Leave it for the Tournament." He waves a hand before his eyes land on me, his lips pulling into a cruel smirk. "Except for our new bride, of course."

I open my mouth and Castor's hand wraps around my wrist at the table, his skin eerily cold.

"Don't you dare question your new king, *princess*. Did your wounds heal so quickly that you've already forgotten your place?"

I give him a smile that challenges the cruelty of the Moon King's, my hand landing on his thigh underneath the table. The small knife hidden in the ruffle of my sleeve slides out and sinks into his skin.

Castor mutters a low curse, his hand leaving my wrist to press against the wound on his thigh. He gives me a smoldering glare and just as he's about to open his mouth–I lean forward to whisper in his ear.

"Careful, *prince*. You wouldn't want to lose another betrothed. I don't think there's anyone left if you want to keep your crown."

His glare intensifies, his lips pressing into a thin line, but he stays silent and he doesn't reach for me again.

As I lean back in my chair, I notice Star is looking at me, an amused smile playing on his lips. I raise my eyebrows as I cross my arms and repeat his first words to me, "Something on your mind, *prince?*"

His smile widens. "There's always a lot on my mind, starlight. But right now, I'm content to just watch you play our little game. It seems the odds have just heightened."

The dinner drags on for so long that the darkness of the sky slowly lightens, the promise of the sun only hours away.

For the most part, I sit in silence listening to the two rulers discuss tedious subjects like competitive trade and Victors through the ages, Solina and Axton eagerly chiming in, both with the attitude of taking over the throne someday.

To my great delight, the twins continue to pester Castor. They ask him about color schemes and fabrics in Luna, about the night-blooming flowers and the magic of the moonlight. Castor grows more agitated with each question. He impatiently taps his fingers on the table while grinding his teeth together, his eyes etched into a permanent scowl.

Star's eyes barely leave me throughout the night, the corners of his lips tugging with amusement every time I grit my teeth or grasp my glass a little too hard.

"You knew who I was all along," I say when I can't take it anymore.

It's not a question but he answers anyway. "Yes."

"Why?"

He takes a sip of his glass, raising his eyebrows. "Why what?" The arrogant smirk playing on his lips tells me he knows exactly what I'm asking.

He's playing with me.

This is all just a big game to him.

I'm suddenly filled with an overwhelming urge to retrieve my hidden dagger, dive across the table, and sink it into his chest.

Star's smirk widens as if he knows exactly what I'm thinking.

I press my nails into the scars of my palms, the pain grounding me enough to ignore the persisting magic of the Tournament. "What do you want from me?"

He taps a finger against his chin, a contemplative humming coming from his lips before the arrogant smirk is back on his lips. "A favor."

I have to bite my bottom lip to keep myself from screaming. Rage is simmering within me, sparks of it sizzling in my fingertips and I'm struggling to keep it all locked away.

"You were right, you know," he says, raising his glass as if he wants to make a toast with me. "Your kingdom did have something better than the meek drink at the tavern."

I only snort in reply, ignoring the twins' questioning looks beside me.

But he doesn't stop there.

"Did you consider–you know." His gaze slides to the side of my neck, to the binding mark hidden underneath my hair.

"I don't know what you're talking about," I mutter, trying to keep my voice low so the others won't hear us and ask questions.

Star smirks and I don't like the knowing look that creeps onto his face. "So you're not going to be wearing black anytime soon? Or do I need to invoke a certain favor?"

A jolt shoots through my heart and the fork in my hand slips from my grip. I blink at the prince, trying to scold my features into a neutral mask, but I can tell it's already too late by the way his smirk widens.

"Again, I don't know what you're talking about. Maybe you should hold back on the wine, or the sky might come crashing down on you," I say, forcing my lips into a smile.

I already knew I shouldn't trust the warrior–Skye–from the market, but I didn't expect her to be working for the prince. Maybe he has offered her a larger prize than the one on my head.

I don't understand what he is planning, but whatever it is, I'm going to figure it out and stop him before it's too late.

If I end his life, he won't need the favor.

"The sky seems fine to me," Star says, tilting his head to the side with a mischievous smirk. "You should know, princess. The sky is home to both the sun and the moon. Without the sky, neither would exist."

I roll my eyes and take a sip from my glass, the wine warming my throat. "As a princess of the sun who recently fell from the sky–" I shake my head, an involuntary shudder running down my spine, "–I'm going to honor the sun in another way. A way that doesn't involve the sky."

Star's smirk disappears along with the silver in his eyes. He rests his elbows on the table, leaning forward so close I can almost feel his breath on my face. "I think that's a mistake."

With a shrug, I glide my finger around the rim of my glass and give him a bored look. "I don't really care about your opinion."

"That's also a mistake."

"I don't care."

"You should."

"I don't–"

"Have you two met before?" Solina cuts in, and I realize everyone has stopped talking and is now staring at us. At the far end of the table, the kings are deep in discussion, thankfully oblivious to their children's bickering.

"Yes," Star says at the same time I say no.

Nails digging into the scars of my palms, I give Solina a forced smile. "We met during the first trial."

"Before you so pathetically fell through the roof?" Castor snorts with a low chuckle.

"Yes," I say through gritted teeth.

"And at the opening festival. The tavern. The masquerade ball–" Star raises his eyebrows at my glowering look. "What?"

"It seems Asteria is not the only one who enjoys skipping her duties and sneaking away," Solina mutters under her breath with a look in Father's direction.

Star studies me intently, as if he can sense the scars aching on my back. "It was a joke. You have those here, don't you? We've only met during the first trial. And yes, before she fell, but fortunately she saw me win it all." The victorious smirk on his face doesn't quite reach his eyes.

I shift in my seat and look away from his searching gaze. I don't want to consider if he just saved me again, even though he was the one who caused me trouble in the first place. His kingdom has a prize on my head, a prize he probably wants for himself and that's why he killed the warriors during the first trial–a prize he no doubt is still planning on collecting, our bargain only making it easier.

"Yes," the Moon King drawls. "The sky lighting silver was a fine sight indeed. Let us make sure we keep it that way. The other princes are training as we speak, yet you insisted on joining me tonight, *Star*." The warning lacing his words sends a series of shivers down my spine and I pray the kings only heard the last part of our conversation.

"Yes, yes." Star waves a hand, much in the same manner as his king did only moments ago. "The sky will shine silver, but it's still a place for both the sun and the moon during these weeks." His gaze flickers to me at the words, still trying to convey the cryptic message I don't want to hear.

The Moon King's glare could cut through bones as he rises

from the table. He fastens the button on his suit jacket, glancing at Father still seated beside him. "I think this dinner has lasted long enough. The Kingdom of the Moon looks forward to welcoming our new bride."

Father gets to his feet and holds out his hand. The firm handshake between the kings is no doubt much harder than it looks, a symbol of the strained relations between our kingdoms. "The Kingdom of the Sun looks forward to continuing our new negotiations."

The Moon King snaps his fingers and his sons shove out of their chairs, ready to follow their king.

As Star rises to his feet, an emotion I can't place flickers across his painfully striking features, as if he's debating saying something else. I only glare at him, ignoring the magic flowing between us, wondering whether our bargain has made it easier for the gods' magic to bring us together.

With a last look, eyes like a starless midnight sky, Prince Star of Luna turns his back to me and walks away, our bargain hanging in the air between us, waiting for the opportunity to drag me into the shadows.

CHAPTER TEN

A large amethyst rests on my finger. The stone is carved in the shape of the moon, the deep purple color reminiscent of the sunset sky bleeding into darkness. The amethyst is wider than my finger, the silver band holding it glimmering in the sunset.

The ring holds the attention of all of Moria.

As does my dress, the luxurious fabric dipped in magic that allows the colors to change in the same manner as the sky above. Crafted to honor both the sun and the moon with the golden shades of Soria in the daylight and the dark shades of Luna in the darkness.

Both are signs of my new promised life, impossible to withstand the attention of the people in the royal city.

"Wipe that look off your face and show them a smile instead," Castor murmurs through gritted teeth, his hand landing on my arm that's hugging his.

I squeeze his hand, making sure the public doesn't see how hard the pressure is, before carefully removing his hand. No need to have more contact than absolutely necessary.

The eyes of the crowd prickle my skin, their hushed whispers reaching my ears.

We must have stopped at every vendor and shop at the market today. The people of Soria are suddenly more welcoming, some of their usual wariness and hatred toward me dimmed, no doubt thanks to the prince at my arm ordering large amounts of whatever they're selling to both kingdoms, a charming smile on his face as he brags about every good we stumble upon.

For a few moments, I'm almost fooled that the union between our kingdoms maybe isn't such a bad idea after all, but then I notice wary and angry glances at my betrothed from people wearing the honorary colors of Luna, and I wonder what darkness I'll find in his kingdom.

There has never been a betrothal between royalty from Soria and Luna. Relations between the opposing people are strictly forbidden, and outside of the Tournament Times, the border is always closed and heavily guarded. That doesn't mean it doesn't happen, but unless you want an early departure to the Shadow Realm, the relationships and encounters are always kept secret. The Sun King giving me away is humiliating enough in itself, but the fact that he's knowingly breaking an ancient law–

I'm no longer the cursed princess who murdered the queen and ruined an ancient temple. I'm the cursed princess who murdered the queen and ruined an ancient temple, now exiled to the enemy kingdom expected to meet her death.

This union between Soria and Luna will go down in history no matter if we survive to see it through.

There is no doubt in my mind this is all just another game–a ploy crafted by the Sun King to distract his people from the ruined Verbena temple and my humiliating display in the Tournament. A ploy that seems to be working very well as all eyes are on our entwined arms and the huge amethyst resting on my finger as we parade around the market.

"That's still not a smile," Castor mutters in my ear, the feel of his closeness giving me the urge to shove him into the nearest barrel or suffocate him in the long fabric of my skirt.

Leaning as far away as possible, I suck in a breath through my nose and give him a well-practiced smile reserved for the few royal duties I've attended over the years.

"Better," he says before leaning in close again to whisper in my ear, the act only looking intimate to the people around us. "As long as anyone doesn't get too close. Don't think I don't know what you're thinking, your eyes betray your thoughts. And, believe me, I'm thinking the exact same thing, only worse." His hand moves from my arm to the small of my back, his fingers digging into my skin.

"Considering the fact you got rid of your last betrothed by shoving her off a balcony, I don't think so," I murmur against the side of his neck, resisting the urge to bite and tear at his skin until I taste his blood.

A low growl resounds from his throat and he leans away far enough for his dark eyes to bore into mine. "Your death will be anything but swift, that I can promise you."

"You shouldn't forget which side of the sky you're currently under," I murmur, gliding my hand underneath his suit jacket and across his chest until my palm lands on his heart. "All it would take for the sun's light to incinerate your heart is a little squeeze–" I dig my nails into his shirt, pressing just hard enough for him to feel it on his skin.

Castor recoils and a pleased smirk spreads on my lips, but then his hand clamps around my wrist so hard I'm afraid he will break the bone. "There is no way you have access to the royal magic," he snarls, increasing the pressure of his hand.

"Maybe, maybe not," I snarl back. "But you should know there is a reason I'm known as the cursed princess, and if you ever touch me like that again—I'll make sure you know why."

Castor glares at me for a second longer before abruptly letting me go, as if he is actually burned by my skin.

I force my lips into a smile for the crowd gathered around us and I'm about to suggest we travel back to the palace when something behind him catches my attention.

"I'll be right back," I say, walking away before he can stop me.

The people part when they notice the princess among them, some of them gasping in awe at my transforming dress. As the rest of the sunlight disappears and the sun dips down on the horizon, the fabric transforms to a darkening blue—a mirror image of the sky above.

"What a pleasure seeing you here, princess." A hand grabs my wrist and drags me into a shadowed alley away from the looking crowd, the touch featherlight compared to my betrothed's.

"I can't say the same for you." I cross my arms and move away from Skye, pressing my back against one of the walls in the narrow alley. "Temporary allies didn't last long."

"What do you mean?" She tilts her head to the side, her features slipping into an innocent mask.

The warrior is wearing the same cobalt blue leathers as the last time I saw her, and two swords are strapped across her back. Her short hair is braided back, some of the blue stripes hanging loosely around her face.

"I know you're working with the prince."

Skye raises her eyebrows with a snort. "Your betrothed? However good-looking he may be, I'd rather sleep with the beasts in the forest than ever speak with him."

That makes two of us.

"I'm talking about *Prince Star*," I mutter, practically spitting his name—the ridiculous nickname he has chosen for himself forever making it impossible to admire the glittering stars in the sky without thinking of him.

"Oh, that." She taps a finger against her chin. "I was hoping to fill you in on the plans myself, but it seems that bastard beat me to it."

"Are you his lover or something?"

Skye blinks at me for a few seconds before barking a laugh. "Heavens no." She shudders and when she looks at me again, a look of pity crosses her features. "Don't tell me you—"

"I don't want anything to do with him," I spit, impatiently tapping my foot as I glance to the sides of the alley. Castor is probably looking for me and I won't have a lot of time before he goes blabbering to Father about my behavior.

"It doesn't matter that he is a prince," Skye says, the look of pity long gone. "Did you know he has seven victories? Yes, seven. But he hasn't competed in a few years. No one has seen him since his last victory."

"So?" I already knew about his many victories, and I expected him to be a good warrior before I knew—winning the first trial was proof of that.

Skye sighs heavily and looks to the sky. "I don't know. It has to be something big. I just haven't figured it out yet."

"I don't have time for all of this! I only wanted to tell you that whatever deal you think we had about a temporary truce—which I never even agreed to in the first place—is done. I'm not getting near that prince."

At least not any more than I have to. If I manage to avoid him for the rest of my life, he won't get any chances to claim our bargain.

The warrior sighs, pinching the bridge of her nose. "Listen. You don't even have to speak to him or look at him. I'll take care of that. We need every advantage we can get and he's a Victor. Of multiple games!"

"We're not allies!" Someone halts at one of the entrances to the alley, and we sink back into the shadows. The next time I speak, my voice is barely a whisper. "You knew about the king's deal with Moon and you matched my dress to Star's suit–"

"That bastard!" Skye lets out a cackle before quickly silencing it with a hand over her mouth. She glances at the street, and when no one comes, she continues in a whisper. "He must've seen me urging you to get that dress and got a suit in the same style just to taunt you."

I move to leave the alley, but she stops me with a gentle hand on my arm. At my glowering look, she retreats with a roll of her eyes.

"Yes, I heard about the deal. Let's just say I might have some other allies that heard a thing or two." She crosses her arms with a victorious smile. "See, I can be useful."

"How was dressing me up to match the wrong prince useful–"

"That was an unfortunate accident. I was only telling you I had ways to find useful information–"

The sound of the distant crowd grows louder, the promised moon prince no doubt in the middle of it. More people are walking past our alley, and it could only be seconds left before Castor or one of the guards finds me. The last thing I need right now is to be spotted sneaking away from the prince to a darkened alley to meet a warrior in the Tournament.

"So, what do you say, princess? Allies for the Tournament?"

I snort. "If you think I'm just going to trust you, there is no place for you in the games–"

"I was right about the dress, wasn't I? And I did get Star to keep an eye on you during the first game, or didn't he rescue you?" She raises her eyebrows, a triumphant smile playing on her lips as if she thinks those words will finally get me on her side.

"Please. You expect me to believe that was because of you? Star is up to something and I won't pretend to understand how allegedly rescuing me when I didn't even need help is a part of that—"

"Exactly!" Skye makes an exasperated sound and glances to the side of the alley.

"And I don't know what you're up to either—" I give her a dismissive once over, the same look I've given countless guards and men to make them remember my status, "—but I don't want to be a part of it."

I start moving back toward the market, but once again, she stops me with a hand on my wrist. Rage boils in my blood from the unwanted touch, sparks of anger shooting down my arms.

"Don't say I never gave you anything useful. I will prove to you that having me on your side is a good move." Skye slips a folded piece of paper underneath the ruffled shoulder on my dress before pushing me out of the alley and into the bustling market.

"There you are, dear. What do you think you're doing running away like that? We're on a date, remember?" Castor's voice rings out behind me, startling me enough to not step away when he wraps a hand around my waist, his fingers painfully digging into my skin. He has a polite mask on for the crowd, but his eyes tell a different story—he's furious.

"I don't know what I was thinking. I'm afraid I've spent too much time in the sun today, even though that shouldn't be possible for a princess of the sun," I say with a chuckle that earns a few smiles from the crowd around us. "I'm so glad you found me, *dear.*" I give him a dazzling smile, the folded piece of paper heavy against my skin.

I pray to the gods no one can see it through the fabric of my dress and that the wind doesn't steal it before I get a chance to look at it.

"I'll make sure not to leave your side ever again," Castor says, the words igniting a fury it's hard to keep back.

I press my nails into the scars of my palms, biting back the insults urging to pass my lips.

"I bought this for you." He holds out a goblet filled with a strawberry pink liquid steaming with a fruity aroma, likely purchased from one of the vendors we passed earlier.

I'm about to reach for the drink when someone bumps into Castor. The goblet clatters onto the cobblestones, the liquid staining the streets and the hem of my dress.

"Oh, my sun and moon! I'm so sorry, Your Highnesses!" A familiar voice shrieks. Skye squats to retrieve the goblet that survived the fall with only a few cracks. "I'll dispose of this for you, Your Highness."

Castor looks down at his pants and mutters a low curse. His pants are stained from the knees down, the dark fabric soaked with liquid reminding me of spilled blood.

"Can I get you a new one, Your Highness?" Skye asks innocently, folding her hands in front of her like an awed subject happening to lay eyes on her rulers.

"No," Castor says, unable to keep the harshness out of his voice. "Just leave us."

"Are you sure?" Skye takes a step forward, her eyes glancing in my direction as she lowers her voice so I'm the only one able to hear the last of her words. "I'll make sure it's not..mixed with..something..this time." She holds up her hands, displaying the pink tint on her fingers.

Something tightens in my chest, squeezing my heart so hard it hurts. The blood in my veins freeze and a loud roaring starts in my ears.

There's a glittering touch to the liquid staining the streets, the prince, and the warrior, as if a drop of magic has been blended with the fruit and berries–the gleam so faint it would be impossible to notice if it weren't for the light of the night shining above.

Poison.

I could've been dead right now–just like that.

I didn't expect the prince to strike before we left for his kingdom, and especially not in a way like this. A dagger to my throat while I'm sleeping seems more like his style, or pushing me off a balcony and deeming me to the same fate as the woman previously promised to him.

Poison is simply too discreet and subtle for someone like him. And that was my mistake–thinking I knew him well enough to see it coming.

I could've been dead right now, my soul gone for the Shadow Realm, my life-binding bargains nothing but forgotten promises.

I would've been dead right now were it not for Skye–

Is this another of their tricks? It is a little too convenient that she was just in the right place at the right time, the only one able to save me from a slow and painful death.

Your death will be anything but swift, that I can promise you.

Was it my threats of burning his heart or the act of running away that made Castor act so suddenly? Or was it the reminder that he is promised to the cursed princess?

I don't know how much time passes before I'm able to move again, before the ice in my veins thaws enough for my heart to come back to its usual rhythm.

"Thank you for your offer," I say, placing a hand on Skye's shoulder. "I'll be sure to remember your kindness."

No matter if this was another trick or she actually saved me– this changes things.

I have a lot to consider before the next trial.

Skye nods and curtsies, the hint of a mischievous smile on her face as she walks away and disappears in the crowd.

I wait until I can no longer see her disappearing back before I turn around to face Castor. For a second, he looks afraid, his eyes slightly widening, a sharp intake of breath sounding from his mouth–but then the scowling gaze is back and anger is the only thing I see.

"I'm ready to retreat to the palace. I believe this *date* is over now," I murmur, leaning against his cheek as if I'm simply going to give him a peck goodbye. My hand follows the same path underneath his jacket until I find his heart, and this time–I don't hesitate. My fingers pop open a button, my nails firmly digging into the skin shielding his heart.

I hope I make him scar.

"I look forward to continuing this at a later time." I give a curt nod to the guards behind us who have been trailing us at a distance all day, before conjuring forth the most wicked smile I can muster.

"After all, the games have just begun."

CHAPTER ELEVEN

The townhouse in the Court of Lavendula is painted and decorated in different shades of pink and purple–the colors a mirror image of the colored fields outside the large windows where rows upon rows of lavender flowers grow, the flower the symbol of the court.

A warm breeze flutters the lilac curtains, the strong herbal and floral scent of the flowers embracing me, a river of memories flowing through me.

I've always cherished the smell of the Lavendula flowers. The scent reminds me of the anticipation coursing through me while venturing through the peaceful fields before slipping into the battleground of the thick forest.

The Court of Lavendula has been the source of many wounds and scars over the years. The court is not only known for its beautiful landscape. During the Tournament Times, the echoes of the beasts' growls can be heard all the way to the royal court in the middle of the kingdom.

Today, Lavendula is hosting the second trial in the middle of that deadly forest, and I feel the same thrill of anticipation shoot through me.

The trial is only hours away and I still haven't found a way to sneak away from the other royals.

"Are you so miserable you cannot find the time to eat?"

I press my nails into the scars of my palms at the sound of his voice, sucking in a few deep breaths before turning around with a neutral expression on my face.

"Sit."

I carefully slip the folded piece of paper into the sleeve of my plum-colored dress before taking a seat next to Solina. The paper is heavy against my skin–the unsolvable riddle making me grind my teeth in frustration.

The paper is filled with swirling ink drawn in strange lines and symbols, magic coating every crinkle and corner. It looks like a ruined map of an ancient temple or city belonging to the gods– the knowledge of how to read it lost to time and war.

I've tried to decipher what it might mean ever since Skye hastily tucked it underneath the fabric of my dress. I've visited the royal libraries and scouted the endless racks of shelves for the old and worn spines, trying to find even a small piece of information I might use. I've even bribed guards and people in the city for gossip about the Tournament. But so far, none of my attempts have been successful.

The magical paper remains a mystery.

Skye claimed she wanted to be allies so my best guess is that the paper has something to do with the second trial. No one but the kings and the highest-ranking generals tasked with making the challenges knows the details of the games. Sometimes, even the kings want to be surprised. So unless Skye somehow has managed to bribe one of them–which no one is able to do and still breathe to talk about it–she shouldn't know anything. It is more likely she's just trying to trick me and make it easier for *Prince Star* to win again.

"What did you think of the wedding dress made of chiffon?" Solina asks as she puts a strawberry to her lips. "The one with the short sleeves."

I sigh and stuff my mouth with bread, ignoring my sister's disdainful look.

It has gotten harder to sneak out of the palace ever since the new bond between the kingdoms was revealed. The palace is brimming with advisers and wedding planners stealing me away for an endless list of wedding duties–getting tailored for not only one but four wedding dresses, cake and food tastings, jewelry fittings, approving color schemes for decorations and dress codes for the guests. I'm almost starting to think Father is making up stuff to keep me locked in the palace.

"Well?" Solina raises her eyebrows, ignoring my glare.

"I want long sleeves," I mutter through gritted teeth.

"Good, at least one thing is decided."

The kings have yet to agree on the location of the wedding, both kingdoms being the logical choice–a wedding in Soria to say goodbye to the princess of the sun, or a wedding in Luna to welcome a new addition to the royal family. The whole thing seems rushed, as if everyone fears the fragile bond will break before we've made our promises to the gods.

I don't know how much time I have left.

"It's a good day for the second trial," Solina says with a smile in Elio's direction. "The sun can't shine any brighter."

Elio swallows the bread in his mouth with a glance in Father's direction. "Any day in Soria is a good day," he says with a bright smile.

I resist the urge to roll my eyes. We all know what they're

doing, and from the exasperated look on the Sun King's face–it's not working too well.

"It is a good day and it will be an excellent trial now that the unworthy warriors are no longer participating," Father says with a pleased smirk.

Elio subtly shakes his head, his hazel eyes boring into mine. *Don't.*

"Do you not agree, Asteria?"

My nails press into my palms so hard I almost break the skin. The pain soothes me, subduing the impulses to throw the hidden Victory Dagger across the table.

He would incinerate me before the dagger left my hand.

"Of course, my king," I say through gritted teeth, forcing a smile onto my face.

Father studies me for a moment, and when gold sparks in his eyes, I quickly look away.

Elio's shoulders relax and he sends me a grateful smile, the sight melting some of the ice in my heart. The relief washing over his features sends a wave of guilt through me, and the wall of ice around my heart thickens, the warmth gone as suddenly as it came.

He doesn't know about my new bargain or that I'm still bound to compete. Too many people know about my secret and I can't take any chances when it comes to my best–and only–friend. I'll do everything I can to protect him. He thinks I need the training to take my mind off everything and ease the tension in my body. Of course, that's partly true. At least that's what I tell myself when the guilt threatens to eat me alive.

The worst part is that I've been using him, not only to help me train. I've been carefully asking him questions about the Tournament, trying to get him to reveal some information about this year's games. I don't know whether the magic of the

Tournament physically prevents him from revealing anything, or if he's just suddenly become very loyal to the gods and kingdoms, or if he simply doesn't know anything, but he refuses to speak of it.

The life of a Victor is a mystery to everyone but them.

"Speaking of today's trial–" Elio says, pushing out of his chair. "I should go prepare. As always, it was a pleasure having breakfast with you, Your Majesty. I look forward to seeing you all at the trial in a few hours." He bows to the king and starts walking toward the door with a last grateful smile in my direction.

I move to follow, thinking this will be my only option to sneak away–

"Sit," Father snarls, the sound of his magic crackling in the air sending a shiver down my back.

I slump back down in my chair, the scars on my back aching as I brace myself for his fury.

"You may leave," he says, briefly glancing at my sisters, the spark of gold in his eyes making it hard to breathe.

They don't look back.

The room turns eerily quiet as the door slams shut, even the guards and servants leaving the room.

I keep my gaze locked on the lavender flowers swaying in the breeze outside the window, praying to the gods the king hasn't found out my secret.

I count one hundred flowers before he clears his throat.

"Asteria."

I don't know if I should look at him, if the sight of the blue in my eyes too dark for the Sorian sky will infuriate him or if my averted gaze is what will set him off.

"Asteria." His voice is surprisingly calm, but I've been fooled by his masks before.

An indignant sigh and my gaze moves to his. The lack of gold in his eyes makes me suck in a small relieved breath, the act making him narrow his eyes.

I shrink in my chair, my fingers grasping the seat to keep myself from running away. What comes out of his mouth next surprises me so much I nearly topple to the ground.

"I think you have earned the right to watch the trial with your friends today. Consider it a last chance at freedom," he says, the hint of a cruel smirk on his lips.

I blink in surprise, certain I must've heard him wrong. He knows perfectly well I don't have any friends except Elio, and he will be too busy with his duties as Victor to have any time for me.

"Or," he continues, straightening the lapels of his golden jacket, the embroidered patterns of the sun shimmering in the sunlight—a king always ready to display himself, "you may take some time to get over the shame of so foolishly binding yourself. Both kingdoms saw the unfortunate outcome of that."

This is not a gift of freedom, but a test and a warning. What he doesn't know is that it will make it so much easier to accomplish my plans.

"Thank you, my king," I say, bowing my head, repressing the urge to burst out laughing as I rise from my chair and turn for the door.

"And Asteria–"

I don't turn around in fear of my face giving away my plans.

"Whatever you decide today, remember that your life is already spoken for. You cannot change your fate."

THE WARRIORS ARE GATHERED in a clearing in front of the thick forest, leather, and armor in every shade of the rainbow gleaming in the setting sun–no longer wearing the honorary colors of their kingdoms, making it hard to discern possible allies from enemies.

I'm not the only one wearing a dark hood to conceal my face, and I'm thankful for the sea of warriors to disappear in.

The sun hangs low in the sky, ready to disappear beyond the thick line of trees. Only a few Lavendula flowers dare to grow this near the dangerous forest–they dance in the wind, their sweet scent a silent warning of the slaughter to come.

The limestone stairs of the Royal Dais clank as the last of the royals ascend, the kings already perfectly poised on their respective sides. A crowd of people mingle with the warriors, the number so great the clearing is too crowded. Some of them crouch underneath the dais, shaking and praying for forgiveness for being too close.

No one will be able to observe the second trial–not even the kings. If you aren't bound, you can't venture into the forest unless you want to risk your life–something the gods are not opposed to. They will welcome every sacrifice–the magic from the souls will seep into the soil underneath our feet, it will be carried away by the wind, restored by the gods to fuel next year's Tournament.

Elio steps forward on the dais, his voice magnified by magic as he delivers a speech almost identical to his first.

Pride makes my heart swell as I listen to my best friend fulfill his duties as the latest Victor. I admire how the sun reflects his bronze skin and the gilded lines of his victory mark, desperately wishing I could stand next to him.

I'm reminded by our countless conversations after our training sessions, both of us so exhausted we collapsed on the ground to watch the clouds glide across the sky.

"One day, we will win together," Elio would say, his hand grasping mine so hard it felt as if we were bound together.

"There can only be one Victor–"

"Not as long as we're together." His hand would squeeze mine, the smile on his face sending a flurry of butterflies through my heart.

"I don't think the gods would like that," I would answer, a smile pulling at my lips.

He would snort with a roll of his eyes as if what he was suggesting was the easiest thing in the world. "You're a princess of the sun. I'm sure they would be thrilled to have you as a Victor. And they'll have no choice but to accept me at your side. We will change history together, becoming the greatest Victors the world has ever seen–"

"Big words coming from someone who begged their forgiveness after picking a too-short Helianthus flower."

"I was seven! And that's beside the point, Ria. There are no rules in the Tournament but one. Survive. We'll have a greater chance if we stick together like we always do. It's you and me forever, Ria. Always."

And then, when we were finally truly ready to bind ourselves–our dreams would be crushed by the fists of the gods as if they knew what we were planning.

"The second trial is a game like no other," Elio says, bringing me back to the present moment. "The Court of Lavendula has crafted an almost unsolvable labyrinth filled with magical traps, beats, and other secrets you can't imagine!"

The crowd roars, the warriors stomp their feet in a thunderous rhythm and Elio holds his hands to the sky–the Victor ready to start the second trial.

"Make it through the labyrinth before our beautiful sun goes to sleep with her last rays of light and the day is covered by the darkness of the moon."

The chorus of cheers reaches its crescendo, the sound so loud it feels as if it bores into my skull.

Elio turns one of his hands toward the forest and the thick branches move away to reveal a dark path. The labyrinth walls are made out of the forest itself, and were it not for its thorny branches, the walls would have reminded me of the sculpted bushes in the palace gardens. The walls are high enough not to reveal anything of the path forward, backward, or to the sides. They snake up so high they nearly block out all remaining sunlight, the construction a cage designed to keep everyone in until the very end.

Excitement shoots through my limbs, my whole being itching to start the trial.

This is what I've been training for.

After the last trial, a little bit of doubt started to cloud my confidence, but this game could've been made for me. Slaying beasts and sneaking around happen to be some of my specialties, and the fact that I'm no longer the targeted princess should count for something.

"As always, the rules are simple. There are no rules in the Tournament of Day and Night but one; survive. May the best Victor win."

Elio claps his hands together, the sound rippling through the clearing louder than the stampede of warriors rushing to the forest.

The second trial has begun.

It feels as if my soul is torn in two–one part yearns to fulfill its bargain to the gods and conquer every warrior, the other is screaming to run far away from the dark entrance of the labyrinth.

Whatever it takes, Asteria.

I run for the labyrinth.

I struggle through the sea of warriors until I find a spot in the front, making sure there's someone in front of me in case of any hidden surprises.

The tactic quickly turns out to be a smart one. At least half a dozen warriors fall through an opening gap in the ground the second they enter the labyrinth, their screams swallowed by the forest.

Instead of trying to jump over the gap, I dart in another direction, the labyrinth opening new paths in the walls as I run. Sometimes the openings are sealed shut behind me, sometimes they linger enough to let more people through.

Other warriors chase after me, fighting each other for space by shoving each other into the bushy walls. Some of the falling warriors disappear, dragged off by some unknown force, while others manage to get up and continue running.

The wind is rushing in my ears as I move. Sounds of battle erupt around me—warriors screaming, bones snapping, swords clanging. It drowns out the sounds from the crowd in the clearing, the cage of the labyrinth making it feel as if I'm in another world far away from my own.

The air is heavy with magic. I feel it seep into my skin, tightening and tugging the invisible string tied around my heart, drawing me forward, urging me to do something. Kill my enemies, sacrifice to the Shadow Realm, conquer–

Win.

No matter how many turns I take or how fast I run, the highest branches of the large oak tree I've been using to navigate don't move. The labyrinth is changing, making it impossible to find a way out by logical navigation.

Elio said the labyrinth was filled with magic, but I didn't expect the labyrinth itself to be alive. It's as if I can feel the walls breathing down my neck, the branches swirling and creaking as the labyrinth awaits to trap and swallow me whole.

A dagger suddenly flies past me, only inches from my head. It flies through one of the walls and lands somewhere on the other side—the metal clanking against the ground the only indication there even is another side and not a gaping hole.

Taking a leap of faith, I jump through the wall.

The branches scrape the bare skin on my hands and face as I push through the bushes, and I'm surprised at the hard resistance I meet.

Today, the labyrinth might be my biggest opponent.

I land on the other side, my body hitting the ground with a thump. Behind me, the branches thicken and tighten to the point of being as solid as a stone wall—impenetrable to the warriors or beasts trying to follow me from the loud bang sounding from the other side.

I pick up the discarded dagger, and a low feral growl reverberates behind me.

CHAPTER TWELVE

I feel the beast hover right above my head as my grip on the dagger tightens. Its foul breath is making it hard not to gag, and I know it's sizable based on the large shadows on the ground in front of me.

Twisting my body, I hurl the dagger straight into its large mouth before rolling away on the ground, the roots of the forest slippery underneath me.

The beast is something out of a nightmare.

Its glossy body is as dark as the night, the size larger than the mightiest stallions in the palace stables. The mouth takes up almost all of its face, the teeth the size of my arm and as sharp as the royal blade. The beast stands on four legs, the paws punctured by sharpened claws that could easily flay the skin off my bones. But the worst part is the eyes–shadows seep out of the empty sockets, the dark mist blocking out the dim sunlight reaching the inside of the labyrinth.

The beast trashes its head with a loud screech, the dagger sticking out at the side of its neck.

I reach for the sword strapped to my back while giving the beast a victorious smirk.

The beast screeches again, its head shaking so violently it's hard to make out in the dark. The dagger clatters to the ground and the misty shadows seeping from the beast's eyes increase.

The sword is ready in my hand just as the beast runs forward, black saliva dripping from its jowls.

I swerve to the right, the beast's teeth snapping for my outstretched arm. It shrieks again, the scream piercing my ears enough for my steps to falter just a little as I maneuver around it.

The beast strikes so fast it's impossible to step away. A long claw slices through the leather on my arm, exposing my skin. Black liquid shoots from the sharpened tip, boiling the blood pouring from the open wound and transforming the skin to a sickly gray color. Some of the beast's poisonous saliva drips onto the leather covering the rest of my arm, burning away the fabric to leave a trail of burn marks on my skin.

The pain erupting in my body is so consuming it makes my vision blurry, and combined with the shadows pouring out of the beast–the room of the labyrinth is so dark it's hard to discern anything.

I scream as I scramble away, the beast tipping its head back to let out a victorious growl so loud it shakes the ground underneath me.

I reach for the sword, my fingers closing around the handle and snatching it away just in time to be missed by a claw-tipped foot.

The beast's shadowy mist now covers half the ground of the labyrinth room, and I'm afraid to find out what will happen if it touches my skin.

Trying to ignore the pain spreading in my body, I roll in the opposite direction of the mist, the beast trailing every move, screeching every time its claws miss my skin. It takes a few tries before I manage to get back on my feet, the poison making me unsteady and shaky.

The beast gallops forward but swerves right at the last moment, the blade of my sword slicing the side of its head. The beast growls as black liquid spurts from the wound and I duck to prevent it from hitting my face. I strike again, and the beast moves to the other side, a wound on the opposite side of its face.

We continue in the same pattern until the beast has several wounds on its face and it's hard to find places on the ground that are not stained by poisonous liquid.

"Alright, it's time to finish this," I mutter, heaving for breath.

I can't keep this up for much longer.

The next time the beast runs forward, I'm ready.

With a clean swipe of my sword, I sever the head from the body. It hits the ground with a thud and rolls away from the collapsing body. The misty shadows vanish and the last of the beast's dark poisonous blood pools at my feet, the liquid sizzling and bubbling.

As I wipe the blade of the sword on the body of the beast, silver light explodes above me, breaking through the thick thorns and branches and lighting up the labyrinth.

The magic on the sky above is like a storm of lightning and a shower of shooting stars and it is so beautiful that for a second, I forget what it means.

Silver for Luna's second victory.

I let out an exasperated sound, my booth kicking the rotting body in front of me.

For some strange reason, I just know the silver light is for him.

Prince Star.

My blood is boiling with rage, the unyielding need to win dragging my soul forward.

He shouldn't be done already. We can't have been here long. Less than an hour. How can he be done already? Unless–

He's a Victor of multiple Tournaments. Having him as an ally would be a really smart move–

The note from Skye is crumpled underneath my leathers, the paper safely tucked between my breasts–the most secure place I could think of this morning when I hastily decided to bring it despite the mystery still surrounding it.

The lines and swirls of ink that only hours ago seemed unintelligible and haphazard are now a shining possibility as bright as the silver stars starting to make their appearance in the sky above.

As I lift the paper to catch the dim rays of sunlight, the ink transforms into something like a moving picture, as if I needed to be right here–in the middle of a deadly labyrinth–for the magic to reveal itself.

It takes me a few moments to figure it out, but when I do–there's no doubt in my mind what this is.

A map.

The thickest lines can be nothing else than the steady outline of the labyrinth, and the swirling lines the moving walls. At the end of the thick lines where the ink is slightly glowing, is a crescent moon entwined with a sun–the symbol for the Tournament of Day and Night and the end goal of the labyrinth.

Shapes and patterns appear and disappear as the labyrinth moves, signaling traps like the opening gaps in the ground and the beast layer I stumbled upon. The symbol indicating where I'm currently standing is a small star that has me grinding my teeth in frustration and cursing the gods for creating the victorious prince.

The sunlight is rapidly disappearing as I pace the small layer, the smell of the rotting beast becoming more unbearable by the second.

It could be a trap. Bribing another warrior to follow me around and seem trustworthy only to lure me straight into a trap is exactly something a prince from the enemy kingdom would do to a princess they want to get rid of. But on the other hand, said enemy prince seems very eager to claim his bargained favor–a favor I won't be able to pay if my life is claimed by the gods.

The wound on my arm is still oozing black liquid and the pain is making it hard to think.

If I don't get to a healer with an antidote before the night is over, there's only one dark path ahead of me.

Whatever it takes, Asteria.

I leave the sword next to the beast but sheath the Victory Dagger back on my thigh, and with the crumpled paper a map in my hand, I move through the opening gap in the wall.

The labyrinth is no longer fighting me.

The paper is not only a map. It is a weapon that makes the labyrinth surrender, the branches easily letting me through as I follow a clear path marked on the map.

The other warriors are nowhere in sight, the ruckus of sounds the only indication I'm not alone in here. Adrenaline thrums in my blood as the sounds of battle fill my ears.

I can only imagine the dangers lurking around the clear path from the sickening sounds occasionally reaching my ears, and a part of me is yearning to join them.

I now understand why so many warriors forget the games and fight each other instead, and I'm afraid to find out how strong that urge will grow as the Tournament progresses.

It's strange that the labyrinth that only moments ago was too crowded and deadly, now feels so empty, like a cage missing its beasts. It's like the labyrinth is shielding me from every possible danger, the paper in my hand ensuring my safety. Even the rooted ground underneath my feet seems smoother.

It feels wrong for a trial to be this easy. Would I have found the way without the map? Now there is nothing stopping me from making it through the second trial–unless the infected wound kills me before I get out.

My arm has gone limp by my side, the bones heavy and skin throbbing. Carefully peeling aside the thorn leather, I mutter a curse at the sight.

The infection has spread. Dark lines snake down my arm as if my very blood has darkened, the burn marks look even more burned and my skin is still a sickly gray color.

I increase my speed, running so fast it's hard to make out the moving lines on the paper. My balance is faltering, my vision blurring at the edges. The pain is increasing too fast, and I wonder what other effects of the poison might be only seconds away.

More and more stars make their appearance in the sky. They twinkle with untold secrets, their silver shine reminding me of the silver in a pair of eyes I can't forget.

Time is running out in more ways than one.

I stumble against one of the walls and the bush catches me like a net, the branches steadying me and preventing me from crumbling to the ground.

The piece of paper is curled in my fist, my hands shaking so badly it's nearly impossible to pry my fingers away to take a last look. A spark of pain shoots through me and the shock of it makes my hands tear it in two, the dark lines dissolving before the rest of the paper dissipates in the air.

A frustrated scream escapes my lips as I clutch my chest. My heart is suddenly too heavy for my chest, my lungs constrict from the lack of air, and I know I don't have much time left.

The branches holding me up transform from friendly to hostile–they become sharp and prodding, the erupting thorns digging into the leather on my back.

I stumble away from the walls. The branches reach for me, the leaves forming into grotesque faces contorted with rage.

"Princess of the sun touched by the moon, cursed and bound, destined for darkness."

"Princess of the sun touched by the moon, shattered and thorn, destiny decided."

"Princess of the sun touched by the moon, burned and frozen, magic collided."

Voices carried by the wind scream so loud they drown out everything else. Invisible hands tear at my leathers and my heart is squeezed so tight it feels like it will break any second.

Black liquid mixed with crimson drips onto the ground. The roots move to collect it, and the liquid sinks into the moss. Even a few of my tears are collected by the hungry labyrinth, the beast thirsting for my life.

My screams are doing nothing to drown out the chaos around me. With my hands pressed over my ears, I do my best to keep moving forward. I stagger and stumble, the labyrinth no longer a friendly ally, but a deadly enemy.

Suddenly, something breaks through the storm–a sliver of light and a shadow of calm making me aware of the invisible strings pulling me forward.

The Tournament may want my life, but it also wants me to slay my enemies.

I can practically see the arrogant smirk and the alluring eyes staring at me, and I wonder if it's the labyrinth or poison playing tricks on me. And then I hear his voice, the deep husky tone breaking through the noise and blocking out the screaming labyrinth.

"Giving up so easily, princess?" A click of his tongue followed by a low chuckle. "And your threats of worthy competition were delivered so beautifully. It's a shame you can't deliver."

His presence, conjured by the Tournament or poison, ignites a spark of fury that fuels me enough to dim some of the pain exploding in my body.

I continue moving forward, willing my senses not to notice the traps around me. The labyrinth is growing more and more frantic with each step I take, and a small kernel of hope blooms in my chest.

I must be close to the end.

Two warriors run past me, their hands tightly clasped together. One of them tries to stop, but the other drags her along with only a glance in my direction.

"Don't bother. That one is on a one-way road to the Shadow Realm."

"Never let your guard down. Ever. No matter what. The most important thing this trial has proven is that even the smallest flower can have the deadliest poison–"

There's something vaguely familiar about them, but I don't have enough strength to figure it out. The pair disappears around a corner, and I grind my teeth together as I follow them.

And then I see it–an opening in the thick bushy walls, the last rays of sunlight shining beyond it. Gilded branches snake up the walls, lavender petals showing the way in patterns that resemble small arrows. A line is drawn in the dirt by something that looks a lot like blood.

The sound of the roaring crowd in the clearing reaches me as I approach the opening. The winner is standing right outside, a silver banner discarded at his feet as he brushes flecks of the silver paper away from his immaculate leathers. The crowd is cheering around him, and groups of beaten warriors are glaring and grumbling at their loss, some of them looking only seconds away from death, others already long gone.

As if he can sense me approaching, the winner tilts his chin up to look at me, unbothered by everything else around him.

Prince Star's lips pull into one of his usual smirks and I resist the urge to give him a vulgar gesture as I struggle to move forward, his eyes glinting silver just as I saw in my mind's only eye moments ago.

A rustling of leaves sounds behind me and I turn around with a hammering heart.

The sight makes me press my nails into my palms and start sprinting.

The labyrinth is closing.

Time is running out.

The sunlight in the distance is so faint I can barely make out anything in the darkness of the cage.

The branches reach for my body, scraping against my leathers, trying to tear them apart and reach my skin.

The ground beneath me moves, rocks and roots rolling and sinking.

A branch catches my ankle.

Vines wrap around my feet.

Another branch emerges from the wall to stab the broken skin at my arm.

I fall to the ground, pain burning through every cell in my body. My fingers reach for the ground past the opening, my fingertips brushing the dirty ground as I let out a bloodcurdling scream.

Crawling to the finish line is not how I wanted to win this, but I'll do whatever it takes–

I twist and turn, trying to wriggle free from the hands of the labyrinth as its mouth tries to swallow me whole. The lavender petals fly from the walls, the gilded branches barely missing me as they fall to the ground one by one. More leaves and branches wrap around my legs, and I try to yank away but the labyrinth's grip is as solid as iron.

I'm stuck–

A hand suddenly wraps around my wrist, a wave of warmth washing over my cold skin. The hand starts pulling, giving me the strength I need to keep moving forward.

I tumble over the finish line just in time.

The labyrinth closes behind me and the last of the sunlight evaporates as if it was never there at all.

I'm out.

A tingling sensation spreads from the binding mark on my neck throughout my body. The blood in my veins vibrates with magic, my heart fluttering so violently as if it is a winged beast ready to fly across the sky.

The feeling is so powerful it's a wonder I missed it during the first trial.

The relief I should be feeling is overshadowed by the pain and dizziness overtaking every part of me, my senses clouded and my mind foggy.

"Is this how every trial is going to end? Your soul is already halfway to the Shadow Realm," Star spits before hoisting me into his arms as if I weigh nothing at all.

I'm too tired to threaten him away, let alone even attempt to move away from his strong grip.

His touch is a cool relief against my burning skin and no matter how much I might hate him, right now, even the slight relief is worth the risk.

If he wanted me dead, why would he bother carrying me away from the stampede of warriors that would eagerly disembowel me, or the king ready to part me with the Royal Sword if he saw me?

I'll deal with the prince later.

"You better hold on, starlight, or I'm dragging you back from the shadows myself, and I can promise you that journey is going to hurt a lot more than this." A low growl reverberates from his chest, the vibration hitting my cheek.

My eyes flutter, glittering stars winking in and out of existence. And then the darkness finally claims me.

CHAPTER THIRTEEN

My dreams are so very strange.

I'm floating in a cold abyss where there is nothing but darkness and hollow silence, but my soul is ablaze with the hottest and brightest flames that won't stop burning until I'm nothing but ashes.

Then suddenly, hands as cold as ice are dragging me out of the empty coldness and pulling my body onto something hard. Long fingers are prodding in my arm, the action sending small sparks of pain shooting through me.

Far away voices slip in and out of my ears, my eyes unable to see anything in front of me.

"–warn her about the poison."

"–as if she would've listened to me."

"It is not only her life at stake here. You would do well not to forget that–"

A low growl followed by a rattle reverberates through me, and it feels as if the whole world is trembling.

The hands and fingers continue to touch my burning skin, the cool touch a soothing relief.

I'm frozen in time, unable to move or speak.

Seconds, minutes, days, or years later, my eyes start to flutter and images move past in a rapid rhythm. It's as if I'm seeing the world through a foggy lens–a strange white gleam clouding my eyes and all my other senses.

I see the moon shining on a starless sky, mountain peaks as tall as the sky, the vast ocean rolling with foaming waves, and a pair of glowing eyes staring into my soul.

I'm seized by a sudden panic at the unfamiliarity, my body jerking against the hands holding me down. Perhaps this isn't a dream at all, but a deadly nightmare–

Nightmares during the Tournament Times are never a good thing.

"Lay still."

There's something vaguely familiar about the voice–

Silver-flecked eyes move into my line of vision, the white gleam glazing my eyes making his face glow in the black night. Shadows ripple off his form, the darkness like an extension of his being.

I open my mouth, but nothing comes out, not even a whisper. My throat is dry as sand, my voice lost to the rushing wind around us.

Star pushes my shoulders back onto the stone underneath me, my skin tingling from his touch.

Another scream is trapped in my throat when I realize I'm naked save for a thin sheet covering parts of my bare skin.

Star snorts and rolls his eyes, his hands holding me still. "Since when are you one for modesty, starlight?"

"Do not rile her, boy. We are almost finished. Just a little longer."

I turn my head to the other side, my eyes landing on the owner of the voice.

The woman's skin is almost as dark as the night and her long black hair flutters in the wind. She is wearing a white dress with no sleeves, her bare arms decorated with white swirls and symbols I can't make out in the darkness. A crescent moon is carved between her eyebrows, the lines a dark crimson. There are no pupils in her eyes, only blood-red irises illuminated by the moonlight.

A witch.

There is no doubt what this woman is. Not a healer, but a witch. She is not one of the witches selling drops of magic at the border markets, long descended from the powerful covens rumored to be residing deep in the Diamond Mountains. No, this woman is radiating magic, her unnatural eyes proof of her immortal soul.

The witch's blood-red eyes meet mine and a shiver runs through my heart. She tilts her head to the side, her fingers closing around my wrist. Words in an unfamiliar ancient language start pouring out of her mouth, her gaze flickering to the moon above.

White lightning flares across the sky, and where the witch touches my skin–magic rushes into me, the pain replaced by a strange tingling.

I struggle against their hold, every instinct in my body screaming to get away. "Let me go or I will–" I gasp as a surge of ice shoots through me, flinching at the stern look from the witch.

"As much as I adore your threats–" Star raises his eyebrows with an indignant look, "–I'm not currently in the mood for them. And I certainly won't waste my favor tonight, which unfortunately means you're going to have to stay alive a little while longer." He reaches forward and trails his fingers over my forehead before closing my eyes.

The nightmare fades into darkness once again.

I AWAKE with a jolt and startle at the familiarity around me. Pale beige walls chipped with gold, a ceiling picturing a summer day, the large windows overlooking the forest–

I'm back at the Sun Palace, in my own bed in my room.

The golden curtains flutter in the summer breeze, the open window revealing the night beyond. The moon is lighting up the dark night, the countless stars around it glittering with a bright silver light.

The sight makes the memories of the previous hours crash into me with a violent force that takes my breath away. I stumble out of the bed, the thin sheet wrapped around my body slipping away and down to the floor.

A faint tingle slithers across the skin on my arm, and a gasp escapes me as I hold my arm up to the moonlight seeping in from the window.

The wounds from the labyrinth are gone. There is no blood, no poison, and no pain.

There is only a dark mark–a mark that shouldn't be there, a mark that should've vanished once I healed from the embarrassing fall through the temple roof.

It is the mark I carved into my skin with forbidden magic after taking the life of a suitor, binding the last of his life essence to mine, giving me another chance should I start the journey to the shadows.

The mark looks about the same as when I carved it into my skin–lines hastily carved into a pattern resembling the ancient runes found in the temples, but new swirling lines have erupted from the mark, snaking from the original mark below my elbow down to the middle of my forearm.

And that's not the only thing that has changed.

The mark that was once blood-red like the binding mark is now as black as the darkest nights.

The dark lines remind me of the ink on the map of the labyrinth. This time not quite alive, but not quite inanimate either. The lines pulse and throb underneath the moonlight, and it feels like a snake is coiling underneath my skin.

Maybe there was some magic left in the mark and that was what healed the poisonous wounds and saved my life. That could be possible, right? I still don't know exactly what the magic did to my body other than keep me alive when I needed it the most—

All magic comes with a cost, girl. You've already been marked. Doing it again may come with a cost too high even for a princess.

Maybe I did buy something with a price too high, unwillingly committing to something more than just a piece of strengthened life force, something that might very well cost me my life. Maybe the gods weren't ready to see the end of my participation. Or worse—the dark mark is now proof of my bargain with the prince.

Whatever it takes, Asteria.

And then there is another possibility, so far-fetched I don't even want to think about

it.

I muffle a scream with the palm of my hand. Too many questions impossible to find

answers to are churning in my mind and it feels as if my head is going to explode any second.

I shouldn't even be here. The royals usually spend most of the week-long break between the trials in the last hosting court and the journey from Lavendula is long enough that it's impossible for me to be back at the palace so soon.

How many days have passed? Is this even real or am I still in the middle of a nightmare or deep in the Shadow Realm? Did

Star bring me back to the palace? Did he bring me to a healer? The last thing I want is to owe him any more favors. And the nightmare–

Whatever or whoever caused me to be rid of the poison and back in my room–I don't have the time to dwell on it.

Too restless to sleep any longer, I quickly get dressed before slipping out of my room.

The Sun Palace doesn't sleep at night.

During the dark nights of the Tournament, the gilded hallways are lit up by lanterns with dancing flames and never-ending swirls of magic lights that float around like petals on water–the kinglights brighter than any flame.

In Soria, day and night, the sun rests in the middle of the sky, and likewise, the palace is located in the very center of the kingdom. The sun might have to sleep for the moon during the Tournament, but thanks to the Sun King's magic–the palace sure hasn't.

The servants' halls are the only places not touched by the king's magic, only a dim light coming from the cracks in the walls and ceiling. I trail my fingers along the walls, following the memorized paths from my room. I've walked through these halls so many times I could do it with my eyes closed.

When I'm forced to leave the security of the hidden halls, I take one of my well-practiced routes past the guards, slipping into shadow after shadow.

The shadows betray you because they serve me.

The voice slithers into my mind so suddenly it startles me, one of my feet banging against the wall. It's as if he is standing right behind me, his breath sending shivers down my neck as he whispers the words into my ear.

A guard passes right in front of me, halting to look around.

I hold my breath, willing my heart to steady.

A few moments later, the guard continues walking, his echoing footsteps disappearing in the courtyard.

I wait a few seconds before following, a relieved breath escaping my lips when I finally feel the summer breeze on my skin.

The moonlight is overshadowed by the lights of the palace, but I can't help noticing the stars that are silently laughing at my loss of balance, blinking like the wink from a prince with feet dangling over the edge of the sacred mountain.

I try not to think about whether or not he is telling the truth about the shadows and the other magic tricks of his kingdom.

Leaving the light of the palace behind, I step into the thick forest, ignoring my hammering heart.

Tonight, I'm not relieved to be free of the palace walls. The darkness makes me paranoid, the moonlight no longer a reprieve from the scorching sun.

It's as if the Kingdom of the Moon has already claimed me.

The dark mark is eerie in the night. The lines bleed into the darkness, and it feels as if a part of the night has seeped into my skin.

I may not know much about the royal magic dormant in my veins—the knowledge of how to use it is reserved for the current monarch, and I'm the last person the king would ever share it with—but I know it's not supposed to look like this.

Soria is the Kingdom of the Sun, of light and sparkling gold. This mark is nothing but unfamiliar darkness, darkness that should not be a part of a princess of the light.

The blade of the Victory Dagger slashes across my skin and I grind my teeth together to not let out a scream that will wake the slumbering beasts in the forest around me.

A sharp pain shoots up the hand holding the dagger and I quickly drop it to the ground followed by a few choice words that would make even the foulest warriors blush.

The dark mark is like steel, the skin impenetrable where the darkness hovers. Not a single scrape or drop of blood leaves my skin by the press of the dagger.

I try again and again, the pain increasing with each slice of the dagger. I try another dagger, a knife, a sword–nothing.

The mark is impossible to remove. At least by sheer force with a blade or another weapon. I wonder if cutting my arm off would get rid of it, and how much more difficult it would be to win the Tournamant like that.

I'll tell you how you can continue your participation in the games for a favor.

The prince's words echo in my head as I claw at the mark, my nails meeting nothing but firm resistance–the skin an impenetrable wall to a mighty fortress.

A bargain.

A favor.

He could ask me anything and I would have to obey, even if it means jumping to my death or clawing my heart out of my chest.

And if the mark is now something worse–a true curse–I have no idea how I'm going to survive this.

I'm trapped.

I'm not free of the cagey labyrinth.

I'm still barely hanging onto the holy mountain.

The Tournament has just begun and I'm in the middle of a never-ending game.

I don't bother holding back my screams any longer as I race through the forest to slay some other monsters than my own.

I'VE NEVER BEEN one to pray to the gods, but in the days following the second trial, I pray to them all–the gods, goddesses, and spirits of the sun. And in my darkest moments, when the mark on my arm throbs and my heart is squeezed by the hands of fear and desperation—I very quietly send a thought to the moon and its unfamiliar deities.

The palace is too quiet without the king. Dread fills me with each step I take through the quiet palace, the remaining staff and guards ignoring my presence as if I'm not there at all, and I can't help wondering why no one is questioning my absence in Lavendula.

It's as if I'm momentarily forgotten.

Maybe Surya has taken pity on a fellow sun warrior trying to prove herself to her kingdom. The deity's story ended in glory and praise as she became the High General of the kingdom's army, a Victor in her own way.

Perhaps the spirits of Lavendula have granted me a pause after capturing me in their maze, or maybe a bloodthirsty god is patiently building up the king's rage, eagerly awaiting my next punishment.

If it's one thing the gods love, it's tragedy. And I'm the most tragic of them all.

On one of my early morning walks, I find Elio in one of our usual spots in the thick woods surrounding Moria. He's sitting on a cliff overlooking the palace in the distance, the rising sun casting the landscape in a magical light.

"You're back," I say, suddenly breathless, my heart beating a violent rhythm against my chest.

Elio turns around to face me. His hazel eyes shine in the morning light, the faint smile on his face warming me more than the sun. "I tried to get back sooner when I realized you weren't in Lavendula but—" he trails off with a shrug, his hands gesturing for me to sit down next to him. "I was hoping you would show up here."

"You know me." Our dangling legs brush against each other, the warmth of his skin reaching me through the fabric of our clothes.

"Of course I do." The smile on his face widens and he grabs my hand, his fingers closing around mine. His hand is no longer as calloused as it once was, a result of less frequent training sessions and more Victor duties.

"I didn't see you at the last trial. I was hoping you'd be at the dais so we could spend some time together. You know, before–"

Before you leave for the enemy kingdom.

"I–"

A wave of guilt washes over me and I suck in a breath before trying again. "The king surprisingly granted me a last chance at freedom and I just couldn't bear seeing the trial considering everything that happened last time–" I swallow against the lump in my throat, locking my eyes on the horizon so I won't have to meet his gaze.

In the far distance, the sun is slowly rising above the Diamond Mountains. Behind them, Luna is hiding its brutality, the Kingdom of the Moon robbed of its darkness for another day.

Elio gives my hand a squeeze. "I'm sorry, Ria. I didn't even think about–"

"Never mind that," I say, forcing a smile onto my face. "I'm just glad you're back."

I feel his gaze on the side of my face, but I keep my eyes on the sun as if it will melt away the ice in my veins.

"Seeing the sun rise has always been my favorite part of the Tournament," he says, his hand releasing mine to pick up a rock and toss it into the forest below. "It almost makes all the darkness worth it."

"I like the difference," I mumble, accepting the rock he hands me and rolling it around in my hands like it's some sort of treasure. "When the sun is always up, sometimes it's hard to appreciate the light."

Elio gives me a strange look and I quickly drop the rock. It tumbles off the cliff, a cloud of debris following as it disappears in the ocean of green below.

"Careful, or you might start sounding like one of them."

"I'll never be one of them. No matter which kingdom I reside in or whose ring is on my finger," I spit, trailing my finger over the faint mark where the ridiculous ring has marked the skin.

The ring is currently discarded in my room. I refuse to wear it any more than absolutely necessary.

"I certainly hope so." His hazel eyes bore into me for a moment before he tosses another rock down the cliff.

"I'm coming back, you know. I'm not leaving for good."

I want to tell him my plans, but I know I can't. Putting him in danger is the last thing I want to do.

"Maybe it would be for the best," he mumbles, his voice so low I'm not sure if I imagined it or not.

"What?" I'm so stunned by his words I have to grab hold of the rocky ground not to topple over the edge.

Elio sighs heavily and rubs his eyes with the heels of his palms. "I didn't mean it like that. Asteria, look—"

"No, I get it. The rumors have finally caught up to you—"

He interrupts me by grabbing my shoulders, his hands turning me to look at him. "No, you don't. Asteria, the last thing I want is to see you leave, but Soria has never exactly been a safe place for you, has it?"

His hazel eyes lose some of their warmth as he looks at me, the sight so unfamiliar it's suddenly hard to breathe. "And especially not now." His hand moves to the side of my neck, his fingers trailing over the binding mark.

"I can take care of myself," I snap and scramble away from his touch.

"Of course you can, Ria. I didn't mean it like that. I just–" he rakes a hand across his short-cropped hair with a heavy sigh. "I'm worried about you, okay? I know you don't want to hear it but I am."

His hands are back on my shoulders, his warmth making it hard to step away. His gaze moves to one of my arms, to a ragged seam on my leathers, and a furrow forms between his eyebrows. "Did you do this?"

Relieved by the change of subject, I let out a chuckle. "I didn't want to part with them. It's just from the binding rounds." I wave a dismissive hand, but the furrow on his face only deepens.

"What happened?"

I blink in surprise, realizing there is so much he doesn't know about me now. "I got a little too confident and didn't exactly watch my back. If I had known he was a prince I probably wouldn't have been so cocky–"

"What?" His grip on my shoulder hardens to the point of pain. He removes his hands when he notices my wince, an apologetic look flickering across his features.

"I got into a sword fight with one of the arrogant princes. Apparently, he's a Victor of multiple games but hasn't competed in a few years–"

"Star. I know him," Elio says through gritted teeth, the hatred in his voice startling me. "Why didn't you tell me?"

"We haven't exactly had much time to talk lately–"

"I should've killed him when I had the chance," he mutters, his face contorted with anger.

A snort leaves me before I can stop it. "I'm starting to doubt whether he can actually die."

Elio shoots me an incredulous look. "Don't tell me you're one of his admirers."

Another snort. "Definitely not. And I'm betrothed now, remember?" I give him a teasing shove, the hatred still evident in his eyes sending an involuntary shiver down my back.

"Yeah, I know. Castor. The fox."

A low chuckle escapes me. "The what?"

Some of the tension in his body vanishes, the corner of his lips tugging upward. "Come on, don't tell me you think his permanent scowl makes him handsome?"

"I guess he is handsome enough," I say, laughing, "but those eyes–you know what? They actually remind me of the beast–" I purse my lips, cursing Surya for my reckless mouth.

Elio raises his eyebrows. "Which beast are we talking about here? Marerit? Bone crusher? Or maybe even a shadow–"

"Whatever the name is of the one I spotted in a book last week. It gave me a really bad nightmare. And I'm sure Castor is going to take its place very soon." I try to mask my raging heart with a weak laugh.

"Still stealing books from the restricted section, I see." Elio chuckles, seemingly unaware of the lies that are slowly becoming easier to tell.

"Burrowing," I correct with a smile that earns another chuckle from him. "And by the way, those books shouldn't be restricted. How else are the people going to be able to defend themselves?"

"Spoken like a true princess," he mutters, laughing when I shove him.

"Never call me that again," I say, raising my chin and looking down my nose in a very princess-like manner.

Elio laughs again. "You know I agree. But that's what the

people have the Royal Guard for, right? You know, protect and serve and all that bullshit?"

I roll my eyes. "I'm sure our training has nothing to do with the lack of beasts reaching the villages."

Elio grabs my arm. The leather of my sleeve has crept up, revealing a long scar on the inside of my arm, thankfully not on the one bearing the dark mark I refuse to think about. "Ten, right?"

"Six, actually. Before you found me and we started copying the guards."

Elio lets out a long breath. "Right. By the sun, no one should meet a beast like that on their own. You could've died–"

"But I didn't." I place my hand on his, giving him a little squeeze. "I'm still here."

"Thank the gods for that."

"I'm not so sure the gods have a say in my fate anymore," I mumble, taken aback by his sudden closeness. He is so close that I can feel his breath on my face.

"I used to like the idea of deciding my own destiny, but that hasn't worked out that great either–"

He closes the distance between us. His hand moves to the back of my neck, his fingers sinking into my hair. "Asteria." He mumbles my name against my lips, his other hand landing on my back to pull me closer.

I freeze.

Elio drops me as if he is burned by my skin, pain flickering in his eyes.

"I'm sorry–"

"No, I'm sorry," he says, dragging a hand over his face before taking a long step away from me, and it feels as if the Diamond Mountains are suddenly between us. "You have a lot going on right now and I–" he sighs heavily, his gaze locked on the sky above, pain still etched onto his features.

"Elio, wait–"

He turns his back to me without another word and disappears between the trees before I can stop him.

The rising sun burns the leathers on my back, the light too bright for this moment in the middle of the forest.

I've been waiting for this moment for so long, craving it with every cell in my body. I don't understand why I turned him away, why I didn't grab the collar of his shirt to pull him closer.

Maybe he's right. Maybe I do have a lot going on.

CHAPTER FOURTEEN

On the morning of the third trial, the king's invisible shackles are clasped closed once again, the tip of the blade too familiar with the skin on my back an unseeable weight crushing my heart.

A package is delivered to my room. A dress with long chiffon sleeves in light shades of yellow and a tin of golden paint. There is no note attached to the package, but the unspoken words are clear.

Play your part as a princess of the sun or face the wrath of the king.

I dutifully paint golden marks on the skin that's not covered by the fabric of the dress, dusting my hair with so much gold I can no longer make out the white strands. My eyelids are painted with a line of golden brown and my lips are smeared with gold as if I've been kissed by the sun herself.

My fingers ache as I braid my hair, my mind churning as violently as the ocean during the harshest storms.

How am I going to complete the third trial when I have to be in two places at once?

No matter how many calming breaths I take, my heart refuses to steady, and my body shakes as if I'm submerged in snow and ice.

As if it can hear my panic, the dark mark sends a pulse through me, reminding me of the price I've yet to pay.

It feels like the magic is trying to break free of my skin, the darkness yearning to be let loose in the kingdom of light.

Whatever it takes, Asteria. Whatever it takes.

I rub some more paint on the mark before tying a strip of golden fabric around my arm just in case. And with a last deep inhale, I leave the security of my room.

The palace is bustling with activity, the usual quiet replaced with resounding footsteps and low chatter. Servants are darting around with heaps of various items in their hands—piles of freshly washed sheets, tailored clothes, wine in crystal bottles, and vibrant flowers.

An elderly woman runs past, one of the few servants I've reluctantly allowed into my room over the years. A decoration of white daisies and pale yellow marigolds is balanced in her hands, some of the petals flying to the ground when I stop her with a gentle hand on her arm. A small squeak sounds from her lips, but she visibly relaxes when she notices it's me and not the king. "Your Highness?"

"Is something special happening today?" I gesture to the hurrying servants around us. "Besides the next trial, of course."

She gives me an incredulous look. "I would've thought you to be the first one to know. The king and a handful of the princes are staying here for the remainder of the Sun Trials before you leave for the other kingdom." Her gaze snatches on the golden paint covering my binding mark, her eyes narrowing slightly, and I can practically hear her disdainful thoughts.

"After your last outing with your betrothed, I was certain your room would be prepared already but I'll make sure someone–"

I don't hear the rest of her words over the roaring in my ears.

"Your Highness?" The servant waves a hand in front of my face, the flowers balanced in her other hand dangerously close to falling to the ground.

"He is not going anywhere near my room," I say through gritted teeth, my nails digging into the scars of my palms so hard I'm afraid it might make me pass out.

The servant gives me a puzzled look but quickly bows her head with a polite smile. "Of course, Your Highness. I'll prepare the best suite–"

"No."

The woman casts uncertain looks around, her mouth slightly agape. "I'm sorry, Your Highness. I didn't mean any disrespect–" she mutters apologetic words, but all I can think about is me in bed, pinned underneath Castor with no way to escape.

This is not happening.

Without another word, I turn on my heels and run out of the palace, my hands balled into fists at my side, the pain from the pressure of my nails making my vision blurry.

The Lunan royals have never stayed at the palace, but there has never been a betrothal between the kingdoms either. The Sun King is rewriting history in more ways than one, and I can't even begin to understand why he would welcome the enemy into his palace.

It can't mean anything good.

Something big is happening and I refuse to be a part of it.

The royal procession is already being prepared in the courtyard when I emerge, the guards creating protective walls around the royals. Today, both kings and their parties will travel together, starting with a march through parts of Moria to where the horses and carriages are packed and ready.

My sisters are all wearing the same yellow dress as me, their postures as regal and poised as ever as they await the start of the procession. For once, I look like I belong with them, my pale eyes the only thing separating us.

A crowd is gathered outside of the palace gates, ready to join the procession and find out where the third trial is located.

It isn't that exciting. The Tournament is made of eight trials, four in each kingdom, and one in each court of the kingdoms. Two trials have been held in Soria, meaning two courts are left. The Court of Light and the Court of Helianthus. And looking at Father–there is no doubt where the procession is headed today.

The Sun King is an incarnation of the sun and its light. A crown of golden leaves rests on his head, his long blonde hair let loose and blowing in the wind. He is wearing a gilded suit embroidered with countless swirls and lines to represent the sunlight–the symbol for the Court of Light.

As light is considered life in this kingdom, the Light Court is dedicated to honor all light and life underneath the sun. It is where the worship of the gods is strongest and countless temples and ancient ruins are scattered throughout the court that's ruled by the priestesses and the High Priestess at the top. The court is located at the far end away from the border to Luna, above Lavendula where I barely escaped the claws of the labyrinth, and next to Verbena where I destroyed the ancient temple.

I'm about to start maneuvering through the crowd of guards and servants when I notice the prince standing in the shadows of the palace. The simmering anger is replaced by an unsettling feeling, my heart beating so hard it hurts.

Prince Star is standing to the side of the other Tournament-bound princes, his usual dark leathers simple compared to his brothers' royal uniforms with silver crested chest and shoulder plates. He is impatiently tapping his fingers on his thighs, a bored expression on his face.

The shadows betray you because they serve me.

You know, one of my kingdom's tricks during the Tournament is visiting people in their dreams—or even better, nightmares.

I'll tell you how you can continue playing the game in exchange for a favor. Do we have a bargain?

The sight of him brings back everything I've been trying to ignore, the magic of the Tournament tearing my soul with a violent wind.

Star gives me a wink when he notices my stare, his lips pulling into one of his usual arrogant smirks as he waves his fingers in my direction, the mark on my arm tingling in reply.

Before I can think it through, I'm walking down the stairs, my gaze locked on the prince who dared to challenge me—

A hand grabs my arm, icy fingers closing around my wrist. I look into the eyes of the last person I wanted to see right now and fury starts vibrating in my blood.

"You forgot this," Castor snarls as he forcefully shoves the amethyst ring onto my finger, the feel of his skin against mine so repulsive I'm struggling not to retrieve the hidden Victory Dagger and shove it into his heart right here in the middle of the courtyard in front of everyone.

Not yet.

I yank my hand away from his, the ring a heavy weight on my finger. "Where did you—"

Ice spreads from my heart, extinguishing the burning fury as fear grips my heart with a clenched fist.

Castor's lips pull into a cruel smile, his dark eyes betraying his triumph. "I expected a certain lower standard for the cursed princess, but to discover that your room was not even guarded at all—"

The cruel smile widens, and he leans close to whisper in my ear, his breath sending unpleasant shivers down my back. "You have no idea how much I enjoy seeing you squirm, *princess*. My promise of making your death anything but swift still stands."

His hand moves to the side of my neck, over the painted binding mark. He squeezes my neck, his fingers painfully digging into my skin. "You're not even safe inside your palace, and especially not in your little room. This might be the most interesting game of them all."

Castor drops me and disappears back into the crowd of people as suddenly as he came, leaving me with a chaos of thoughts and churning emotions.

Noticing the looks of the people around me, I force myself to keep moving until I'm standing behind my sisters.

As if he can sense my presence, Father turns around from his position at the front

to give me an assessing look, seemingly pleased with my appearance from the lack of sparkling gold in his eyes.

"Let us begin." The Sun King's booming voice breaks through the noise of the crowd, and at the sound of it, everyone falls silent. Even the chirping birds and howling wind seem to quiet, the courtyard so still I'm afraid to breathe too loudly.

The king nods to his High General and the gilded gates fly open, the crowd beyond parting to make room for the royal procession.

Moria is magnificent underneath the sun. The road winding through the outskirts of the city is decorated with a rainbow of colors, the flowers dusted with glittering gold that sparkles in the sunlight.

People of all ages are celebrating the Tournament–their loud cheers echoing off the cobbled streets as they dance around the procession, their arms reaching for the sky above.

I count each step forward, trying to ignore the pull of the magic urging me to take out the competition behind me.

I can practically feel Star's silvery gaze trailing my every move, the Tournament-bound princes around him stoking the magic in the air.

And then there's Castor walking beside me. His mahogany eyes glance in my direction every time my steps falter, the feel of his fingers on my neck still lingering on my skin.

I pray I'm not forced to share a carriage with any of them. I don't think I would be able to hold myself back all the long hours of the journey.

At the end of the city, the road transforms from cobblestones to dirty forest ground, the thick forest parted to let travelers through, the roots long stomped into the ground.

An army of guards are standing around a chain of carriages. On one side, the Sun King's golden carriages glimmer in the sunlight, the white stallions' shiny coats dusted with gold. On the other side, partly shielded by the thick forest, dark horses looking as if they've been carved out of darkness are standing in front of black and silver carriages, the shadows of the forest seeming to cling to the Lunan procession.

I'm about to step into a golden carriage with my sisters when a hand lands on my shoulder. Rage sparks in my fingertips, and I turn around to scream at my betrothed–

"Will you give your future king the honor of your company on this journey, Princess Asteria?"

The hairs on my arms rise at the sound of his voice, my body stiffening beneath his touch. "Father expects me to stay with my sisters–"

"Oh, I am sure Helios will not mind me getting to know my

future daughter," the Moon King says, his hand wrapping around my upper arm to steer me away from my sisters' shocked faces and in the direction of the darkness of his kingdom.

Father's carriage at the front of the procession is already closed and Elio is nowhere in sight.

None of the guards or servants move to save me from the enemy king.

No one even glances in my direction.

I am all alone.

Being alone with the enemy is the last thing I should do, but it would be a grave mistake to deny a king no matter which kingdom he rules over.

I swallow against the lump in my throat and force a polite smile onto my lips, allowing the Moon King to steady me as I step into his carriage.

The interior of the carriage is all black, from the velvet benches to the intricately carved ceiling picturing the night sky. There are no lit candles or floating lights, the only light the sunlight seeping in from the window.

The sound of the door closing sends a jolt of fear through me and I will myself not to tremble underneath the king's dark gaze.

The carriage feels too small for both of us.

I glance out of the window, hoping I'll see Elio or one of my sisters come running to save me. I only get a glimpse of the forest before the black curtains blow shut on a phantom wind, startling me so much that my back slams against the wall.

"Forgive me, but I am not one to spend any more time than absolutely necessary underneath the sun," the king says, his voice sending shivers all over my skin. "Oh, how it pains me to endure the presence of the dreadful light during these weeks and months."

Only faint traces of light escape the curtains, casting the

carriage in even more darkness, the king the darkest shadow of them all. There's a subtle smirk on his lips and a gleam in his eyes that has fear gripping my heart so hard I'm struggling to breathe.

It feels as if his dark eyes can see through my skin and bones and into my very soul, as if he knows about the secrets I'm desperately trying to hide.

I give him a curt nod in reply, my lips still strained into a polite smile as I allow myself to study the king in front of me.

A crown of silver thorns sits atop his head, the same dark hair as Star's reaching down to his shoulders, the black assorted with a few strands of gray so faint it's impossible to see from a distance. The king has the same cold eyes as Castor, only pure black, the irises indiscernible. There's a slight stubble to his sharp chin, and a brutality to his features that hints at his immense power. It's easy to tell he has created a line of warrior princes, his black suit doing little to conceal his robust frame.

"You know, the mountains surrounding my city do not often allow the sunlight to settle, so it would be prudent for you to start lowering your exposure to the sun as well," he says as the carriage starts moving forward. "Of course, once the Tournament ends, that will not even be an option."

"I'll be sure to keep that in mind," I say, clearing my throat and digging my hands in the skirt of my dress to hide my clenched fists.

The Moon King studies me for a moment, his eyes pausing on the binding mark peeking through the golden paint. "Tell me, *Princess* Asteria, are you looking forward to the third trial?"

"Of course. As always, it is a great honor for my kingdom to host the Tournament of Day and Night–"

The Moon King clicks his tongue in disappointment. "Do not insult me by lying in my presence, at least not away from prying eyes and curious ears."

"I'm afraid I don't know what you mean, Your Majesty—"

It happens before I've even finished speaking.

Something stirs in the shadows behind the king.

A black mist seeps out from the walls.

Darkness and shadows swirl together and a pair of smoky hands shoot forward, the dark fingers wrapping around my throat as solid as stone.

I struggle against the shadows, gasping for air as I try to yank them away, but my fingers are unable to grasp them. It's like trying to reach for the wind or the sunlight—impossible.

The Moon King is sitting as still as a statue, not a single sign of strain to be seen. "Do not pretend you are some meek pathetic little girl when I can see your vicious mind working behind those frosted eyes," he snarls, his voice seeming to rattle the bench underneath me.

The shadowy fingers tighten and a fear unlike anything I've ever felt before slams into me. My chest is constricted from the lack of air, my vision is starting to blur, and it feels as if I'm only moments away from the Shadow Realm.

The Moon King clicks his tongue again before straightening the lapels of his jacket. "Now, let me ask you again—"

The shadows dissolve and I gasp for air, sliding along the bench and pressing myself against the corner wall to get as far away from the king as possible.

"Are you looking forward to *participating* in the third trial, Princess Asteria?" He gives me a challenging smile, the shadows around him darkening ever so slightly.

I don't understand how he figured it out. I didn't see any of the princes during the last trial—

Star.

"I—"

The king raises his eyebrows and I snap my mouth shut, my

mind racing and my heart beating so heavily I can hear the drumming in my ears.

"Yes?"

Will he kill me if I deny it or just strangle me until I can't take it anymore and beg him to end me? And if I tell him, will he kill me himself or boast to Father until the Royal Sword is cutting so deep into my back there is no chance of survival?

This is just another game.

This is just another game I need to survive.

Whatever it takes, Asteria. Whatever it takes.

"I've dreamed of the Tournament for as long as I can remember," I say, willing my voice to be steady and resisting the urge to rub my aching throat. "And I know very well what happens if you don't follow the rules or lack of them. The binding is eternal and if you fail to participate in what you signed up for–" I trail off with a shrug of my shoulders, swallowing against the lump in my throat.

"And?" The king leans forward, eyebrows still raised. He moves the hand resting on his thigh palm up and a faint black smoke emanates from his fingertips.

"Yes," I say through gritted teeth, praying I'm making the right choice. "I do look forward to participating in the third trial."

The Moon King sighs heavily, a pleased smile spreading on his lips. "That was not so difficult, was it?"

"What do you want?" Anger slips into my voice and I can't help muttering a low curse aimed at the gods for my reckless mouth.

The smile on his lips widens. "There is the princess I have heard so much about, the one radiating trouble and defiance."

I'll give him defiance.

I straighten my posture, giving him my best glare. "Go ahead, tell Father about my little secret if you're so afraid I'll beat your princes. From what I've seen so far, that shouldn't be very difficult. Maybe I'll gift you their black hearts so you can decorate this gloomy carriage."

I hold my breath, my heart beating so hard I'm convinced he can hear it.

The Moon King looks at me for a heartbeat before tipping his head back with a hearty laugh, the sound more terrifying than his silence. "Do not worry, princess. I have no plans to rob my kingdom of entertainment by blabbering to Helios. No, I am going to enjoy seeing you try to keep this secret while fighting to stay alive in the games."

He taps a finger on his chin and I notice his nails are painted black. "As you very well know, I do not mind letting my fellow royals compete although we have a little game of our own." A sinister expression crosses his face as he leans back against the wall.

"Another game?"

"Yes."

"And let me guess, you're not going to tell me what it is?"

"No."

A few drops of blood escape the skin in my palms from the pressure of my nails, forcing me to curl my hands together to not spill it on my dress.

"I can only guess this game has something to do with me?"

The king shrugs, seemingly finished with our conversation. "Yes and no." He waves a dismissive hand, a burst of black smoke exploding from his fingertips. "But I can say there is definitely an added prize this year."

I shrink back against the wall, not daring to chance my luck any further.

The long journey is mostly spent in silence. I'm too agitated to sleep, and I know that will cost me later. I try to peek behind the closed curtains, desperately avoiding looking at the king and the shadows around him.

Occasionally, the Moon King will mutter something ambiguous about the Tournament or his kingdom, only some of the words intelligible to my ears.

"... sacrifice to the Shadow Realm."

"... the army stationed in NAR."

"... those bloody witches."

I can't tell if he's trying to intimidate and scare me, or whether he's just thinking out loud or even speaking to the darkness. It wouldn't surprise me if his shadows were somehow able to deliver messages. The power I felt was only a fraction of the magic in his blood.

Without the sun's presence in the sky to tell the time, I'm forced to count my breaths, but with each word or movement from the king, I lose count and have to start all over again. The darkness of the carriage is making me paranoid, and the longer I stare at the shadows, the more faces and beasts I see.

If I'm struggling this much in only hours of darkness, I fear what it will be like to be in the middle of a kingdom of inescapable darkness.

When I'm certain I'm going to go insane from the cramped space and brooding king, the carriage finally comes to a stop.

The Moon King moves his dark gaze to me, a wicked smile slowly appearing on his brutal face. "Let the third trial begin."

CHAPTER FIFTEEN

The Court of Light is gilded by the sun. The pale stone of the temples and ruins in the center of the court is reflected by the sunlight, the stone lighting up the spiraling roads with a bright light.

The normally subtle magic of the court is vibrating in the air, the power blowing through the city caressing my face and sending shivers down my neck.

Filled with remnants of the gods' reign, this is where the god's presence is the strongest.

I can almost feel them scrutinizing me from the clouds or the cracks in the temples, cursing me for bearing their blood and destroying their legacy.

When I was a child, I was certain the large statues were secretly alive and ready to crush me with their cold arms, and right now, with the Tournament magic racing through the court, I'm half convinced that actually might happen.

The Light Court is an eerie place and the scorching sun is not enough to warm my icy resentment.

The royal family has a place in every court. I've always hated the one in Light.

This is where Mother died.

This is where priestesses and witches attempted to save her life as she was dying, whispering and snarling as she cradled me to her chest. It is the only real memory I have of my mother–her warm skin going cold and the echoing sounds of her dying screams.

The next time I stepped into this court, years later, Father abandoned me and demanded the priestesses cleanse me of my troubled soul and reckless behavior.

Two years passed before I was able to leave.

I've not been back since. Not until today.

The howling wind ruffles my dress and I can almost hear the screams of the late Sun Queen. It's as if a part of her lingers in the court that last felt her living presence, the summer breeze blowing against my skin feeling like her invisible hands reaching for my face.

Something tightens in my chest. I glance at my sisters, wondering if they feel her too.

The Sun King leads the procession through the city of ruins, his gilded frame shining as bright as the sun above. Some of the priestesses peek out of their temples as we pass, their whispered prayers echoing off the wind.

May King Helios the first and holy bless our sacrifices and brighten our sun.

May the light of the sun shine through our souls and dispel every bit of darkness.

May the Gods of the Sky hear our grateful prayers and continue to bless us with their light.

Goosebumps prickle my skin and a shudder rocks through me. It may have been a long time since I stepped into this court, but not long enough for the memories of the priestesses' harsh words and cruel punishments to fade.

More and more people join the procession, their shouts and cheers resounding off the limestone walls. We wind our way through the city, the stone underneath our feet soon replaced by grass and rocks. In the distance, the vast ocean is basking in the evening sun, the water glittering like a thousand crystals.

A wave of salty air brushes my face, and my heart sinks as I realize where we're headed.

The long beaches in this court were once a familiar escape from the humid rooms of the Light Temple, the cool water a soothing touch against my heated skin. In the winter, the ice coating the surface was the only place I could see my eyes staring back at me, the snow-covered dunes a good hiding spot from the long-robed priestesses searching for me.

The Light Court may be the home of the brightest light, but I'm not eager to dive into its waters. I've seen various creatures slither along the seafloor, monstrous bird-like creatures hide in the caves of the cliffs, and felt slimy tentacles brush against my legs as I desperately fought my way back to the surface.

I can only imagine what monstrous beings are summoned for the Tournament.

We reach cliffs overlooking one of the lagoons along the shoreline and the crowd of people divides. Some of the warriors run down the cliffside toward the beach, others gather on the edge of the cliffs, and some follow the front of the procession that's headed for the Royal Dais tucked into an outcropping in the rocky cliffs.

The sun is slowly making her descent in the sky, the roaring waves of the ocean a trashing storm underneath.

There is no way to tell how much time is left before darkness washes the sunlight away from the sky. That is the way of the

Tournament. The time of the trial could be hours, minutes, or just seconds, the last one believed to be only a myth.

I'm about to climb the steps of the dais when a hand lands on the small of my back, a spark shooting through me at the contact.

Star leans forward when I turn around, his face so close I can count the stars sparkling in his eyes. "Breathe."

"What?"

"Breathe," he repeats, the corners of his lips tugging. "Breathe. Don't fight it. Remember that." He gives me a wink before sauntering off to join the other warriors gathered in the sand below the cliffs, his black leathers disappearing in the crowd.

"Asteria."

Father's warning tone drags me out of my stupor. He is standing at the front of the dais, his eyes flaring gold, the rage of discovering me emerging from the Moon King's carriage still evident in his features.

I quickly ascend the stairs and choose a place at the far end next to Davina, the king's gilded eyes trailing my every move.

There is a ledge in the cliffs above the dais that casts half of the dais in shadows perfect for the Moon King and his princes, the other half lit up by the sun. The ledge is the perfect spot to watch today's trial, and I look up just in time to see Elio step forward, his Victor's armor casting gilded shapes onto the floor of the dais.

It's hard to pay attention to his usual speech about honoring the gods and the sky when all I can think about is the last time I saw him and the way he whispered my name against my lips.

"Today, we are gathered in the Court of Light that will grant us the honor of the third Trial of the Sun. Let us all strive to impress the gods looking down on us today, and pray they approve of our usage of their gifts."

As always, the Victor's voice is magnified by magic, and if I didn't know better, I might've mistaken Elio's voice for one of the gods. The sound of it is carried by the wind and the earth, the sound reverberating through the crowd and all the way through the Kingdoms of the Sky.

"The third trial is this–"

A wide grin spreads on the Victor's face as he looks down at the crowd of cheering people. Once again, I see Elio as the sun–a golden presence looking down on everyone, unreachable and magnificent.

"There is a treasure in the ocean. Find a part of it and reveal it to the light before our beautiful sun goes to sleep with her last rays of light and the day is covered by the darkness of the moon."

The warriors standing on the cliffs scurry, shoving away the audience to find a clear path down to the ocean. The warriors on the beach below are restless. They impatiently stomp their feet in the sand and turn around to mark possible targets, various weapons gleaming in the setting sun.

"And remember–" Elio raises his hands above his head, "–as always, the rules are simple. There are no rules in the Tournament of Day and Night but one; survive. May the best Victor win." He claps his hands together, the sound as loud as thunder, and the warriors dive into the water from all angles.

The warriors thrash and struggle in the water, the white foam on the rolling waves quickly colored by their blood.

"This should be fun," the Moon King mutters, casting a glance in my direction to give me a little wink.

I can't wait for long.

I have to be in the water as soon as possible. There's probably not enough treasure for all the warriors and the gods know what kind of traps or beasts are guarding it.

I need all the time I can get.

I place my hand on Davina's arm, forcing a look of pain onto my face in case the king should glance our way. "I need to go. I'm pretty sure I just got this month's bleeding."

Fear flickers in her eyes when she meets my gaze, and for a second, I'm terrified she is going to deny me and break the lifelong deal between us.

"Hurry," she whispers, glancing at the king standing as an immovable statue at the front of the dais, his eyes locked on the ocean. "It would be a shame to ruin how good you look today, like a true princess of the sun." She squeezes my hand before ushering me away, her eyes returning to the king with determination.

My heart aches at her words.

A true princess of the sun. Not the cursed princess, not the princess who stole the life of the Sun Queen in this very court.

"Go now, Asteria!"

I jump down the side of the dais, hiding in the shadows of the Victor's ledge before starting on a narrow path in the cliffside that leads down to the ocean, my mind racing with too many thoughts.

I don't have time to run back to the carriages to search for my fighting leathers hidden among my belongings. The servants might have already moved them to the royal housings and I definitely don't have time to search through the many hallways of the eerie temple.

I curse myself for not thinking this through. I can't show up soaking wet after the trial, that is too hard to explain away.

Whatever it takes, Asteria.

With a heavy sigh, I drag the yellow dress over my head and stick it between some large rocks in the sand, praying to the gods it will be there when I get back. I leave my chemise on, grateful it ends in shorts and not a skirt.

I can't do anything about the golden paint on my skin. The paint is blended with a little bit of magic and has to be forcefully scrubbed off with various rounds of soap and water, one of many reasons I don't like to paint my skin. But without the dark fighting leathers to conceal myself, maybe the paint will help hide my identity.

A wave crashes against the shore, the water reaching my bare feet. The ocean is warmed by the sun, but still cold enough for chills to prickle my skin.

Thank the gods I didn't wait until next year's winter solstice to bind myself.

I take a few deep breaths, trying to calm my erratic nerves before diving underneath the waves.

The underwater currents drag me toward the cliffs where streams of small fish are swimming around vibrantly colored reefs, the water as clear as glass. My feet brush against sharp rocks and corals that scrape my skin, my head barely missing the stone of the cliffs.

I struggle back toward the surface, gasping for air when I emerge in the middle of the crashing waves.

The ocean is not going to make this trial easy.

My hands gripping the slick stone of the cliffs, I slowly swim forward, fighting the strong streams trying to drag me out to the deep, ignoring the alarming thoughts that something or someone is going to grab my feet and drag me down to the bottom any second.

The waves crash against the cliffs, hitting my head with a force that takes my breath away. My hair sticks to my face, and the salty water leaves a bitter taste in my mouth. But I keep moving forward, knowing the worst is yet to come.

Whatever it takes.

I duck beneath the waves when I near the cliff with the Royal Dais. I'm not taking any chances in front of the king's sharp gaze.

The world beneath the surface is so colorful and alive that it feels as if I'm in another realm. The sunlight from above casts everything in a magical light, the crashing waves only a distant sound.

Countless warriors are searching for the treasure below the sun. Some of them are wearing their usual fighting leathers, others have ripped pieces of the fabric to move more freely. I even spot a couple of warriors swimming completely naked with only a dagger in their hands.

My dagger–Elio's Victory Dagger–is tightly clasped in my hand, the only form of weapon to defend myself against the beasts around me.

It will be enough. It has to be.

My gilded hair flows around my head as I swim, the locks swirling in front of my eyes and blocking my view. Frustration builds inside me, and I'm tempted to just cut it all off with the Victory Dagger.

I place my feet on a reef high enough to allow me to stick my head above the water, the stone of the cliff banging against the top of my head. With the handle of the Victory Dagger between my teeth, I reach down and tear a strip of fabric from my chemise and tie my hair back.

Where I'm standing, the sea foam floating on the water is more red than white. At least a dozen warriors are lying face down in the water, the crashing waves dragging their unmoving bodies away from the shore. Around them, other warriors dive and emerge in between the waves, gasping for air either from the water or an opponent trying to drown them.

Today, the ocean is a battleground in more ways than one.

Only a small part of the sun is visible on the horizon beyond the vast ocean, the sky above tinted with pink and orange hues.

I have to find the treasure. Fast.

With a sharp intake of breath, I dive back below the waves. I make it a little more than halfway to the bottom before my lungs are straining for air and I'm forced to kick back to the surface. The water tastes bitter in my mouth as I gulp down the salty air, my eyes burning and heart racing.

I try again and again and again, only getting a little closer each time, the bottom still unreachable.

The seafloor beneath me is too deep, impossible to reach with my human lungs.

There has to be another way. The only rule of the Tournament is that you have to survive, and the gods demand a Victor. That means at least one of us is going to make it through this trial.

There is a treasure in the ocean. Find a part of it and reveal it to the light before our beautiful sun goes to sleep with her last rays of light and the day is covered by the darkness of the moon.

Maybe the treasure is not at the bottom of the ocean. Maybe it's floating somewhere in the waves, maybe it's hidden among the reefs close to the surface, maybe it's hidden in one of the caves in the cliffs only getting splashed by the ocean.

The trials of the Tournament are known for their trickery and almost impossible goals. A treasure could be anything, it doesn't necessarily need to be something fit for the royal treasury or a large chest hunted by pirates, but why wouldn't it be?

I suck in another deep breath and rub my eyes. The increasing wind mixed with the salty water is making it hard to see anything beyond the vast ocean in front of me. The magic of the Tournament is making me paranoid and it's getting harder to discern my own thoughts.

I need to start simple and assume the purpose of the game is exactly what Elio said. I need to look for a part of the treasure small enough to carry through the waves and light enough to hold above the surface.

One last deep breath and I dive underneath the next wave crashing against the cliff.

I search through rainbow-colored reefs, my fingers fumbling with rocks and shells, hoping I'll find a golden coin or pearly necklace.

A fish slithers along my skin and the feel of its scales startles me so much that I disturb a stream of silver fish floating between the corals. The fish scramble away, revealing a large hole in the middle of the reef.

The hole leads to a cave submerged in darkness. Something glimmers on the sandy bottom, the faint traces of the setting sun barely breaking through the dark water.

The cave doesn't seem to be as deep as the bottom I tried to reach earlier, but it's still deep enough that I fear I may succumb to the darkness.

Can it be a part of the scattered treasure?

I have to take the risk it will be.

I'm running out of time.

I brace my feet on the reef and stick my head above the water, filling my lungs with as much air as possible. And with a silent prayer to the gods, I slide my feet away from the reef, allowing my body to fall back into the water toward the sunless bottom of the cave.

My eyes are locked on the spot in the sand where I previously noticed something that could be a part of the mysterious treasure as I swim through the hole in the reef.

The rocks and corals scrape my skin, sending small sparks of pain through my body. Seaweed and underwater vines stick to my skin and wrap around my legs, the feel of their slick texture against my skin making every instinct in my body scream to turn around and swim toward the light above.

The sand on the bottom of the cave shifts from the

movements of the ocean. A small white pearl sparkles in the dim light seeping through the small cracks in the cave.

A victorious thrill shoots through me, overshadowing the increasing pressure in my lungs and head.

I reach for the pearl, my fingertips barely brushing against it. One more kick of my feet and flailing of my arms and my hand finally reaches the sand.

My fingers close around the pearl and the vines around my ankle tighten.

A whoosh of air erupts from my lips, a storm of bubbles dancing up to the surface.

The vines pull me backward and my head hits the wall of the cave with a thud.

More strands of green shoot from the walls, wrapping around the rest of my legs, my arms, my stomach, my chest, my throat.

I'm trapped.

I frantically thrash against the strands, the pearl in one hand, the Victory Dagger in the other.

I manage to free the hand with the dagger enough to start cutting the strands around my thighs, but as one loses the battle against the dagger, another appears somewhere else even tighter than the first.

The vines are like ropes. They dig into my skin, squeezing and caging me more aggressively than the labyrinth ever did.

The pressure in my chest is starting to become unbearable. My lungs are screaming for air, the panic filling my body making everything worse.

I'm trapped. I'm trapped. I'm trapped.

The darkness of the cave is as suffocating as the arms of the ocean that refuse to let me go no matter how much I fight.

A scream escapes my lips, the sound dulled by the roaring

ocean, another stream of bubbles floating to the surface that's suddenly too far above me.

There's no way to tell how much time I have left before the sun sets, but it doesn't matter.

My body is going to give out first.

Something glows on the opposite side of the cave and another scream erupts from my lips, the stream of bubbles vanishing as I struggle in the water.

A pair of yellow eyes are peeking at me from the shadows of the cave. The eyes are as large as my head and they glow with anticipation and satisfaction.

A shrill voice bores into my skull, pain exploding in my head from the sound of it.

A little golden princess visiting my cave. What a nice little surprise.

A trap.

The pearl was a trap, a scheme to lure me into the cage only to be trapped and served as a meal to whatever is lurking in the shadows.

Oh how good the little golden princess will taste.

I'll save your heart for last.

This is it. There is no way out.

As my vision starts to blur, I hear another voice, this one only a faint whisper in my mind.

Breathe. Breathe. Don't fight it. Remember that.

What a strange thing to say to someone before diving into the ocean.

What a strange thing to say to someone with human lungs who needs fresh air to breathe and survive.

If he thinks I'm so stupid I'm going to open my mouth and just–

Magic. The Tournament is made of magic that bends the rules of the world to the point of there being no rules at all.

Don't fight it.

Fighting the plants only makes it worse. I cut one away and another appears. I thrash and flail and their grip tightens. The more I fight, the stronger they get.

Now, with barely any strength left, the fight slowly slipping away, I notice the strands suddenly seem looser and I'm certain I would be able to gently pull away if only I had some air left.

The last time I used unwanted advice from so-called allies, it helped me survive. And it's not as if I have many other options at the moment, not if I don't want to give my life to the water or the beast, whoever comes to claim me first.

Whatever it takes, Asteria.

And so I open my mouth and welcome the ocean.

CHAPTER SIXTEEN

Water rushes into my mouth, the pressure in my lungs and head increasing so much it feels as if my whole body is going to explode, but then, a second later–magic.

Streams of gold and silver glittering bubbles dance in front of my eyes, the light of the magic dispelling the darkness of the cave. The magic surges through me in a violent rush, starting with my mouth and lungs before spreading in my entire body, the glittering bubbles gone as suddenly as they came.

The pressure in my chest and throat disappears. My lungs expand as if I'm breathing the freshest air in the world. My vision clears. The pain in my body is gone.

I no longer feel on the brink of death.

The ocean feels lighter, warmer, the water flowing into my lungs even better than the air above the surface.

It's as if I was meant to spend my life here among the bright and vibrant colors of the coral reefs, swimming with the sea creatures and only observing the sunlight from the deep.

The large yellow eyes study me with curiosity, the beast's voice no longer hammering against my skull.

The sea plants previously caging me are now caressing my body, the strands soft against my skin.

I push away from the wall.

They don't follow or move to trap me again.

As if I passed the test, the unknown beast blinks one last time before vanishing in the darkness. A long gilded tentacle slips into the light before it disappears, the only indication of what's hiding in the shadows.

I let out a relieved breath, and this time, there is no stream of bubbles.

I'm a part of the ocean now.

Moving into the center of the cave, I open my palm to the dim light shining through the water. The white pearl is shining with an inner glow–a faint silver gleam similar to the magic bubbles granting me the ability to stay underwater.

Magic. It has to be.

This is it.

The pearl is a part of the treasure and what I need to make it through the third trial of the Tournament.

I let out a cry of victory and feel my lips spread into a wide grin.

I did it.

At the bottom of a dark cave in the roaring battleground of the ocean, I feel invincible, unreachable, powerful.

Everything is unbelievable. That I'm suddenly able to breathe underwater, that I found the treasure, and that I've made it through another trial.

I kick out of the cave, my body threading through water so easily it's a wonder I wasn't born in the ocean.

The beings of the sea greet me as I swim past. Small fish and crabs emerge from their hiding places in the reefs to look at me. A stream of silvery fish floats underneath me, unbothered by my presence. A small shark brushes up against the bare skin on my arm, its mouth pressed into a line that looks a lot like a smile. A large turtle swims past my face, its deep blue eyes giving me a small wink.

For once, I feel as if I truly belong, the ocean welcoming me as one of its own.

I move away from the reefs along the cliffs and see another part of the ocean.

The water is not only calm and vibrant. It is an agitated, bloody battlefield filled with things that don't belong.

Strips of fabric and discarded leathers are floating around, daggers and swords are glinting in the faint sunlight, and warriors are frantically thrashing and fighting. Many are still searching for a part of the treasure–some of them diving up and down, others swimming around as easily as me, magic running through their veins. Many warriors have lost all the light in their eyes, their bodies limp as they drift by. And then there are the ones who have taken up an entirely different trial, replacing the search for a treasure with a search for revenge and bloodshed.

I pass a ledge on the seafloor, the deep below filled with various beasts.

A giant snake-like creature with green scales is coiled around half a dozen warriors, its mouth working to remove the warriors' heads.

Hundreds of dark blue fish flutter together, creating a pattern of a sword that chases a warrior with a handful of pearls in his hands.

A massive blood-red octopus is squirting black liquid on a group of warriors hacking at its head, their dying screams lost to the sounds of the countless battles.

In the middle of the chaos, I spot a warrior in cobalt blue

clothing crafted for swimming, a pearl gleaming between her fingers.

I study the chaos underneath me and something dark flashes in my peripheral vision, gone when I turn my head to look at it.

The magic wrapped around my soul is screaming, the invisible strings pulled so tight it feels like my muscles are going to snap any second.

My soul is screaming to join the fight, the urge so strong it drowns out everything else.

Kill.

Take.

Conquer.

Win.

Destroy the enemy kingdom. Let their blood stain the ocean and their bones rot in the sunless deep. Tear out their hearts and feed them to the churning sea.

I feel the ongoing battles in my soul and body, the sensation so strong I feel some of the warriors' wounds on my skin.

We're all a part of the ocean now.

I let the magic and currents draw me forward, the water caressing my skin, power vibrating in my blood.

Right now, slaying every warrior around me is the most important thing.

Nothing else matters.

I vaguely wonder if this was how my mother felt before she became a Victor and then later queen, if this is not only the magic of the Tournament, but a part of my very blood—an unyielding urge I have no choice but to fulfill.

Whatever it takes, Asteria.

I raise the Victory Dagger above my head, a smile playing on my lips. Excitement bubbles through me as my eyes land on the closest warrior struggling toward the surface.

Something is digging into the skin of my other hand, my fingers firmly closed into a fist.

I don't understand what it is.

I don't care.

It doesn't matter.

All that matters is the warrior in front of me and the urge for bloodshed coursing through me.

The warrior is getting closer, his back only inches from my blade–

My knee bangs against a rocky outcropping in the seafloor and the hilt of the Victory Dagger digs into my palm, the carvings scraping against my skin.

The small twinge of pain clears away some of the magic and suddenly, the ocean is not so warm anymore.

I blink in confusion, the Victory Dagger slipping from my hand. It sinks in front of my eyes, down my chest and stomach and I barely manage to catch it between my thighs before it's lost to the depths.

I'm about to reach for the dagger when I notice I'm holding something in my hand. I open my palm, revealing a single white pearl.

What–

Everything comes crashing back in violent waves. The trial. The cave. The vines trapping me against the wall. The pearl.

It's as if my mind has been submerged in murky water, the magic desperately trying to break back into my soul.

I forgot what I was fighting for.

A current hitting my face snaps my attention away from the pearl. The warrior I only moments ago was intent on killing is moving toward me, no longer struggling from the lack of air.

I tuck the pearl back in my palm and grab the dagger with my other hand.

The warrior's face is pulled into a sneer, his hands reaching for my throat. His fingers graze my skin and I shove the dagger into his thigh.

The warrior lets out a cry of pain and I yank the dagger out of his skin. I place my hand on his chest, allowing a fraction of the Tournament's magic to gift enough strength to give him a hard push.

The warrior floats away, his mouth agape, hands pressed over the bleeding wound on his thigh. He moves from the ledge and into the darkness of the depths, his blood oozing out into the water.

Something dark emerges from the darkness so fast it's impossible to see what it is and the warrior disappears, lost to whatever is living in the deep below.

I move away from the edge back toward the cliffs, my bare feet grazing rocks and sand, my eyes locked on the darkness in the distance.

I reach a reef in pink and orange shades, the colors reminding me of the sky during sunset, and once again, I'm drawn out of the murky water dulling my senses.

Only a faint trickle of light is visible where I'm floating and I crane my neck to look at the surface far above.

I don't want to give up the miracle of the Tournament—the water soothingly rushing against my skin, the exhilarating sensations of my body filled with magic, and the feeling of belonging. The sunless deep is surprisingly comfortable, but I can't risk losing the trial and my chance at proving myself to the kingdoms.

I can't forget what I'm fighting for.

Whatever it takes, Asteria.

I force my feet to push away from the reef, but the ocean doesn't want to let me go.

The current grows stronger the farther away I get from the bottom, the water thick and heavy around me.

My movements are no longer effortless and flowing, but clumsy and inadequate.

It is no longer easy to swim with my hands clenched, but I can't let go of the dagger or the pearl.

What will happen if I stay here until the trial ends? Will I be forced to live the rest of my days underneath the surface, my body slowly transforming into one of the mythical merfolk? Or will my magical abilities vanish with the sun, the ocean or the Shadow Realm claiming my soul?

Swarms of fish try to block my path, their rainbow scales obscuring my vision. Below me, vines are reaching for my legs, the strands grazing my toes.

And then there's the magic, its silent voices begging me to stay just a little longer, reminding me how great it feels to be a part of the ocean.

Streams of glittering bubbles caress the bare skin on my arms, and for a second, I'm tempted to just give in, but then a sliver of light breaks through the water and I'm reminded of the sky above.

A scream erupts from my lips, the sound echoing in the water as I struggle to reach the surface. It takes all my strength and will to keep moving forward, the ocean and magic straining to keep me in their grasp.

Another scream and I'm a little closer.

A strain of curses aimed at the gods and my ascension slows, the water a sluggish stream almost impossible to move through.

An unbearable pressure is building in my chest.

Invisible hands are back around my throat, the fingers squeezing and digging into my skin.

My eyes sting from the salty water, my vision blurring at the edges.

My limbs are heavy and there's barely any strength left in my body.

The magic gifting me life underwater is seeping out of me.

My body is starting to return to its natural state.

I'm running out of air.

I stretch my hands toward the light above, and I can't help thinking of the many statues in the City of Light, their stone arms always reaching for the sun.

If I don't make it out of the ocean, there will never be a statue in my honor. I will be nothing but a tale of caution, the cursed princess who perished in the games.

I continue to struggle toward the surface, feet kicking and arms flailing. I'm unable to keep my mouth shut any longer, my body fighting to find air. Water rushes into my mouth, the salty taste making me choke.

All I see is darkness, all I feel is the pain bursting through my body.

I'm dying–

Just when I think this is it, this is how I die, my head breaks through the surface and I'm gasping for air.

My head bangs against the stone of the cliff, the pain threatening to make me pass out. A wave crashes against the cliff, the force of it sending me back underneath the water.

Panic seizes my heart and I'm so afraid of being captured below the surface again that it takes me a few moments to remember the dagger in my hand. My fingers fumble with the hilt, my arms shaking so much it's difficult to do anything but allow the waves to slam my body against the rocks.

It takes a couple of tries, but I find a fissure in the cliff to embed the dagger. I desperately hang onto the hilt, chest heaving and body trembling. The muscles along my neck are screaming from the effort of keeping my head floating above the waves. My mind is slow, the thoughts churning just beyond my reach.

It feels as if I left something important in the sunless deep, as if the ocean has stolen a piece of my soul.

I lean my forehead against the rock to shield my face from the rolling waves, gulping down as much air as possible. When my heaving chest has slowed a little and my mind has gotten enough air to function again, I finally remember what I'm supposed to do.

The sun is creeping down on the horizon, barely visible among the agitated sea. With my fingers firmly curled around the hilt of the dagger, I extend the other hand to the sunlight.

The pearl lights up with a glow so strong I have to squint my eyes to keep looking at it. It's warm against my cold skin, its glow casting iridescent shadows in my palm.

Golden light erupts in the sky above. It flares across the sky, the streaks of light exploding in cascades of glitter that fall to the ocean, momentarily lighting up the darkness below.

The sight is so mesmerizing it takes me a moment to realize what is happening.

Did I just win this trial?

My heart beats a violent song against my chest and something stirs deep within me as the binding mark on my neck throbs, the pain confirming that I succeeded in another trial.

A victorious scream ending in a choked laugh bursts from my lips. I spit out salty water, the triumphant smile on my lips vanishing with the golden light in the sky.

I need to get back to the Royal Dais.

Staying close to the cliffs, I slowly swim back the way I came, moving the Victory Dagger along the rocks, the pearl between my teeth.

Without the magic flowing through me, my body quickly

tires. My arms are aching, my neck is throbbing, and the muscles along my back are screaming.

Angry waves threaten to drag me under, the salty water stinging my eyes. I try to not think about the beasts and warriors underneath me, praying something or someone won't drag me down to the sunless deep.

A large wave crashes over my head, and I nearly swallow the pearl from the pressure.

Just a little bit longer.

Just a little bit farther.

Whatever it takes.

I repeat the words in my mind, focusing on the chanting instead of the increasing pain and panic wringing my heart.

When I finally reach the shallow beach, I collapse on the sand with a thud, the waves crashing against my feet angrily roaring at my escape.

I spit out a mouthful of bitter water and the pearl rolls in the sand, threatening to disappear back into the ocean it came from. Crawling on my hands and knees, I catch the pearl before it can disappear with the waves, the feel of its warmth grounding me as I roll around on my back.

The world is spinning around me, the sky above a plethora of colors so serene and captivating it is a miracle that it is a part of this world.

The light sky so familiar to Soria is almost gone, leaving only a faint trace of pale blue and pink in its wake. A red so deep it's almost black has started to creep up on the sky, mingling with the yellow and orange dipping down into the horizon.

A couple of stars appear as I try to catch my breath, the faint outline of the moon right above me.

When my body has stilled enough for my head to spin a little less, I heave myself off the ground, stumbling to my feet. My body desperately needs rest but I can't linger a second longer.

I peel the wet fabric of my underclothes away from my body, shivering in the salty breeze, my teeth chattering so loudly I'm afraid Father can hear it back on the dais.

Each slap of the waves against the shore serves as a ticking clock, reminding me that I've already run out of time.

A loud rumble from the ocean reverberates through the sand and a shudder rocks through me.

The battle in the ocean is far from over and I need to get as far away as possible from the persisting magic trying to lure me back in.

I bury the soaked underclothes in the wet sand, the grains like silk slipping through my fingers. The discarded dress is thankfully still in the same place I left it, untouched by the water. Wringing salty water out of my hair, I hastily pull it on, hiding the pearl in between my breasts, the treasure now cold against my skin.

The golden paint on my skin is still as polished and gleaming as it was when I left the palace, the gold only smeared in a few places. Stripes of white are peeking through the gold in my hair and my fingers are stained with gold when I touch the binding mark on my neck.

It has to be good enough.

The sand swallows my feet as I waddle across the beach, the ocean screaming behind me.

I don't look back.

The ascend of the cliffside is slow, each step exhausting and painful.

On the top of the cliff, the Royal Dais is a towering figure. Hundreds of kinglights are floating in the air on the Sorian side, the king trying to suppress the darkening night with his power.

Dread fills me as I near the Royal Dais. The pearl feels leaden against my skin, and the dagger strapped to my thigh is now slightly visible through the thin fabric of my dress without the undergarments. I can't do anything about my wet hair but I try to hold it away from my dress as I walk, not wanting to leave wet splotches on the fabric.

This is just another trial.

This is just another game.

I climb up the side of the dais, the same way I left, straining as I try to pull myself up. A warm hand wraps around my wrist, effortlessly pulling me onto the raised platform.

Prince Star is grinning at me, mischief glimmering in his eyes. His hair is wet from the ocean, some of the dark strands sticking to his forehead, and drops of salty water are running down his face. His fighting leathers are soaked, the fabric clinging to his broad body.

"I don't need your help," I hiss, breaking free of his arm and smoothing out the wrinkles on my dress.

Star's grin widens. "Keep telling yourself that, starlight." He tilts his head to the side, his binding mark gleaming in the sun. "You seem to be alive and *breathing*, or do my eyes deceive me?" He gives me a wink before retreating into the crowd of royals.

Father is standing at the front of the dais with the Moon King, gesturing and pointing at places in the ocean, their immaculate suits illuminated by the floating kinglights.

Relief washes over Davina's features when she notices me. "Asteria–" She lets out a heavy sigh, her gaze raking over me, eyes narrowing when she notices my wet hair. "I can only do so much–"

"I know. I'm sorry. It was a disaster. Blood everywhere. I even had to rinse some out of my hair. I–"

Her gaze flickers to the side and she raises her voice. "You should know better by now. Maybe you should ask the servants to count the days of your cycle if you're unable to do so yourself." She mouths a silent *good luck* before turning around to join the rest of my sisters, her hands balled into fists at her side.

I curse the sun and drag my fingers through my tangled hair, some of the gilded dust staining my fingertips.

Maybe my participation in the Tournament will be the end of the union with my sisters. If this gets too dangerous for them—

"Asteria."

I freeze at the sound of his voice, my breath a shallow thing in my chest as I turn around to face him.

Both of the kings are right in front of me. The Moon King scratches his chin, a smirk playing on his lips and a hungry gleam in his eyes as if he can taste the potential trouble in the air. The Sun King, on the other hand, is fuming, his golden suit blinding in the light of his magic.

I can almost feel the Royal Sword slicing across my back. The old scars will open, leaving blood running down my back, and new lines will be added to the collection.

The Moon King speaks before Father can even open his mouth to scold me. "Asteria. You missed Star's grand entrance through the surface. He puts all the other warriors to shame. Even the sun warriors from the Royal Guard—"

"Yes," Father says through gritted teeth, his hand reaching out to move a long strand of damp hair from my shoulder. "You were certainly missed. I almost thought I saw some white hair beneath the surface at some point."

I swallow against the growing lump in my throat. "Sadly I'm not the only one with hair like snow in the kingdom."

"No, although that lack of color is a rare one," the Moon King croons, his smirk widening.

"I'm sad to say I missed a lot of the trial," I say, forcing a smile onto my lips, "but I didn't miss the magnificent sky of gold."

"Ah, yes." The Moon King clicks his tongue in disappointment, the sound sending a shiver down my back. "Soria may have won this one, but there are still many trials left where my kingdom will gift the sky with our colors."

He takes a step forward, the smirk widening into a grin that gives me the urge to grab my dagger and slice it off his face. "I am sure you and your sisters are going to enjoy having a Victor stay at the palace. And the other princes, of course. Who knows? Maybe we will have more alliances than we think."

"Asteria," Father says through gritted teeth, stepping in front of the enemy king. "Go join your husband-to-be. And the next time you have *an accident,* make sure to let the servants help you. We can not have a princess going around looking like—" he gestures to my body, a look of disgust on his face, "—like that."

I make a low curtsey, nails digging into the scars in my palms. "Your Majesties."

"Soria already has a Victor staying at the palace. And soon there will be another one," I mutter as I pass the Moon King, the words intended for his ears only.

I don't join Castor at the front of the dais. There is another prince I need to talk to.

At the back of the dais. hidden in the shadows of the cliff ledge, Star is leaning his bare forearms on the railing. His skin is marked with swirling lines and symbols, not silver but dark—the same shade of black as the mark on my arm hidden by my dress.

According to rumors, a Victor will gain a permanent victory mark somewhere on his body, the image supposedly representing something from the Victor's Tournament.

I've never heard of anyone winning more than once, and I have never seen a victory mark. The knowledge of what happens to a warrior after winning the Tournament is a well-kept secret I've been dying to figure out.

But if the markings on Star's skin are his victory marks—should they be as black as the darkest nights and not silver like the moonlight of his kingdom?

"Already here for more?" Star purrs, starry eyes briefly flickering to mine before returning to the ocean in the distance.

"How did you know?"

He gives me a tired look. "I know a lot of things, princess. You're going to have to be a little more specific."

"You know exactly what I'm talking about."

He opens his palm and reveals the pearl resting there. Where mine had a silver gleam, his is golden, as if our destined pearls got mixed up and landed with the wrong warrior.

The last of the sun disappears on the horizon, and a ruckus of sounds erupts around us. The crowd of people cheer and shout, the applause drowning out the devastated screams of others.

"Like I said, I know a lot of things," Star says, seemingly unbothered by the chaos around us.

The markings on the inside of his wrist are reflected by the moonlight above, but before I have the time to study the rest of his marks, Star pulls up the sleeves of his leathers, hiding a secret I'm dying to know.

A secret that might explain some of mine.

"As much as I would enjoy seeing that pearl where it currently is, I bet it would make an even better necklace." He nods to my chest and heat spreads through my body.

His gaze moves to the large amethyst resting on my finger and he snorts. "It would definitely be a better ring than that one. It pains me for you to think that's the best my kingdom has to offer." His midnight eyes move to my lips and the heat in my body intensifies. "I can promise you it's not."

"I don't care about your kingdom," I snarl, pressing my nails harder into the skin of my palms.

"You should." He moves away from the railing to lean close to my ear. "After all, it's going to be your new home. And save that anger for the Tournament. I might claim my debt sooner or later."

"I owe you nothing."

His hand shoots out to capture my wrist. "Yes, you do," he practically spits. "You would be dead if it weren't for me." His grip is like a shackle around my wrist–cold and unmovable.

"I didn't ask for your help. And I thought you didn't care whether I lived or died–"

"I told you, to claim my favor I need you to stay alive long enough for me to do so," he growls, his eyes nothing but pure darkness as he glares at me.

"It must be a very important favor for you to go to all this trouble in keeping me alive."

"Oh, it will be." Silver flares in his eyes, his grip tightening before he releases me so abruptly I wonder if I burned his skin.

"Not if I can stop it."

"You've stepped into the darkness. There is no way out now."

CHAPTER SEVENTEEN

"Which one of the handsome warriors gave this to you, my dear? Was it the one with the pretty blue eyes?" The woman in the jewelry vendor in Moria beams at the magnificent pearl as she holds it up to the sunlight, squinting one of her eyes to study it in the light.

"Yes, the warrior with the beautiful eyes of dawn," I gush, forcing a dreamy look onto my face, ignoring the image of another pair of blue eyes flickering in my mind.

"Lucky girl," the woman says, her smile widening as she starts pulling out various strings of thread, presenting me with options for the necklace. I choose a simple black string, wanting the pearl to be the center of attention.

"A good choice," she remarks and walks out of her stall toward me. "Here, I'll help you put it on."

Before I can protest, she places the string around my neck, her warm hands fumbling with the lock.

The necklace is an unfamiliar weight against my skin. The pearl rests in the same place I hid it underneath my dress after the trial, close to my heart. It sparkles in the sunlight even brighter than it did underwater, and it feels as if a part of the ocean is living inside it, as if the churning waves aren't ready to let go of the treasure.

A memory of my victory and proof that I can overcome whatever the gods throw at me.

"There. Beautiful. Don't let anyone tell you otherwise." The woman's hand lingers on my neck in what I would imagine to be a very motherly gesture and the smile on her face looks so genuine it makes my heart swell a little.

The woman doesn't know who she is touching.

My hair is concealed underneath a golden scarf that hides my eyes and parts of my face. I don't show my face up close to the public very often, and when they glare at me from a distance, my snow-white hair is my most distinguishable feature. Without it, no one bothers looking too closely.

Is this a tiny glimpse of how my life could've been if only I weren't known as the cursed princess? Is this how my life can be when I become the next Victor and Sun Queen?

"Thank you." Unshed tears prickle my eyes as I place a generous amount of golden coins in her hands.

The woman's eyes widen and before she can protest, I close her fingers around the gold. "Thank you."

I spend hours at the market, browsing through vendors filled with exquisite spices, lush fabrics, objects claiming to contain magic, and various weapons. I avoid the more crowded areas, mainly keeping to the dark and narrow alleys, half expecting Skye to jump out of the shadows every time I choose the latter.

She never does. And I'm not sure if I'm disappointed or not.

Moria is thriving underneath the sun, the royal city soaking up the sunlight. The familiar streets are decorated with colorful banners and flowers, music and laughter echo through the city, and magic sparkles in the air.

I can't help wondering if this is the last time I'll see the city like this.

It is only when the last of the sunlight is almost gone from the sky, that I reluctantly move back toward the palace, each step heavier than the last.

The guards stationed outside of the gilded gates are not happy to see me. When I got close enough to be spotted by the ones hidden in the forest, I moved the golden scarf from my hair to my neck, letting the fabric hide the aching binding mark reminding me the games are far from over. Now, the guards send me glowering looks as they open the gates to let me pass, enraged that I once again managed to leave the palace without permission, afraid that they'll be punished by the High General or even the king himself.

I can't resist blowing a few kisses just to infuriate them even further as I make my way to one of the palaces' smaller entrances hidden in the shadows.

"I can't deny I get a little envious when your taunting isn't directed at me."

A shiver runs down my back at the sound of the deep voice and I dig my nails into the scars of my palms to brace myself against the magic pulling me forward.

Star's arms are braced on each side of the open doorway, a smirk playing on his lips.

"What are you doing here?"

He broadens his stance to block me. "I live here now, remember?" His arrogant smirk gives me the urge to just tackle him to the ground and be done with it.

"How could I ever forget? The palace will probably soon reek from your infestations," I mutter, moving to the side to try and walk past him.

Star moves with me, his arms and legs stretched as far as

possible. He leans forward so close I can feel his breath on my face and his smirk widens. "Everything smells divine to me."

"Move. Or I will–"

His hand shoots forward, his fingers grasping the pearl dangling in front of my heart. "I thought you said you didn't need my help. You're not very convincing as you keep taking my advice." His fingers stroke the pearl, his eyes narrowing slightly.

"I have never needed your help and I never will," I snarl, yanking the pearl out of his hand.

Star shrugs, folding the sleeves of his loosely fitted white shirt that's so at odds with his usual dark clothing, revealing the dark marks I'm dying to study. "We'll see."

The smirk is back on his lips. He knows he is taunting me. He knows he has information I desperately need.

"Is there something I can help you with, Asteria?" He steps away from the door, eyebrows raised in question, eyes glimmering with mischief.

I shove past him, ignoring the magic urging me to turn back and the questions churning in my mind as angrily as the ocean during the last trial.

The marble hallways are cooled by the breeze blowing through the open doors and windows. But the palace that is usually calm and quiet, is different now.

The palace is awfully crowded these days, and it is a wonder the enormous space could ever feel so. There's always more activity and people in the palace during the Tournament Times, but never before have the enemies been in the middle of it.

The shadows that are not reached by the kinglights feel darker, as if some of Luna's darkness has seeped into the palace along with the unexpected guests. Not only are there numerous people planning the upcoming celebrations, generals seeking out the king's approval, and servants preparing for our travels to

Luna, but more guests have moved into the gilded palace–five more Princes of the Moon, in addition to Castor and Star.

As I move through the palace, a ruckus of sounds echoes from the guest wings and I vaguely wonder if the princes are redecorating the furniture.

I'm not the only one rattled by our new guests.

Servants with frightened expressions run through the palace with various items stacked in their hands–freshly washed linens in a dark fabric I've never before seen in the palace, clothes in Lunan colors, bath salts with unfamiliar scents, and steaming bowls of soup a dark red that reminds me of blood.

More guards than usual are patrolling the hallways, weapons gleaming at their sides as they escort unfamiliar faces through the palace.

Magic tugs at my soul and the sound of clashing swords draws my attention, my feet moving onto one of the balconies on the upper level of the palace.

In the shadows of the night, the princes are doing their usual training with parts of the Lunan Royal Guard. Their fighting is distinguishable from ours, the movements sharp and fast, occasionally broken up by long elegant sweeps.

Some of the princes have their father's dark hair and eyes, but the others look as different from each other as the two sides of the sky. What they have in common is their warrior appearance and relaxed but alert behavior, all handsome smiles and sparkling eyes to lure you into their traps.

My sisters frequently giggle and bat their eyelashes in response to the princes, twirling strands of gilded hair around their fingers and handing out dazzling smiles as if it were air.

If any of the princes are fooled by my sisters' innocent and flirty behavior, they're in for a big surprise.

Every instinct in my body is screaming to join the fight, the magic of the Tournament whispering into my soul.

Not yet.

In this part of the courtyard, there are no kinglights. There is only the darkness of the night and the sliver of moonlight breaking through the thick clouds obscuring the moon.

Something white flashes in my peripheral vision. Away from the other princes, a figure in a white shirt and black pants is in the middle of an ongoing battle.

He is not only fighting one opponent like an average person might do. No, Prince Star is fighting about a dozen guards.

At the same time.

Star's movements blend into the night. He uses the shadows of the night to hide his next move, his white shirt the only thing always visible. The marks on his body blink in and out of existence in the darkness, the blood-red of his binding mark and the black of the marks peeking through the fabric of his shirt a stark contrast to his pale skin. He dances between the guards, his steps never faltering.

The guards are nowhere near striking him down.

The magic coursing through me yanks me forward so hard I have to brace my hands on the railing.

Waves of violent magic yank and pull at every limb in my body.

My heart is beating so hard it hurts.

My soul is fighting to be free of the cage that is my body, shrieking and roaring to kill the enemies in my palace.

Never before have I seen anyone move like that.

The prince below me belongs in another world.

He looks like a god of the moon.

"He's good, isn't he?" The voice drags me out of the trance, startling me so much I nearly tumble over the railing.

A woman in a white servant's uniform is standing behind me, but unlike the rest of the servants running through the halls, her hands are empty, and a mischievous smile is spread across her face.

"You–"

Skye makes a ridiculous curtsey, some of the blue strands springing free from the bun tied at the back of her neck. "Your Highness."

"What are you doing here?" My fingers grasp the hilt of the Victory Dagger hidden underneath my shirt, my feet slipping into a fighting stance.

A snort escapes her and the last of the servant act disappears. "A girl has to earn her gold somehow, you know. Not everyone is a princess of the sun living in a beautiful palace–"

I hold up a hand to silence her and she gives me an impish grin at the very royal act. "You can't expect me to believe you've been working here the whole time."

She shrugs and tucks the loose strands of hair back into her bun. "Why not? I'm sure you don't know the names of every servant in the palace."

A small flame of guilt flickers in my chest. "I don't. There are so many people working here I would've lost count every time I tried to count them."

"Exactly."

I give her an indignant look. "But that doesn't mean I don't recognize someone who doesn't belong here."

The smile on her face disappears as she narrows her eyes. "And you do? Belong here, I mean. Truly belong here?"

I only cross my arms in answer, waiting for her to deliver whatever nonsense she has planned for today.

Skye rolls her eyes. "I just wanted to say hello. So, hello." The smirk is back on her face, widening at my glowering look. "Come on, this will be fun! You can show me all the secret paths and best cakes and–"

"No."

"Fine. You still don't trust me. I get it. But now that I'm here–" she gestures to the palace behind us, to the ornate ceiling and intricately painted walls, "–I will have more opportunities to prove myself to you."

"I know this palace a lot better than both of you. And I'm going to figure out what you're up to," I snarl, taking a step forward.

Skye makes another absurd curtsey and on any other day, I might've laughed. "I look forward to it, princess." She starts to retreat into the palace, her voice echoing off the marble tiles. "I love the new jewelry by the way. Maybe I'll have to do some shopping of my own."

As I tuck the pearl beneath the fabric of my shirt, I realize the courtyard has quieted.

The clouds obscuring the moon have vanished, leaving the courtyard illuminated by the moonlight. An ocean of glittering stars is twinkling in the sky, the light of the stars even brighter than the moonlight. The princes and guards are gone, only a lone figure left. The wind ruffles his hair, the fabric of his shirt fluttering to reveal dark marks covering the lower half of his stomach.

The prince of the moon lifts his hand in a wave and I would bet with the gods the wave is accompanied by one of his usual taunting smirks.

The palace is filled with enemies and I'm not safe anywhere.

IN THE WEEK following the third trial leading up to the fourth, I spend as much time as possible training.

My body is constantly sore, every muscle is aching, my skin is full of scratches, and my whole being is highly paranoid. I'm constantly tired, and my body is never able to fully recover from the long training sessions.

It's hard to sleep when my body startles at every sound and my eyes conjure shapes out of the shadows in my room. Every sound or movement may come from the enemies living in the palace. It doesn't matter where I go.

I'm not safe.

With my opponents so close, the magic of the Tournament never quiets. Invisible strings yank and pull in every direction as if I'm nothing but a puppet to be molded and moved. Unseeable weapons stab and slice my skin for seconds, minutes, or even hours at a time.

Elio never told me the binding mark would work like this. The Victor is nowhere to be found so I train alone, unable to learn any of the Tournament's secrets.

Star and Skye are gone too, but I'm always walking on my toes, waiting for either of them to emerge from the shadows.

Time ticks by on a swift wind, each passing day a reminder of the unknown dangers to come. The day of the fourth trial arrives quicker than I would've liked, starting with an unpleasant breakfast.

For the first time since moving into the palace, Star is present. He chose a seat across from me, in the middle of the gilded decorations, seemingly unbothered with being the only Lunan amid the royals of his enemy kingdom.

The prince is already wearing fighting leathers and the gods know how many concealed weapons. From his tense body and the way he grips his fork, it seems as if he expects the fourth trial to start any second and not during sunset in its chosen court. His gaze never moves from my face and I wonder if he is plotting the most efficient way to kill me.

I ignore his midnight eyes, trying to swallow the leaden piece of bread stuck in my mouth.

I deemed it wise to join the others for breakfast today, especially when I can't fulfill the king's orders. Being present for the start is one thing, but sooner rather than later I have to disappear and join the rest of the warriors. Each lost second might be the end of my participation in the Tournament of Day and Night, and if I cease to try—the Shadow Realm will gain a new soul.

"We're all wearing chiffon honey today," Delia whispers beside me, pointedly looking at my faded, ripped white shirt and leather pants streaked with dirt from my early morning training.

"And I suggest braiding your hair back. Maybe put some gold in. Tell the servants to make sure the short strands in front of your face are–"

"I got it," I mutter through gritted teeth. Father's stare bores into the side of my face and a shiver runs down my spine.

Delia narrows her eyes. "And don't forget your diadem. The golden one with glittering small suns. You know what that is right? Not quite a crown, but not quite a headband either–"

The sound of my chair scraping across the floor drowns out the rest of her words.

Delia, the youngest of the triplets and last in line before me, always strives to be better than me. It is not difficult with my bad reputation, but it always makes me want to strangle her.

"She's probably still on her monthly bleeding. I'll make sure someone from the medical wing tends to her before the trial tonight–"

Footsteps so light I would've missed them were it not for my highly alert senses trail me as I walk away. When I reach the hallway with my room, I spin around and pin my stalker to the wall with a dagger to his throat.

Star smirks and wraps his fingers around the blade. "Go on then, starlight. Afraid you're going to lose tonight? Again?"

I press the tip of the dagger hard enough to summon a drop of blood. His smirk widens, his fingers still wrapped around the blade. "Careful, prince. Or you might lose your favorite body part just in time for the fourth trial."

He leans forward and more drops of crimson trickle from his skin, the blood running down the blade to stain my fingertips. "I would love to see you try. And I'm sure my favorite body part would very much enjoy that too."

The dagger clatters to the floor, a splash of blood drowning the carvings on the marble tiles.

Star snorts and bends down to pick up the dagger. "If you're going to survive the games, you can't let anyone rattle you like that." He holds the hilt of the dagger toward me, his blood still coating the blade.

"Keep it. You need every advantage you can get. This time I'm not letting you win," I snarl, relieved the Victory Dagger is safely tucked away in my room.

As I turn to leave, the prince throws the dagger. The blade flies through the air and bores into the wall only inches from my head.

"I don't steal from pretty girls like you, starlight. But–"

A warm hand lands on my hip, drawing my back against his chest. His other hand grips the dagger and pulls it out of the wall before slipping it into the pocket of my pants.

Star sweeps away the hair on my neck, his breath tickling my skin as he leans forward to whisper in my ear. "I'm going to give you another piece of advice. The fourth trial–"

"I told you I don't need your help!"

He lets out a low chuckle as he moves away just in time to not injure his *favorite body part*. "That's bold coming from someone who thinks the moon is the sun's shadow. And I said I don't believe you. It's different this time–"

I hurtle the dagger over my back, a small part of me disappointed when I hear it clatter to the floor.

Before he can say anything else, I open the door to my room and slam it shut behind me. Leaning my forehead against the heavy door, I take a few deep breaths to calm the raging storm inside me.

In. Out. In. Out.

I don't know how much time passes before a hand lands on my back, startling me so much that I scramble away from the door and fall to the floor.

"How on the brightest sun did you get in here?"

Star is standing above me, arms crossed and eyes narrowed. "You're not the only one familiar with the shadows, princess."

"Get out of my room before I take you up on the offer involving that body part," I spit, moving to get off the floor.

He squats down, a hand landing on my chest to keep me on the ground. "Are you always this stubborn? Did I not help you survive the labyrinth? And from drowning in the ocean and–"

"Get away from me." I dig my nails into the exposed skin on his wrist, bracing the soles of my feet on the floor.

"No."

The magic simmering inside of me roars. Waves of it crash through my blood, sparks shoot through my heart, and flames ignite in my bones.

It would be so easy to just give in.

With a little bit of luck, I could take him. And luck seems to be on my side lately. And with the magic rocking through me like the fiercest storms—

"Let's end this once and for all. Right now."

A low growl reverberates from his chest as he removes the hand from my chest. "Believe me, I'm very tempted at the moment. Killing you would be easy. It's keeping you alive that seems to cause all my troubles."

"Why do you even care?" My gaze rakes over his towering body, trying to decide where to strike first.

"You and I have a bargain to fulfill."

I struggle back onto my feet, deciding to go for his favorite body part.

"If you could only listen for a second—Asteria?"

My eyes are suddenly not working right. It's as if I'm trying to see through murky water, the prince in front of me a flickering image.

A prickling sensation starts at the side of my neck and darkness seeps in at the edges of my vision.

"Sky above—" Stars grabs my elbow, steadying me against the swaying motions overtaking my body.

It's as if all the strength in my body is seeping out and my bones are getting too heavy to stay in my skin. The magic that was only seconds ago urging me to fight is now a heavy anchor making it impossible to do anything but try and keep steady in the storm.

"What did you do to me?"

His reply is lost to the roaring in my ears, his face obscured by my blurry vision.

Something blue flashes in the distance. "Did you do it?" The voice is far away, the only tangible sensation Star's warm hands pressed against my skin.

"No." Another voice, more familiar. "I told you she wouldn't listen to me. She's the most stubborn woman—"

"I specifically asked you not to threaten her—"

"Don't you dare question me."

A snort mixed with a frustrated sigh. "Don't go all royal on me. Not now. Did you at least—"

"Our marks will activate any second—"

The rest of their words blur together in a mass of murmured sounds I can't decipher. The mark on my arm and neck ache in rhythm with my rapid heartbeats, my chest constricting with shallow breaths.

The warm contact at my elbow spreads to my back, as if a warm blanket is embracing me and holding me together.

Something safe. That's what it feels like.

The thought is so ridiculous a strained chuckle escapes me, only causing my throat to tighten and my eyes to water.

The hair sticking to my clammy forehead is swept away by gentle fingers. They linger on my bare skin, tracing idle lines down the sides of my face.

"Asteria?" The voice is barely a whisper in the thunderous tempest.

The dark sky with silver stars flickers in front of my eyes, the sight so beautiful I let out a content sigh.

My eyes flutter shut to welcome the darkness, and I wonder if this time it will truly be my last glimpse of this world.

CHAPTER EIGHTEEN

There's something strange about the sky.

Something is blocking my view of the sunset. A pattern of rope tied together in an intricate system, reminding me of the netted traps used to catch fish and crustaceans where the ensnared quarry is forced to wait for their death.

My head and body are throbbing and aching as if I just woke up from a century-long slumber. All my senses are groggy, and there is a heaviness in my body unlike anything I've ever felt.

A warm breeze ruffles my hair, dragging my attention to the side. The netlike strings of ropes and threads are blocking my sides too. Beyond the ropes, rocky ground juts out from all sides as if I'm floating in the middle of a mountain.

The breeze blows against my fingers and I notice one of my arms is hanging through one of the holes.

I slowly turn around on my stomach, each small movement sending sparks of pain shooting through my body. And then fear slams into me in a violent bang.

I am trapped in a cage.

Below me, there is nothing but darkness. It's as if a gaping black hole has swallowed parts of the earth and carved a path to the Shadow Realm.

A loud growl reverberates from the darkness, the sound so loud it rattles the cage.

"About time you woke up, princess," a familiar voice shouts beside me.

Hundreds of cages are dangling from a cliffside that goes around in a circle so vast I can barely glimpse the cages on the far side. Skye is sitting in the cage closest to me, her feet dangling through holes in the bottom.

A snort sounds on my other side and I turn my head, the muscles along my neck screaming.

Star is standing in his cage, his elbows casually leaning on the net, his hands folded on the other side of the cage. The posture reminds me of how he leaned across the railing of the Royal Dais after the last trial.

"What did you do to me?" My voice comes out as a rasp. My mouth is desperately in need of a bucket of cold water. It feels as if I haven't spoken in years.

"No, this is all you, princess," Star croons with a smirk. "Or we kind of did it together." He tilts his head to the side, his Tournament mark glistening in the setting sun.

"What?"

"It's probably worse for you since it's your first time. But don't worry, it'll wear off eventually. Unfair yes, but the Tournament has no rules," Skye says in a singsong voice on the other side.

The hammering in my skull intensifies, the pain in my head so overwhelming it gives me the urge to claw my eyes out. "The Tournament? No that can't be–" I snap my mouth shut as I notice the roaring crowd in the far distance, barely visible on the furthest cliffs.

The Royal Dais is so far away I have to strain my eyes to see it. Elio's victory armor gleams in the sunlight, his victory mark shining the brightest.

"Why?" I ask, glaring at Star, the action probably not as intimidating as I would like it to be from my sprawled position in the cage.

The prince rolls his eyes. "The thrill of the Tournament is that you never know what comes next," he says, mimicking the ceremonial speeches of the Victors.

"I tried to warn you but you were too busy thinking about my favorite body part." The usual arrogant smirk doesn't quite reach his eyes and if I didn't know better I might've mistaken it for worry.

"You better snap out of it, starlight. You're lucky you weren't in the bath when the mark activated. No matter how much I would've loved to see you naked–" he trails off with a wink before his eyes scan the arena around us.

The mark.

I press my hand to the aching mark on my neck. The skin underneath my palm is tender and sore, and it feels as if I've been beaten repeatedly with something heavy.

"You're saying you didn't drug me so I wouldn't have any time to prepare—"

"Yes," he says, pulling out the word slowly, as if I'm a child that needs clear instructions.

A string of muttered curses escapes my lips.

Skye snorts behind me. "Exactly what I was thinking, but please avoid cursing the gods in the middle of one of their games."

I open my mouth to say something more, but the sound of Elio's magnified voice makes me snap my mouth shut.

"The fourth trial is this. Escape from your cage and climb to the top of the cliff before our beautiful sun goes to sleep with her last rays of light and the day is covered by the darkness of the moon. Or before the beast gets to you."

Another growl reverberates from the darkness, the sound closer this time.

"As always, there are no rules in the Tournament of Day and Night but one; survive. May the best Victor win."

Elio claps his hands together in a thunderous boom that rattles my cage. And then, the second the sound of his clap stops, something emerges from the darkness below.

Something gigantic and dark shoots out of the black hole so fast I'm unable to see what it is. It swallows one of the cages in the distance, the rope holding it breaking with a loud snap, the warrior's dying screams cut off by the darkness. But the screams from the warriors nearby–desperate, panicked, terrified, as if they'd rather spend eternity climbing the rope instead of encountering the beast deep below.

My head is so groggy and my body so full of pain it's impossible to move from my position on the bottom of the cage. When I finally manage to lift my head, I notice Skye is already halfway out of her cage. She jabs the net with something that looks a lot like a fishing knife, her movements fast and efficient, her lips pursed in concentration.

As if the warrior can feel my stare, she looks up from the net. She meets my gaze and worry flickers across her features. "Roll to the side," she shouts and continues slicing the strings keeping her trapped.

"What?"

"Roll to the side and then back again," Star shouts from my other side.

I turn my head toward his voice, wincing at the pain in my muscles.

The prince is already out of his cage. His feet are planted on the top of the cage and his hands are folded around the rope, ready to climb to freedom.

A rope snaps in the distance.

A shrill scream pierces my skull.

Another rope snaps. Then another. And another–

"If you can't get out with the dagger in your pocket, roll to the side so the cage starts moving! We'll catch you and help you out!" Skye's shouts nearly drown in the storm of sounds around us.

I grit my teeth as I continue struggling. My muscles are unable to hold me. My limbs are too heavy to lift.

It's as if my body has stopped working.

The black hole below is widening, as if each sacrifice is fueling the darkness.

"What other choice do you have, starlight? It's either trusting us this once or waiting for the beast to come for you."

"Asteria, please," Skye pleads, the earnesty in her voice sending a jolt of fear through me.

A rope snaps so close I can feel the breeze from the beast as it devours the cage.

"Asteria, please–"

"Now would be a good time to move, princess–"

I can't move. I'm frozen to the bottom of the cage. My body refuses to obey my commands.

Screams echo in the distance only to be silenced by the hungry beast below.

One. Two. Three.

Each snap of rope sends a wave of panic through my heart.

I'm going to die here.

"Asteria," Star snaps. The sound of my name on his lips startles me so much that for a second, it's all I can hear. He is still standing atop his cage, his gaze locked on me. A storm of emotions flares across his features–frustration, anger, confusion, and something that looks a lot like fear.

What an important bargain it must be for him to fear for my life.

"You need to move. Now."

"I can't," I say through gritted teeth.

I'm barely able to move my head to look at him. There is no way I'm going to be able to escape the cage and climb up the rope.

"You have to!"

"I can't!"

He lets out a frustrated sound, his eyes frantically looking around as he drags a hand through his hair. His frantic state is so unlike his usual calm and confident demeanor that panic seizes my heart with an icy fist, squeezing so hard it's hard to breathe. "Fuck!"

"Do something!" Skye shouts.

I'm too tired to even try to look at her.

The darkness growls and screams. It has extended up the walls of the cliffs, the reverberating sounds so loud it feels as if my head is going to explode any second.

Snap.

Snap.

Snap.

"Asteria!" Star's voice is stronger now. Silver flashes in his eyes. A muscle ticks in his throat. "I order you to move."

I let out a strangled sound, but he speaks again before I have the time to curse him. This time, it feels as if he is speaking into my very soul.

"By our bargain sealed by the gods and their magic, I invoke my favor and order you to move! NOW!"

Magic rushes through me in violent waves, the force so strong it takes my breath away.

The power melts some of the ice in my veins, lifting parts of the weight in my limbs. Fresh air fills my lungs. The pain lessens.

Instincts I can't deny urge me to move forward, drawing on strength I didn't know I had.

The magic of the bargain is impossible to resist.

I roll over and the cage sways with the movement.

"Good. And now the other side." The pure command in Star's voice speaks to a primal part of me.

I couldn't deny him even if I wanted to.

My body listens to his orders as if it's more important than breathing or keeping my heart beating. Every cell in my body screams in pain, but still, I move.

I roll to the other side, the momentum of the swaying cage increasing slightly.

"Again."

The rope digs into the skin on my back, the thin fabric of my shirt doing nothing to subdue the cutting strings. The wind is howling in my ears and blowing my hair in front of my face.

Snap.

"Again."

Snap.

"Again."

Snap.

Snap.

Snap.

"Again–"

The frequency of screams and falling cages increases with rapid speed, each snap of rope sending a jolt of fear through me. The darkness below is reaching for me, the beast feeding the warriors to the unfathomable dark hole.

I don't want to figure out what kind of creature is big enough to swallow the cages and warriors within.

"Asteria. Focus."

Star's voice tethers me to the present moment. It channels strength into every part of my being, allowing me to quicken the rolling motions of my body.

I focus on the sound of his voice and try to ignore the growing dizziness.

Blurred images flicker by. The cascade of colors on the setting sky. The vast darkness below. Cages plummeting into the black hole. Warriors struggling to climb the ropes. And the prince leaning forward on top of his cage, his arms extended.

"Almost there!" Skye's hands reach for my cage, and two rolls later, her fingers close around the net. With a grunt, she gives my cage a hard shove.

The cage flies through the air with a rush. My body is thrown sideways with a painful thud, the netted rope digging into my skin.

Star grabs the cage and hooks his arms through the net. "Hold onto the floor," he says through gritted teeth before he starts sawing through the ropes with one hand, the other gripping the cage with white knuckles.

Snap.

Snap.

Snap.

I focus on the sound of Star's dagger slicing through the net, holding onto the floor of the tilted cage with all my strength. Around me, more and more warriors fall to their deaths, some taken by the beast, others unable to climb.

Only a few seconds pass before Star stops cutting and tucks the dagger underneath the leather covering his chest.

There's now an opening in the net big enough for me to fit through—a way to possible freedom. But the magic of the bargain is slipping out of my soul, and I feel my body start to freeze again.

I can't do this.

"Grab my arm."

Snap.

The falling cage is so close that the growl that follows rattles my heart.

I'm going to die–

"Grab my arm!" Star's hand hovers in the air, his fingers twitching in my direction.

"There's no way you're going to be able to hold me," I rasp, fingers tightening around the net.

"This is not the moment to underestimate me," he snarls, impatiently waving his hand.

"It's not going to work–"

"Now, Asteria, before we both become dinner. I know you don't want that for my favorite body part."

With the explosion of colors of the sunset behind him, the prince once again looks like a god of the moon. His black hair gleams in the light, the silver in his eyes sparkling like the brightest stars I've ever seen.

"You can spend as much time as you want admiring me when we get out of here," he hisses, extending his hand even more as if he's debating just grabbing me himself.

"Let's go!" Skye screams behind us, and I turn my head to see the warrior already halfway to the top of the cliff, her body dangling from the thin rope holding her cage.

"Asteria. Take my hand. Now."

"No–"

A growl louder than ever before shakes the cage so much I can't help screaming.

Five cages fall at once.

Something dark flashes on the side of my cage.

"Asteria."

Snap.

"Look at me."

The last magic of our bargain grips my soul with a force so strong that it feels as if my heart is no longer mine, but a part of both of us.

"You need to trust me," Star almost screams, his voice drowning out the chaos around us.

"I no longer owe you a favor. You don't need me alive anymore–"

Our bargain is done. He used it to save my life.

Whatever it takes, Asteria.

His eyes bore into me, the magic of the bargain giving my heart a last squeeze.

Whatever it takes, Asteria!

Please don't let this be a mistake.

I reach for his hand, a spark shooting through me when our fingers meet. He clasps my hand for a moment before his fingers move to my wrist. I follow his movements, my nails digging into the leathery fabric covering his arm.

"Let go of the cage on three."

I can't breathe.

"One."

A scream is swallowed by the darkness.

"Two."

The beast's growls rattle the earth.

"Three–"

My fingers slide from the net.

Star releases his hold on my cage.

I slip through the opening in the net and the cage swings away with great force.

I'm suspended in the air, my feet dangling in the roaring wind. If I fall, there won't be a temple roof to catch me. There won't be any magic restoring me to life.

The only thing keeping me from plummeting into the darkness is the prince of the enemy kingdom.

The prince's gaze is still locked with mine. Behind him, the sky is lit up by golden light. The magic crackles across the sky with thousands of glittering sparks as bright as the sun, the sound of the magic louder than the chaos of the Tournament's trial.

Another victory for Soria.

An emotion I can't place flickers across his features and I strengthen my hold on his hand.

If I fall, he goes down with me.

But then, as the golden light disappears, the unfathomable emotion is gone, replaced with a look of sheer determination.

Star hauls me to the top of his cage so effortlessly I'm half convinced he actually is a god in disguise. I fall onto his chest, my fingers clinging to the leather covering his heart.

A swoosh sounds behind me and I wish I didn't turn my head to look at my cage swinging back toward us.

Something dark shoots out of the black hole and a massive jaw closes around the broken cage.

Snap.

Teeth so large they could easily devour the Sun Palace break the cage into tiny pieces. A river of gray saliva sizzles the rope into dust, a shrill scream exploding from the beast's mouth as it realizes the cage is empty.

The beast is a snake–like creature so enormous it shouldn't be possible. It is an extension of the darkness it inhabits, crafted from all evil in the world. Its gigantic shape twitches between something solid and misty, and where there should've been eyes, there are only hollow sockets with swirling shadows.

The beast's head dives back into the vast hole, its tail dragging half a dozen cages down with it. The world shakes and the beast disappears in the darkness.

My body is trembling so badly I'm afraid I'll tumble after the beast. Anxiety rushes through me in violent waves, my heart beating too heavy for my chest.

The beast's growls of fury will haunt my nightmares for the rest of my life and the sight of its mouth will be burned into my mind every time I close my eyes–

A warm hand forces my gaze away from the darkness, bringing my face back to the chest of the enemy and my biggest opponent.

Star's arms embrace me in a tight hug, crushing my cheek to his heart which is beating just as rapidly as mine. "Can you climb?"

"What?"

"Can you move?" His voice is urgent in my ear, his breath cold against my flushed skin.

I try to stretch my heavy limbs and pain erupts in my body. "Just a little," I say, voice barely a whisper.

There is no way I'll be able to climb a rope.

Star is quiet for a few seconds and I almost feel the sunlight slipping from my fingers.

The time of the trial is coming to an end.

Star's arms release me from their tight embrace and he pulls me away from his chest, his fingers moving to my arms. "Put your arms around my neck," he says, bending down so I can reach him.

My hands fall onto his shoulders. "What–"

He grabs my waist and twists his body so I'm hauled onto his back. His hands wrap my legs around him, his fingers moving my hands so I'm embracing his shoulders and collarbone.

"Hang on." Star grabs the rope with his hands, readying

himself for the steep and difficult climb. "I don't want to dive into the darkness to get you," he mutters, rolling his shoulders.

I tighten my grip.

If this is my only chance out of here, I'm going to take it, no matter how humiliating it is to depend on my enemy.

Whatever it takes, Asteria.

"And don't look down."

Pressing my forehead to the back of his neck, I close my eyes.

He starts climbing.

I try not to think about the frail rope that wasn't made to hold two warriors at the same time, the beast that could catch us any second, that Father could see me from the dais, or any of the other chaotic thoughts racing through my mind.

"I must admit it's nice to have you follow my orders without objecting for once."

"Shut up and climb, moon boy."

"You good back there?"

"Mhm."

"Maybe you should move to the front so you're closer to my favorite body part."

"Do you want me to feed you to the beast? Because that is what will happen if you don't stop saying those words."

The muscles on his back move as he climbs, and I feel his heartbeat against my skin.

We move through the trial together, heart to heart, with no bargain between us.

I don't want to think about what this might mean.

"I'm only trying to keep you awake, starlight," Star says with a chuckle.

"Why do you keep calling me that?"

He chuckles again. "You–"

A ferocious roar erupts from the darkness below.

The cage rattles.

The rope sways.

Star tenses underneath my hands and I tighten my hold even harder.

"Take the dagger from my chest and throw it down." His voice comes out in a rush, the howling wind trying to tear it away.

"What–"

"Just do it. NOW!"

He increases his tempo, moving us faster and faster to the top of the cliffs. My fingers reach the bare skin on his chest, gliding along chiseled muscles and deep scars.

"Hurry, Asteria!"

My fingers fold around the hilt of the dagger, my arm shaking so badly it's a wonder I can move at all.

Another growl resounds, closer this time.

Almost there.

The tip of the dagger stabs a small hole in the leathery fabric, halting my movements. It's stuck.

"Asteria–"

I grind my teeth together, flames of pain licking across my skin.

The cage rattles again and the swaying of the rope increases. Star curses and stops climbing, his body curling around the rope. His hands are red, his knuckles white. His sweat trickles down my hands, making it harder to hold on to the dagger.

Just a little longer–

I finally manage to free the dagger from his leathers and with the last of my strength, I hurtle it down into the darkness.

Star lets out a strangled sound. "You couldn't throw it the other way? You nearly took out my favorite body part for good."

The next growl transforms into a shrilling scream, but the sound is more distant.

Star continues climbing.

We've stolen a little bit more time.

But the sky above is not waiting. The pink and orange are replaced by a darkening blue, only faint traces of sunlight visible behind the dais in the far distance.

"We don't have a lot of time—"

"I'm perfectly aware of that, princess," Star says through gritted teeth. It's a miracle that he is still able to go at this pace, especially with me on his back.

How much longer can he hold on?

When the top of the cliff is only a few moves away, the cage below rattles with a violent force and I can't stop myself from looking down.

The cage has already disappeared into the beast's mouth. The snake-like creature extends upward, the gray saliva disintegrating the rope. A foul stench hits my nostrils as the beast closes in, the swirling shadows in its eyes reaching up—

Star jumps off the rope just in time. I tumble off his back, my side hitting the rocky ground with a painful thud. He drags me away from the edge, my head cradled against his chest.

At the edge of the cliffs, a large chunk of the mountain crumbles, and the last of the rope slips away. An enraged growl reverberates from the deep, the mountain shaking from the force of it.

Invisible daggers stab the binding mark on my neck, the blades twisting and turning in my skin.

Star's fingers against my cheek are the last thing I feel before everything fades to black. "Until next time, starlight."

CHAPTER NINETEEN

A warm breeze carrying an earthy smell wakes me. My eyes flutter and I shield my face against the blinding sun. The sky is nothing but a cloudless blue, the sun shining down on the fields of yellow and brown around me.

I'm lying in the middle of a sunflower field, deep in the Court of Helianthus.

With a groan, I roll around on my stomach before slowly heaving myself to my feet. My hands and shirt are stained yellow from the Helianthus flowers, the fabric clinging to my sweaty skin.

I press my palm against the aching binding mark on my neck. The skin is still tender and sparks of pain shoot through my body when I touch it.

A bee sizzles past my ear before disappearing behind a sunflower, drawing my attention to the vast fields around me.

At least a dozen other warriors are scattered in the fields, some still deeply asleep, others already on their feet. I search for familiar faces, and I don't know whether to be relieved or disappointed Skye and Star are not among them.

I have no idea where the beast's black hole is located so I can only assume the rest of the warriors are waking up all over the court.

The sunflowers around me barely reach my knees and I know I'm closer to Moria than the ocean or the border beyond the Helianthus Court. The fields closer to the borders and the mountains can have flowers as tall as the royal palace, the faces of the flowers always reaching for the sun.

Something rustles behind me and a pair of warriors emerges from the hill. A woman with a long blonde braid hanging down to her waist and a man with black hair tied at his neck, both wearing brown fighting leathers.

There's something vaguely familiar about them and I rack my brain trying to figure out if they're someone from the first game determined to claim the life of the cursed princess for a generous prize, but my mind and body are still affected by the magic and it's hard to remember anything at all.

I slip into a fighting stance, cursing the gods for my lack of weapons and disguise. I have no weapons but my skin and bones, and my body is in no condition to take on two opponents at the same time.

The warriors stop a few paces away without reaching for their weapons.

The woman gives me a bored look. "Pay up, little brother. I told you the princess was still competing."

The man mutters a low curse before reaching into his pocket. He retrieves three shining golden coins and slaps them into the woman's open hand. "You might've won this bet, little sister, but I've still got you beat by a couple hundred."

The woman snorts before tucking the coins into a pocket on her chest. "I'm not in the mood to bring up that discussion again." She tilts her head to the side, her gaze trailing from my head to my feet and back up again. "You sure have an interesting life, princess."

"I assume there's not even a slight chance you'll wait until the next trial to try and kill me," I snarl, trying to will some strength back into my beaten body.

"Killing is not the honorable part of the Tournament. We have no issue with you, and you shouldn't have any with us. Let's just leave it at that," the man says, his pale green eyes giving me a dismissive look.

A humorless laugh escapes me. "So you're hoping to win the king's favor by spilling my secret–"

The woman takes a step forward, eyes identical to the warrior beside her narrowing. "We have no interest in your royal affairs. You're not as important as you wish to be," she practically spits before sauntering past me.

"Until next time, princess." The man gives me a mock bow before following his sister.

They may claim to have no cruel intentions, but every limb in their body is on high alert.

I keep my eyes locked on their backs.

They don't interact with anyone else, only each other, their steps and movements perfectly aligned as if it's a practiced dance. I don't move until I can barely glimpse their forms among the vibrant colors, the brown fighting leathers blending in with the fields.

I debate following them for only a second before I turn around and walk in the opposite direction of the royal court.

My fingers brush against the yellow petals, their earthy aroma filling my senses. It has been years since I was able to walk through these fields.

Helianthus has a special place in my heart.

I've always thought the warmth of the sunflowers lingers in

Elio's soul. It's as if some of the vibrant colors swirl between the hazel of his eyes, serving as a constant reminder of his heritage. Elio's father is the High Lord of the Helianthus Court, living in the center of the court in a large mansion challenging the royal housing next to it. Elio's mother, Vera, left the city for a quiet life spent in solitary.

It has been years since I was able to visit Vera in her small cottage by the stream amid the Helianthus mountains. Despite the passing of time, it's easy to find the path, my fingers continuing to brush the leaves of the bright flowers just as I did as a child.

The ragged cottage is located at the bottom of a hill in the middle of a forest, hidden between tall sunflowers reaching for the sky. The yellow flowers grow glued to the wooden walls, some of them reaching beyond the grass-lined roof. A pair of goats are grazing peacefully in front of the cottage, a herd of chickens screeching around them.

The forest around the cottage is filled with traps to alert Vera of any unwelcome guests and a smile pulls at my lips whenever I notice a new one. Elio has spent long periods away from the Sun Court after he became a Victor, and now I finally know where he has been hiding.

The large black dog that always eagerly greeted me as a child slumbers on the porch in front of the small house, only lazily blinking its eyes in greeting. I give him a quick pet before raising my hand to knock at the worn door.

A faint creak sounds behind me. Something sharp pokes my back.

"My home is not part of the Tournament," a familiar voice snarls, the pressure of the sharpened tip increasing.

"I'm not here for the Tournament."

A shuffling sound and the weapon disappears. "Turn around, slowly."

Vera is standing behind me, a garden knife in her hands. Her hands are streaked with dirt, her overalls covered in green splotches.

She looks about the same as the last time I saw her except for a few new lines on her face and a slight graying to her chestnut hair. But as always, the most prominent feature is her eyes. They are the same shape as her son's and they might've been the same shade of hazel were it not for the white obscuring the colors.

Vera is blind. She stabbed her eyes again and again when the world became too much.

I've always been terrified to find out what she saw.

Vera takes a step forward, the garden knife still clasped in her hand. "Don't speak. Don't move."

I stay silent and still as Vera steps so close I can feel her breath on my face. Her eyes gleam in the sunlight, the obscuring white like a fog seeping out of the shadows.

"Asteria?"

"Yes–"

"Asteria. Is that really you?" The garden knife clatters to the ground and her hands reach for me. She presses her fingers against my cheeks, a wide grin spreading across her lips.

"It has been too long." Vera drags her fingers over my face before combing through my tangled hair. "Is it still as white as snow?"

"Yes," I say with a relieved sigh.

"And trouble still follows you wherever you go."

She moves my hair away from my shoulders and her fingers brush across the binding mark. The grin disappears and her face transforms, a storm of emotions flickering across her features. Shock, anger, worry, fear. "Asteria–"

I move away from her hands, smoothing my hair back over my shoulders to cover the mark even though she can't see it. "It's nothing. It's over."

Vera opens her mouth to say something, but another voice beats her.

"That's not true. It's far from over."

Elio emerges from behind the cottage. His victory armor is replaced by a simple beige shirt and pants, and a bundle of carrots is dangling from one of his hands. His eyes are narrowed and anger radiates off his broad form.

Vera grabs the carrots from his hands and stands on her toes to give him a peck on his cheek. "I'll get the soup started. You two work it out before you come inside." She gives us a stern look before disappearing inside the cottage, as if we're still children arguing about something meaningless.

Elio crosses his arms, his victory mark blinding in the sun.

"What?" I shift the weight from one foot to the other, glancing at a tree behind him.

"The Tournament," he snarls, the rage in his voice startling me. "I saw you. In your cage."

"I don't know what you're talking about," I say, moving my gaze to the ground where a sunflower's head is drooping.

"Don't lie to me, Asteria. Not about this," he pleads, and something cracks in my heart.

"I'm sorry. I couldn't tell you. I–"

"You should've told me! You failed in the first trial! I don't want to know what kind of dark magic you've found to get back in–"

"I didn't fail! My fingers touched the crown of the holy mountain. I didn't have a choice."

Elio snaps his mouth shut, his eyebrows creased with confusion. "So the last trial wasn't your second. You've been in the games this whole time." The hurt flaring in his eyes breaks my heart even more. "You can't be sure the gods didn't grant you another chance at life without forcing you to continue in the games—"

"I didn't have a choice. Are you saying you wish my soul was in the Shadow Realm right now?" I ball my hands into fists, nails digging into the scars in my palms.

He lets out a frustrated sound. "Of course not. I'm relieved you didn't search for dark magic but I'm furious you didn't tell me. Do you know how dangerous—"

"I'm perfectly aware of that," I snap, causing him to take a step backward.

We've never argued like this.

"You trusted the *enemy*." The anger is back in his voice and when he takes a step forward, I'm half tempted to slip into a fighting stance.

"Just enough to survive. Again, I didn't have a choice. I could barely move because of the magic—"

"If you had told me about your plans we could've prevented that—"

"If I had told you, you would've tried to stop me."

Elio purses his lips and drags a hand over his head. His hair is shorter than the last time I saw him, the strands so short they're impossible to grasp.

"Don't lie to me. Not about this," I say, throwing his words back at him. "You're the one who's supposed to support me. You even told me you were going to help me—"

"That was before you ruined a temple and the king made a deal with the enemy kingdom. Things are different now. You know the risks—"

"This is my choice. You know I've trained for this my entire life. I'm not giving up now."

We glare at each other, neither of us willing to back down. Minutes tick by in silence, my mind churning as violently as the roaring waves of the ocean.

I want to scream that he betrayed me by binding himself without me and that none of this would've happened if only he had waited for me–

Elio breaks the silent battle with a heavy sigh. "You're not going to be able to sneak around like this when the Tournament moves to Luna." He plops down on the porch, his head in his hands.

I cross my arms, leaning against the doorway. "Sneaking around has never been a problem. No matter where I am."

Elio's face hardens, a muscle shifting in his neck. "It's the enemy kingdom, but it seems you may have forgotten who the enemies are."

"All I've done is follow the only rule of the Tournament. I've done whatever it takes to survive, and I'll continue to do so," I say, voice laced with warning.

"You've never even left the kingdom, Asteria."

"Yes, I have–"

"The border bridge doesn't count."

I let out an exasperated sound, my hands slapping against my thighs. "What exactly are you trying to say, Elio?"

He studies me for a moment, his fingers rubbing his temples as if I'm causing him the biggest headache of his life. "I want you to stop competing."

The words are like a slap to my face and a dagger to my heart. Fury sparks at my fingertips, wrath fills my heart, and my blood roars with rage.

Elio lets out another heavy sigh. "I know. I just had to try, at least." He rises to his feet and rests his hand on my cheek, his fingers stroking along the side of my face. "I'm sorry, Ria. I just want you to be safe. No more lies, please. Just–just please let me help you." His fingers twirl my hair, sending a small tingle down my neck.

For so long this was everything I wanted. To rekindle our relationship and lose myself in his arms.

"Elio–"

His hand drops from my face, his eyes avoiding my gaze. "If you think the games in Soria were brutal, you're not prepared for the ones in Luna," he says through gritted teeth, all signs of atonement gone as if it was never there at all.

"I'm sure I'll be fine."

He moves past me, his hand closing around the handle of the door.

"Elio, please," I grab his arm with a strained smile, desperately trying to keep together the now very fragile threads of our friendship. "I would love your help. You're a Victor."

"But not a multiple times Victor or a prince. I'm not like him."

I drop his arm, not able to mask my anger anymore. "Jealousy doesn't look good on you, Elio. You were the one to end everything between us without so much as a word–"

"Just make sure to train in the dark," he snaps, ending the discussion of our brief relationship. "With your eyes closed."

"I'll make sure to keep that in mind," I say through gritted teeth before following him inside.

The moment I step over the threshold, the smell of freshly made soup fills my nostrils.

Vera's cottage feels like a home, warm and comforting and far from the silent marble halls and rooms that always feel too large, too empty. The small space is overflowing with plants and herbs. Pillows and rugs in every imaginable color litter the floor and furniture, as if Vera couldn't bear to part with the colors outside of the cottage even for a second, or maybe she wants to keep the vibrant colors through the winter when everything will be drowned in white.

I allow myself to study the swirls of paint that cover every crinkle and corner of the walls, floor, and ceiling. Vera may not be able to see the explosion of colors, but she paints and decorates as if she could.

Vera's life always seemed like an impossible dream to me, a dream I would yearn for during the lonely nights and brutal punishments served by the king. A life far away from prying eyes and inescapable duties and expectations.

"Come eat, Asteria." Vera's voice brings me out of my trance and I walk into the kitchen where Elio is already seated by the small table, an angry line still bulging across his forehead.

Vera smacks him playfully with her wooden spoon, conjuring a small smile from her son. "What did I say? None of that inside. I may not see it, but I can feel your brooding all through the house." She gestures for me to sit down next to Elio, and I quickly obey, my stomach grumbling from the delicious smells emanating from the stove.

Vera hums as she places steaming bowls on the table, her fingers reaching forward to smooth away the creases on Elio's forehead.

He sends me an indignant look behind her back and I give him a relieved smile, grateful there's still something left between us. It might not be much, but it's all I have at the moment.

"Let's eat," Vera says, one hand resting on top of Elio's, the other on mine. "I'm so happy you're both finally home. However brief it may be."

And for now, I'm content to live in the dream, willing away the thoughts of the impending darkness waiting to sweep it all away.

THE VICTOR OF DAY AND NIGHT

WE DON'T SPEAK on the journey back to Moria.

The days pass in a blur, the sun a constant companion during the day, the moon peering at us as we toss and turn on the hard ground during sleepless nights.

I cling to Elio atop his horse, my body still beaten and sore from the last trial. I don't know how I would've made it back to the palace without him.

The Sun Court is cold compared to the vibrancy of Helianthus despite the Sun Palace's glow. The marble hallways chill my skin with dread, each sound sending a jolt of fear through me.

I make it into the servant's halls without encountering anyone, and I'm so exhausted I have to steady myself against the walls. I tumble into my room, halting when I notice my reflection in the large mirror next to the wardrobe.

The clothes I hastily washed in the river behind Vera's cottage are dirty and ripped. My hair is a tangled mess–leaves, pine needles, and small twigs are clinging to the white strands. There are dark circles underneath my eyes, the pale blue color hollow and glassy.

As I scrub my skin clean in the bath, the memories I've been trying to suppress come flooding back.

The cage.

The sounds of the ropes snapping.

The growls from the beast rattling my bones.

The hundreds of warriors sacrificed to the gaping black hole.

The unexpected end to a dangerous bargain.

When memories of *his* skin against mine start to resurface, I let the water seep out of the tub before putting on a simple white dress, every movement slower than usual.

The sun has disappeared from the sky when I finally make my way to the patio reserved for tonight's dinner. Each step fills me with a panic that grips my heart, and I mutter prayers to every god I can think of.

The table is more crowded than usual and the servants have just started to place platters with heaps of various food onto the decorated table.

As I hesitate in the open doorway, someone walks past me, warm fingers brushing against my frosty hands.

"Glad to see you back on your feet, starlight," Star mutters before sauntering to the table and taking a seat next to a prince with dark brown hair streaked with black.

My heart leaps at the sound of his voice. I force myself to ignore it and sit down next to Davina, as far away from Father as possible.

The Sun King is talking with his opposing ruler, a pleased smirk on his lips. "The dark night sky is nothing but a joke compared to the gilded sky of the last trial."

The Moon King takes a sip of his large silver goblet with a glare, a faint black smoke emanating from his fingertips.

I lean toward Davina to whisper in her ear, "Was the sky golden the last trial?" The second the words leave my lips, a memory resurfaces–Star looking down at me with the golden sky at his back, his hand clasped around my wrist.

My sister gives me a wary look. "Yes, you would've known that if you for once did as you were supposed to. You need to stop this–"

"Yes, *Star*," Castor cuts in, a cruel smirk on his lips. "Why didn't you win last night?"

Star waves a dismissive hand, a bored expression on his face. "I have to leave some victories for the others."

The Moon King slams his goblet down and the table rattles. The princes don't even flinch.

Star is gripping his fork so hard it seems to bend a little. His gaze flickers to mine for a fraction of a second before he puts a bite of buttered bread in his mouth, chewing so slowly it looks like he's in pain.

Guilt slams into my heart and I ball my hands into fists underneath the table.

"And where, dear betrothed, have you been these past days?"

It takes a moment to realize Castor is speaking to me and I press my nails into the scars in my palms to keep from screaming at the sound of his voice.

"I'm afraid I was unable to leave the palace. I'm still bleeding. Probably just wedding nerves. I didn't want to bleed all over the dais–"

"Enough," Father says, slamming his hand down on the table so hard the cutlery rattles. Gold flares in his eyes and a faint light starts to seep out of his hands.

The scars on my back start to throb. My heart is suddenly too large for my chest. Waves of panic crash through me so violently it feels as if I'm going to shatter into a million tiny pieces.

I can't breathe—

"I'm so sorry, Your Majesty."

Elio emerges from the open doorway, his golden jacket gleaming in the kinglights. "I found her in the medical wing before the procession left and told her I was personally going to tell you, but due to the incident in the crowd–" he trails off with a vague gesture with his hands, his lips pursing into a thin line.

"Very well," Father snaps with a glowering look in my direction that screams he will punish me at a later time.

"What incident?" The words leave my mouth before I can stop them, the panic squeezing my heart slackening its grip enough for my voice to function again.

"Oh, just the usual sort. Ridiculous so-called rebellious forces," Moon croons with a sinister grin that sends a shudder down my back.

There's a wicked gleam in his eyes that makes it clear the dark king has already delivered some punishments of his own.

Uproars during the Tournament are not unusual. The rebellious parts of the two kingdoms never stop, no matter the increasing number of public executions and forced bindings. They don't respect the gods or the tenuous treaty between the kingdoms. And they don't honor the Tournament and its magic.

"I do hope you will be present for the rest of the games, Asteria," Moon says with a pointed look at Castor. "As a future bride of the moon, I expect you to show your support." His cruel grin widens, his dark eyes staring into my soul.

"Of course, Your Majesty," I say, willing my voice to be steady.

"After the wedding, you will not be my problem anymore. Perhaps not to anyone in this world either," Father mutters in a low voice, but not so low as to keep everyone at the table from hearing the scalding words.

My chair scrapes across the balcony ground, my body flushed with anger and shame.

"Stay." Magic crackles in the air, the kinglights floating above the table flickering like thousands of small flames ready to burn me alive.

"I have a lot of preparations to do before we leave tomorrow," I say, ignoring his heated stare. "I wouldn't want to forget my linens. You know, for the bleeding."

The corners of my lips tug at the disgusted look on his face. "Oh, and my dear betrothed–" I turn my head to look at Castor.

"I'm sure you'll show me where to find linens in your kingdom. You know for your–I mean my–bleedings. You probably have some good *glittering* remedies too."

"Definitely," Castor mutters, his contorted face challenging the king's.

"I'm leaving too." Elio stands from the table, bowing to the kings. "The halfway celebrations are only days away. I'll make sure it's a celebration worthy of the gods."

I don't release the pressure of my nails until we're back inside the palace. We walk in silence for a while, our footsteps echoing in the silent halls.

"Thank you," I say, brushing my fingers against his hand.

Elio's steps falter from my touch, his lips pressed into a thin line.

"Elio–"

"Was that proof enough that I can help you? If only you would have let me sooner."

"I was only trying to keep you safe–"

"I'll see you later, Asteria." He recoils from my touch and walks away without glancing back.

I swallow against the lump in my throat, willing away the ache in my chest. I run, my shoes loudly clicking against the marble floor, the passing servants averting their eyes from the frantic cursed princess.

When I reach a hallway unlit by the kinglights, something changes in the air and I notice the prince leaning against a shadowed corner.

"Trouble in paradise, starlight?"

My dagger is buried in the wall beside his head before I have the time to blink.

A wicked grin spreads on Star's lips as he yanks the dagger from the wall. "Again, a thank you would be more appreciated."

He offers me the hilt of the dagger, the blade resting in his palm.

"Are you sure you don't want to keep it? Our bargain is done, you have no reason to keep me alive anymore."

Silver flashes in his eyes and the grin disappears.

I don't know how to feel when I look at him. The prince of the enemy kingdom so insistent on a bargain, desperate to keep me alive so he could claim the favor he used to save my life.

I may no longer owe him my half of a life-binding bargain, but I certainly owe him my life.

"Why?"

A muscle twitches in his jaw. Another flare of silver in his eyes. It looks as if he is fighting a war with himself, as if an invisible battle is raging in his soul.

"I wish you would just thank me and move on," he says and reaches forward to grab my hand.

The feel of his skin against mine makes my heart skip a beat, and a small part of me is disappointed when he only places the dagger in my hand.

"Thank you," I snap, slipping the dagger into the bodice of my dress.

Star chuckles. "I never thought I'd hear those words from you."

"And I never thought the enemy eager to kill me would save my life." I take a step forward and I'm instantly engulfed in his heady scent. "Why?"

"A momentary lapse of judgment perhaps." He doesn't back away and I don't stop walking until our faces are only inches apart.

"Why?"

He sighs, his breath hot on my face. "I have my reasons."

"Which reasons?"

His gaze flickers to my lips and my heartbeat quickens. "Reasons I'm keeping to myself."

I let out a dry chuckle. "You still know my secrets. How do I know you won't tell the king now that I no longer owe you anything?"

"You owe me your life."

I ignore him. "Why shouldn't I just kill you now?"

"You won't."

"Don't underestimate me." I reach for the dagger, but he grabs my hand, his fingers locking around mine.

"I'm not." His other hand reaches forward and cups my cheek. "You won't kill me because you like me too much and I just saved your life. Again."

"I don't like you—"

"Maybe I want an ally in the games. Maybe I want to make sure someone will help me when the time comes." He tilts my head up, his face so close his lips graze mine.

"You have Skye for that—"

"I want you."

I suck in a breath, my eyes involuntarily fluttering shut.

His lips are featherlight against mine as his hands leave my skin. When I open my eyes, he's gone, only shadows left in his wake.

CHAPTER TWENTY

The fourth trial in Helianthus where the beast of darkness devoured countless warriors was the last Trial of the Sun and marks the halfway point in the Tournament of Day and Night. The Tournament will move across the Diamond Mountains to Luna during the month-long break before the four Trials of the Moon, and as a last chance for the sun to outshine the moon, the Sun Festival is celebrated in Moria before the departure.

Today, the royal court has opened its gilded gates to the entirety of the Kingdoms of the Sky.

The open area in the market square used for the fighting rounds following the binding ceremonies is crowded with dancing people, the vendors, taverns, and dining areas around it bustling with activity. An orchestra of musicians is playing festive and joyous tunes, their breaks overshadowed by music reverberating from nearby buildings.

The royal city is decorated with vibrant colors. Flowers in every shade imaginable color the streets, the petals littering the cobblestones. The celebrating people are dressed in vivid colors that swirl together in a cascade of colors as they dance between each other. Large banners with ornate pictures of the Tournament symbol—the sun entwined with a crescent moon—are hanging in the air between the roofs, the fabric fluttering in the warm summer breeze.

A fanfare rings through the city and all the sound and movements quiet, everyone halting mid-celebration to hear the words of the king.

The Sun King's speech will be heard anywhere and everywhere in the two kingdoms, his voice magnified by so much magic that his words will rumble like thunder across the sky.

Even the gods will be listening.

In the middle of the open square, feet planted on the circle picturing the sun, the king raises his hands. His hair is let loose, the blonde locks flowing to his shoulders. A gilded crown sits atop his head, the yellow gemstones giving his features an eerie glow. His golden suit is blinding in the sunlight, and gilded rings glimmer from his ears and fingers.

I've always thought Father is more suited as a king of ice and snow, but today he looks like the perfect King of the Sun, glowing in all his glory.

"The Tournament of Day and Night is the result of a bargain between our ancestors and the gods. Once a year, starting on summer or winter solstice, we host games in their honor to keep the truce between the two kingdoms of the sky. It is a way to keep the balance between the two sides of the sky. The light and the dark, the sun and the moon." Gold flares in the king's eyes as he speaks and a faint light starts seeping out of his chest.

"The gods gift us their land and magic during the Tournament Times, and thus the warriors shall gift them back with their sacrifices. Eight games, eight chances for each court to prove themselves worthy to reign underneath the sky."

I resist the urge to roll my eyes as my gaze wanders away from the king. Everyone knows the true purpose of the games is the exact opposite of his well-practiced words.

The Tournament is war.

Castor pinches my arm that's interlaced with his, his eyes boring into the side of my face until I redirect my gaze back to Father.

I hate that I have to stand next to him. I hate that I have to wear the stupid ring, and most of all I hate that he has to touch me.

"The Trials of the Sun are unfortunately over–" a large part of the gathered crowd boos and a pleased smile pulls at the king's lips, "–for now."

The unsatisfied sounds transform into applause and cheer and the king opens his raised arms as if he is going to tear the sun off the sky. "But the games are far from over for our warriors of the sun!"

Elio steps forward, his Victor's uniform almost as bright as the king's attire. The Crown of Victory rests on his head, and his hazel eyes glow from the reflections of the crown and the victory mark on his neck.

"And may the people of the sun join us as we travel across the border to follow the rest of the games and welcome our next Victor. Let the celebrations continue!" The power of his title is evident in his voice. The people cheer louder as he bows his head and the Sun King lowers one of his hands from the sky to place it on the Victor's head.

Golden light erupts from their bodies. The wind blows the magical light in magnificent swirls before it seeps up to the sky, some of it breaking apart into tiny pieces of light that float away like gilded ashes.

The crowd roars. The rhythmic thumping of their feet and clapping of their hands shakes the earth beneath us.

I feel the thousands of people push forward, the armor of one of the guards caging the royals brushing against my back. It feels as if Castor's hand is not only on my arm, but on my throat and chest, squeezing so only shallow breaths can escape my lips.

The guards shift their positions to allow parts of the crowd to greet the Sun King and the Victor and I slip away from my sisters, ignoring Castor's protesting words and scowling eyes.

I push my way through the crowd, gaze locked on the ground. Hands reach for me, fingers tugging at my dress. Angry eyes prickle my skin and shouted curses slam into my ears. Someone yanks my hair and my eyes water.

It's too much–

I barge through the door of the first building I see, gulping down air, my hand pressed against my raging heart.

The tavern is dimly lit and only a few people are scattered on the wooden tables and benches. Stearin stains are permanently etched onto the planks, and pieces of wood are torn off and full of splinters. The tavern looks as if it's going to crumble any second, the room more ruined than not.

It is not a place for celebration. This is a hiding place tucked away from the crowded parts of the city center.

Bracing my back against the wall, I suck in a relieved breath. Away from the large and angry crowd, my body calms enough for my mind to start working again and I'm suddenly aware of someone calling my name.

"Asteria!" Skye's voice breaks through the silence of the tavern and she winks me over to a table tucked into a dark corner.

The other guests don't bother glancing up as I pass, their gazes locked on the drink in their hands. All except for two of them.

The pair of warriors from the Helianthus fields raise their

glasses in a silent toast. The man gives me a wink, the woman beside him only giving me a bored look.

Skye is not alone. A bulky man is sitting wide-legged on a stool beside her, a mug nestled between large hands crisscrossed with scars. A crescent moon is stitched onto his chest, the uniform of the Lunan Royal Guard a stark contrast to the clothes of the other people in the tavern.

"It's okay," Skye says with a sly smile when she notices my wary look. "This is Thunder." She gestures to the man who raises his mug with a cursory glance.

I wonder if Thunder is a nickname to hide his true identity, the name well suited for his thundering appearance.

"Come, sit down. You look like you could use a drink." Skye drags out a chair across the table, patting the seat.

The echo of the crowded market seeps in from the open door behind me and an involuntary shudder runs down my back.

I sit down.

"Relax, princess. I'm not in the mood to bite anyone today," Thunder drawls before giving me an impish grin. A thick scar runs across his face, cutting through his lips and barely missing his left eye.

"Shouldn't you be outside guarding your royals?"

He shrugs and downs the rest of his drink. The man might be giving the impression of a slightly drunken guest, but I can tell all his senses are on high alert. His hand is casually angled for easy access to the sword strapped to his side and his gaze occasionally flickers across the room, his back slumped against the wall so he can see the entire tavern at all times.

"How are you feeling?" Skye asks, leaning forward to peer at me in the dim light.

"Fine."

A waitress appears with a glass of red liquid and puts it down in front of me without so much as a glance.

"Good." Skye leans back in her chair, tucking a loose strand of blue behind her ear. "You're ready for the next game then."

Thunder is still pretending to not pay attention to anything else than his now-empty mug, but I know he is listening to every sound.

"I'll be ready," I mutter, my eyes scanning the room for what he could be looking for.

Skye opens her mouth to speak but purses her lips when something knocks against one of the walls of the tavern, the force rattling the glasses on the inside.

Another bang and a dark-cloaked figure barges through the open doorway. The figure slips into the shadowed corner on the opposite side of the tavern, the table concealed by a wall and unreachable by my searching gaze.

"That's my cue." Thunder grabs my glass and swallows the liquid in one large gulp.

"Later, ladies." His chair scrapes across the wooden floor, his heavy steps making the floor creak as he moves to follow the dark-cloaked figure.

Skye chuckles nervously, eyes darting around the room. "Duck."

"What?"

A thud followed by a crash echoes behind me and Skye pushes my head down. A glass hits our table and tiny shards clatter to the floor around us. Another crash followed by a muttered string of curses and Skye drops her hold on me.

Thunder thumps down in his chair and reaches for Skye's glass which is miraculously still standing. His knuckles are bruised and there's a small cut on his forehead. Blood drips from his hands, staining the glass. "That got a little messier than planned but not nearly enough. Moon, I miss a real fight." With a heavy sigh, he gulps down the liquid before shattering the glass on the floor.

Skye hisses something I can't hear over the chaos of sounds. A waitress runs around with a broom, desperately trying to collect the broken glass. The other guests move to leave, shouting as a crowd of people rush through the open doorway.

On the opposite side of the tavern, a limp hand is lying on the floor, the rest of the body hidden behind the wall where the dark cloaked figure and Thunder were only moments ago.

"What–" I slam my palms on the table, instantly regretting it as the shattered glass cuts into my skin.

"I suggest you get out of here, princess," Thunder mutters before pushing away from the table, Skye following just behind.

"Yes," she hisses, casting a glare at the towering man beside her. "That's a good idea, unlike all your other thoughts."

Thunder snorts and wipes his bloody hands on his stomach, staining the dark fabric of his uniform.

Skye grabs my arm and hauls me out of the chair. "Here, take the back door." She points me in the direction before pushing me away with a hard shove.

Fights break out behind me, the tavern suddenly as loud as the crowded market square outside. Shouts and screams followed by crashing and banging reverberate behind me as I hurry through the door, and I vaguely wonder if the old tavern will be able to survive this.

Outside, the moon has taken over the sky, the city colored by a white gleam. An ocean of stars sparkles in the darkness and a dark fog seeps from the ground. The chaos of the tavern is muted by a magical atmosphere of alluring music and exquisite smells, this side of the building nothing but serenity.

"There you are. We've been looking everywhere for you," Erina says, suddenly appearing to link her arm with mine.

"You're lucky Father is too busy dealing with the rebels to notice your absence," Arina snarls, appearing on my other side to form a cage with her twin.

"Rebels?"

They start walking toward the pier overlooking a small pond in the middle of the city, dragging me along with them.

We walk past families and warriors showing off their binding marks, and my sisters put on their most dazzling smiles, politely waving to the small children gawking at the princesses.

"Yes," Erina says and bows her head to a passing noblewoman.

"A couple of them destroyed one of the shrines before escaping. They're probably gathered in one of those disgusting taverns as we speak," Arina mutters in a low voice, the hand that's not linked with mine waving in the direction of a handsome man wearing a suit fit for a royal.

"Oh," I say, forcing a neutral expression onto my face.

"Don't act so innocent," Erina snaps, increasing the pressure of her arm. "You were the one who started all of this. Today was not the first ruination of ceremonial places, after all." Her perfect mask slips just long enough to send a subtle glare in my direction.

"At least someone appreciates my bad reputation—"

The twins glare in unison, their arms squeezing me so tight it's hard to breathe.

"This has to stop," Arina hisses. "The sun knows what kind of beasts you might run into in Luna."

"We can't help you there. All of us agree," Erina says, forcing a smile onto her face as we reach the guards waiting by the pond to escort us back to the palace.

Like their caging arms, their words wring my heart, the betrayal cutting through me.

"I want this taken care of before we leave tomorrow."

I stiffen at the sound of Father's voice and I curl my hands into fists to keep anyone from noticing my broken skin. The king is angrily gesticulating with one of his generals, his magic crackling in the air around him, small pieces of gold fluttering in the wind.

"Enjoying the celebrations, Princess Asteria?"

The Moon King startles me with his presence. The usual cruel smirk is plastered on his face, his black eyes even darker than the shadows around him.

As if they didn't just warn me to stay out of trouble, the twins release their hold on me, bowing to the king before stepping away.

"Yes," I say, willing my rapid heart to steady. "I very much enjoy the celebrations."

"Good." He folds his hands behind his back as the procession moves forward, signaling for his guards to keep a distance with a curt nod. "Of course, I think Luna outdoes everything you have seen so far, but I guess I am a little biased."

"I look forward to figuring that out for myself."

There's a gleam in his eyes that hints at the brutality of his kingdom, and the sight sends a jolt of fear through my heart.

"I am sure my prince will be eager to show you around. You two seem close enough now."

"Prince Castor will be a good husband," I say, ignoring the need to spit his name.

The king's cruel smirk widens into a grin. "I was talking about my other prince. I am sure you know which one."

Something tightens in my chest. "I'm afraid I don't know what you mean, Your Majesty. I've barely been introduced to the other princes–"

"Do you need a reminder of how I feel about lies? Do not play stupid with me, girl. It will not do you any good in my kingdom."

His voice is sharp enough to cut glass and I feel more than see the tendrils of darkness reaching for my throat. "After all, the rules of the Tournament have changed."

"There are no rules in the Tournament."

A dark cloud obscures the light of the moon and the dark fog thickens. In the middle of the darkness, the Moon King is more terrifying than any beast. There's not a trace of color to be found on the king, and the shadows of his eyes threaten to drag me into the Shadow Realm. "Oh, all but one. You have to survive."

His power vibrates the air around me, and a hand emerges from the darkness to tuck a strand of hair behind my ear. The feel of his power on my skin is so horrifying I wish he would just kill me and be done with it.

"And a princess of the sun surrounded by darkness, cursed to live in the shadows? I think we both know her chances are not very good."

The shadowy fingers stroking my cheek are as solid as stone. The hand moves down to my throat, the fingers teasing the skin.

"You're wrong," I whisper and the fingers halt.

I know perfectly well that I shouldn't argue with a king, but I know he would hate my silence and lies even more.

As I turn my head to look at the Moon King, a prickling sensation starts at my neck, and it feels as if I'm being watched from the shadows.

"This princess of the sun has enough light to survive the dark."

CHAPTER TWENTY-ONE

The carriage rattles along the uneven road. The room is suffocating and too small, cramped with bags and suitcases that bump against each other, barely missing my head or legs when they tumble off the racks. The doors are locked on both sides and the windows are sealed shut to block the view.

The outside of the carriage might be fit for a royal procession, but the inside is so old and ragged I'm afraid of falling through the wooden floorboards any second, but perhaps that would be a relief.

I might finally be able to cross the border of the kingdom, but the king will certainly make sure it isn't a pleasant journey.

The journey to Luna has already stretched over several days and nights, the only breaks from the carriage brief to take care of my most necessary and urgent needs. The general who delivered my stale meals and allowed me to slip away for a few minutes only gave me gruff orders, not bothering to answer any of my nagging questions.

A royal treatment indeed.

There's only one official route between the Kingdoms of the

Sky. In the middle of the Diamond Mountains—the two chains of mountains creating a border and separating the sun from the moon—there is a bridge built over the coursing river that divides the land.

The last and only time I was near the border, all I got was a glimpse of the sparkling water, my fingers reaching for freedom as I was dragged away.

I've always yearned for something more, to see more than the familiar landscape and cities basking in the eternal light.

I won't let Father take that away from me too.

As the night drags on, I'm debating slipping out of the carriage to steal a horse or just walk on my own feet. Anything to get away from this smothering place.

My head bangs against the wall as I drift in and out of sleep, my dreams haunted by dying warriors and beasts lurking in the shadows.

I don't know how much time passes before I snap awake to a scratching sound coming from the roof.

The hatch in the ceiling that was sealed shut from the outside the last time I checked pops open to reveal the dark night. A breeze of fresh air blows through the opening, a cool relief against my flushed skin.

A dark figure jumps down and elegantly settles on an overpacked suitcase in front of me. The figure pulls down the hood concealing their face, revealing midnight eyes and an arrogant smirk.

I cross my arms and lean back against the wall. "What a surprise," I say, willing my voice to sound bored instead of disappointed. "What are *you* doing here?"

Star crosses one ankle over the other, his broad form making the carriage feel even smaller. His outstretched feet reach the bench beside me and if I were to just slightly lean forward, our faces would be mere inches apart. "From the pleased look on your face when I opened the hatchet, I would've thought you were happy to see me."

I roll my eyes. "I was enjoying the fresh air and the possibility of finally getting out of here."

The prince's smirk widens, mischief glinting in his eyes. "Let's go then."

A snort escapes me. "I'm not going anywhere with you."

He tilts his head to the side. "Are you not on the way to my kingdom? With me, might I add?"

I roll my eyes again, ignoring the small part of me that is disappointed Elio still hasn't shown up.

"And besides, are you going to let a night like this go to waste?" Star gestures to the open sky above us, to the countless stars taunting me with the challenge, glimmering like the silver in the enemy's eyes. "Your kingdom is deprived of the night's beauty for so long it would be a shame to let it go to waste."

"Don't you have some enemies to torture or something?"

His gaze flickers over my body, to the long dress clinging to every dip and curve. "Yes," he repeats, more slowly this time. "So let's get out of here."

Another snort leaves me.

"What?" He leans forward, resting his elbows on his knees. "Here I am, thinking you would use every opportunity to train. Training underneath the moon is far better than under the sun, but I'm sure you know that by now, seeing as you've spent the last few nights doing exactly that. And with your eyes closed. Impressive"

"Are you following me?"

"Maybe."

"Why?"

He leans forward even further. His breath is hot on my face

and I'm absorbed by his scent–citrus mixed with something I still can't place. "As you said, it's important to keep an eye on your enemies."

The hidden mark on my arm tingles as his gaze once again rakes over my body, the secret burning on my skin. I resist the urge to place my hand over the mark or do anything that might make him curious about what I'm hiding.

"I thought you wanted to be my ally," I mutter through gritted teeth.

"Enemies, allies, friends, *lovers*. it really doesn't matter." He shrugs with a smirk. "Like I told you the last time we spoke, I have my reasons."

That is not the only thing he told me the last time we spoke. He also kissed me.

I allow myself to study him for a few moments. He is wearing another set of leathers today–the dark fabric stitched with swirls of silver and the phases of the moon. His skin has a faint silver gleam, iridescent from the moonlight above. A lock of dark hair curls down to his forehead, and for a second, I'm tempted to sweep it away.

"See something you like?"

"Maybe," I say, smirking when he blinks in surprise.

He opens his mouth to say something but quickly snaps it shut. My smirk widens.

I shouldn't be doing this. He is the enemy and my strongest opponent. And yet–

"I need to get out of here."

I can't pass up an opportunity for freedom, no matter which hand offers it.

Star straightens, the arrogant smirk back on his lips as he lowers his head to not bang against the ceiling of the carriage. He holds out a hand, the tally marks peeking out of his sleeve, the scarred lines a red so dark it's almost black.

I ignore his hand. My limbs are stiff from sitting in the carriage, the muscles along my back and neck aching from the hard wall. "I said I'm not going anywhere with you so scurry back to wherever you came from."

It's only then that I notice the carriage has stopped moving. It wouldn't surprise me if Star somehow managed to sneak in while the procession moved forward, but the last carriages are not as heavily guarded as the rest during the night.

Only the king and a few of his generals share the knowledge of my whereabouts.

And apparently also Star.

Star effortlessly hauls himself through the opening in the ceiling, hinting at the strength that helped him win multiple Tournaments.

Missing a great amount of his height, I place a few of the suitcases on top of each other to create a wobbly stool. With a clumsy leap, I manage to get the upper half of my body onto the roof, my legs helplessly dangling underneath me.

"Need some help, princess? You only have to ask," Star croons as he looks down at me with one of his usual smirks.

"And risk being tricked into another bargain? I don't think so." I grit my teeth as I try to swing my legs and crawl farther onto the roof, refusing to even consider asking him for help.

Star sighs and taps his foot in impatience. "Working on your climbing skills should be at the top of your list. You know, after last time. The temple roof and the rope–"

"Shut up," I sneer, finally able to rise to my feet.

Star chuckles and jumps down from the carriage, his hand extended once again.

"Leave me alone," I hiss before carefully scaling down, glancing around to make sure no one has seen me.

The Diamond Mountains are towering in the distance, and I suck in a relieved breath when I realize we've yet to cross the border. By my calculations, we should be at the border between Verbena and Helianthus, the passage in the mountains nearing.

A group of horses grazing nearby are the only ones close enough to see and hear us. Tents have been set up for the night, another luxury I've been deprived of. A crackling fire and low chatter echo in the distance, the cool breezes rustling the long fabric of my dress.

Star chuckles beside me. "Relax, princess. No one worth mentioning will see us as long as you stick with me." He stalks through the tree line without looking back to see if I follow.

And for some reason I do. Maybe it's the magic of the Tournament urging me to kill him, or maybe it's my curiosity drawing me forward.

We emerge in a clearing in the dense forests, the canopy of trees parting to reveal the night sky.

My breath catches in my throat, the sight above so breathtaking it feels like a dream.

I can't even begin to understand what I'm seeing.

Swirling rivers of silver and gold dance across the sky, shifting from nearly translucent to strikingly vivid waves of color.

The lights are brighter than the moon and stars behind, brighter than the kinglights, and perhaps even brighter than the sun. It reminds me of the sky during the Tournament's trials, but even that doesn't compare to this.

Never before have I seen the colors of the two sides of the sky together like this.

"Magnificent, isn't it?"

The swirling lights are reflected in the prince's eyes, the intensity of his gaze making my heart skip a beat.

"What is it?"

"Magic, of course." He gives me a strange look before moving his gaze back to the sky above. "Don't tell me you've never seen it like this before."

"There are a lot of things I haven't seen."

"It would seem so."

I'm about to snarl something very insulting but he continues speaking before I get the chance. "The magic of the Tournament never disappears. It's not lying dormant waiting for the next game. The magic is in everything around us. In all of us."

"I know that," I snap, moving to leave him. "You don't have to insinuate at stupidity—"

His hand wraps around my wrist, his skin cold in the summer night. "I didn't. Don't judge me so quickly, starlight."

"Why do you call me that?" I repeat the question I didn't get an answer to the last time I asked it as I try to wrangle free of his grasp, anger evident in my voice.

His fingers stroke the inside of my wrist before he releases his grip with a wink. He backs away and slips into a fighting stance. "Beat me and I'll answer any question you want."

"And if you win?"

His lips pull into a smirk that tells me he plans on doing exactly that. "Let's just say I'll collect my prize at a later time."

I roll my eyes and move my stiff shoulders. My body and soul have been screaming for a fight ever since I was stuffed into the cramped carriage. "You know, your threats aren't all that effective when you keep hinting at the vague future."

I shouldn't bother, but I'm bored and angry and in desperate need of a distraction. And maybe I'll learn something useful from the victorious prince.

Star holds out his hand, motioning for me to make the first move. "The most powerful threats don't always have to involve action."

I give him a bored look but every nerve in my body is humming with built-up adrenaline. "You only want to tire me before the next game. Don't pretend otherwise."

When he opens his mouth to answer, I kick out my foot to tackle him to the ground.

Star jumps away, his eyes glittering with amusement. "If you tire this easily, maybe you should just give up on the Tournament."

"Never," I say through gritted teeth, my hand flying through the air as I aim for his throat.

Again, he moves away. "Why is this so important to you? A princess should already have everything she desires."

"I thought you said you knew all the rumors."

Star clicks his tongue. "Yes, but you're a princess nonetheless. It's been a very long time since one of you participated in the Tournament."

"Then it's about time."

The silver and gold waves dance across the sky as time drags on, casting the clearing in an enchanting light. The moon is only a faint figure in the sky, its light overshadowed by the magic.

With every attempted kick or strike, Star moves away, his moves mimicking the dance of the lights above. Not once does he try to strike back.

He's taunting me. And it's starting to make me very angry.

The movements feel good on my stiff and aching limbs, the days spent on the road nearly forgotten in the hours with the prince. When my muscles start to grow weary, I let out a scream of impatience and rage.

He's playing with me, refusing to attack.

"I thought you wanted to win."

The corners of his lips tug upward, and in the next heartbeat, at a speed that shouldn't be possible, he does exactly that.

His foot wraps around my ankle, yanking me to the ground. His hands wrap around my waist, easing the fall. I'm pinned to the ground, trapped beneath his body.

"There. I won," he purrs, his face so close I can count the silver flecks in his eyes.

"How did you access the royal magic?"

Star blinks at me for a second before scolding his features back into his usual arrogant mask. "No. You lost. Again. You didn't earn the right to an answer."

"It wasn't a fair fight. My long dress got in the way–"

He snorts. "A queen would know how to fight at any moment. Especially in a dress."

I try to ignore the way my heart speeds up at his words. I would hate to think he somehow knows about my deepest desire.

Star's eyes flicker to my lips, his nose grazing mine.

I still remember the first time we were this close, an ornate mask hiding his identity as we devoured each other. And I haven't forgotten the last time we were this close, the memories haunting my mind during long sleepless nights.

I want you.

No–

I shove at his chest until he reluctantly moves away, his fingers briefly touching my cheek. Ignoring the tingling where his fingers touched my skin and the thundering beats of my heart, I lean on my elbows, listening to the sounds echoing in the distance.

The swirls of dancing lights are gone as suddenly as they came and the dark night is rapidly growing lighter, the sun starting to rise behind the thick trees.

The procession is getting ready to move again.

"I have to get back to my carriage," I mutter, dread filling my chest at the thought of the cramped room.

"You have to?" Star tilts his head to the side, the binding mark peeking up from the high collar of his leathers. "You don't have to do anything, starlight. It's time you realized that. Join me on my horse instead. It would be a great way to start the rumors about you in Luna."

I roll my eyes as I heave myself to my feet. "As much as I would enjoy seeing the look on the guard's faces, it's not worth the punishment that will follow."

His face hardens, the flecks of silver vanishing so his eyes are nothing but a dark storm. "The Sun King has no right to punish anyone in my kingdom." His words are practically a growl, and it's almost as if the shadows behind him darken from his fury.

Something tightens in my chest. "And the Moon King?"

"The Moon King would relish every possibility of seeing his enemies squirm."

A shudder runs down my back and I try to remind myself that the dark king *wants* to see me in the games.

"But he is not the one who condemned you to ride in the carriage." The glimmer of mischief is back in his eyes, the smirk on his face eager to cause some trouble. "I won. Stay with me. I'll even agree to do this again. You are in desperate need of more training."

I narrow my eyes.

"Or you could always owe me a favor–"

"Absolutely not."

Star chuckles, a low sound that sends a shiver down my neck.

"Why? Why would you want to...train me?"

I want you.

Something flickers across his face, there and gone so fast I don't know if I imagined it. He raises an eyebrow, his eyes glittering like the brightest stars I've ever seen. "I can't have an ally unable to fight in a dress."

I glance behind me to the awaiting carriage barely visible through the trees, and just the thought of spending another second in there is enough.

The urge to see the Diamond Mountains and the coursing river in all their glory overshadows every screaming instinct to step away.

And when was I ever one to stay away from trouble?

"You know what, moon boy? Fine."

The smirk widens into a wicked grin and a wave of anticipation rocks through me. He extends his arm, the promise of trouble crackling in the air.

And so I link my arm with the enemy prince underneath the brightening sky, eager to meet the next trial ahead.

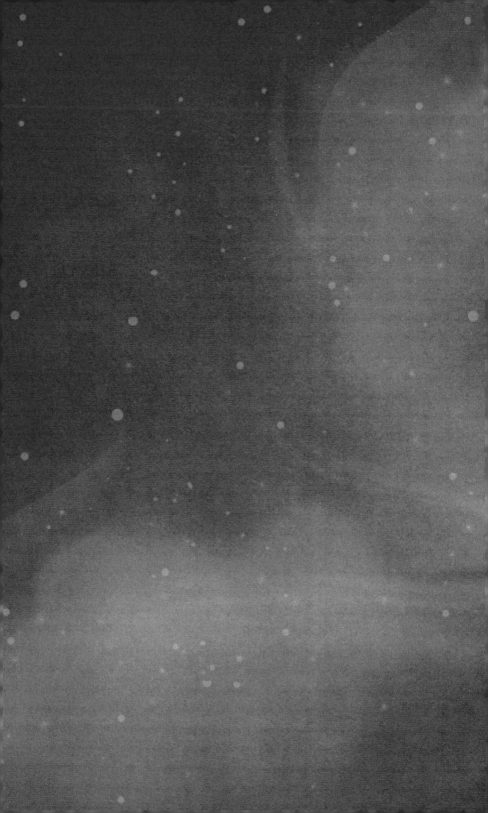

PART 2

SHOOTING STAR

CHAPTER TWENTY-TWO

"Remove your hands or I'll kick you off the horse."

The sun dips lower in the sky, her last rays of light not quite reaching my face amid the darkness of the Lunan army. Still, I relish in the freedom of the fresh air underneath the open sky, grateful to be far away from the stuffed carriage, the closeness of the prince behind me a small price to pay.

Star's chuckle reverberates through my back. His hands linger for a few seconds longer before he releases the grip on my hips. "*The horse* is called Esra. Call her anything else and you'll be the one kicked off."

"Esra," I murmur, stroking my hand along the side of her neck. Thin strands of silver threads are woven into her black mane, matching the silver symbols on her harness and saddle.

The black mare didn't protest when I climbed onto her back in front of Star and took the reins. But the Sorian Royal Guard did when we pushed forward between them. The Lunan Soldiers barely spared a glance at us when we chose a place amid them, everyone seemingly familiar with the prince's antics. The rest of the royals were thankfully seated inside the carriages, unable to spot us for at least a while.

The hours since have passed in a blur, only occasional snide remarks breaking the silence between us.

Esra makes a content sigh as I drag my fingers through her mane, huffing a breath and nudging her neck closer to my hand.

Star snorts again. "You're lucky she likes you. She tried to kick every stable worker that attempted to groom her in Soria and she is not pleased that she has to wear riding equipment."

"Is she yours?"

"Yes."

My grip on the reins tightens, the leather digging into my skin.

"Don't tell me you don't have at least half a dozen horses of your own, princess."

"I don't," I mutter through gritted teeth. "I had one, once. A beautiful stallion with dark spots in his white coat."

"And?"

"I don't have him anymore."

My heart aches at the thought of the magnificent horse. I found him in one of the villages a day's journey from the palace when I was about fourteen. I only got to enjoy his company for a few days before Father brutally took him away from me.

"He doesn't fit in with the rest," the king snarled as the Royal Sword dug into the skin of my back, each slice and cut a reminder that I didn't fit in either.

That the horse didn't look like the rest of the polished horses in the royal stables was what had drawn me to him in the first place. That, and the fact that he was destined for the slaughters–also a fate much like mine.

We fall back in silence, the only sounds around us the clacking of hooves and grinding of the carriage wheels. There are nothing but towering mountains around us. They reach for the sky, the setting sun barely visible between them. Flashes of gilded armor and arrows gleam in the fissures and crevices, the border between the kingdoms never unguarded.

It has been hours since the procession started to travel the long road between the mountains. We should be nearing the river soon.

The thought of it makes the dark memories stuffed into an iron box in my mind rattle, my heart leaping into my throat.

Two hours pass before I hear it and two more before I see it.

The river cuts through the rocky ground with jagged edges lined with slippery stones. The water sparkles like thousands of clear and bright crystals colored a magnificent blue, the rushing current roaring in the silent evening. The water splashes against the sides of the bridge, staining the stones even more. Splotches of crimson color the stones, some almost black, others still glistening in the faint light.

It is not as much of a bridge as a stack of stones piled on top of each other, flattened enough for carriages to roll, but still dangerous enough to not allow everyone to pass.

An army of gilded soldiers guards the area from all sides, and at the far end of the bridge–silver armor gleams in the faint sunlight.

A tremor rocks through me, the hands curled around the reins shaking as a million butterflies swarm in my chest.

Finally.

The border does not only mark the end of my kingdom. It also marks the end of my life as it has always been, carving out the rest of my new beginning that started the second I defied the king's orders and bound my life to the Tournament. Or maybe even before then, when the life essence of someone else was tied to mine with forbidden magic.

The procession shifts, the Sorian side parting to let the Lunans through. They will lead the rest of the way.

A Lunan General is the first to cross the bridge. The bridge is wide enough for half a dozen carriages to pass side by side, the ancient stones sturdy despite the cracks and holes.

It can only be magic holding it together.

"Are you ready for this, starlight?" Star's breath against my ear sends a shiver down my back. "It's not too late to back down–"

"Never." I tap my heels against Esra's side and the horse moves forward, following the general. She doesn't hesitate, her hooves easily finding a path on the bridge, avoiding the sunken and broken areas as if she has traveled the path numerous times before.

My heart is screaming in my chest, a part of me terrified that the iron box in my mind will be filled with more dark memories.

Star scoots closer, his chest grazing my back. I focus on the annoyance flickering inside of me, shoving the fear and panic aside.

We cross the bridge without problem.

Esra's hooves touch the ground of Luna and we continue moving forward.

It is not until hours later when we finally leave the Diamond Mountains behind, I notice the difference. There is a shift in the air and for a second, it feels as if we are emerging into a different world.

The magic in the air feels different. It tastes like something savory and delicious. It slithers across my skin like a veil of translucent glitter flickering in and out of existence, and a faint rhythmic humming pours into my soul.

The night is darker and the stars are brighter. There's an edge to the night–the promise of something more lurking in the shadows. Even the thick woods and roving mountains seem sharper and more brutal than the Sorian side. And the moon–the moon lights a path with glorious swirls of white light that enchant the land to something ominous and magical.

I gulp down breaths of air, all my senses ravenously taking it all in.

The Lunans don't stop for a break until the sun has started to creep back into the sky, already deeming the light side unworthy of their waking hours.

Star takes one long look at me before retiring to his tent tucked in front of the thick forest, the arrogant smirk and glimmer in his eyes clearly stating an unspoken offer.

I don't bother telling him it's never going to happen.

Refusing to even think about going back to the carriage, my only option is curling up on the ground next to Esra, the Victory Dagger tucked into my palm.

My body is so exhausted I quickly succumb to the sleep tugging at my mind. When I wake hours later, a blanket is draped over my shoulders and a canteen of fresh water and a bindle filled with bread and fruit is lying in front of me. I devour the food, hoping one of the servants brought it.

I don't want to owe Star anything more than I already do.

A little while later, I steal a sword from one of the guards and find a secluded spot to practice. I've already lost too many days cramped in the carriage, and I can't lose any more.

The month-long break at the halfway point of the Tournament is known to make many warriors lazy and careless, and I'm determined not to let it happen to me.

I only wish Elio was here to train with me.

When dusk approaches, I hear the procession start to pack up and I'm already seated on Esra when Star appears from the shadows.

Ride. Sleep. Train. The same cycle of events is repeated every day. Sometimes Star joins me when I sneak away to train, taunting me until I attack and we end up sparring for hours. Other times, I practice alone, imagining Castor's face on my invisible opponents.

I stay away from the Sorian side of the procession, not wanting to find out if Father has noticed my absence, yet desperately hoping Elio will find me. With every passing day and week, it seems more and more impossible that we will ever spend time together again, the promise of his help hanging onto a very fragile thread.

Star orders Esra to stay with the soldiers, steering away from the royals, but I have a feeling the Moon King wouldn't care if he were to notice me among his people. It would only be another part of his games waiting to be played.

We don't talk much, the only breaks in silence as we ride my warnings not to touch me and his condescending remarks about my skills. I refuse to talk about what I'm screaming to find an answer to and he doesn't speak of it either.

The road to the royal court passes by in a blur, the scenery only changing from vast fields to mountains and thick forests, the Lunans purposefully choosing paths that don't reveal too much of their kingdom to the enemy.

On what I've calculated to be one of the last nights of the journey, Star sighs heavily behind me, startling me from my churning thoughts and making me aware that I've slumped against his chest.

I quickly adjust my posture with a glare over my shoulder.

He leans his head on my shoulder, his breath tickling my neck as he whispers in my ear, "I'm bored."

I roll my eyes, leaning away from the warmth of his body. "I'm sure that's very difficult for a prince. Poor little warrior."

He clicks his tongue, his hands sneaking around me to grab the reins.

"I warned you to keep your hands to yourself–"

Esra bursts into a gallop at Star's command, the soldiers' shouts echoing after us.

Star laughs, the sound reverberating through me so different from his usual dry chuckles.

He sounds *happy*.

He leans forward and pats Esra's neck, his voice light and affectionate. "You can outrun them, dark beauty," The horse neighs appreciatively and the speed increases.

The wind ruffles my hair, the white strands blowing everywhere and blocking my view. It feels like we're flying away on the wind, the swarm of butterflies slumbering in my chest waking in a flurry of movement.

Warm hands grasp my neck, gathering the unruly hair away from my face and I see the landscape blur by so fast that it's nothing but darkness.

"The reins! You can't just drop them." My shriek is swallowed by the wind as I frantically try to grasp the flying reins.

Star laughs again, the sound carried by the roaring wind. He cradles me to his chest, his hands tucking my arms tight so I'm unable to reach for the reins. "Relax. Enjoy it."

My heart leaps into my throat as Esra jumps over something I can't see in the blurry darkness. It's as if the horse is a part of the night, the only thing visible the flickering silver of her harness.

"I should've let her loose weeks ago. And I would have if you decided to back down on my offer for trouble. But here we are. Finally."

His words don't make any sense. I clench my feet around the horse, my nails digging into his arms.

We could fall off any second.

Star extends our arms to the sides so nothing but our feet is keeping us secure.

I scream, my voice choked by the wind rushing into my

mouth. Tears well in my eyes and I snap my eyes shut, internally cursing and screaming.

Star lets out a cry of ecstasy as he moves our arms up toward the sky. I scream again, terrified by his sudden insanity.

He keeps our arms suspended in the air a little longer before he embraces me back against his chest.

I suck in a relieved breath, a stream of curses rushing from my lips.

"Maybe next time you won't be so stiff." His lips brush against the bottom of my ear as he speaks.

"There will never be a next time. We're probably way off course by now." I have to scream for my voice to be heard over the roaring wind.

"Esra knows the way home."

"Home?"

Esra halts and the abrupt movement would've sent me tumbling to the ground if it weren't for the prince holding me upright.

"Open your eyes, starlight."

I open my eyes and my breath gets stuck in my throat. My heart threatens to break out of my skin and I'm tempted to rub my eyes to make sure I'm not dreaming.

"Welcome to Nyx."

Built into the valleys between a towering range of mountains, Nyx is a beacon in the darkness, the brightest light in the night.

Most of the buildings are concealed between the towering stone, the rest of them spiraling upward like blooming flowers. A river cuts through the middle of the city and disappears underneath the highest peak which at the top rests a gigantic palace made of obsidian stone. Silver-tipped spires rise from the dark palace, the stone casting eerie shadows over the city.

It's the most beautiful place I've ever seen.

I can't do anything else but gawk in awe as we near the enormous silver gates guarding the city, the doors already flung open to welcome the royal procession and all the people who will follow.

We pass through the gates in silence, the guards in silver armor bowing their heads when they notice the prince. Behind the gates, the city is bustling with life despite the late night or early morning–depending on which kingdom one asks.

The buildings not made from stone are painted dark to blend into the night, some of them with glassy roofs to allow the moonlight to seep into the rooms. The rest of the buildings are made of stone, some of them extending into the mountains, others carved into the mountain itself. And then there are places similar to Moria, but the feelings that arise are nothing like what I've felt before.

Something that reminds me of kinglights illuminates parts of the city, but where the Sun King's lights are golden, these lights look as if they've been crafted from moonlight. White and silver lights float through the city like stars fallen from the sky, the light so different from the kinglights it's a wonder I ever thought it was the same.

For the first time, it strikes me that Luna might not be only darkness.

The city is decorated with dark flowers that gleam in the night. Tournament banners are hanging in the air between the buildings and festive music pours out of places I'm dying to explore.

The scent of lavender and jasmine mixed with unfamiliar spices blows against my face, the sensations strange and intriguing.

Crowds of people are celebrating in the streets. They dance and sing, their joyous sounds echoing through the city. Small children are running around, giggling as they reach for the stars above.

Freedom. That's the word ringing through me as we move forward.

Some people stop when they notice us, their mouths gaping and eyes widening. I try to sit as straight as possible, my gaze aimed high.

Star drops my hair, letting the locks glide down one side of my neck, his fingers briefly lingering on my skin.

"--the cursed princess promised to the wretched prince-"

"--both of them are going to ruin the entire kingdom-"

"--I heard she stole all the life left in her mother after she was brought into the world. The late Queen of the Sun didn't stand a chance against her curse."

"--and then she cursed the kingdom! We better get rid of her before she curses us all!"

"What on the moon is she doing with the Victor?"

"--and then she fell through the roof! A disgrace ruining that ancient temple. If only the gods-"

Trouble indeed.

I grit my teeth and grab the reins, the leather digging into the palms of my hands. Star is tense behind me, his hands once again on my hips.

"Why is everyone awake?" I mutter to Star, instantly regretting the words the second I've uttered them.

I have to remember I'm in enemy territory now.

Everything is different.

I can't be fooled by its beauty.

"Would you expect anything else from the kingdom of darkness? You'd do well to remember that we thrive in the dark and our days are not usually obscured by your light."

We wind through cobblestoned pathways snaking out in

narrow alleys, the coursing river a constant companion. The city is much larger than I expected. It is the heart of Luna, the royal city everything Moria is not.

I'm terrified for Soria's future should the inevitable war finally break out, but still, I breathe in every image, every smell, every sound, every emotion surging through me, relishing in a dream finally coming true. No matter the nightmares that await.

Too soon, we reach the end of the city and halt in front of another silver gate, the doors sealed shut and heavily guarded this time. Beyond the gleaming gates is the tallest mountain topped with the palace. There is only one road to the palace–a steep road carved out of the mountain that goes around in circles all the way to the top.

The gate swings open on silent hinges and dread fills my chest.

The sounds of the city fade as we ascend the mountain, the view beneath getting farther and farther away. And when I thought Nyx couldn't get any more beautiful, I was wrong.

The city underneath us is an ocean of glittering stars, and I want nothing more than to dive into it.

Esra moves quietly up the mountain, her steps never faltering. The road is dark, unreachable by the lights of the city.

A million questions are racing through my mind, but I can't find my voice to ask them. Fear grips my heart as the palace comes into view, squeezing so hard it feels as if my heart is going to shatter into tiny pieces.

The palace is both magnificent and ominous. The dark stone gleams in the light of the moon, reflecting the stars above. Parts of it are built into and out of the mountain and I wonder how much of the ground underneath us is reached by the palace.

The Moon Palace is sculpted out of the night–an embodiment of the sweetest dreams and deadliest nightmares.

"Welcome home, princess."

CHAPTER TWENTY-THREE

Star leads me through a palace carved from darkness.

Dark blue and ebony walls blend into the deep gray and black of the mountain, the onyx floors ranging in the same shades. On parts of the walls and floor, there are glittering silver fissures that remind me of oozing blood. A dark fog clings to the high ceiling and seeps down the large tapestries and paintings on the walls, Star walking so swiftly I don't have time to study the ornate pictures.

The moonlight shines through large windows that take up whole walls, the same lights I saw down in the city floating through parts of the dark palace. There are no other lights.

The Moon Palace welcomes the darkness of the night, the towering building carved from and into the mountain only an extension of it.

There is a prickling at the back of my neck that sends shivers all over my body. It feels as if various beings are watching me from the dark corners, and it wouldn't surprise me if there actually are beasts hiding here.

There's an unnerving silence between us as Star leads me past darkened hallways moving deep into the mountain, and with each leaden step forward, my mind comes up with another reason why this was a mistake.

The prince hasn't given me any indication he no longer wants me as an ally–or whatever he chooses to call me–and instead wants to remove some of his competition in the Tournament by killing me. Yet.

Should I just kill him now?

"Your thoughts are loud, starlight."

His voice startles me, the sound of it echoing in the quiet halls.

The shadows betray you because they serve me.

For a second, I'm terrified he can hear my thoughts, but if that were true–I would've been dead already.

"They are not."

Star snorts, his eyes giving me a brief look. Shadows dance across the planes of his face, his black leathers bleeding into the darkness.

How much more powerful will he be now that we are in his kingdom?

A shudder runs down my back and we continue walking. My boots click against the stone floor. Star's steps are silent.

"Where are all the guards?"

The palace is too empty. The Sun Palace is always brimming with guards ready to halt my escapades, and with the enemy moving into this palace–it doesn't make any sense.

"Just because you can't see something, doesn't mean it's not there," he says, voice laced with warning.

Another shudder rocks through me and fear knots in my stomach.

"You should keep that in mind at all times here." He puts a

finger to his lips when I open my mouth to speak, the other hand pointing to his ear and then the shadows on the walls.

Point made. It's not safe to talk about anything I don't want anyone else to hear.

I'm not safe.

We emerge into a stairway that winds around in a circle. The lower levels are nothing but darkness and again I wonder how much of the mountain is a part of the palace. Black fog reaches for my feet and I step away, my heart in my throat. A sliver of pale light breaks through the darkness above.

"A princess in a tower, how original," I mutter, thinking of a ridiculous story Arina used to tell me when we were children and I had caused more trouble than they could help me cover up. It was a story about a lonely princess trapped in a tower for years before a prince came to her rescue by using her very long hair as a ladder.

"If you would rather sleep in the stables with Esra, I would be happy to show you the way," Star says, one foot on the first step, a mocking smirk on his lips.

Lifting my chin, I give him my best glare, and with a low chuckle, he starts walking up the stairs.

The long stairway is wide enough to accommodate us both, but Star's arm occasionally brushes against mine. White orbs of light flutter past us, accompanied by faint, light hums reminding me of the sounds from insects.

"I didn't think the Moon King would have kinglights lighting up the darkness," I say as a light sizzles past my ear and a shudder rocks through me.

I learned early that touching the Sun King's lights leaves a burn unable to be mended by healers. There is a lot I don't know about his magic, but I know the strongest of his lights can easily suck out all the light of one's soul.

Star's eyebrows rise. "They are not *kinglights*." He plucks a passing orb with two fingers, the light so small it almost disappears in his hand.

My mouth falls open.

"They are called *skylights*. And they are nothing like what you Sorians call *kinglights*." He adds the last part at the stunned look on my face, rolling the orb around in his palm to further prove his point.

"It is unclear where they originally come from—my bet is the witches—but today, they are used by almost every person in Luna. Some say they are stolen from the moon, others claim they were gifted by a mischievous god."

He extends the light toward my face and I stumble down a step. He rolls his eyes and tosses the orb toward the ceiling where it disappears in the darkness. "There are only a few people able to wield them, but the trade of them is very common."

"Skylights," I murmur, my gaze locked on the place the light disappeared. "They seem almost...alive."

Star shrugs and continues walking up the stairs. "Is not all magic alive?"

I snap my mouth shut and follow him up the stairs, my mind churning with all the new information I never thought I would learn.

The tower is much larger than I expected. The spiraling stairs break off in different levels, but Star doesn't stop until we reach the highest floor.

At the top of the tower on the far end of the hallway, there is a large window that spans over the entire wall. Beyond it, dark waves of the vast ocean glitter underneath the stars, the sight making a twinge of envy jostle my heart.

There is only a handful of doors scattered in the hallway, all of them black with silver constellations carved into the frames. A large chandelier filled with skylights gleams in the darkness of the high ceiling, the orbs of light flickering like stars.

As Star leads me down the hall, I can't help peering into the dark corners, my hand resting close to a dagger in case any hidden guards or beasts are waiting to jump out of the shadows to kill me.

"Your room." Star halts in front of an obsidian door with small stars carved into the stone.

I cross my arms. "This doesn't look like a guest wing large enough for the rest of the royal family."

"It's not."

My eyebrows rise. "And it doesn't look like a dungeon or prison either."

Star rolls his eyes. "It's not."

I tap my fingers in annoyance, tempted to reach for the dagger. "Then why did you bring me here?"

"Again, if you would rather stay in the stables with Esra–" he trails off with another smirk, his hands shoved into the pockets of his pants.

For a second, I actually consider taking him up on that offer. I would be much safer outside underneath the open sky than locked up in a tower in an unknown palace. But if Star is the only one who knows where I am–

The handle of the dagger digs into my palm. It might not be the smartest–or safest–choice, but right now it is the best option I have. If he decides to go back on his offer, I'm not going down without a fight.

"I've spent enough time next to Esra's snores for a while."

The corners of his lips tug upward. "You should get some rest before dinner," he says with a pointed look before turning to walk back to the descending stairs, but then he halts and turns back around to give me another look that sends an involuntary shiver down my back. "I'm warning you not to wander around before someone has shown you where you *can* go."

He turns his back to me and I'm about to retort something back about not being willing to wait until my hair grows long so he can rescue me, but then I notice he's right.

I am exhausted and I do need rest.

Without another word, I open the door and cross the threshold.

There are no skylights in the room, only the light of the moon and stars seeping in from the open window. A warm breeze scented by the ocean and unfamiliar flowers flutter the long drapes, the dark blue color the same as the silky sheets on the bed that's covered by a canopy veil of a nearly translucent fabric shimmering with thousands of tiny stars. Clad in various shades of blue, the room is larger than my room back at the Sun Palace, but that room was not really suited for a princess. This one certainly is.

The twinge of envy grows, squeezing my heart.

After checking every dark corner and the marble-tiled bathing room multiple times, I jump into the bed without a second thought, my body quickly succumbing to deep sleep.

It is only when I wake hours later I wish I didn't let myself sink into the soft mattress.

A musty smell tickles my nostrils and something cold is pressed against my cheek. The softness of the bed is gone, replaced with a hard surface that scrapes my skin.

"About time you woke up," a familiar voice spits, and I feel something sharp and cold on the bare skin of my back.

Terror slams into me, the fear so strong I'm struggling to breathe. I open my eyes and desperately wish I didn't.

A kinglight floats an arm's length away from my face, the only light in the darkness of the musty room seemingly carved from the mountain.

The Sun King drags the Royal Sword across my back, and I can't stop myself from hissing in pain.

I'm usually more prepared for this, my mind already long gone to distance myself.

The sword continues across my back, cutting again and again, the king ignoring the small whimpers coming from my lips.

I've already lost count. Blood is trickling down my back, pouring from the newly opened scars. The pain blurs my vision, threatening to drag me into the darkness if I don't hold on to the scars in my palms hard enough.

He is not holding back.

"This is for not showing up to the last Trial of the Sun–"

The sword cuts a long line all the way from the top of my shoulder down to my lower back.

"This is for sneaking out of your carriage–"

Another slice next to the previous one.

"And this is for making a fool of yourself and our newly formed alliance," he practically growls as the sword makes three slices in one, pain erupting with each one.

"Riding a horse and leaving the procession with the enemy! You are nothing but a disgrace to your kingdom." The Sun King clicks his tongue in disgust, pressing the sharpened tip deeper into my back.

My nails dig into the scars in my palms so hard I'm convinced I've broken the skin and I bite down on my lip in order not to scream. Tears are welling in my eyes, threatening to break the promise I made to myself years ago.

Don't cry. Don't scream. It will only make it worse.

It is, after all, my fault he is this way. I was the one who took away his queen. Without me, she would still be by his side.

"I warned you many times, *Asteria*." Again, my name is the foulest insult he could think of as the sword continues traveling the map of scars marking my back.

"Why do you insist on defying my orders and humiliating the entire kingdom? I should have gotten rid of you years ago. Not even that precious Victor of yours would have missed you." He spits on the ground next to my head before pressing the tip of the blade so hard into my back I'm starting to see stars.

"It will not be long before Soria forgets about the pathetic princess. The temple will rise again. Who knows how long you will survive in the dark? " He sighs wistfully, as if my demise is his greatest dream. "It's too late for me to kill you now. But if you're still breathing when the games are done–" the blade grazes the bone of my shoulder and it feels as if he is tearing out a piece of my soul.

Gods, I wish he would just kill me now and end this torture.

"Do not think this will be my last chance at disciplining you, *Asteria*. As long as the Tournament is going, you are still mine," he snarls, cutting one last long line across my back before I hear him wipe the blade of the Royal Sword with his handkerchief.

The Sun King found a way to punish me in Luna and no one is going to stop him from doing it again.

I keep my head low as I hear him slip the sword into the sheath at his hip. And even if I wanted to look at him, I couldn't. The pain is keeping me glued in place, my blood staining the ground underneath me.

I learned a long time ago it's better to keep quiet and not move before he has left the room. Any small movement might provoke his anger–the king is a beast ready to pounce on its prey any second.

"Take a single step out of line and I will no longer bother negotiating with the Lunans and gladly revoke my bargain. As tempting as that may sound for you, remember this—" he yanks my head back until my eyes land on his glowering face, on his eyes that are nothing but liquid gold, "—you will wish you died that day in the ruins."

He drops his hold so abruptly my head slams against the stone floor. The tangy taste of blood fills my mouth and my vision blackens.

"Remember my warning, *Asteria*. I expect you to be on time and presentable for dinner. No more bleeding excuses." The kinglight flickers and disappears from my line of sight, the sound of the king's bootsteps growing more and more distant.

I'm left in nothing but darkness. All I feel is the blinding, all-consuming pain exploding through my body.

Is this how I die?

I don't know how much time passes before I'm able to move. It could be seconds, minutes, hours, years, centuries. The quiet darkness is all that exists.

My nails scrape against the stony ground as I crawl forward until I find a hole in the wall that has to be the doorway.

I can't see anything in the darkness and pain obscuring my vision, but it *feels* as if I'm in some kind of underground tunnel. From the lack of agonized sounds and screams, it's not a prison or a dungeon, but it might as well be with the king's cruel punishment burnt onto my back.

It wouldn't be the first time he locked me away.

The ground is wet against my skin, the blood running from my back making my hands and knees slip. It takes numerous attempts and falls before I manage to get on my feet. I lean against the wall, my body shivering in the cold darkness.

Please let me be alone down here. If someone or something finds me now—

Pressing my forehead against the wall, I force myself to take a few deep breaths in through my nose and out through my mouth.

I can do this. This is nothing I haven't endured before.

This is just another trial.

This is just another game.

Whatever it takes.

When my head has stopped spinning enough that I'm not afraid I'm going to pass out any second, I shove away from the wall, blocking the pain and fear, focusing on the goal of the trial.

I need to get out of here. I need to find a way to tend to my wounds. And I need to be ready for dinner. If there ever is a time to follow the king's orders, it's now.

I squint my eyes in the dark, trying to locate the way with a little less darkness, hoping it will lead me somewhere else than this suffocating tunnel-place.

Choosing the path to the left, my hands steadying me against the walls, I slowly walk forward until my feet bang against a stone step.

I start to crawl.

My fingers fumble on the steps, leaving handmarks of blood unseeable in the darkness. The rough stone scrapes against my skin. The fabric of my dress tangles my feet.

It takes everything in me to keep going and not tumble back down the steps.

Everything hurts.

Drip.

Drip.

Drip.

The sound of something dripping and my ragged breathing are the only sounds in the darkness.

There is nothing else. Only everlasting darkness.

I don't know how much longer I can take this.

My head bangs against the next step and a scream rises in my throat. I bite my lip so hard I taste blood. But I keep pushing forward.

Whatever it takes.

When I think I can no longer take this torture, I see a sliver of light in front of me. The stairs change from dirty stone to cleaner stone, the musty smell replaced with a faint herbal and flowery aroma.

A strangled breath of relief pushes through my clenched teeth.

I climb a little farther and the stone stairs start breaking off in different paths. I follow the pleasant scent and barge through an open doorway. The dress barely hangs onto my shoulders as I wobble forward, and blood drips from the open wounds on my back, staining the floor with splatters of crimson that seep into the stone.

Hallways lit with scattered skylights wind out in a labyrinth of corridors and stairwells.

Not again. If I have to survive another labyrinth without a map–

A strange sound snaps my attention and before I can stop myself, I walk around the corner toward the sound, praying to the gods I don't run into one of the princes.

A child no older than two years is playing with a bucket, his small hands splashing water onto the floor. A woman with copper hair braided to the side of her neck is hanging up sheets above him, wearing what I assume is the servants' uniform of Luna.

The child stretches his hands toward a dark sheet and the woman chuckles before redirecting him back to the bucket. "We don't want to get it dirty and wash it all over again. We never know if the prince receiving it might be your–" She slams her mouth shut when she notices me standing in the doorway, eyes widening in fear. Her gaze flickers to the boy before frantically darting around the room, as if she is debating hiding him underneath the dirty sheets lying in heaps on the floor.

"Mama?" The child looks at his mother before following her eyes.

That's when I notice it.

There is no mistaking it. Even in my groggy and wounded state, I know it without a doubt. Deep green eyes with traces of blue. Dark brown hair. Even the freckle above his brow is the same.

This is the son of Prince Axton, the prince favored to be the next king of Luna.

If no one finds out about this dangerous secret.

The woman has started to tremble. She picks up the boy and cradles him in her arms, pressing his face against her chest to keep him from looking at me.

I don't blame her. I probably look half-dead.

"You– Your Highness– P–please–"

I hold up a hand to silence her, wincing when the movement sends a jolt of pain to my shoulders. "I won't tell anyone if you help me. Believe me, I have some dangerous secrets of my own. I'll keep yours if you keep mine. Do we have a deal?"

Auren is the name of my first lady's-maid and the mother of Prince Axton's illegitimate child.

The servant leads me through the stone halls until we emerge in a kitchen where she hurriedly hands the child to an older lady, promising to be back to tuck him into bed as usual before she ushers me out of the kitchen.

We walk through hidden servants' halls to not let anyone see the bleeding princess, Auren steadying me when the pain becomes too much.

We don't speak of either of our secrets, the unspoken deal between us hanging in the air.

"I'm taking you to a healer and then–"

"No," I say through gritted teeth. "No healers. No one can know about this. I need to make myself presentable for the welcoming dinner."

Auren gives me a strange look but doesn't object to my orders. "Fine, but we need to do something with your back."

I don't have an objection to that. "As long as I'm ready in time."

We continue walking through the dark and narrow halls. There are a few skylights on the walls, but most of the time the small cracks in the walls and ceiling are the only sources of light.

I vaguely wonder if the Lunan people have eyes better suited for the dark, and whether my eyes would adjust after time.

"Stay here," Auren says when we enter a dusty room with sheets draped over the furniture. "I'll go find something for your back and something you can wear to dinner." She guides me onto a small couch where I collapse on my stomach, and at my stern look she adds, "I'll be quick, I promise."

I close my eyes against the waves of pain washing over me and only realize I must've passed out when something cold touches my back, jerking me awake.

"I'm sorry, Your Highness, but we don't have much time so I thought–"

"It's fine, just do it," I hiss, bracing myself against the sting. "And please just call me Asteria, we're way past niceties at this point, *Auren*."

"Your wish is my command, *Asteria*."

The fabric of the ruined dress sticks to my skin, and it takes a lot of wiggling and muttered curses to remove it. Auren washes the wounds with cold water that has me biting into the cushion in order not to scream. I can almost feel her growing list of questions, but she stays silent as she washes and bandages the wounds.

"Do you know where you're staying?"

"In a blue room in one of the towers."

Auren makes a contemplative sound. "I'll ask around and make sure your things are brought to it during the dinner. For now, you'll have to wear the dress I found." Her fingers halt. "Is that okay?"

"Please," I say with a strangled chuckle. "I don't know what you've heard about me, but I can assure you I'm not used to being treated like a princess so there is no reason for you to start now. We both have a stake in this."

"Fair enough," she mutters. "I've never been a lady's-maid."

"Then I won't treat you like one."

She chuckles and helps me to an upright position. Resting my head against the seat of the couch, she starts brushing my hair with a wet brush to untangle the unruly curls and wash away the dried blood.

"Is this something I may expect in the future?"

"Yes, but hopefully not."

She purses her lips for a moment, her fingers moving through the white strands. "I'm of course more than happy to do anything you want considering our... deal, but I have two conditions."

I raise my eyebrows, repressing the urge to remind her that she currently needs this deal more than I do. Of course, that won't be true for long.

"Aico, my son. I need to be there for him so I'm not going to recklessly risk my life for you. If that's something you expect, you need to tell me now so I can find a way to leave before you send the king after me. And, if you agree to my condition and we're really doing this, I need something more than your word that you won't tell anyone."

Her boldness surprises me, but considering I just asked her not to treat me like a princess, I can't blame her.

"What do you want?"

"You didn't answer my first question."

I give her a weak smile. "No, I'm going to be the one to recklessly risk my life, not you. I just need someone I can trust enough to help me do it."

Auren's eyes lock on the binding mark on my neck and understanding flashes in her eyes. "I see. It seems you have more secrets than how you got the scars on your back and why you don't want anyone to know."

"Yes."

She studies me for a moment before speaking. "That sort of secret may challenge my own, so yes, I'll do it."

I let out a relieved breath. "And your other condition?"

"I want silver. Or gold, it doesn't matter. I need as much as possible in case I need to leave the palace and bring Aico to safety."

"That won't be a problem."

"Good." She sighs in relief. "Then we have a deal."

I take her outstretched hand.

This is a deal I won't regret making.

Twenty minutes later, Auren leaves me in front of enormous iron doors with a crescent door handle. The guards in front of it barely glance at me and I half expect I have to shout a plea for the royals inside, but they haul the doors open and let me pass without further inspection.

Inside, there is a dining room that widens my eyes with awe. The walls are so high I have to tilt my head back to see the ceiling where an opening has been carved into the mountain to allow the full moon to light the room. Swirls of white light seep into the mountain, casting shadows onto the table that spans the entire length of the room. Dark flowers decorate the table where the dinner has already started. Not only are royals seated throughout the room, but Generals, High Lords and Ladies, and other people hungrily absorbing everything around them.

The sounds of chatter and scraping cutlery stop when I step over the threshold. The musicians stop playing and every eye in the room turns in my direction.

"You are late," Father says from his seat at one side of the table, the pleased look in his eyes giving me the impression that was exactly what he was aiming for. "And that is not very nice considering this is your first night in your new home."

I mutter my apologies and find the only available seat–across from Star, in the middle of Castor and Davina. My so-called ally only gives me a lazy once-over before he continues sipping his drink–a silver liquid reminding me of fallen stars.

The pain of my wounds only increases throughout the dinner, the liquor doing nothing to numb my senses. I'm served the usual red wine from Soria, and as Father raises a toast in my direction, I know he takes great delight in my pain. What he doesn't know is that it's not as bad as it could've been, thanks to Auren's help and the healing remedies she poured down my throat before we left the abandoned room. Without it, I would've been screaming on the floor by now.

At one point, Castor reaches behind me to rest his hand on my back, his fingers digging into the raw wounds. His touch sends a wave of pain through me so sharp it nearly makes me pass out. I can't help flinching at his touch, an action that only makes the prince press against me even harder.

"Still sore from the fall, princess?" Castor's breath is hot on my skin as he leans close to whisper in my ear, his fingers trailing over the bloody lines on my back.

I'm about to answer with a threat when Star clears his throat. "I see that you still can't take a hint, *little brother*."

Castor moves away to lean back in his chair, his hand still lingering on my back.

Star's gaze is locked on me, his hands balled into fists at the table. At my glance, he quickly moves his hands to his lap, a muscle ticking in his jaw.

"Save it for the games," Castor snarls with an icy glare across the table.

Star's lips curl slightly, a cruel smile playing at his lips. "I would if you had joined them. But you didn't, so here we are."

Castor raises his glass to his lips, fingers curled tightly around the stem. "We all have a place in this kingdom, although it has been rather crowded lately."

Star rolls his eyes. "Don't flatter yourself. It's not as if you're playing a rather important role at the moment and it's not as if you were unable to bind yourself. Your so-called duties came after." He raises his eyebrows in challenge, relishing in the anger radiating toward him.

"Careful, *Star*," Castor spits, "you've gained a lot of enemies over the years you didn't bother to make an appearance in the games, so I wouldn't scheme so loudly if I were you."

"Then it's a good thing you're not me."

Castor rolls his eyes before muttering another insult I can't hear over the roaring in my ears. Their sibling rivalries are doing little to distract me from the growing pain.

I didn't dare drink too much of the healing remedies in fear of it making me pass out during dinner, and what I did drink was hardly enough. It's going to run out soon.

The sound of a chair scraping against the floor snaps my attention back to the princes. Star rises from his seat with a smug look at Castor before turning his attention to me. "Why don't I escort you to your room, princess?"

A quick glance around the room and I notice the rest of the party has started to leave the table, some of them gathering in groups to continue their loud chatter and excessive drinking. Father is already moving in the direction of half a dozen important-looking people, his gaze nowhere near me.

With a heavy sigh, I heave myself out of my chair, briefly closing my eyes when the room starts spinning before me.

A hand lands on the small of my back, another on my arm as I'm dragged away from my sneering fiancé and the loud room.

"You really need to learn some manners," I say through gritted teeth. "Silence is not the same as consent."

He rolls his eyes but continues to escort me down the hallway. "Of course not. But seeing as you looked like you were either going to pass out or throw up all over the table–" Star shrugs, one of his fingers brushing away the hair sticking to my face. "And despite how much I would love to see you do the latter in Castor's lap–"

"Shouldn't you be in bed already? Isn't the first sign of light practically your bedtime?" My voice is tired and clipped even to my ears.

"As should you."

"And where do you think I'm going? Certainly not to Castor's bed."

"I would hope not," he practically growls, looking at me so intently I have the urge to run away. "Especially not when I've made sure you don't have to."

Yet.

"I'm not thanking you for that."

Silver flares in his eyes. "Fine, but at least let me show you the way back–

"That won't be necessary."

The pain in my back is so intense my vision is starting to blur again. My knees buckle as I take a step forward and Star grabs my waist to steady me.

A humorless chuckle escapes me. "I thought we established the fact that I would throw you off the horse if you kept touching me."

"Esra is not here right now and like I said, you look like you're about to pass out."

"And what if I am? That would be none of your business."

"It is when many people would be happy to find you passed out on the floor. I said I wanted you as my ally. I need you alive for that."

He is about to say something more when a shaky voice interrupts him. "There you are, Your Highness. I've been looking for you."

Auren is carrying a basket with clean towels and what looks like different bottles of soap and bath salts. When she notices Star beside me, she gives a quick curtsey, the basket expertly balanced on her hip.

Star glances at the servant before raising his eyebrows in my direction, his hand still wrapped around my waist. "I'm assuming I'm not the Highness in question."

"No, this is Auren, my lady's-maid."

"Really?" A hint of amusement creeps into his voice.

"Yes," I say, forcing myself to take a step away from him and his steadying arms. "And *she* will be escorting me to my chambers."

"How wonderful that someone who has been working at the Moon Palace for years can be your lady's-maid," Star says, the corners of his lips tugging upward.

I can't help thinking back to Skye's condescending words

when I found her wearing a Sorian servant's uniform. Her claim that royals don't recognize their workers is apparently not true for everyone.

"Because I appointed her. Do you object to it? Are you going to tattle to the kings?"

"No." His lips pull into a smirk. "I'm not."

"Good." Before he can suggest another bargain, I bid him goodnight and practically drag Auren along with me.

CHAPTER TWENTY-FOUR

There's only a slight ache throbbing on my back when I wake. My eyes snap open to dim light seeping in from the open window and a wave of relief washes over me.

I'm still in the bed in the blue room. Alone. Safe for now.

The stone floor is cold underneath my bare feet as I wobble to the open window. Far beneath, the royal city is slowly starting to wake up. People open barricades over the windows and doors in the shops and vendors, bakers shuffle past with steaming pastries on platters, and parents chase after their half-dressed children. A pink and orange hue casts an ethereal light over the rooftops and mountains, and in the distance, the sun is slowly starting its descent behind the vast ocean.

It's strange to witness life like this, and it once again strikes me how different the two kingdoms are from each other.

Light and dark. Two opposite sides of the sky. Two ways of life.

The door to the bedroom opens with a small creak and I turn around to see Auren striding into the room. "I see the potion worked."

Before I promptly fell asleep, she poured more liquid down my throat, the taste so strong I nearly threw it all up. But it worked so well I'm furious I didn't find anything like it sooner.

Auren doesn't wait for my answer. She strides across the room and through the door that leads to the adjoined bathing chamber. Seconds later, the sound of running water echoes through the wall.

I sit down on the edge of the bed, marveling at the lack of pain shooting through my body. After the king's harsher punishments, I can barely move the days after. "Can you get more of it?"

Auren emerges from the bathroom with furrowed brows. "Maybe, but you can't take it too often. And you don't want to know what's in it." She purses her lips and moves to the large armoire on the opposite side of the room. Beyond the silver tinted doors, there's a room filled with clothes—not a single garment from home, but a whole new wardrobe in the shades of Luna.

"As long as it works, I don't care what's in it," I say, ignoring the resurfacing memories of glittering poison.

She needs me alive. For now.

"There's a ball tonight," Auren says, browsing through sparkling gowns of unfamiliar fabrics.

The Lunan part of the Tournament has always been a mystery, far-fetched rumors my only source of information.

My sisters have accompanied Father many times, but all I've gotten in reply is that I would've known the answers if only I did as I was told.

As if the king would ever let me leave the kingdom without a binding bargain.

"The starting ball is one of the biggest events of the year," Auren continues, her fingers halting on deep blue fabric. "Of course, it's nothing like the final ball, but it's a magnificent night nonetheless. I'm sure the king plans on spectacularly introducing you. And as your *lady's-maid–*" she smirks at the word, "–it is my job to make sure you look the part." She holds out the dress for my approval, eyebrows raised in question.

The dress is a blue so dark it almost looks black, only the reflecting light bringing out the color and faint traces of silver that gleam like the stars reflected on the ocean waves outside. Sheer sleeves extend from a tight bodice with a plunging neckline that ends in a billowing skirt that would've been nearly translucent were it not for the layers of silky fabric flowing like waves to the floor.

"It's–" I snap my mouth shut and continue staring at the masterpiece dangling from her hands, unable to find the words to describe it.

"Shadow silk, one of the most exquisite fabrics in the entire kingdom. It's so rare I haven't seen it in ages. I wonder where it came from." Auren looks as transfixed as I feel, her fingers brushing over the shifting fabric. "So you'll wear it?"

I give her an incredulous look. "Of course I'll wear it. But I'll need some paint for my arms. My back is not the only place that has to be concealed–"

"Done." She carefully folds the dress, and as she closes the doors of the armoire, something catches my attention.

The braid on her neck flutters in the breeze from the window, revealing parts of her skin not covered by the fabric of the uniform. Thick dark scars mark her skin, the pattern haphazard and distorted. And in between them, so faint it would be impossible to see without the moonlight pouring in from the window, are traces of silver.

"You're a Victor–"

The dress slips from her hands, but she catches it before it hits the floor. Her eyes widen in terror and she sucks in a breath, her hands trembling slightly.

"I was, once." Her voice is barely a whisper. Pain flickers across her features, the far-away look in her eyes giving me the impression she is reliving something she is desperately trying to forget.

"The mark—"

Her eyes snap to mine and she lifts her chin. "I'm not saying anything more about it."

"But—"

"This is where I draw the line," she says, voice firm, sheer determination slipping into

every part of her being.

I could order her to answer me. I could demand her to tell me all her secrets.

But I won't.

My head dips into a nod. If anyone can understand what it's like to be surrounded by dangerous secrets and dark memories, it's the cursed princess.

"Your bath should be ready any second and I'll make sure the dress is ready for the ball. Is there something else you need before I go, *miss*?" Her eyes are pleading now, begging me to forget I saw another of her secrets and go back to the easy rhythm between us.

Heart hammering in my chest, I force a smile onto my face as I roll my eyes. "I need some fighting leathers. With a hood, preferably dark. And please don't steal some from the Royal Guard. I need you to be very discreet."

We may have a deal, but that doesn't mean I'm not going to remind her. Many of the servants in Soria are nothing but gossiping busybodies and that is one thing I don't expect to be different in Luna.

This time Auren is the one to roll her eyes. "Discretion is not a problem. Your needs are my duty," she says with a mock bow before walking out of the room.

The next two hours pass too slowly. I pace around, lean out of the window to study the city underneath, and leaf through a couple of books I find in the adjoined seating room while I soak in the large bathtub.

When Auren finally comes back, she hands me a wrapped package with a sidelong glance. "Dark fighting leathers with a hood. And something special. I figured it might be useful," she says with a shrug.

A dagger clatters to the floor. The silver blade gleams in the dim light and the black handle is carved with pictures of the night sky. It's smaller than the Victory Dagger and perfectly sized to slip underneath a sleeve.

It might not fill the void of Elio's Victory Dagger I left behind in Soria–I didn't want to risk losing it and figured it also served as a promise of my return–but it will undoubtedly be a cherished weapon in the games.

I blink in surprise, my heart swelling with gratitude. "It's–"

Auren looks at me expectantly, arms crossed in front of her chest. "You're welcome."

"Thank you."

Her arms fall to her thighs and she smiles. "Now, let's get you ready for the ball. I'm not taking no for an answer."

She raises her eyebrows and I snap my mouth shut. "Princess or not, this is your first time in Luna and who knows how you would've showed up to one of the kingdom's most important events without me."

It seems I have more to learn from my unexpected lady's-maid.

"Remind me when the next trial is. The count of days is a little lost to me at the moment," I say as Auren smoothes the skirt of my dress with her hands. The shadow silk feels amazing against my skin. It clings to every curve and dip in my body as if the dress was crafted for me and no one else.

"At the break of dawn the day after the ball." She adjusts the sheer sleeve of my left arm, making sure the silver paint is still covering the dark mark she painted without comment. "And it has to be completed before the sun rises and the darkness disappears, the opposite of the Sorian games."

A contemplative sound leaves my lips and Auren ties half of my hair back with a silver crescent clip before fastening small glittering stars throughout the lengths.

When I suggested dusting my hair with silver when she painted the marks on my skin, she only gave me a strange look. "You should stop hiding your beauty. It's hard to appreciate the colors of the world when you've spent all your life surrounded by gold. Your hair looks stunning combined with the Lunan colors and the dark shades make your eyes even more radiant."

Now, placed in front of the large ornate mirror in my room, I see it.

It terrifies me how much it looks like I belong here.

Auren places a silver diadem in my hair, her eyes shining with something I can't understand. "You look like a queen of the night."

Something tightens in my chest.

"I doubt Castor will ever be king," I say with a snort and twirl the large amethyst ring on my finger.

"That doesn't mean you're not going to be a queen someday." She adjusts the diadem and pulls out a few strands of hair to frame my face, her lips pursing into a thin line.

My heartbeat quickens at her words–the reminder of what I'm truly fighting for.

Auren steps away to study me, walking a circle around me to make sure every little detail is as she planned. "There. All ready for the next fight. And–" she gives me a knowing smile and pulls a bag of fabric out from the pocket of her dress, "I'm going to leave this somewhere safe for you to change, and then I'll retrieve it and put it all back as if nothing ever happened."

A smile pulls at my lips.

I knew this was a deal I wouldn't regret making.

We walk down the stairs of the tower, through silver and black corridors, Auren assuring me she's going to show me the servants' halls later before telling me to just stick to the shadows when I sneak back after the fifth trial.

If I survive it.

To my great dismay, there is going to be a private gathering reserved for the most important guests before the starting ball.

A deck is carved into the palace mountain high above the royal city, and a table with an assortment of drinks has been brought out underneath the starry sky. There are no railings or boulders around the ledge and it's too crowded even with the low number of people.

Gods, I hope Castor doesn't try to push me off.

Auren lingers in the doorway for only a second and I can't help glancing at Axton. The servant ignores the prince, but Axton's forest eyes briefly look her way.

If I didn't know about their shared history, I'm sure I would've missed it.

Star is leaning against the side of the mountain, his dark suit blending into the shadows of the night, the silver liquid in his glass sparkling in the moonlight. There's a hard expression on his face, but when his gaze lands on me, a delighted smile spreads on his lips, his midnight eyes practically devouring me.

Heat flares in my chest and I bury my nails in the scars of my palms to keep steady through the waves of memories washing over me. The last time we were together at a ball and the feel of his lips on my skin–

"A princess of the sun transformed into a bride of the moon," the Moon King croons, replacing the heated memories with cold dread. "What a pleasure to finally have a woman among us." He sips his large silver goblet, his eyes pausing on my dress.

One of the princes I don't remember the name of snorts. "Let's see how long it will last."

"Hopefully not long enough to tie us together," Castor mutters, his voice so low the Sorians are unable to hear him.

"We'll see. As long as the sun is still gilding your sky, there is still time left to burn you alive," I mutter back. Raising my glass to my lips, I let my eyes wander to Elio standing next to Solina on the other side of the deck, ignoring Castor's scowling threats.

The Victor doesn't meet my eyes but the grip on his glass tightens, his knuckles going white.

The Moon King's low chuckle snaps my attention back and sends a shiver down my spine. "What exciting games all of us are playing. I expect we will toast to another silver victory tomorrow, *Star*. Or perhaps one of my other princes will finally catch up?"

The princes grumble low replies, but it's another voice that holds all the attention.

"We will see which color the sky glimmers when the head of the beast falls." Elio takes a step forward, his gaze flickering to mine so fast I'm not sure if I only imagined it.

The Moon King's black eyes move to the Victor, and my heartbeat stutters when a faint smoke emanates from his lips. The king's eyebrows raise slightly, his eyes studying Elio for a brief moment before his head tilts to murmur something to Axton.

I let out a relieved breath.

"Did you know Luna has a whole lot of beasts that haven't

been seen in Soria in centuries or never at all?" Elio continues, raising his glass to his lips.

It seems he's just throwing the question into the air to see who will bite, but I know he's talking to me from the way he is slightly angled in my direction, his other hand scratching the victory rune at his neck.

"If you're worried about the security at the palace, *Victor*," a prince I haven't been introduced to says, "I can assure you that you have nothing to worry about. You're in Luna now. I'm not sure how you do things over there under the sun but–"

"Good," Elio mutters through gritted teeth. "I suggest going for the artery behind the left ear if it has a purple sheen to its flesh, and a stab in the throat is a good choice for the scaled ones whereas the winged beasts usually need a snap before–"

The unknown prince waves a hand. "None of us are in a mood to listen to so-called advice from a Victor who didn't even win a Moon Trial before he cheated his way through the finale."

Glass shatters on the mountain, some of the shards falling to the ground far below. Blood drips from Elio's fingers and a murderous gleam flares in his eyes as he takes a step toward the prince.

The prince moves to meet Elio halfway but a hand shoots from the shadows and yanks him back.

"Save it for the battleground," Star growls, slamming his brother against the wall of the mountain without so much as a glance. "After all, going for the heart is always the best choice. No matter the beast."

A delighted laugh resounds from the Moon King's throat and he raises his glass in a toast, glaring until all his princes do the same. "Cheers to bloody games and vengeful gods."

"Go for the heart," Star mutters again, his gaze briefly flickering in my direction. "No matter the beast."

THE STARTING ball in Luna is held in an enormous ballroom at the lowest level of the palace, the room taken out of the sweetest dream, momentarily relinquishing the Moon Palace's claim to be carved from the deadliest nightmares.

The ballroom bleeds into the dark night, and if I didn't feel the summer breeze blowing from the garden blooming with glowing flowers, it would be hard to distinguish where the true night begins. Thousands of skylights gleam above, the high ceiling a mirror image of the night sky.

At the start of the ball, the Moon King's booming voice announces the new union and bargain between the two kingdoms of the sky with a tiny fraction of his magic. Shadowy figures glide across the floor with swift movements, gesturing for me and Castor to start the dance floor.

For a moment, the crowded room is deathly quiet. Castor takes me into his cold and stiff embrace, and I try to ignore all the inquisitive eyes around us. Then eerie music breaks out in the room, the tones unlike anything I've heard before.

"Try to keep up," Castor snarls in my ear before leading me into the unfamiliar dance, his movements effortless and practiced as he follows the music.

I stumble for too long before finally getting into the rhythm, hating every second I'm forced to be the center of attention. Mocking snickers and condescending words reach my ears, the eyes of the crowd burning my skin. I try not to look at their faces, my eyes studying their attire instead.

Luna's fashion is so different from what I expected and I thank the gods for Auren.

There are no spikes, claws, or teeth sticking out from the

ornate gowns and not every garment is black. There are mostly dark shades of color, but the fabric seems crafted for the light of the night. When the fabric shifts from the movements of the dance, it reveals hints of bright color visible even in the dark night. Some of the clothing looks as if it is taken straight out of a battleground, the wearer ready to battle whatever comes for them, but most of it is so marvelous and elegant that I can do nothing but stare in awe.

The rest of the party joins the dance and a blur of colors swirls through the room, the cursed princess and murderous prince suddenly only two of many dancing guests of a wondrous ball.

"Which court are you from?" The question leaves my lips before I'm able to stop it.

Castor's dark eyes snap to mine, his lips curling into a sneer. "That's not really any of your business, is it?"

"It is if this alliance is going to work," I snarl back. "Or do you want me to tell my people you're from the beast fields?"

"Your people?" He snorts. "Since when have Soria ever claimed you as theirs?"

I'm unfazed by his words. "I could say the same for you. I'm not the only source of rumors. You wouldn't believe the things I've already heard about you." He swings me away from his chest and I force a smile onto my face that quickly disappears when his dark gaze is back on me.

"Consider this a warning, *princess*. Stick to your room. Because out here and out there–" he leans forward to whisper in my ear, his fingers digging into my waist, "you're nothing but a prize anyone would love to claim."

He releases me enough to place his face right in front of mine. "And if I happen to find a lonely princess wandering around in the dark–I certainly won't claim you as mine. There's nothing more I would love than to see a dagger in your heart and your gilded blood pour from your veins."

The pressure from his hands increases so much that I'm certain he is leaving a mark on my skin. "You're in my territory now. Go ahead and taunt the darkness. It has already started to seep into your soul. The gods know how long it will take before all your light is gone and there is nothing left of the high and mighty little princess who can't even climb a fucking mountain."

The music fades into another song and Castor drops me so abruptly I nearly tumble to the floor. He dips his head with a cruel smirk on his lips and walks away without another word, his threats lingering in the air.

I move away from the dance floor until my back hits the wall of a secluded corner. My hands are balled into fists at my side, fury sparks at my fingertips and it feels as if my heart is going to break out of my skin.

Focusing on my breathing does nothing to soothe the raging storm inside me or dim the urge to murder my betrothed, so I let my gaze wander over the enemies, imagining all the ways I'll beat them in the next trial.

The magic of the Tournament drags my attention to the princes with binding marks gleaming on their necks and I can't help wondering if they bound themselves willingly or if it's another of the Moon King's games.

Some of the princes are so far away it's hard to tell if their marks are fresh or old, but there are at least four other princes besides Star who are competing this year. They all look like brutal warriors who have done nothing else than prepare for the games their entire lives.

Identical twins with long blonde braids lean against a wall with crossed arms, hungrily studying a drunken Sorian warrior.

A prince with bluish hair in a silver suit nibbles at a

woman's neck, a dagger gleaming from the pocket on his chest, another prince with coppery skin tangling his fingers in her hair.

The prince with long chestnut hair has two warriors pinned against the wall, his strikes concealed by flickering shadows.

And then there's the one with short hair a mixture of brown and black and striking eyes of cyan blue that somehow seem a little *warmer*. His eyes are crinkled from the slight smile on his face and his posture is so relaxed it's a wonder there's a binding mark on his neck.

A nice little trick to lure his enemies straight into his arms.

His smile widens when he notices my gaze and he strides across the dance floor until he's standing close enough to extend his arm in invitation. "Will you do me the honor of this dance, Princess Asteria?"

Unlike his brothers, the prince waits for my reply, his eyebrows raised in question.

It would be unwise to refuse him in front of all the prying eyes, something I'm sure he's very aware of. Invitation or not, I don't have another other choice than to take his hand.

"Of course."

I let him guide me into the dance, his hands resting respectfully on my ribs, not too high and not too low.

"I'm sorry I haven't been able to introduce myself yet," he says as we maneuver through the crowded room, the slow melody absorbing us in its tunes. "My name is Cyan, Prince of the Moon, number twelve, gifted from the Court of Silver."

"Gifted?"

His eyes twinkle as another smile breaks across his lips, surprisingly not cruel or cunning like the other smiles I've been granted by the rest of the Lunan royalty. "Yes. Our kingdoms are as different as the two sides of the sky."

A disgruntled sound leaves my throat, the anger coursing through me rising in intensity.

Cyan chuckles. "Since you so graciously agreed to this dance, I would be more than happy to dive into your questions."

"That's unusually kind of you. And what would you want in return?"

He chuckles again, tipping his head back. "This dance will be more than enough."

For now.

"What do you mean by gifted?"

"Unlike you and your sisters, the Princes of the Moon don't share the same mother. We're all gifted to the king by women in the different courts originating from the most powerful bloodlines."

An unsettling feeling rocks through me.

Gifted.

"And you said you're from the Court of Silver?"

Cyan dips his chin into a subtle nod. "Yes. As Soria, Luna has five courts, one of them being the Moon Court, the royal court you're currently residing in."

"Tell me something I don't know," I sneer, my hold on his shoulders tightening.

Cyan is unbothered by my anger. "I don't mean to insult you, Asteria. Your... reputation... has followed you across the border, and to be completely honest, I didn't know if you had received the same education as your sisters."

Heat prickles my cheeks and the anger roars.

I've never gotten the same treatment as my sisters. The lessons from the tutors at the palace quickly vanished in favor of the king's punishments, and when I was banished to Light, the priestesses only preached their rituals and favored gods. Every skill I have is nothing but hard work.

"I'm sorry," Cyan mutters, a crease forming between his eyebrows.

"What are the names of the other courts?" I ask, ignoring his attempted manipulation.

Cyan seems grateful for the change in subject, the corners of his lips tugging upward again. "Moon, Silver, Night, Shadow, and NAD."

"NAD?"

A sheepish smile this time. "The Court of Nightmares and Dreams."

"Sun, Light, Verbena, Lavendula, Helianthus," I mutter, adding the names in Luna to the small pool of knowledge I have about the kingdom.

"Yes, your people are very fond of flowers."

I can't help rolling my eyes. "I guess so. Your names aren't any more impressive or creative. How many synonyms for darkness are really necessary?"

Cyan laughs, a light hearty sound like a bell ringing a celebratory tune. "You know, you're much more pleasant than your rumors make you out to be."

"Oh, but you've barely seen anything yet," I murmur, giving him a secretive smile.

"So you do disintegrate people into ash with your eyes?"

"Yes." I lower my head and look at him through my lashes. "And directly touching my skin will set you on fire."

He chuckles, leaning in a little closer. "That might actually be possible with your royal blood."

I blink at him. "What do you know about royal magic?"

The prince moves his gaze away from mine to sweep over the crowd around us. "It seems the dance is ending. How unfortunate."

"And I assume you want something in return for your

answers," I say through gritted teeth, all signs of peaceful and polite conversation evaporating into thin air.

"Stop working with Star." His words are rushed and clipped, as if he fears said prince will somehow hear him.

"I'm not working with anyone. I'm only here to be an observer of the games and a dutiful bride to your half-brother."

Cyan cocks his head to the side, revealing a binding mark identical to my own. "You don't need to lie to me, Asteria. I saw you. And I can only assume my brothers did too."

"I don't know what you think you saw," I mutter in a low voice, my nails digging into his shoulders, "but you saw wrong."

The prince rolls his eyes. "None of us may ever understand Star's mind, but I know he is up to something, and that something is usually something very bad. He has never helped anyone like he did you. I've seen him play the game plenty of times, and he is not usually so...cordial." His blue eyes bore into me so intently I'm tempted to look away.

"Like I said–I don't know what you're talking about. I don't know your brother and I'm definitely not *working* with him. I only met him during the first trial and then at these dreadful events." I shrug, willing my grip on his shoulders not to waver as I keep my gaze locked with his.

Cyan gives me an indignant look. "I know what you think of me, Asteria. I can see it in your eyes. I'm only another enemy prince scheming my way around, but I'm not like them."

My eyebrows raise and I purse my lips–a silent challenge to continue.

He sighs heavily. "I only wanted to warn you. It's up to you whether you believe me or not. Star is...different. And he is definitely not someone you should trust."

"I don't trust anyone, especially not any of *you*," I mutter, narrowing my eyes.

Cyan's eyes darken slightly. "Like I said, I only wanted to warn you. It's up to you whether you heed that warning or not. And when it comes to Star–you should be *very* careful. There is a reason the king never took another heir from the Shadow Court after him." The last note of the song ends and he gently releases me from his arms, folding himself into a bow before walking into the crowd.

I blink at his disappearing form, my mind racing with every new piece of knowledge I've gained tonight.

"May I have this dance, princess?"

A man clad in an elaborate blue and silver uniform with a hungry gleam in his eyes blocks my line of sight, his hand extended in the air as if he is only seconds away from grabbing my throat.

"No," I snarl, before quickly scolding my features into a polite mask when I remember the role I'm supposed to play. "My apologies. I'm afraid the princes have tired me already. I'll save you a dance at the next ball." I give him a sliver of a smile before walking away, dismissing his protests.

The prickling sensation of being watched slithers across my skin as I make my way out into the garden where I'm greeted by dark flowers tinted with every color of the rainbow, some of them glowing in the darkness, their sweet scent enveloping my senses.

Only a few people are moving around in the garden, the music from the ballroom spilling outside. The fresh air is a relief compared to the crowded room and I gulp down as much of it as I can, willing my raging heart to steady.

I don't find him, but I'm sure he is watching me from the shadows somewhere. A beast waiting to pounce, a prince yearning to ruin the princess.

I just need to figure out how to destroy him first.

CHAPTER TWENTY-FIVE

The Court of Nightmares and Dreams glimmers in the night, the land cast in silver by the haunting moon. Growls and screams from unknown beasts and warriors reverberate off the mountains and the trees rattle in the roaring wind. Weapons clash against each other, the steel clattering to the ground as warrior after warrior falls.

My eyes scan the ground underneath me, my head resting against the thick trunk of the tree I'm currently perched on. A branch snaps in the close distance, and I grip the long knife strapped to my thigh, thanking the gods for my lady's–maid.

The starting ball celebrations lasted the whole night and well into the morning hours, the palace still brimming with guests indulging in all sorts of activities when I woke up in the early afternoon to get ready for the leaving procession.

Auren barged into my room before I even had the time to come up with an escape plan, urging me to hurry as she handed me an assortment of weapons I strapped on with raised eyebrows. Instead of answering my questions, she pulled my hood up and led me out of the palace, ushering me into a carriage reserved for servants and baggage, promptly telling the people to stop staring and mind their own business.

If I didn't know better, I almost would've thought helping warriors sneak around unnoticed was a common occurrence for Auren. The servant easily maneuvered around the procession, guiding me to the back of the crowd in time for the Victor's words.

I didn't ask what it took to arrange it and she didn't tell me, the deal between us enough for me to trust that none of the kings would come snooping, how I would avoid the punishment that was sure to follow a problem for another time.

The court that my betrothed may be *gifted* from turned out to be one of the courts closest to the Moon Court, the location for the first Moon Trial only a few hours' journey from the palace. The Royal Dais was raised at the beginning of the thick forest, the shadows of the night clinging to the pale limestone to blend it into the dark night of Luna.

Ferocious growls reverberated from the treeline as Elio delivered practiced words that sent a shiver down my back, the Moon King's frame almost indiscernible from the darkness behind him, a silver crown of thorns glittering at his brow.

"As always, there are no rules in the Tournament of Day and Night but one; survive. May the best Victor win."

It wasn't until after his speech that I realized the Victor kept his promise. As if he could sense my fading hope and growing frustration, Elio found a way to help me by warning me about the trial to come even in the midst of the enemy kingdom.

Slay a beast and retrieve a bone before the sun rises. The fifth trial in the Tournament and the first game in Luna. A task that shouldn't be too difficult with the enormous herd of monstrous creatures that have been summoned to the woods in a court that is starting to live up to parts of its name.

Now, hidden between thick branches bursting with leaves, my fingers trace the bulging mark on my neck, the binding mark that is brimming with magic that lures the beasts to the warriors.

The bitter taste of disgust coats my tongue as I'm reminded of the mark rendering me unconscious during the last game.

I never want to feel that helpless again.

Jumping onto the next tree, I listen for the footsteps of the beast I've been trailing for the last hour, fear and excitement coiling in my stomach at the thought of what might be behind the heavy footsteps.

A slight rustle in a nearby tree snaps my attention and I grind my teeth together to not let out a scream of frustration.

If we weren't in the middle of a game of life and death, I might've laughed at the ridiculous sight of such a large warrior squatting in a tree like a squirrel.

I wave my arms with a glare, silently telling him to back off before I decide to hunt him instead of the beast.

The corners of Star's lips tug and he places a finger on his lips in a shushing motion, his eyes darting to a point behind me.

It feels as if my heart stops beating when I realize why he is signaling for silence. The air behind me shifts and a low growl reverberates through me.

Something silver glimmers from Star's hands and I fumble for my own weapon, determined to beat him to the win.

My hand closes around the handle of the knife and another growl sounds behind me, closer this time. The sound rattles the branch underneath me and a flock of birds scatter from a tree in the distance, screeching as they hurry away from the battleground of the forest.

Slowly, inch by inch, with my breath caught in my throat, I turn around.

What I see behind me has me biting my lip to keep myself from screaming.

This is the Court of Nightmares. And the beast is carved from the deadliest of them all.

It's as if the darkest shadows have come to life, as if the most terrifying and haunting parts of the darkness have been molded into something that shouldn't be alive, something that shouldn't exist beyond unfathomable nightmares.

The beast is the size of a small house—a house that would be considered large in any rural village in Soria—and as it moves, it tramples the trees back into the earth they came from. Sharp spikes jut from shiny flesh, the tips dripping with blood, and the sword-like teeth protruding from its large mouth carve lines in the ground as if the rock is nothing but soft butter.

This beast is nothing like the one I encountered in the labyrinth. That was an easy kill. This certainly isn't.

I look up at Star for a fraction of a second, but it's enough to see the hard look on his face and the slight shake of his head. *Don't.*

I smirk and tighten my grip on the knife. The sky will be golden tonight.

Star's dagger flies forward in a perfect arc and the blade bores into the part of the tree where my branch is connected.

The branch snaps.

I plummet through the air, my hands grasping the passing branches to try and ease the fall. They scrape the bare skin on my hands, the leaves fluttering around me in a blur of dark green. My body slams to the ground with a thud, my ribs taking the worst of the impact.

The beast's head snaps in my direction, shadows swirling around it as it takes a deliberate step forward. The sword-like teeth clang against each other as it opens its massive mouth, and in the empty sockets where its eyes should've been, familiar gilded honey blinks at me.

I'm wheezing for air, pressing a hand to my aching ribs, a few of them undoubtedly broken or at least fractured. Pain shoots through my body as I roll, desperately trying to put some distance between me and the nightmarish beast that is slowly prowling closer, circling its prey and enjoying the hunt.

What was it Elio said again? Go for the artery behind the left ear? Or was it the right ear? This beast doesn't seem to have a trace of purple but it's hard to tell in the dark.

It doesn't matter. I'm not going to hit any artery behind its head from where I'm lying on the ground, and the pain in my body will make it hard to move into the right position. The dagger previously strapped to my thigh is nowhere in sight, lost to the dark forest on my way down to the ground, the long knife in my hand gone with it, and I can't reach the shortsword on my back. I have nothing to defend myself with–

In my writhing panic, the silver dagger gifted by Auren slips from the leathery sleeve into the palm of my hand, the sharp blade prickling the tender scars.

I'm about to prepare to aim for the beast's heart when a shadow shoots through the air.

Star lands on the back of the beast, a sword shining in his hands. The beast growls and squirms to shake off its attacker, the large teeth moving from the ground and exploding through its head in an attempt to skewer the prince above.

The eyes that only moments ago were a mirror image of the Sun King's glowering stare, transform into silver eyes speckled with tiny dark spots, and misty shadows seep out of the jagged mouth.

A prince and beast of shadow battling in the darkness.

Unfazed by the thundering beast, Star stands steady and raises his sword. The silver blade gleams in the faint moonlight breaking through the thick canopy of trees, and with a glance in my direction, the prince of shadow pushes the sword down, right into the heart of the beast.

The beast's dying growl rattles my heart and the earth quakes when it slumps to the ground. Black liquid spurts from the sharp spikes and the same shadowy mist that only moments ago seeped from its mouth bursts from every part of its body, the smoke rising to the sky.

A frustrated scream breaks free of my throat, the pain in my ribs flaring in protest.

Vengeance erupts in my veins and fury sparks in my fingertips. I see red.

"You sabotaged me!"

Star jumps down from the beast, dragging his sword loose. "This is a competition, starlight. You shouldn't forget that." He wipes the dark liquid coating the blade on one of the spikes before sheathing it across his back.

"That was my beast—"

"Then you should've been faster. And we both know that beast came for me. You didn't have a chance against it."

Another frustrated scream leaves my throat as I try to get to my feet, the pain making my legs wobbly.

"You're trying to shake me off," I snarl, leaning against the trunk of the tree behind me. I may not look as threatening as I want, but the message is clear.

I'm done playing whatever this game is between us.

"Of course I am," he snarls back, taking a step forward. "Like I just said, this is a competition."

I let out a strangled chuckle. "You said you wanted me as an ally—"

"I changed my mind," he snaps. His chest is heaving and

there's a ferocity in his eyes that makes me hesitant to move. "You will die in the games without me. It's time you relinquish your participation and this trial is the best opportunity you'll get. All you have to do is fail and you'll be out of the Tournament, your life still intact."

The anger inside me roars as viciously as the dead beast between us. Magic crackles in the air, the invisible strings tugging so hard it feels as if my soul is going to be yanked out of my body. Every part of me screams to bury the dagger in his heart.

"I'm never giving up," I snarl, my body shaking with the built-up anger. "There is nothing more cowardly than failing a trial on purpose and besides, there are no guarantees my life would be mine if I did. That's the risk of the binding. I gave up my life the moment the ceremonial dagger pierced my skin–" I wince at the pain shooting through me and the fury that boils my blood.

After the last game in Soria, when he actually *saved* me by using our bargain–a fragile bond of trust formed between us, enough so that I've let myself forget who he really is.

I want you.

I'm never going to fall for his tricks again.

He is the enemy. He is the one standing in the way of my victory–

"Good luck completing the game in your condition," Star practically spits and unsheathes a dagger strapped to his thigh,

"This isn't over–"

"Unfortunately not." A heavy sigh leaves his lips as he squats to retrieve his victory bone.

"Haven't you been a Victor enough?" I struggle to stand upright. "What was it, five times?"

"Seven. But who's counting?" He gives me a bored look before he starts slaughtering the beast, the dagger cutting through the flesh on its chest.

When I don't answer, he looks up with raised eyebrows. "You really should get going if—"

"You just said you wanted me to fail," I snap, pushing away from the tree with a grunt.

Star shrugs and blood sprays around him as he tears at the flesh with his hands, probably aiming for the most impressive bone.

"This isn't over," I repeat, each step away leaden with pain, his whistling tune behind me only infuriating me further.

As much as I would love to kill him right now, I have to save my strength for the trial. I'm not losing the Tournament because of him. Later, I will find a way to end this once and for all.

Whatever it takes.

I can practically feel my aching ribs grinding as I maneuver through the battleground that is the forest, slipping in and out of the shadows to avoid encountering any bloodthirsty warriors.

There's so much noise around me I'm almost tempted to submerge my head in one of the crimson puddles on the ground. The echo of the booming crowd beyond the forest. The roaring wind blowing up a storm. Growls and screeches from countless beasts. Raging battles between warriors. Victory screams bleeding into the dying screams of others.

It's too much.

A fetid smell seeps from the ground and I press my arm over my nose to keep from gagging. Scattered remains of beasts and warriors litter the ground, the roots and moss splattered with their blood.

I will not be one of them.

I lean against the trunk of a tree to catch my breath and look up at the sky that's barely visible between the thick canopy of trees. A light blue has started to form cracks in the darkness, the first ray of sunlight perhaps only moments away. And as I watch, silver light flares across the sky, lighting up the darkness around me.

Another victory for Luna.

The anger blazes, pushing away the exhaustion, pain, and desperation numbing my senses.

I don't even want to consider if Luna's victory is because of *him*.

I push away from the tree, the rage dragging me forward.

The Tournament's magic yanks and tears at my soul, but no beasts come to find me. It's as if the gods heard the prince's demand for my failure and they are not happy.

The shadows of the forest are retracting, the darkness more gray than black. The sky lightens rapidly, the light shades of blue shoving away the dark to prepare for the presence of the sun.

Time is running out. Fast.

I run faster, biting my lip against the waves of pain threatening to drag me down.

I will not fail. I will not fail. I will not–

A screeching dark figure the size of a very large bat flies toward me, an arrow protruding from one of its wings. The wounded wing causes the beast to wobble through the air, the arrow dragging it toward the ground.

No. I'm not finishing what someone else started. I'm not stealing something I didn't earn. The small beast would probably be harder to catch if it weren't for the wounded wing, but it's nothing compared to my first target.

Whatever it takes, Asteria–

With a muttered curse aimed at the gods, I extend my hand and close my fingers around the bat-like creature's throat.

Glossy green eyes stare at me, a mouth the size of my hand snapping with thousands of tiny sharp teeth. Unlike a bat, its skin is a very dark green, so dark I easily mistook it for black in the darkness.

I shouldn't do this, but with the approaching sun and my aching body, I don't have much of a choice.

With another muttered curse to the gods, I snap its neck with my hands.

There's an old witch legend that wearing the bones of your kill will enhance your senses, gifting you with the victim's powers. That is what I think of as my dagger cuts through the small beast.

There is no honor or power in this. The witches would be mortified by my weakness.

It is a good thing I decided to wear a disguise for the rest of the Tournament because this is nothing but a disgrace to my ancestral warriors.

A sigh of relief escapes my lips when the dagger finally meets the thin bone on the outer rim of the wounded wing. I crack it off and stick it in the pocket of my leathers.

The confirming tingle in the binding mark comes a second later.

Another trial completed, but this time the win doesn't feel so good.

The first ray of sunlight hits the decaying corpse at my hands, shining light on the lone warrior princess who is barely a warrior anymore.

CHAPTER TWENTY-SIX

My footsteps are light and quiet as I move down the hallway outside my room, the magic wrapped around my soul telling me where I need to go.

Ignoring the fear that someone or something is watching me from the shadows, I carefully open the door, thanking the gods it glides open on silent hinges. Perhaps this will grant me some of their favor.

The room within is different from what I expected. It is sparse, as if the owner hardly spends any time in here besides a few hours sleeping. A sliver of sunlight breaks through the black curtains covering large windows, a breeze carrying the faint scent of the ocean fluttering the fabric. The high ceiling is painted as an exact replica of the starry sky, and a dark mist rises from the bed underneath where pale skin is peeking out from rumpled black sheets.

He looks peaceful asleep, so unlike the arrogant warrior and scheming prince I've come to know. He is lying as still as a statue, his lips slightly parted, his skin illuminated by the dim light. Some of the dark locks curl down to his forehead, and for a second, I'm tempted to sweep it away with my fingers.

I grit my teeth and move my gaze away from his face. The lower half of his body is concealed underneath the sheets, and my breath catches in my throat when my eyes land on his bare chest.

The skin is a map of scars much like the one on my back, some lines faint and shallow, others ragged and deep. And then there's the myriad of marks etched into his skin, some of them perhaps his victory runes.

Dark, all of them. Just like the mark on my arm.

The prince might possess secrets I desperately need, but the need to win the Tournament is stronger.

I'll do whatever it takes.

I'm about to reach for my dagger when suddenly, at a speed that shouldn't be possible, I'm pinned to the bed, the tip of my own dagger pressed against my throat. My heart leaps into my throat and I can do nothing but blink at him, willing myself not to glance at his very naked body.

Star leans down so close I can feel his breath on my face. "If you wanted to be restrained in my bed, you only had to ask, starlight," he purrs, pressing the tip of the dagger a little harder into my skin.

I snort, and the movement makes the dagger sink deeper into my skin, a drop of red running down my throat. "In your dreams, moon boy." Snatching the dagger from his hands, I roll over, flipping our position.

Star folds his hands under his head and looks up at me with an expectant look, amusement glimmering in his eyes. "So tying me up would be more to your liking? I have no objections to that."

I move the dagger to his throat. He is not taking me seriously, just like everyone else. The thought ignites an inferno of wrath inside me, my hands shaking with fury.

"Is that your last words, princeling?" I slice a shallow line across his throat and his blood stains the tip of the blade.

Star doesn't so much as flinch as he bares his teeth. "I can think of a few other good uses for my mouth." His tongue slides along his bottom lip, his gaze moving to my lips.

"I've had your mouth on me on more than one occasion and I can't say I was very impressed."

"You sweet little liar."

With a frustrated scream, I raise the dagger above his heart.

This ends now–

The dagger flies away with a slap of his hand, and I am once again pinned underneath him.

Star smirks as I struggle against his hold. His hands are wrapped around my wrists, pinning my hands to the mattress above my head, and his body is pressed against mine. His *naked* body.

"You're not trying to kill me, are you, starlight?"

"Don't call me that," I growl, slamming my knee into his favorite body part.

He lets out a small hiss but his grip on me doesn't budge. "That's not very nice, princess. Now tell me, is this your master plan? Kill the princes one by one?" He snorts and I glare at him.

"Yes. And I'm starting with you." I slam my head against his, ignoring the pain as I finally manage to wriggle free and tumble to the floor.

He chuckles, the sound unnerving in the quiet room. Blood drips from his nose, staining the silky sheets on the bed, and a wicked smile spreads on his lips. "I guess I can let you try."

Giving him the most feral grin I have, my foot swings out to tackle him to the floor.

Star grabs my foot, yanking so hard it takes every part of my strength to keep my balance. My nails claw at his arm and he pushes me away, my back slamming against the wall.

He prowls closer and I punch him in the chest, on the place where his black heart is beating underneath his scarred skin. Pain shoots up my arm and I curse, ducking when he moves to strike me back.

"Was all our training for nothing?" he says, catching my fist in his palm when I try to punch his face. "If you really wanted to kill me, I should've been dead by now. Is this how you plan to defend yourself when the first person jumps at you from the shadows?" He twists my arm before releasing his hold and I fall back against the wall.

Star tilts his head to the side and opens his arms wide, daring me to glance lower than his chest.

I keep my gaze locked on his face, my mind churning and chest heaving.

This is just like every time we trained together on the journey from Soria when he got bored and decided to taunt and tease me instead of fighting back.

"Everything would have been so much easier if you'd only taken my last advice."

Fury sparks in my fingers, the flames licking up my arms. The string around my heart tugs and I run forward, straight into his awaiting arms.

My hands wrap around his throat, but before I get the chance to squeeze the life out of him, he yanks my arms away and pulls me to his chest, my hands trapped between us.

"Cute, but you need to learn a few more tricks if you plan on taking out the other princes before I beat you to it."

"What?"

The wicked smile is back on his lips, and the words he

whispers in my ear send shivers all over my body. "Let's make another bargain."

He abruptly releases me and starts pacing around the room, one hand tapping his bloody chin, seemingly unfazed by his lack of clothing. "We both want the same thing. So let's have some fun."

"You want to kill your brothers?" My mouth falls open and I rack my brain trying to remember if I heard him correctly.

He halts pacing long enough to give me an exasperated look. "They're not really my brothers, and even if they were, we do things a little differently in this kingdom, you should know that by now." He waves a hand dismissively and continues pacing.

"You tried to sabotage my last trial. I will never bargain with you. And especially not after the last one you tricked me into," I snarl, glancing at the discarded dagger on the floor between us.

"Didn't our last bargain allow you to continue in the Tournament?"

"You tricked me–"

Star stops pacing and his dark gaze bores into me. "You've already made bargains you shouldn't have made so quit your whining."

The hidden mark on my arm tingles as if it can hear the words spoken about it.

"I don't know what you're talking about," I say, crossing my arms.

It has been long since he has hinted about knowing my secret. He can't possibly know–

He's in front of me in an instant, even faster than he unexpectedly pinned me to his bed. "I'm sure you don't." His fingers trail along the binding mark on my neck.

"Oh that–"

"Yes, that," he mutters through gritted teeth, fingers still lingering on my skin as his eyes darken even further.

"I'm not the only one who has made bargains," I snap, pushing his hand away. "Don't think I haven't noticed that you always seem to know what's going to happen in the Tournament—"

"Make a bargain with me and I'll spill some of my secrets, starlight."

"Never," I snarl, racing forward for the discarded dagger on the floor.

Star snatches the dagger before I even have the chance to dive for it. He twirls it in his hands, the sharpened tip barely missing his skin. "I don't think so, princess. None of us are dying today."

I let out a frustrated scream and dart forward, tackling him to the floor. With my thighs around his chest to keep him on the floor, I extend my arm to finally wipe the arrogant smirk off his face, but his hand effortlessly blocks me, his fingers closing around my wrist.

"Make a bargain with me." Blood is still running down his face and he leans forward to wipe it on the fabric of my shirt, staining the white a deep crimson.

"Never." I swing my other arm, barely missing his chin as he catches me with his other hand, the dagger clattering to the floor.

He holds my hands against his chest, his fingers like shackles around my wrists. I'm about to lean forward and tear his heart out with my teeth when something catches my attention.

One of the dark marks covering his body gleams in the flickering darkness. On his arm, at the exact same spot as the one hidden on my arm, one of the marks stand out from the others, the swirls and lines a little darker and less scarred. Where mine is alone, his mark is accompanied by numerous others that bleed into each other, but the brighter mark looks suspiciously similar to mine.

My heart stutters and air leaves my lungs in a rush. It can't be–

Has he used the same spell as me, borrowing the life essence of another? And if he has, did he pay the price I'm horrified to pay, the cost of which is still unknown? Can he tell me why the mark didn't disappear along with the magic?

If it's the same mark, it changes everything–

Momentarily caught off guard by the mark, I'm not able to stop him when he flips us around and pins my arms to my sides against the floor.

Silver flares in his eyes and a muscle ticks in his throat. "Make a bargain with me."

His growling order is only a faint sound among the roaring in my ears and beating of my heart. "What is that mark?"

Silver flares again and his eyes narrow. "Make a bargain with me and I might tell you."

"No."

"Why do you always have to be so stubborn?"

"You don't know me–"

"Oh, starlight, I know you better than you think."

"You're wrong." I struggle against his hold on me, but it's like trying to move an ancient mountain. Impossible.

"Make a bargain with me," he repeats, leaning down and resting his face in the crook between my throat and shoulder. An involuntary shiver runs through me at the contact, another kind of fire igniting in my body.

"Why?" I hate how breathless my voice sounds, and the way I shiver at every puff of his breath on my skin.

"Why not? We both want the same thing. It will only make it easier."

"And why would you want your brothers dead?"

He is silent for a moment, his lips grazing my skin. "I want the princes gone so I can take the throne, of course."

I suck in a breath at his words. "And the king? It doesn't seem like he's going to step down any time soon–"

His lips nibble at the sensitive skin on my neck, each touch sending a scorching flame through my body. "I'm saving him for last."

"And you think that's what I want? To help you become king?"

"Not particularly, no. But you want to be queen. And I can make that happen."

I feel his arrogant smirk against my skin and a dry chuckle escapes me. "No thanks. I'm going to be the Queen of the Sun, not this dark place. And if you think I'm stupid enough to believe that you wouldn't get rid of me the second you were crowned king–"

His teeth bite down on my skin, hard enough to cause a small jolt of pain before his tongue licks over the same spot. "Fine, I'll help you win the Tournament so you can be the next Victor and prove yourself to those boring sunflowers."

"You tried to sabotage me–"

He lets out a heavy sigh that tingles my skin before he moves his head to look me in the eyes. "And before that, I helped you. Numerous times. And even when I didn't explicitly help you, I nudged you in the right direction."

"You almost killed me–"

He rolls his eyes with a snort. "Believe me, princess, if I wanted you dead, you would be nothing but ashes right now. Your death would be a minor inconvenience, that's all."

"A minor inconvenience–" a string of curses leaves my lips as I desperately wriggle against his hold.

Star tilts his head to the side, his eyes glittering with untold secrets. "Do you pray with that mouth?"

I curse him a little more, fighting a little harder.

He rolls his eyes and lowers his head, his tongue licking across the column of my throat before moving to the side of my neck.

Heat coils low in my stomach and when he presses his body a little harder against mine, need and desire explode in every part of my being.

The next yank of my arms is for an entirely different reason.

Star smiles against my skin, and the fingers wrapped around my wrists ease their grip to stroke the sliver of bare skin between my shirt and pants.

My fingers dig into his shoulder to pull him closer, marveling at the feel of every hard ridge in his body pressed against the soft parts of mine. I glide my fingers along his back, feeling the jagged lines of countless scars, and he leaves a trail of smoldering kisses from my jaw to my collarbone, his fingers inching higher on my stomach.

A groan reverberates against my skin, the sound fueling the inferno of flames inside me. His teeth nibble at the bottom of my ear and I shiver, a moan working its way up my throat. His lips move to the side of my face, my chin, my jaw, my cheek, halting right in front of my lips.

"Do we have a deal?" His lips graze mine, the sensation only a hint of the pleasure my body desperately needs.

"What?" His heady scent is so intoxicating I can't think straight, and there is nothing else than the feel of his skin against mine–

"Let's seal the bargain." His lips are pressed against mine now, but he doesn't move, waiting.

"Hmm?"

He smiles against my lips, one hand coming up to tangle in my hair, the other cradling my neck to pull me closer—

A crash sounds outside the door and some of the lust clouding my senses slips away. Something is tugging at the edge of my mind, but Star whispers my name against my lips, drawing my attention away from the thoughts that are just out of reach.

It doesn't matter anyway. All that matters is releasing the tension in my body by finally giving in to the desire—

The door flies open with a loud bang and a guard stumbles into the room, freezing when his eyes land on the entwined royals on the floor.

The need disappears as quickly as it came.

I push away from the prince, ignoring his disgruntled sounds, forcing myself not to look at the chiseled bare skin that almost tricked me. Again.

I curse myself this time. For being so reckless and allowing him to almost seduce me into a bargain that could very well claim my life. It horrifies me how easily he slips past my defenses.

"I will never make another bargain with you," I snarl as I get to my feet. "I would rather burn myself alive than make a deal with you—"

"Fine," he growls, picking up the dagger and pushing away from the floor. "But when you come running back and want the bargain because you realized you actually need me—there's going to be an even higher price to pay."

"I won't come running."

A vicious smile spreads across his lips, the silver in his eyes vanishing as his eyes darken to a starless sky. "We'll see about that, princess. And next time, wake me up wearing something more interesting, or preferably, nothing at all." He crosses his arms over his chest with a wink that makes me see red.

"I'll find another way to kill you that doesn't involve getting in your bed," I snap, striding across the room to the open doorway where the guard is trembling with fear, his gaze darting between us and the hallway behind him.

"Then maybe I'll have to sneak into yours."

I slam the door shut, his laughter echoing through the halls before a terrified scream renders the air.

CHAPTER TWENTY-SEVEN

The streets of Nyx are bustling with activity despite the afternoon sun and I wonder if the royal city ever sleeps during the Tournament Times.

The city carved from darkness and starry skies is surprisingly glorious in the sunlight, the lack of dark days doing nothing to subdue its beauty. The shadows from the towering mountains bleed into the city, and where the streets and buildings are lit up by the sunlight, the silver details sparkle like the missing stars.

I pass a crowded outdoor eating area and I avert my gaze to the ground, pulling on the dark scarf concealing my hair to make sure no strands of white have sprung free to reveal the new and only Moon Princess.

My face, neck, and hands are painted with silver, and I'm wearing a simple shirt and pants in an attempt to conceal myself from prying eyes, Hopefully, no one will recognize me this far away from Moria, but riding into the city pressed against one of their Victors and princes probably wasn't the best idea.

An invisible string tugs me in the direction of a darkened alley and I spot a dark-cloaked figure hurrying along on silent feet. A sudden urge to follow overwhelms me–a sign from the gods or the Tournament's magic urging me to get rid of some competition–and that's exactly what I do.

We move farther and farther away from the bustling city center, the sounds growing more and more distant as we emerge in the outskirts of the city where the smaller and more ragged houses make Nyx look more like an average village than a royal city. Mountains surround us on all sides, the vast ocean or thick forest peeking through the occasional gaps. Behind us, the Moon Palace looks down from the highest peak, a gray mist obscuring everything but its silver spires that are blinding in the sunlight.

The dark-cloaked figure moves toward a tattered house tucked into the mountainside. The figure disappears around the corner and I race forward to see them run down stairs that are missing large chunks of stone before slipping into a well-concealed hatchet in the wall.

I hesitate at the top of the stairs, my mind racing and heart hammering, some unseeable unknown force telling me this is exactly where I need to be even though I have no idea why.

"Are you going in or not?" A deep voice says behind me, annoyance laying every word. A man in dark fighting leathers accentuated with gold is standing behind me, an indignant look on his face.

"Of course," I say, willing my voice to be steady as I straighten my posture and lift my chin, praying he doesn't recognize me.

"Well, come on then. I don't want to miss this meeting." The man lets out an exasperated sound as he impatiently taps his fingers on his thighs.

This is just another game.

The words ring through my mind as I walk down the stairs with sure steps, the curiosity bubbling within me overshadowing the fear.

There is no handle in the concealed door, but there's a hole large enough to place my hand and tear it open. Skylights flicker in a long narrow passageway that seems to lead into the very mountain.

The man behind me sighs and I step into the darkness.

The tunnel breaks out in different directions, but I walk straight ahead, following the sounds of a crowd that grows louder the deeper into the mountain I get. And from the lack of protest behind me, I must be going the right way.

After a few minutes, the tunnel expands into a large cave lit up by numerous floating skylights. Benches, tables, and chairs are scattered throughout the cave, and barrels and boxes filled with various items are stacked along the walls. An assortment of weapons gleam in the dim light and heaps of coins sparkle when a skylight floats by.

Crowds of people are cramped into the cave, some seated at the benches around the tables, some slumped on the rocky ground, and others leaning against the walls.

There are so many different people it's easy to slip in and find a place in the shadows against the wall.

No one bothers acknowledging me so no one recognizes the princess among them. I'm just one of many blending into the crowd, insignificant and anonymous.

A dark-cloaked figure steps onto the table in the middle of the cave. He holds up a hand and the crowd falls silent, and then he pulls down his hood to reveal a wicked smile on his scarred face.

Thunder.

The man drinking with Skye at the tavern in Moria. The man who disappeared and came back with a bloody hand seconds before chaos broke out. A general in Luna's Royal Guard.

This is dangerous. I shouldn't be here.

I glance back to the entrance, but the cave is so packed with people it would be impossible to leave unnoticed.

The princess of the enemy kingdom can't be seen here.

My eyes search the faces, but there are too many. The gods know who may be waiting for the perfect opportunity to kill me.

I can't leave. I'm trapped.

"Where there is light there is darkness, and where there is darkness there is light." Thunder's deep voice rumbles through the cave, the crowd instantly echoing the words, and the sound of their combined voices is so loud it feels as if the mountain is shaking.

The words remind me of the priestesses' chanted prayers before I fell through the temple roof and the witches' murmurings before I permanently marked myself with dark magic, but these words are forbidden and secret and should not be uttered underneath the open sky.

A shiver runs down my back and dread coils in my stomach.

"Rowan." Thunder waves a hand to someone in the crowd and discards his long cloak before sitting down on the table and leaning back on his arms.

He is wearing simple black pants and a black shirt rolled up to his shoulders, revealing chiseled skin that's more scarred than not, his scars seemingly trophies he's proud to show off, each line a reminder of something he doesn't want to forget.

A man in a black soldier's uniform steps forward. "The fifth game took out about 226 warriors, 56 injuries that will likely result in death sooner or later, and 43 minor injuries to the ones that are now out of the competition. Then there's the 36 that lost because of sabotage or lack of game or–"

Thunder waves a hand, gritting his teeth so hard it's a wonder they don't break. "And our own?"

Rowan swallows, his gaze locked on the ground. "72 last night, and 36 the previous at the—"

Thunder waves his hand again, eyes locked on the ceiling as if he's trying to glimpse the sky through the cave so he can properly pray to the gods. "They will not be happy to hear this."

Rowan swallows again and fear flickers across his features before he regains his composure and transforms back to a loyal soldier ready to serve however is giving the orders.

Thunder nods curtly and Rowan steps back, the soldier replaced by a woman also wearing a uniform. She lists a lot of things that don't make any sense to me. Names of places I've never heard of, names of people dead and alive, costs and assets, and other information I don't understand but that seems to mean a lot to the people around me.

"And then there's the upcoming royal wedding—"

The low chatter of the crowd halts and my heart leaps into my throat.

"Yes, what's the latest news regarding the alleged attempt at a union? As if that's not what we've been working for this whole time." Thunder snorts and leans forward with his elbows on his thighs.

The guard retreats into the crowd and a servant steps forward. "The wedding will be rushed to take place any day now. Most likely right after the next game, or maybe even before, depending on the actions of the princess."

A skylight drifts by, lighting up her face when she lowers her hood. Her copper braid gleams in the dim light and a small smile plays at her lips.

Auren.

A jolt rocks through my body, my heart hammering so hard I'm afraid it's going to explode out of my chest at any moment.

This isn't happening. It can't be—

Not even a royal wedding is important enough to overshadow the Tournament. It would be a disgrace to the gods to arrange one in the middle of the games.

This can't be happening. I was supposed to make sure it didn't happen when I was crowned Victor. The next game is only days away.

And Auren–It seems I have to renegotiate the terms of our deal.

Thunder frowns and taps a finger on his scarred chin–a finger that is missing a large piece at the top, as if a beast has taken a bite out of it. "That changes things, yes. Can we hope the princess will take care of it on her own?"

Auren looks momentarily uncertain, and in that moment I see why she is a good spy for whatever this is. Now, she looks like one of many servants, submissive and obedient, leaving no trace of the strong-willed mother and Victor hiding the child of a prince.

Thunder raises his eyebrows. "There can't be a wedding without a groom." The corners of his lips tug upward and he angles his head in my direction as if he is personally speaking to me.

Maybe the general knows I'm here and this is some sort of test.

Do I want to be a part of this?

In the middle of one of their secret meetings, I still don't understand the rebellion.

I've witnessed executions both secret and in public, heard Father curse their hatred for the Tournament, and observed his elation at their deaths after forcefully binding them to the games they despise, and yet their true purpose is still a mystery.

I think of my sisters and their anger that my ruination of the sacred temple stirred something in the rebellion. Am I already a part of this, willing or not?

The Tournament is the most sacred thing in the Kingdoms of the Sky, and it has always been my destiny. I should stay far away from anyone who wants to ruin my chances, but if they want to stop the wedding then maybe it wouldn't be so bad to be a part of it for just a little while?

I can't marry a prince of the enemy kingdom with a broken reputation. And it's not like it would be the first time I got rid of a potential husband.

"Are we absolutely certain the wedding is going to happen that soon?" A voice shouts from the crowd, voicing a question I'm dying to know the answer to.

Thunder moves his gaze to the servant in front of him.

"Yes. I heard the kings arguing last night at their private dinner." Auren winces at the memories, and I can only imagine what it must be like to be a servant in the presence of not only one but two raging kings. Especially when one of them is the grandfather of her child.

"If everything goes according to their plans–and I'm sure it will unless the princess has anything to say about it–there will most likely be a wedding at sunset after the second Moon Trial," Auren continues, folding her hands at her back.

"Most likely?" Someone else shouts from the crowd, a murmur of angry voices following.

A knowing smile spreads on the servant's lips. "That is if the princess doesn't stop it. She doesn't strike me as someone willing to be just a bride."

"Let's hope not." Thunder's snort is lost to the chaos of voices erupting in the cave.

"The royals can't be trusted!"

"She is cursed!"

"The royals are the reason for all the suffering–"

"We would be better off just getting rid of her ourselves–"

"Kill her now before the wedding! There can't be a wedding without a bride–"

The crowd continues arguing, shouting a few rumors even I haven't heard before. Then they go on to discuss if I fell on purpose, arguing whether it was an attempt to end my life or the worship of the gods. And apparently, there is an ongoing bet about me and Castor. Who will kill the other first? Will he push me off a balcony or will I destroy another temple with his body? The latter gives me the urge to laugh or scream, whichever comes first if I decide to open my pursed lips.

"Please tell me you're going to get out of that ridiculous deal. I've bet all the gold I earned back at your palace."

I startle at the sudden presence next to me, cursing myself for letting my guard down. Again.

Skye is leaning against the wall, arms crossed and a mischievous gleam in her eyes.

"Of course you're here," I mutter, glancing around to make sure no one else has recognized me.

Skye raises her eyebrows, awaiting my reply.

"I'm not getting married to that wretched prince," I say through gritted teeth, trying to keep my voice low.

"Thank the gods and the sky above," she says with a sigh. She's not wearing her blue fighting leathers today, but a simple white shirt and brown pants paired with a darker shade of boots. Her short hair is pulled to one side, barely covering her binding mark, the blue stripes hidden or washed away.

"I'm not doing it for you," I snarl, nails digging into the scars of my palms. "And why do you even care if there's a wedding or not?"

Skye shrugs, her eyes narrowing slightly. "We have our reasons. Reasons I'm not going to tell you. At least not yet, not before I know we can trust you. You're lucky I don't agree with the majority, or you wouldn't even have made it through the city. Of course, none of that matters right now as it's clear you don't trust us either."

"I don't trust anyone."

"And you shouldn't. Me, however–" She shrugs, her eyes glancing from the silver marks on my skin to the scarf concealing my hair. "We'll see."

Thunder claps his hands together to silence the crowd before jumping to his feet, the hard look on his face hinting at the general, and perhaps even the leader of the rebellion, lurking underneath his skin.

"Let's give the princess a chance to prove herself. If she doesn't, we'll have a fun night destroying a wedding." A wicked smile spreads on his lips as he bares his teeth, the crowd cheering in reply.

THEY COME AS SUDDENLY as the stars blinking into existence in the darkening sky.

As quiet as the wind blowing through the city, they burst from the narrow alleys and jump down from the roofs of the buildings. At least a dozen people all clad in fabric as dark as the night, weapons gleaming in the light of the moon.

I don't have time to catch my breath or do anything at all before the first one is upon me. One of them lands a harsh blow to my stomach, another boot cracking my back from behind. A punch to my face sends me tumbling to the ground, my blood coloring the cobblestones.

I roll onto my back, a boot barely missing the point between my eyes. Another kick to my stomach, my legs, my sides, and it's as if I can feel every bone in my body on the brink of breaking.

I'm surrounded with no way to escape. Every time I try to reach for a hidden weapon or rise to my feet–they strike me down, each blow or kick more painful than the last.

They don't speak. The night is quiet, the only sounds my grunts of pain and the beating of my body.

They don't reach for their weapons, and even with all the chaos, do I realize they want to make this last before they kill me.

They want to make me suffer.

There's a growing list of people who could have ordered this, each person as likely as the next. The scarf concealing my hair has been yanked off during the attack so there is no longer any doubt this is coincidental.

They want to kill Princess Asteria of Soria. And there is nothing stopping them.

I press my hands over my head, doing my best to shield myself. It's hard to see anything past my teary vision.

A sneer and a murderous look. The gleam from a silver knife and golden sword. Bloody knuckles and shiny boots. Dark cloaks fluttering in the wind.

I focus on the sky above, remembering how I thought the morning sky would be a good last glimpse of the world when fire ate the body of the dead lord before me.

The night sky will be my last glimpse of the world.

The starlight is obscured by dark clouds gliding across the sky, the moon delighting in the looming darkness. A shooting star disappears behind the palace mountain and I close my eyes, praying my death will be quick.

But then, as suddenly as the attack started, the quiet night is transformed into an inferno of screams. A thunderous crack resounds from the sky and a cold wind sweeps through the alley.

The beating stops, and when I open my eyes, I see nothing but darkness.

Is this it? Is this the end?

I squeeze my eyes shut, desperately praying there is something more to the Shadow Realm than this empty darkness.

The next time I open my eyes, I'm not alone.

The dark-cloaked figures that only moments ago were beating the soul out of me are lying scattered on the ground, heaving for breath, eyes wide with terror.

I follow their line of sight, my head muddled from the pain in my body.

A towering figure of shadow is standing right in front of me. The large form bleeds into the night and it's impossible to discern where one begins and the other ends. Tendrils of shadow ripple of its form, reminding me of the Moon King's magic reaching for me in the carriage.

Fear slams into me so fast it's hard to breathe. I fumble on the ground, my hands slick with blood.

The dark figure strides forward, and just as I'm about to open my mouth to either scream or pray to the gods, it bends down, transforming into a familiar face.

Star.

"Tell me who did this," he demands, reaching forward to grab my chin. His hands are shaking, his eyes nothing but darkness as he looks at me.

"Which one did this to you?" His fingers brush across a scrape on my cheek and I wince. He narrows his eyes and removes his hands. And as he rises back to his feet, the night darkens and the people on the ground shudder, their screams cut off by a phantom wind.

Star's chest is heaving, rage and fury evident in his features. He looks like an angel of death conjured from the darkest parts of the night.

"Who?!" His voice is so loud it's closer to a growl, the sound of it echoing off the buildings and reverberating through my chest.

The prince glares at the dark-cloaked figures one after one, daring them to even breathe too loudly. It's like they're glued to the ground, their fear keeping them locked in place.

No one speaks.

"Fine," Star says with a heavy sigh. "All of them, then." A sinister smile spreads on his lips, his eyes sparking silver like lightning crackling across the night sky.

A dark cloud blocks the light of the moon, leaving the alley in impenetrable darkness, and when the cloud passes in the next heartbeat—they're all dead.

A river of crimson runs over the cobblestones, staining the tips of Star's boots. He steps over the lifeless bodies lying around him, the blade of a knife gleaming in his hand.

"Come," he says, one hand held out for me to take.

I can't move.

"Asteria." He moves closer, the coldness in his features slipping ever so slightly, some of the dark blue back in his gaze.

My eyes dart to the dozen bodies behind him, to the soulless eyes and open mouths. There are no signs of a struggle, only a clean line sliced across their throats and the steady flow of blood.

"They will be gone before the sun rises. As should we," Star says, his hand beckoning.

I still can't move.

Star heaves another sigh before he effortlessly gathers me in his arms. "Consider this a favor and proof that a bargain with me could be *very* helpful."

The steady beating of his heart and the warmth radiating off his body allow the darkness to finally claim me.

Time doesn't exist in the abyss of my dreams. I don't know

how many days or nights have passed when I'm awoken to a tangy liquid being forced down my throat.

I spit and choke, but gentle hands tilt my head back with softly murmured words. "Go back to sleep, Asteria, and all the pain will be gone the next time you wake up."

The flickering image of a copper braid and jagged scars is the last thing I see before I'm once again swept away by darkness. And this time, there is no pain.

CHAPTER TWENTY-EIGHT

Two nights before the second Moon Trial, one of the palace's ballrooms is so elaborately decorated that I'm terrified a priestess is going to emerge from the shadows to bind me to Castor any second, but so far nothing has happened to suggest the rebellion wasn't right about the time of the ceremony.

I still have time.

If someone doesn't kill me first.

The flickering skylights make the long skirt of my silver dress pool around me like a sea of sparkling stars, the fabric reflected by the lights making me the brightest person in the room. I'm only waiting for the moment when someone steps on my dress and I go crumbling to the floor in a heap of glittering fabric.

Perhaps that's the way I'll be claimed by the shadows.

The amethyst stone is heavy on my finger during the dinner that seems to go on for an eternity, the ring clinging against my large silver goblet as I gulp down wine so fast that some of the servants send me concerned looks.

Nobility from both kingdoms are seated at the large table that covers an entire side of the ballroom, the guests not worthy of a seat milling around the rest of the room, some of them gliding across the dancefloor.

At the end of the Lunan side of the table, I sit next to Castor, grinding my teeth every time he moves or speaks to the guests on his other side. The Sorians are so far away I have to squint my eyes to spot the familiar faces among the ornately clothed guests, the gold of my kingdom barely visible in the darkness.

The wine burns my throat, but I continue drinking, ignoring the prince across me trying to catch my gaze.

Every time I flinch from Castor's proximity, roll my eyes at his snide remarks, or wave at the servants to refill my glass–Star glances in my direction, his midnight eyes glittering underneath the skylights. A single silver star glimmers from his left ear, the same shade of silver lining the hems of his black suit.

During course four, I notice the warrior prince might not be as nonchalant as he claims to be. He may be absentmindedly twirling his goblet and sending bored looks at the other guests, but there's a tension to his body and features I didn't realize I'd started to notice.

Is he really unbothered from last night? When I woke up in my bed this morning, I almost managed to convince myself it was all a nightmare, but the map of bruises on my body speaks otherwise. Another large dose of healing potion was standing on the bedside table and I gulped it down without another thought. Only stiffness and tenderness remained when I got dressed for the ball hours later, my lady's maid nowhere in sight.

If the prince is going to pretend nothing happened, so will I.

May the person who ordered the attack see that I'm still standing.

"Are you sure you should drink that much right before the next game, starlight?" Star croons, raising a perfectly sculpted eyebrow, a smirk tugging the corners of his lips.

"She shouldn't," Castor says beside me, casting a glowering look at the both of us.

"She can decide for herself," I snap, draining the rest of the glass in emphasis.

Star's smirk widens into a grin and he raises his glass to his lips. "This is going to be a very interesting night. The king has brought out his extra special wine tonight."

A servant leans forward to refill my glass, and I notice the dark liquid is swirling with small pieces of glittering silver.

A very un princess–like snort escapes me and I glance at the prince beside me. "Are you trying to poison me again?"

His answering glare would've sent a shiver down my back were it not for the wine numbing my senses. A muscle ticks in his throat as he turns away to mutter something–probably that my curse has started to make me insane–to the man seated on his other side.

Star leans his elbows on the table, his head resting in his hands. "Poison." He snorts. "Not very creative."

"That's what I thought," I mutter with an exasperated look in the direction of my betrothed who only ignores me.

"There is no poison in the king's special wine. Only a little touch of magic to make it a bit little more...magical." He reaches forward to tuck a loose strand of hair behind my ear, the feel of his skin against mine sending an involuntary shiver down my spine as something ignites inside.

It has to be the special wine, right?

"Care to dance, starlight?"

"You're actually asking this time? How unusual."

With a shrug, he pushes away from the table, straightening the lapels of his jacket when he gets to his feet. He disappears from my blurry vision, and in the next heartbeat, he's behind me, dragging my chair out and linking his arm with mine.

"What do you think you're doing?" Castor seethes, his hand twitching as if he is considering strangling me in front of everyone.

"Escorting Luna's future princess to the dancefloor, of course," Star says with a mock bow that makes an embarrassing giggle bubble from my lips. "If she'll let me." His eyebrows rise, a teasing smirk on his lips.

I reach for the glass on the table, downing the rest of the glittering liquid, welcoming the burning sensations that follow.

Right now, I can't remember a single reason as to why I should deny him.

"You know what? I want to dance. After all, that's what this dress was made for." I place my hand on our entwined arms, allowing the prince to guide me away from the table.

The room falls silent when we emerge onto the dancefloor and I can practically feel the eyes boring into me, some of the looks more scorching than others.

Star clears his throat and the music begins anew, a slow and alluring tune echoing through the large room, the skylights above flickering in the same rhythm.

I wrap my arms around his neck as his fingers dig into my waist, pressing my body flush against his. The warmth of his body seeps into me, his heady scent increasing the magical daze clouding my senses.

The room blurs as he spins me around, the gowns of the other dancing guests a haze of colors. Skylights descend from the ceiling like a flurry of snowflakes, the orbs of light singing their own melody.

My feet stumble in the long fabric of my dress, and I would've tumbled to the floor if it weren't for the prince holding me upright.

"Falling for me already?" Amusement glimmers in his eyes and he dips his head toward mine.

"In your dreams, moon boy–"

"In my dreams, you're already in my bed, wearing absolutely nothing this time. Other times I've used the dagger you threatened me with to cut away all that fabric in the way."

Heat blazes in my core at his words and the way he slides his tongue over the binding mark on my neck. "And I bet you dream about it too. You've only gotten a little taste of what we could be."

He bites the bottom of my ear before twirling me away from his chest, and when I'm back in his arms, his face is so close I can count the stars in his eyes. "You look absolutely divine tonight, starlight. As always."

Starlight. That's what I resemble in the shadows and flickering lights. The silver dress casts a magical light around us, the silky fabric shining brighter than the sun. My white hair is as luminescent as the stars outside and I can only imagine the glow of my frosted eyes.

Star lowers his head to my throat, his lips grazing the sensitive skin. "But I have to admit I miss your other dress. You know, the one that matched my suit. We looked so good together even the gods were envious. If only you would make another bargain with me." He sighs, his breath making me shiver.

"A bargain?"

The dance is making me dizzy, the wine making it hard to think beyond the flames licking up my spine from his sultry looks and touches. A distant part of me is screaming to remember something that's just out of reach, but then his lips nibble at my skin and I can't think of anything else.

"Yes, a bargain. In addition to the one we already have, of course." One of his hands leaves my waist to stroke along my arm, his fingers landing on a painted mark where black peeks through the silver. His forehead is pressed against mine, his lips only inches from giving me what I want–

Cold arms wrench me away with a painful grip, dragging me across the dancefloor and through the crowd. Castor curses in my ear, his hands like frigid shackles around my wrists.

"Where are we going?"

Fear grips my heart and dread coils in my stomach, all the magical wine in the world not enough to forget the ring on my finger and the wedding that could happen any second.

What if the kings want to bind us before the ceremony?

If it weren't for the magical wine slugging my senses I would've pushed away and retrieved the dagger hidden in my bodice, but I can barely keep myself from tumbling to the floor as he drags me out of the ballroom and into the long dark hallways of the palace.

"Where are we going—"

"I'm not going to let you humiliate me any longer. Your king agrees." A cruel smile pulls at his lips, his mahogany eyes blazing with fury. "He has left a special surprise for us."

"No." I try to yank away from his grip around my shoulders but he doesn't budge. He may not be a warrior like Star, but he is certainly strong.

"Consider this a warning," Castor snarls as we barge through a door leading to a stairwell descending into darkness. "I only need you to stay alive until the Tournament is nearing its end, then a few wounds won't be your only punishment."

A musty smell hits my face. The scars on my back ache as my heart speeds up to an uncomfortable rhythm. I regret every drop of magical wine as Castor carries me down the stairs and into the same empty dungeon where the Sun King delivered his last punishment.

A single skylight hovers in the upper corner, its dim light

flickering as fast as my panicked breaths coming in and out of my mouth. And leaning against one of the walls, gleaming in the flickering white light, is the most sacred artifact in all of Soria.

The Royal Sword.

The sword that doesn't belong in the darkness, discarded by its bearer and king, waiting to be maltreated by the enemy.

If only the gods could see their king so recklessly *misplacing* such a holy relic and leaving it for the enemy to find. The consequences it could have for Soria if the sword is lost or destroyed—

A scream is stuck in my throat and tears are welling in my eyes as tremors rock through my body.

No. Anything but this—

Castor throws me from his arms and my body slams against the hard ground. The back of my dress is ripped open before I even have the chance to try and lift myself off the ground.

The scars that no one is supposed to see, bared to the enemy. My deepest, darkest secret the king has held in a tight fist, revealed to the enemy as if it was nothing at all.

I shrink onto the ground, internally screaming and cursing the gods as if they're the ones who ordered this.

Castor laughs and the sound echoes in the quiet room. "Not so high and mighty now are you, *princess*?" He clicks his tongue in disgust as he walks around me to the gleaming gilded sword. He glides a finger across the ornate handle, over the carved pictures showing a piece of Soria's greatest history.

Gritting my teeth, I manage to push up on my elbows. The long dress is a suffocating blanket, the silver fabric no longer as magnificent as it once was.

Castor picks up the sword, weighing it in his hands. The golden blade is eerie in the hands of the enemy, and I hold my breath, waiting.

Nothing happens.

No vengeful gods emerge from the shadows. No gilded power rises from the sword. The Sun King does not come running.

Castor is still alive and breathing.

"One day, I'm going to get my hands on the real deal," he says with a snort, "this is a joke compared to the one of the moon." He looks at me, a malicious smirk on his lips, and takes a step forward, ready to carve me open.

I roll onto my back, the moist ground sticking to my bare skin—to the scars that will never heal.

Castor stabs the tip of the sword into the ground beside my head, barely missing my ear. "If you want the punishment to be more visible, by all means. I'm sure we could find a veil thick enough to cover your face for the wedding," he snarls, turning the sword around and causing a cloud of dust to emerge from the ground.

"I'll gladly make sure no amount of paint can cover it up," he scoffs, baring his teeth in a menacing smile. "No amount of healing potions can remove scars."

"You—"

"Of course it was me." He spits and turns the tip of the sword around in another circle on the dusty ground. "I don't know how you managed to escape, but I can assure you it will not happen again. The only mistake I made was not seeing it through myself. I'm going to enjoy giving you a taste of what's to come."

My gaze flickers across his towering body, to the sword in his hand and the dagger still hidden in the bodice of my dress.

"Don't even think about it," he warns, his eyes as dark and soulless as his king.

I move my hand to reach for the dagger, but I'm not quick enough.

Castor thrusts the blade of the sword into my hand, the tip

clanging against the stone as it punctures right through my hand and pins me to the ground.

Pain explodes in my palm and I scream.

"I warned you." He twists the blade around and it feels as if my screams reverberate through my soul. "This wasn't exactly a part of the deal. This was all you." He yanks the sword away and blood pours from the wound in a steady flow.

I press the bleeding hand to my chest to stanch the running blood, the pain bursting through me blurring my vision.

"Now, unless you want to repeat that for all your limbs—let's start the punishment." Castor taps the sword in impatience, the sound of the bloody tip clanging against the ground sending a jolt of fear through me.

It's hard to think past the pain and liquor still clouding my senses, but I know I have to stop this.

I need more time.

"Two lines," I say through gritted teeth, trying to will the wine to evaporate from my system, focusing on the rapid beating of my heart instead of the burning pain.

Castor narrows his eyes. "We can start with that. Two long lines for failing to show up to the first Moon Trial." He motions for me to turn around, the sound of the Royal Sword cutting through the air sending a tremor through me.

"Fine." I bow my head in an attempt to appear submissive, but as I turn around, I grab the hidden dagger with my uninjured hand, quickly shoving it into the sleeve of the dress.

I don't have to pretend to struggle to get up on my knees. My hands are slick with blood, the pain making me more dizzy than the wine ever did.

Castor makes an impatient sound behind me. "I told you that you shouldn't drink so much. Now the punishment will have to be prolonged to ensure the wine isn't doing anything to subdue the pain." He lets out a heavy sigh, but he doesn't reach for me.

He wants to make this last, just like the assassination attempt in the city.

"Gods, your back is horrible. And from now on, every time you look in the mirror, you'll be reminded of this moment and how you'll never get rid of the mark I've left on your skin."

When I finally manage to get up on my knees, he lets out a dark chuckle. "Two lines to start. I've been told you know how to count."

Anger roars inside me. Sparks of fury flicker in my fingertips, evaporating before I can grasp them. I suck in a breath and with each hammering beat of my heart, I let wrath and hatred fill every part of my body until the pain is only a distant distraction.

In the shadows of the flashing skylight, I see Castor raise the Royal Sword behind me. The gilded tip presses against my skin-

I turn around and slam the dagger into his thigh.

Castor's eyes widen in surprise. He lets out a roar and stumbles backward, the sword clattering to the ground as his hands fumble for the dagger.

Rolling away, I reach for the sword. My fingertips graze the rough handle and I brace myself against the rising panic. Tears threaten to spill from my eyes and my heart is beating so hard and fast it feels as if it's going to burst through my skin.

May the gods forgive me.

I close my fingers around the carved pictures, ignoring the part of me that is screaming how wrong this is.

Nothing happens.

Castor curses me excessively before yanking out the dagger, his face contorted with rage. "How dare you–" His gaze snaps to the sword in my hand and he gives me a cruel smirk. "Fine. Let's finish what I started yesterday." He takes a step forward, the silver dagger poised in his hand.

I struggle to get my feet underneath me and he prowls closer, slowly, the cruel smirk widening.

The sword's carvings dig into my skin, the sword too heavy for my weakened body. The blood from my injured hand makes it hard to hold on and I hesitate for too long before swinging the sword forward.

Castor jumps away. He twirls the dagger in his hand, ignoring the blood pouring from the wound on his thigh. "No wonder you didn't last in the Tournament. You're nothing but a pathetic little princess too afraid of daddy to make any real impact on the world–"

The tip of the sword scrapes against the stone underneath us, the heavy weight threatening to drag me down.

Castor laughs. "You should consider yourself lucky you managed to kill your mother before she could see the disappointment you turned out to be."

Fury explodes in every part of my being, pulling on strength I didn't know I had.

This time, I don't hesitate. The gilded blade lights up the darkness as I thrust it forward and into his chest, aiming straight for his heart.

"Not so high and mighty now are you, *princeling*?" My snarl fuels the last of my strength and I push the blade deeper until the tip clangs against the wall behind him, twisting it around until I've made a full circle–a carved picture of the sun.

I lean forward until I'm so close I can feel the last breaths he will ever take in this world.

His mouth is screaming silent words and the deep brown of his eyes is gone, leaving nothing but darkness. His blood paints the ground underneath us in messy strokes, seeping into the stone and leaving a mark in the mountain that will never fade.

His head falls to his chest and I grab a fistful of hair with my bloody hand, yanking his face up so his last glimpse of the world will be the hatred and anger in my eyes.

I don't let go until he stops breathing and I'm sure the last of his life essence has slipped into the Shadow Realm.

After a while, exhaustion and pain pull me to the ground, my entire body shaking with aftershocks. Only an empty darkness remains in my heart, the last embers of fury extinguished by the cold breeze that shatters the dying skylight.

"Well, well, well," a familiar voice drawls from behind me. "It seems you actually won for once."

"You were the one who said to always aim for the heart. No matter the beast."

CHAPTER TWENTY-NINE

"We need to seal the bargain with a kiss."

"No."

Star takes a step closer, midnight eyes flickering to my lips. "You should know how this works by now. I told you there would be a bigger price this time." He tilts his head to the side, the marks peeking up from his collar glistening in the dim sunlight.

"What is it with you and your obsession with bargains?" I ask, stalling the inevitable.

My gaze flickers to the lifeless body of my betrothed discarded on the ground beside us, to the eyes that are staring at the morning sky, glassy and unseeing. His blood is staining his deep purple suit, and the lower half of his body is submerged in the coursing river that ends in a thunderous waterfall that nearly drowns out our voices.

"They're fun," he says with a shrug, silver glimmering in his eyes. "And usually very....helpful."

I swallow against the growing lump in my throat, the tangy taste of healing potion still coating my tongue. My hand is bandaged with silver fabric ripped from my dress, and Star's jacket is covering the bare skin on my back.

A tiny favor included in our bargain, he called it.

We left the palace through a labyrinth of narrow dark tunnels, Star effortlessly carrying his brother on his back. We argued all the way out, the prince threatening to turn around and display my mess to the party if I didn't agree to his bargain.

With our last bargain finally over, the last thing I wanted to do was forge another, so I kept demanding he let go of the body so I could take care of it on my own.

"No can do, princess. I'm a witness and you are way too drunk to manage anything beyond causing more trouble," he said, increasing his speed. "Just drink the potion. It's the last I'll be able to get in a while. Perhaps you should beg the witches for a magically refillable bottle."

Star takes another step forward, the gray fog clouding the mountains parting to let him through, the sight reminding me of the shadowy beast in the woods ready to pounce on me any second. "The party is not over. I can still shout for every guest and king to come see–"

"No."

A muscle ticks in his throat as he takes another step forward. Then another. And another. "So stop walking away so we can get it done."

"I'm not walking away–" I purse my lips at his raised eyebrows when I stagger back as he takes another step toward me.

"Do you need a reminder about what will happen if the kings find out about this?"

As if I could forget his endless pestering and warnings about exactly what could happen if anybody found out.

"No." I grind my teeth together and force my body to be still as he strides forward until he's close enough to reach for my face.

"So you're finally ready for this?"

I'm not. This is the last thing I should be doing, but do I really have another choice? Our last bargain didn't turn out so bad after all, and if this means he'll stop trying to sabotage me and actually be *bound* to help me—

Whatever it takes, Asteria. Whatever it takes.

"I'm ready."

A smirk tugs at his lips, and I can practically feel the delighted arrogance radiating off him. "I will help you win the Tournament and become the next Victor and you will help me get what I want."

Magic crackles in the air between us and silver flares in his eyes.

"Do we have a bargain?"

The magic roars in my ears, its invisible hands tearing at my soul.

"Yes."

The magic yanks harder and my heartbeats stutter.

Star's fingertips graze the skin of my jaw as he lowers his face, his breath hot on my lips.

"Magical bargains are sealed with blood," I snap, fumbling for my dagger before realizing it's gone, probably left in the dungeons with Soria's Royal Sword.

Star's smirk widens. "That's one way, yes, but there are others. Other ways I would rather do in bed but wouldn't mind doing right here and now. But if you prefer the bloody messy way–" he shrugs and drops his hands, his lips still only inches from mine.

The fury slumbering in my chest blinks an eye open.

I grab the collar of his shirt and roughly press my lips against his before biting down on his bottom lip hard enough for the bitter taste of blood to coat my tongue. "There. A kiss *and* blood."

"That's not fair." His eyes darken and he grabs my head, his fingers tangling in my hair. "We have to blend together. I'll have to take some of yours too."

His lips crash against mine before I have the time to protest.

The kiss is gentle at first, and I make an angry sound in the back of my throat while slapping his chest, startling when his teeth pierce my bottom lip. His tongue glides along my lip and I allow him to kiss me just a little bit longer to make sure our blood is blended before firmly pushing him away.

Star's chest is heaving and his eyes swirl with black and silver as his bleeding lips mutter a chain of silent words I can't hear over the roaring coming from all sides—the waterfall behind us, the power vibrating in my blood, and the screaming of my soul.

A throbbing sensation explodes on my arm, the skin where the dark mark is hidden aching in rhythm with my pounding heart.

I tear away the sleeve of my dress and gasp when I see the dark swirls expanding, coiling like a snake as they extend from my forearm down to my wrist. A single small star appears in the middle of the mark, resting in the crook of my elbow.

A star for Prince Star, whose life is now tangled with mine— our lives bound to the bargain between us. If one of us fails to fulfill it–

I look up into his eyes and see nothing but cold, ferocious darkness. All signs of taunting and flirtation have vanished from his features, leaving nothing but a bloodthirsty warrior ready for battle.

"What have you done?" My words are barely a whisper. Regret grips my heart so hard I'm struggling to breathe and an unsettling feeling spreads through my body.

What have *I* done?

"It's the mark of our bargain. It will disappear when the bargain is done," Star says, his voice void of emotion.

"You said nothing about a mark. There wasn't one the last time—"

"Our last bargain was nothing but a joke," he snaps, anger slicing through his words. "This bargain is real. As will the consequences be if we fail to complete it." A muscle ticks along his jaw and fury blazes in his eyes.

"Isn't this what you wanted?"

The world will end before I will understand his shifting moods.

Star doesn't answer. He turns toward the river where the water is tearing at the dead body—the symbol of a fragile bond finally snapped in two, leaving no chance to mend the relationship between two kingdoms in an ancient never-ending war.

"What are we going to do when the king notices he's gone?"

We.

I hate that we're a we now, however fleeting it may be.

"Which one?"

"Either one."

I need to put on a good show of being hurt so Father won't try and punish me himself. And what will he think when he realizes Castor is gone? He may not have cared about my previous suitors, but Castor was a prince and he will certainly be missed.

Star squats down and pushes the body toward the edge of the cliff.

For a moment, I'm brought back to another place with another dead body–pewter eyes instead of mahogany staring at the sky.

Only this time, I'm not alone.

"A prince always has a lot of enemies."

With one last push, the heavy body rolls off the cliffs and down into the rush of raging water.

A prince of the moon—gone, his soul commended to the Shadow Realm, the magic in his royal blood back to the sky it came from.

The muscles on Star's back shift as he stands from the ground, the fabric of his dark shirt doing little to conceal the sculpted body underneath.

It's terrifying how someone can be so unbothered by death.

"And what are you going to tell your king when your brothers disappear one after one?"

He turns his head in my direction and a sliver of sunlight breaks through the mist, lighting up his impassive face. "Luckily for us, a few of them are competing in the Tournament where there are no rules."

"Is that why you bound yourself?"

He doesn't answer. He glances at the vast ocean, to the crashing waves basking in the morning sun.

"Is this how it's going to be now? You still haven't told me why you were so persistent on the bargain. Couldn't you just get rid of them yourself?"

"I have my reasons," he says through gritted teeth, still refusing to meet my searching gaze.

"Reasons you said you would reveal if we made a bargain." I cross my arms against the shivers rocking through me. It might be a warm summer day, but the sun is doing nothing to melt the ice in my heart.

"That was last time. I told you the price would be higher this time." He drags a hand through his disheveled dark locks before smoothing the fabric of his rumpled shirt. There are dark splotches on his shirt barely visible on the dark fabric, and his hands are stained with blood—his blood through his half-brother.

"And what exactly is that price?"

"You'll see."

Star strides past me and his arm brushes against mine—the touching arms sharing something more than the life-binding bargain between us.

Just like Castor said, the next time I look in the mirror, I'll see a mark on my skin and be reminded of this night. But it won't be his mark.

"And how will you fulfill your end of the bargain?" I call after the prince disappearing in the thickening mist.

"You'll see," he repeats, anger and frustration building within me at his words. "I'll see you at the next trial, starlight. Winning a Tournament is nothing I haven't done before."

The Shadow Court is dark, eerie, and empty. A thick layer of fog is seeping down on the land, blocking nearly every trace of light from the sky above. The magic is thick in the air, and with every step I take, it feels as if I'm being watched–as if the gods of death are yearning to claim my soul.

And the sixth game in the Tournament, the second Moon Trial, is exactly that—waiting to see who will survive the night and who will be claimed by the shadows.

Elimination round. Survive the long night and stay alive until sunrise.

It's a weak excuse for allowing the kingdoms to kill each other without repercussions. Not a very creative trial, but very efficient nonetheless, especially using the Shadow Court as the arena.

I've come prepared this time. A bow and numerous arrows strapped to my back. A sword at my side. A few daggers and small knives hidden throughout my body underneath my dark leathers.

All thanks to Auren.

There wasn't any time to reveal I knew another of her secrets and she didn't give me a single hint if the rebellion might know that I—accidentally or not—did exactly what they wanted.

Not only did Auren trick Father into thinking I'm currently immobilized back at the palace, but she helped me travel unnoticed. And the means of transportation was not a carriage this time.

At the bottom of the palace mountain in Nyx, a gaping black hole was swirling with shadowy tendrils of magic, a black smoke seeping out of the mountain. The Moon King was the first to step into the darkness, and one after one, people followed. Even the Sun King walked into the hole without a second thought, but flares of gilded light erupted after his departure as if he was fighting the darkness with his light.

Heart in my throat and the hood of my leathers tightly secured over my head, I followed the procession. It was perhaps the most terrifying minutes of my life, but I emerged by the Royal Dais with my soul still intact, following the warriors across the border to the court hosting tonight's trial.

The second we passed the border to the Shadow Court, I could tell this place was different from the entirety of the two kingdoms.

The opposite of the Light Court in Soria, it honors the afterlife and is rumored to have a direct link to the Shadow Realm. A mountain range extends from the Diamond Mountains, the rocky landscape lush with thick woods rumored to be the home of the ancient witches. Besides the lingering presence of the gods and the souls of the deceased, the court is nothing but empty darkness.

There are no beasts and no people.

The Shadow Court is not a place you want to be.

Ever since the Tournament was created, there have been endless discussions about whether this court should host a trial. No king, Victor, or general wants to plan it, and the people of both kingdoms are hesitant to even go near the court. The bargain with the gods won in the end, and the warriors are forced to enter the dark court once a year. But the observers—even the royals and Victors—will stay outside the border, unwilling to risk their souls being claimed early if they cross it.

Lined with glittering silver paint enchanted to kill anyone who crosses, the elimination arena is a large part of land at the edge of the court—a combination of woods and mountains with a large lake in the middle.

The hordes of warriors are currently gathered around the lake, the crowd of onlookers detained behind a line of guards in the distance. The Royal Dais is barely visible through the fog, the magnified voice the only sign of the Victor.

The sound of Elio's hands clapping together reverberates through the clearing. A chorus of battle cries erupts from every direction and countless battles explode around me.

The court that only moments ago was eerily quiet transforms into a storm of sounds. Steel clashes against steel. Fists and feet slam against leather and skin. Blades clang against bone. Arrows whoosh through the air. Magic crackles in the air as the Shadow Realm greedily welcomes the sacrifices.

I do the one thing I haven't been training to do in the face of battle.

I run.

I dart for the thick forest, moving in a zigzag pattern to make it harder for the flying arrows to hit me.

Stay out of trouble. Only fight when you have to.

Elio's words of advice ring through my mind as I put as much distance as possible between me and the raging battlegrounds in the clearing, making sure to stick to the paths going in opposite directions from the other fleeing warriors.

My feet thump against the ground, the roots and rocks trying to drag me down while my heart beats a painful rhythm against my chest. A cold breeze carrying the stench of death blows against my face, not even the warmth of summer able to warm the darkness of the Shadow Court.

When I've run far enough to dim the sounds of battle, I choose a tree with leaves thick enough to conceal me and high enough to provide an overview of my surroundings.

I unsheathe the quiver and bow at my back, resting it against the large trunk. Willing my heart to steady, I suck in a deep breath and study the darkness around me.

There's only a faint glimmer from the stars and moon in the distance, the gray fog blocking the light from the land. Or perhaps even the sky is reluctant to shine its light in the Shadow Court.

Footsteps crunching on the ground snap my attention. A man crouches down behind a tree. Blood is pouring from a deep gash in his forehead and pieces of the leather on his arms are torn away.

A strange sound I can't place sounds from his direction.

"Shh, Adie. You have to be quiet, remember? Silence is our most important rule." He heaves something off his back and when I realize what it is, it feels as if my heart stops beating.

There's a child in the middle of the most dangerous and deadly game in the Tournament.

The girl looks to be about eight years old. Splatters of blood are smeared in her blonde hair and there are bruises all over her face and throat. She is not wearing fighting leathers like the man beside her, but simple brown clothes dirty from struggling through the forest. A black string is tied around her throat, its emerald stone pressed against her chest above her heart, and a tiny teddy bear dangles from her fingers.

The child turns her head to look at the man and terror slams into me so hard I nearly topple from the tree.

There's a binding mark on her neck.

No—

I desperately pray this is just an illusion conjured by the shadows trying to lure me to my death. A child can't possibly survive in the Tournament this long when I barely managed to get through the games myself.

I squeeze my eyes shut, but when I open them five heartbeats later, the man is dabbing his bleeding face with a cloth and tears are running down the child's face.

This is real—

"You said it would be over by now." The girl's bottom lip trembles as she speaks and she rubs the tears away with firm motions that leave red splotches on her cheeks.

The man sighs and squats so he can look into her eyes. "Listen to me, Adie. I promise I'm doing everything I can to get you out of here, and I pray every day and night that I'll finally prove myself to the gods. Words can't even describe how sorry I am that you got dragged into this. We will get through this. Together, you and me. Just like we always do. Okay?" He strokes a hand over her head and she gives him a slight nod, her small hands balling into fists.

"You and me. And Tawny." The child lifts the teddy bear and the man pats its head with two fingers.

"You and me. And Tawny," he says, a sad smile on his lips.

The girl opens her mouth to say something more but a twig snaps behind her and the man quickly shoves her behind his back.

A woman in blood-red fighting leather stalks forward. Daggers gleam in each of her hands, the sharpened tips dark with dried blood. There's a murderous gleam in her eyes and sheer determination marks her every movement.

She won't hesitate to kill a child.

The man reaches for the sword strapped to his side, his gaze darting around as he slowly moves backward, the child following his movements without a sound.

Silence is our most important rule.

"There is no place for children in the games," the woman snarls, twirling the daggers in her hands. "Or cheaters!"

"Leave us and I won't kill you." The man's voice is calm, but the hand gripping the child behind him trembles.

The woman's eyes narrow, her upper lip curling in disgust. "Cheaters deserve death. There can only be one Victor—"

"There are no rules in the Tournament but one. The child has done nothing but survive and my only goal is to get her out of the games. Leave us and we'll cause you no trouble."

The woman tips her head back and her laughter sends a shiver down my back.

Stay hidden. Only fight if absolutely necessary.

The man has managed to keep the child alive through dangerous trials. He doesn't need my help—

It happens so fast that I don't see it coming.

And neither does the man.

One dagger hits his head. The other bores into his heart.

A bloodcurdling scream shatters the darkness.

The man falls to his knees. His eyes are wide and blood runs from his mouth. The last breath that leaves his lips is accompanied by one word.

"Adie."

Another scream that ends in a shrill cry echoes through the darkness.

The girl is drenched with his blood, the tree behind her soaking up the crimson liquid.

Not a single drop of life essence is wasted in the Shadow Court.

The child wails as if a part of her soul has left with the man. She stumbles against the tree, her hands holding the teddy bear tight to her chest.

The woman tilts her face to the sky as if she is waiting for the gods to praise her, unbothered by the anguish she just inflicted.

The child thumps to the ground and crawls to the man, her hands and knees slipping in the blood pooling on the ground. She takes his hand and presses it against her heart, the teddy bear between them.

"You and me. And Tawny. Always." Between each word, a sob forces its way from her throat.

The woman snaps her gaze to the child and a sinister smile spreads on her lips. She takes a step forward and I leap from the tree.

I will not let the gods steal the soul of this child.

The woman startles and turns from the girl, her eyes narrowing in my direction.

Ignoring the twinge of pain shooting up my legs, I unsheathe the shortsword from my side. The magic urging me to slay my opponents is stronger than ever before, and I allow it to fill every part of my body, fueling the wrath and vengeance boiling inside me.

"Run." I glance at the child to make sure she heard me but she only tightens her grip on the man.

"I'm not leaving him—"

The woman darts forward and tackles me to the ground with a harsh kick to my stomach. The sword clatters to the side and she grips it before I even have the time to reach for it.

"The darkness is full of cheaters tonight," she snarls, taking a step in my direction. "The gods will be pleased with my cleansing."

I cough against the pain, my hands fighting for a grip on the slippery ground.

The woman raises the sword and I extend my foot, hitting her shin. She curses and drops the sword but not without kicking my ribs.

My chest slams against the ground, the hard impact knocking the air from my lungs.

"You have to run!"

The child is still sobbing next to the man. She rubs her splotchy face, her big round eyes meeting my gaze.

She shakes her head.

"Run. Now!"

The woman yanks me by the hood, turning me around before slamming me back onto the ground. "Are you blind to the fate of the other cheater?" She dips the tip of the sword in the blood on the ground before smearing it across my cheek without slicing my skin.

"You're the one who can't see she's just a child—"

The woman tips her head back, the cackling laugh erupting from her throat sending a shiver down my back. "Don't you see? There are no children in the games. Only warriors." She lowers her head and her gaze bores into me, her lips curling into a sneer. "And apparently a lot of cheaters."

"Run!" I roll away just in time, the sharpened tip of my sword boring into the ground where my heart was only seconds ago.

The woman lets out an angry sound and I scramble to my feet, leaping over the dead body and pushing the child away. We tumble away from the bloody tree and the child screams and thrashes in my arms. Her nails bore into the leathers on my arms and I cradle her head to my chest to shield her from the boulder we crash into.

Pain erupts in my skull and the edges of my vision blur. The child scrambles from my grip and I'm too weakened and hurt to get her back.

"Run—" my voice is cut off by a strangled cough.

The girl is screaming words I can't hear over the roaring in my ears. She crawls back toward the dead man, the emerald stone tied around her neck banging against her chest. The teddy bear is lying on the ground and her small hands grab it, clutching it back against her chest just as the woman emerges from the darkness behind her.

A scream works its way up my throat.

I can't move. I can't breathe.

I can do nothing but watch as the woman yanks the child by her hair to expose her throat.

"You're next." The warrior glares in my direction, the sinister smile back on her lips. And then she lets out a battle cry and drags the tip of the sword across the child's throat.

Blood pours from the girl's throat in a violent gush. A single tear runs down her cheek, her screams lost to the howling wind.

The teddy bear falls from her hand and the child crumbles to the ground.

Fury roars inside me. Faint gilded sparks explode from my fingertips, extinguished by the darkness a second later.

I push away from the boulder, ignoring the pain throbbing in my head.

I'll tear the woman apart with my hands if I have to.

The warrior steps over the dead body without a single glance, her eyes moving to the sky above, a satisfied smile on her lips.

"And now, the last cheater—"

She raises the sword to the sky and I fumble with the dagger hidden in my sleeve. The sword gleams in the dim light and the dagger slides into my palm.

As I prepare to throw the dagger, the woman lets out a startled cry. Something black and sharp emerges from her heart and she falls to her knees. A dagger as black as the night is protruding from her back, its bearer a towering shadow behind her.

"There are no rules in the Tournament of Day and Night but one; survive." The shadowy figure reaches forward and yanks the dagger from the fallen warrior. "The only disgrace here is you."

He wipes the blade on her back before spitting on her as he pulls down his hood, revealing a scarred, furious face.

Thunder.

The presumed leader of the rebellion and a Lunan General in the middle of the Tournament protecting a Sorian princess.

The collar of his dark leathers is so high it's impossible to make out if he has the binding mark, but I would bet all the gold in the world that the only thing marking his neck is scars.

It shouldn't surprise me that he knows about my secret, not when he knows about other parts of my life unknown even to me, but I can't even begin to understand why he would risk his life by doing the most treasonous act in the two kingdoms.

My death would ensure that the rebellion succeeded in their plans of stopping the royal wedding. Does he know I already did that? And if he does, why would he even care whether I live or die?

"Hello, princess. You might want to lower that dagger now." He raises a scarred eyebrow and tucks his own dagger away.

My chest is heaving and anger clouds my vision. "Showing up a little earlier would've been nice."

He glances at the child next to the woman and a muscle ticks in his throat. "You can't save everyone."

A strangled chuckle bursts from my throat.

"You should focus on surviving the night. Nothing else. The real games are just about to begin." He turns his back to leave and I throw the dagger. It flies through the air right past his head before clattering to the ground.

Thunder spins around with a glare. "Nothing else means not attacking the person who just saved your life."

Exhaustion slams into me with a sudden force and I shrink back against the boulder. "Fine. But you can't just leave her—" I choke on a sob when my eyes land on the child's face buried in the ground and the bloody puddle around her.

"This is war, princess. It's the way of the gods." He practically spits the last word, his glare moving to the sky above. "The shadows will claim her when the trial is over—"

"No. I refuse to leave her like this."

Thunder sighs but reaches into a pocket on his chest, his fingers revealing a small glass orb with a flickering skylight.

"Are you sure you want to tamper with the gods' magic?"

No—

"Yes."

The corners of his lips tug and he shatters the glass in his hand before tossing it onto the dead body between us. The flickering light explodes into flames and I force myself not to look away until her entire body is submerged in fire.

"The man too. They came together so they'll leave together."

You and me. And Tawny. Always.

"As you wish, Your Highness." Thunder bows his head with a heavy sigh before moving to the bloody tree where the body of the child's protector lies alone in the darkness. He heaves him onto his shoulder, the dagger still protruding from the man's heart.

I let out a relieved sigh when Thunder gently moves the man down next to the child and the fire engulfs him in its flames.

The man and child. And Tawny. Together until the very end.

"I assume you won't ask me to help her soul." Thunder casts a glare at the woman, his feet kicking her away from the flames.

"No. I will pray to the gods she will rot before the shadows can claim her soul."

Thunder snorts. "Remember my words, princess. And a last little word of advice. Always remember to watch your back. You never know who or what you might find in here." An impish wink and mock bow later, he saunters away into the gray fog, leaving me with countless questions to keep me awake for the night.

The rest of the night is uneventful, except for the strange magic in the air. I make sure to keep moving, and despite how much I try not to think about what happened, Thunder's warning rings in my head.

Always make sure to watch your back, princess. You never know who or what you might find in here.

An obvious advice, but one that makes me highly paranoid throughout the night. My every instinct is screaming to join the fight. Invisible strings pull me in all directions. My whole body is trembling, my fingers twitching to nock an arrow or reach for a dagger.

Even though I'm not doing anything else than hiding, it's as if my soul is constantly in battle. I startle against invisible blows hitting parts of my body, my muscles tiring as if I'm in an ongoing war. When a scrape appears in my palm out of nowhere, I'm convinced the magic is thoroughly messing with my mind.

And then another thought slams into me, and it's so terrifying I wonder if it's not only the magic messing with my mind but the shadows and darkness of this court.

What if it is the curse in my body—the forbidden magic marking my skin black—that's forcing me to feel the wounds of the warriors around me, never knowing who it comes from or when it will happen? What if one of them dies and I do too?

Perhaps that's the price I have to pay.

The mark on my arm throbs as if in answer.

The sounds of battle never subside and I wonder how many lives will be claimed by the Shadow Realm tonight. I try to not let my gaze linger too long on the ground.

When the darkness around me finally seems to lighten a bit, I'm so restless it feels as if my blood is vibrating. I make my way toward the clearing where the game was opened in what seems like a lifetime ago, each step heavier than the last.

The sight that greets me gives me the urge to scream and claw my eyes out.

This is not a game.

This is war.

This is not a competition to find the best warrior and Victor, but a war between two kingdoms that have been battling for centuries, always on the brink of a full war that will destroy both of them.

The Tournament is a bloody battleground, and tonight, the Shadow Realm has stolen countless lives.

The first ray of sunlight hits the hand of a still warrior, a hand shielding a bloody face, a hand that will never move again.

A wave of nausea surges through me, my heart sinking at the thought of all the lives *wasted*.

And then the gray fog clouding the sky parts enough to reveal silver lightning crackling across the sky.

Silver for Luna.

Silver for the Lunan warriors sacrificing the most to the Shadow Realm.

The mark on my neck tingles, a silent confirmation of my success in overcoming the sixth trial.

Only two to go.

There is nothing good about this win.

Hordes of guards sweep into the clearing, swords and shields raised and ready to stop any warriors trying to break the fragile rules. When the sun rises and the trial ends, so does the slaughter.

At least that's what they want us to think.

Warriors emerge from every direction, some looking as if they've slept the entire night and others as ragged as the dead before them.

I linger in a tree until most of the warriors are gone from the clearing and the Royal Dais has disappeared in the distance.

As I jump down from the tree, a twig snaps behind me.

A shadowy figure steps into the dim light and something tightens in my chest at the sight of the warrior prince.

Star's dark hair is disheveled, and all traces of silver and midnight blue are gone from his eyes, only pure darkness left behind. There are shadows underneath his eyes, and there's a tiredness to his features that makes me question how he's still alive. His leathers are ripped in various places as if numerous beasts have attacked him at once, and crimson streaks the dark fabric. His face and hands are smeared with blood, but not his blood as there are no wounds on the prince.

My breath catches in my throat and my heartbeats stutter as he approaches me. I can't help wondering if the reason the Moon King never took another heir from this court is because some of the shadows' darkness is living inside the prince in front of me.

Death and shadow incarnate–the Prince of Shadow and Darkness.

He halts a step away, his dark gaze flickering across my body before landing on my face. He extends a hand, his fingertips grazing my right cheek.

"It's not my blood." I take a step back and he drops his hand.

I cross my arms against the eerie wind blowing through the fog, locking away the night's dark memories. "What happened to helping me win the games? I haven't seen you since..."

Since I killed your brother and we made a life-binding bargain.

A muscle ticks in his throat and he moves his dark gaze to a point behind me. "I always kept an eye on you but I was... occupied...enough to not have time to let you know. But it seems you did quite well on your own."

His eyes snap back to mine and a shiver runs down my back. "You should be glad no one knows the princess is still in the games," he says, voice so hollow it's a miracle he's still breathing. "This trial is why you should've left when you had the chance."

I open my mouth to say something but snap my mouth shut when he takes a step forward.

"Everyone wants the prize of killing the prince. Sadly for them, attempting that means no longer having a beating heart." He steps aside to reveal a limp body behind him and my breath catches in my throat.

I barely recognize the beaten man lying on the ground. His long brown hair is soaked with blood, and only a sliver of his cerulean eyes are visible through his swollen eyelids.

"You really went through with it. You killed–"

"Why do you think the Princes of the Moon participate in the Tournament? Our prize is not becoming a Victor, but eliminating the competition of inheriting the throne," Star practically spits, rage flickering across his features as silver flares in his eyes.

"He foolishly chose to go after me. I only defended myself. Prince Ciron is out of the games and there are now only nine princes separating me from the throne."

CHAPTER THIRTY

My nightmares are haunted by bloody blades, bloodcurdling screams, a teddy bear soaked in blood, and a warrior prince looking like death itself. And then there's Castor, his face contorted with rage, the Royal Sword protruding from his heart.

When my eyes blink open, I'm drenched in sweat and my heart beats a violent rhythm against my chest. For a second, all I see is the forest of shadows, but then I blink again and notice the sun streaming through the open window in the blue room in the Moon Palace. And instead of the putrid smell of fire, I inhale the sweet and musky aroma of flowers.

I'm not in the middle of a trial. I'm safe.

For now.

There is a careful knock on the door, and without waiting for an answer, Auren stalks in with a basket of freshly washed sheets.

"Morning, princess. Or should I say night?" She sets the basket on the bench in front of the bed before walking into the adjoining bathroom to turn on the faucet in the porcelain bathtub. "At least you got a good half-hour sleep."

After Star escorted me through the black hole in the mountain and back to the palace, I was so exhausted I rolled into bed and promptly fell asleep, dirty leathers and weapons and all. A bath and clean sheets are exactly what I need.

"You better hurry," Auren shouts over the rushing water. "The palace...well... It's a mess. Chaos, actually."

"What?" Dread coils in my stomach and all thoughts of confronting her about her role in the rebellion evaporate into thin air.

She emerges from the bathroom and gently grabs my arm to drag me with her. "As you know, Prince Castor is...*missing*. And then there's the unfortunate loss of Prince Ciron last night."

"Yes," I say, dragging out the word and looking for any sign she might know about the princes' true fates. The only sign is a slight hitch in her breathing, but I'm too anxious to question her right now.

"The news has reached the kings and they are not very pleased." Auren helps me remove the dirty fighting leathers and the weapons clatter to the floor.

The warm water that should be soothing and comfortable fails to thaw the ice in my veins.

"Have you seen Star today?" My gaze flickers to the expanded mark on my arm, to the lines that somehow feel *alive*.

I hate that I have to ask her.

I hate that I might have to depend on him.

And I hate that I don't know what he is planning.

My fingers trail along the new parts of the mark, over the single black star that serves as a reminder of the prince I'm now bound to.

A magical bargain is life-binding, but our bargain wasn't as specific as it should've been.

He could still trick me.

He could still kill me.

It's a good thing I plan on beating him to it.

But tonight I actually need his help.

"No," Auren says, untangling the knots in my hair with a silver brush. "I haven't seen him since the trial ended, but I'm sure he had something to do with the sky glittering silver." She purses her lips, her gaze briefly flickering to the mark on my arm and I hide it underneath the soapy water.

"And what about the other one? The prince who fell during the game? Ciron, was it?"

Auren shrugs as she rinses the soap out of my hair. "It's part of the games. They all know the risks. He will be claimed by the Shadow Realm just like the rest of the warriors."

"So there won't be a proper ceremony for him? He was a prince–"

"No." Her words are clipped as she speaks. "The only ceremonies for the fallen warriors are the common burnings. But since the prince lost in the Shadow Realm, there won't even be a fire. The shadows will take care of him."

A shudder runs down my back and I'm unable to stop the thoughts of my death being treated the same if I hadn't survived the fall through the temple.

Auren shrugs again. "It is the way of the gods." She moves to the porcelain sink where the ridiculous amethyst ring is discarded. "I guess you won't be needing this anymore," she mutters, studying the large rock.

"Take it."

She gives me an incredulous look.

"I mean it. Wear it, destroy it, sell it. I don't care. I just never want to see it again."

"I can't do that–"

"Consider it part of your payment. Don't make me order you to take it." I give her a sly smile as I step out of the water.

"Fine," Auren says with a sigh, slipping the ring into a pocket in her uniform before wrapping a towel around my body.

In the overfilled armoire, the wedding dress is hanging on display. It is a heap of white and silver fabric cinched tight enough to squeeze the life out of me.

"There's not going to be a wedding today," I murmur, shoving away the wedding dress in favor of a simple dress in a deep shade of blue so dark it's almost black. "This is a day for a grieving bride."

CHAOS IS an understatement to the state of the Moon Palace that afternoon.

One of the smaller ballrooms is decorated for a royal wedding, the light and dark shades of both kingdoms blended into swirls of colors. Banners hang from the high ceiling and silver and gilded pendants shaped into various forms dangle from sparkling chains, clanking and clunking when they brush against each other in the slight breeze flowing through the palace.

On one side, clad in matching dark suits with silver circlets resting on their brows, the princes are waiting and alert, their eyes locked on the kings arguing at the far end of the room. On the other side, with duplicated outfits of yellow and gold, my sisters' solar diadems gleam in their golden hair.

"Asteria! Why aren't you wearing your wedding dress?" Solina grabs my arm, steering me away from the black carpet lining the middle of the floor.

"Why should I? My wedding isn't until after the

Tournament," I say, willing a mask of innocence onto my face, one I carefully perfected in the bathroom mirror.

"It's a surprise wedding," Erina mutters, glancing at Father who is still deep in a heated discussion with the Moon King. "But you already knew that."

"Oh wow, then I'm really underdressed. And at my own wedding." I trail my fingers along the firm skirt of my dark dress before dragging a hand through my loose hair.

My sisters' reply is lost to the sound of bootsteps thundering into the ballroom and I turn around to see Star and Thunder accompanied by a few guards.

Star doesn't even look at me as he saunters toward his king, but his side brushes against me and his fingers briefly squeeze mine.

The kings stop talking when they notice the prince. The Moon King takes a step away from Father and Star says something in a low voice that causes the Moon King to lock his jaw as a murderous expression crosses his face.

With a snap of the dark king's fingers, Thunder walks forward and bows down on one knee as if he's going to beg for forgiveness.

"Your Majesty. It has been confirmed. The body found in the shallows of Sapphire Bay is indeed the missing Prince Castor. The death wound a sword to the heart. Likely the rebellion." Thunder's deep voice echoes through the quiet room and a low murmur breaks out between the other princes.

My heart beats so hard I'm afraid it's going to give me away and I press my nails into the scars of my palms to keep myself from passing out.

"How convenient that the groom is found murdered on the day of the wedding," Father spits, golden eyes glowering in my direction. "Where were you during the last game, dear daughter?"

I swallow against the growing lump in my throat as I force

myself to lift my chin and straighten my posture. "In bed. Healing. The last time I saw Prince Castor was the night of the last celebratory ball. As I'm sure you very well know, my king."

A flare of gilded light erupts from his eyes and his fingers twitch in the direction of the Royal Sword strapped to his side–the sword that only days ago murdered the prince in question and is now back where it belongs as if nothing ever happened.

The Moon King makes a sound very much like the growls of the shadowy beast in the Court of Nightmares. "Perhaps this is the work of your kingdom, Helios. An attempt to break away from our contract."

"How dare you even suggest such a preposterous thing–"

Star steps between the two raging kings, holding out his hands, and the gilded light erupting from Father's eyes is doused by a dark smoke seeping up from the Moon King's feet. "There will still be a union between our two kingdoms–"

"There cannot be a wedding without a groom," Father practically screams, unknowingly repeating the words of the rebellion. His hand is now fully closed around the hilt of the Royal Sword, the golden sparks emanating from his fingertips increasing in number.

"There will be a union between our two kingdoms," Star says again, a small trace of silver light flickering to life in his dark eyes.

Father lets out a furious cry and starts unsheathing the Royal Sword, but a shadowy hand shoots from the shadows behind him and halts right in front of his face.

"Wait." The Moon King's voice is pure warning. "As much as I would love to see our magic clash together, I am curious to see where this is going." His gaze snaps to mine and it feels as if my heart stops beating.

Father is shaking with fury but he takes a step away from the shadowy hand, his grip on the handle of the Royal Sword whitening his knuckles.

The only reason he is not unleashing the full force of his magic is the palace caging him from the sun, but even that won't stop him for long.

This is not going to end well.

"Continue." The Moon King waves a hand, his gaze moving to his son.

Star gives him a curt nod before striding through the room until he is standing right next to me. His midnight eyes bore into me, whispering silent words I can't decipher over the thundering beating of my heart. A muscle ticks in his throat and he grabs my hand, his skin unnervingly cold.

And then he holds up my hand with a ring I didn't even notice he slipped on. A simple black band with a stone in the shape of a glittering star, the blue so pale it's almost silver.

No–

"I've asked Asteria to marry me and she has accepted."

No one speaks. No one moves. No one dares even breathe too loudly. The only sounds are the fluttering of the banners and the clanking of the chains and pendants.

It feels like an eternity passes before Star lowers our hands and slips his fingers between mine.

Magic roars inside me. It vibrates through my blood and tears at my soul with a violent force that takes my breath away.

The Moon King is the first to speak, his dark eyes narrowing at his son. "And when, exactly, was this deal made?"

Star's voice is loud and confident when he answers, unfazed by the raging kings in front of him. "Before I went into the last trial and when I started to suspect something might have happened to the prince. It's important we keep up appearances at this time, especially with the increased attacks of the rebellion and now that we've lost two in our ranks."

Moon studies him with cool indifference, a stark contrast to the fuming king beside him and the shocked expressions around them. "I suppose," he says finally, dragging out the words while tapping his chin.

Father opens his mouth to speak but the shadowy hand slams against his face, silencing his voice and the golden light radiating from his head. The Sorian guards closest to their king bristle, but they don't move.

The Moon King turns to his opposing king, eyebrows raised and a smirk on his lips. "Does it really matter which one of my princes fulfills the contract? As long as there is still one left, our bargain still stands."

The shadowy hand retreats and Father coughs as gilded sparks splutter from every part of his body. "The next time you lay your magic on me, it will be your last."

The Moon King rolls his eyes. "Let us just get this over with–"

"We can't have the wedding today," I blurt, ignoring every screaming instinct to run away. "I mean," I continue, forcing my voice and body to be steady as I speak. "We just agreed it's important to keep up appearances. The people need time to adjust, to grieve, and to celebrate a new union." I almost blurt out the word bargain when the mark on my arm tingles as Star's thumb strokes across the back of my hand, either in warning or encouragement–I can't tell.

The room falls silent again and I count ten painful heartbeats before the oldest prince pushes away from the wall.

"She's right."

Hope sprouts in my chest and I suck in a silent breath.

Axton continues, his voice loud in the quiet room. "The people need time. And we can't let the union be overshadowed by the Tournament or the other way around. The best choice would be to hold the wedding after the games are done, perhaps even at the final ball."

It's not real. The ring on my finger, the proposal, the wedding. None of it is real.

It's only a ruse to hide what happened, not a part of the bargain. It can't be. I refuse to bind myself to any of them more than I already have.

I just need time. Time to win the Tournament and become a Victor.

A Victor doesn't need to be a bride.

A Victor can be queen.

I just need time to make it happen.

Whatever it takes, Asteria.

The Moon King claps his hands together. "It is my kingdom hosting the wedding in question, so I will make the final decision." He casts a warning glance at the king beside him.

Father doesn't so much as flinch. His gilded glare is locked on me and his fury seems to warm the air in the room.

I can't breathe—

Star squeezes my hand and I lift my chin, moving my gaze to the other king and the cruel smirk on his lips.

"Fine. The wedding will be postponed until further notice." The relieved breath working its way up my throat is strangled by a gust of dark wind blowing through the room.

"But you better convince the people you are deeply in love," he snarls, the cruel smirk vanishing as fast as it came. "I am warning the both of you. Mess this up and it will be the end." A sinister smile breaks across his lips and he rubs his hands together, another gust of smoky wind hitting my face.

Star bows his head with another squeeze of his hand, silently urging me to do the same. Avoiding the scorching eyes of the room, I follow his lead, willing my body to stop trembling as he drags me away.

As we walk out of the room, the wedding banners seem to droop in answer to the canceled ceremony.

My new betrothed leads me through the ornate doors and into the cool hallways and shadowed corners of the palace.

We walk in silence until we emerge onto one of the many balconies, and I can't help wondering if this is the one Castor's previous bride fell from. No matter if it was out of desperation or if her betrothed pushed her, she didn't have a bargain with another prince to save her.

"Breathe, starlight," Star murmurs and tucks a strand of hair behind my ear. He tilts my head up to look at him, and I blink and release a breath I didn't know I was holding, easing some of the tension in my chest.

"I told you making a bargain with me would be a good idea." A smirk plays at his lips as his dark gaze searches every inch of my face.

"Marrying you was not a part of the bargain," I snap, backing away until my back hits the stone of the palace and his hand is no longer touching me.

Star gives me a bored look. "You were the one who said we didn't have time to make a specific written contract," he trails off, raising a dark eyebrow.

An exasperated chuckle escapes me and I rest my head against the wall. I'm suddenly so exhausted I can barely stand, let alone fight a pointless battle.

The prince moves forward so fast it startles me, his hands landing on the wall making a cage around me. "Help me get what I want and I'll help you win the Tournament. That was our bargain. This is me helping you." His breath is hot on my face, his citrusy smell as enticing as ever.

"And what do you want?"

His eyes darken as they flicker to my lips, sending an involuntary shiver down my neck. "For now I just need you to play along."

My eyes narrow. "Right, be the obedient bride and stay out of trouble–"

"Oh, starlight, I would never ask you to stay out of trouble. I am trouble. And you and me together?" His dark laugh reverberates through me, his eyes glittering as bright as the stars behind him.

"Unstoppable."

CHAPTER THIRTY-ONE

The grieving color of Soria is an earthy brown meant to symbolize the earth where the essence of life will be given back before it seeps back to the sky.

Brown is not the grieving color of Luna.

It is a deep shade of forest green, also meant to represent the circle of life, honoring the energy borrowed and now given back. The soul of the deceased will move on to the Shadow Realm, but the life essence will fuel the magic keeping our world alive.

Castor's lifeless body is already burning on a pyre, concealed underneath a draped fabric in the same color as my dress–moss green with a veil in an even darker shade to hide my face. At least it keeps out the many looks in my direction, giving me an excuse not to force myself to shed a few tears.

The amethyst ring previously residing on my finger is gone along with the marriage contract to the dead prince, replaced with a bargain with another prince, the proof an obsidian ring hidden in the long sleeve of my dress.

Hours ago, when I got ready in a townhouse in a border city in the Court of Night–the court Castor was *gifted* from–Auren told me a little about the royal death rituals in Luna. Sometimes it's the color green and a ceremony in one of the forest temples, other times it's the color blue accompanied by a ritual in one of the ocean temples, but never black. The color usually associated with the night is honorary and celebratory, the pride of the kingdom.

And for some, there are no colors or ceremonies at all.

Perhaps Castor's last night is in the forest because the ocean has already claimed some of his essence.

"From the earth and the sky were you gifted and made, in the earth and the sky will you stay, from the earth and the sky will you rise again." The priestesses' chanting is haunting underneath the moonlight, the familiar words prickling my skin.

The flames from the large fire warms my skin, sticking strands of hair to my cheeks and forehead while the veil threatens to smother me. Large amounts of flowers have been added to lessen the stench of death, their dark colors bleeding into the night.

The Moon King has already given his last speech to his son, and his words were followed by a ceremonial throwing of rocks soaked in moonlight by his other sons.

My roving gaze lands on my new betrothed leaning against a pillar of the temple. Like the rest of the royals, Star is wearing green, the shade so dark the color almost disappears in the dark night. His dark locks are swept away from his forehead and emerald stones glimmer from the bottom of his ears.

The prince raises a hand to straighten the lapels of his jacket and my breath hitches.

There is a ring on his finger. A black band with a pale blue and silver stone that sparkles in the darkness—the counterpart to my own ring.

If we were to stand next to each other, we would've matched in more ways than the clothes and rings. A magical bargain is now between us, binding our lives together in the form of black lines pulsing on our arms and invisible strings tied around our souls–not to be broken until both ends are fulfilled.

I'll die if I fail to fulfill my end.

Whatever it takes, Asteria.

There's no weeping or screaming as we watch the fire burn. There's only silence and the crackling of the flames eating away the life of a prince and the dreaded promise of my future.

A FEW DAYS after the burning ceremony in the Night Court, a grand soiree is held in one of Moon Palace's gardens.

There is little time for mourning during the Tournament Times.

The limestone statues of the gods are decorated with dark flowers and silver glitter, and thousands of tiny skylights fly through the garden. Small tables are brimming with drinks in all shades of the rainbow and hundreds of different pastries and cakes stuffed with fruit and berries.

The garden is crowded with people from all over the two kingdoms because tonight, the palace is open to everyone. At least in theory.

There's a long line of people waiting behind the gates, the guards letting in a few people at a time as others are ushered away after barely catching a glimpse of the palace. The long mountain trek up to the palace is so packed I'm half afraid people are going to topple over the edges any second.

Anticipation and excitement stir the summer air, the ecstatic chatter of the guests echoing off the mountains.

Nyx has been quiet since the death of the princes. There were no festivities after the last trial, as there never is in the Shadow

Court, so even the Tournament has been at a pause. But tonight, something big is going to happen. That much is clear from the opulent event and the open invitations.

I fidget with the sleeves of my dress as I descend the stairs to the garden, the stone on my ring casting swirls of light onto the billowing skirt. It is the same dress I wore the night I found out that the unknown warrior I fought in the binding rounds was a prince–the prince I'm now bound to.

It feels like a different life.

The starry dress was delivered to my room this morning along with a single dark flower I've never seen before, the emanating sweet and musky aroma all too familiar.

"Are you ready for this, starlight?" Warm fingers wrap around mine, and sparks shoot from our touching fingers.

Star is also wearing what he did the night of our first dinner together on the palace patio in Soria. A dark suit embroidered with the same stars on my dress, the flecks of silver lighting up his dark appearance.

I'm about to pull away when Star leans forward and presses a soft kiss to my cheek, the faint stubble on his chin scratching my skin.

"Remember what the king said. We have to appear madly in love for this to work." He snorts and his breath is hot against my cheek.

I let him lead me onto a stone path in the shortly-trimmed grass, ignoring the urge to shove him away. "One would think that wouldn't be appropriate considering my previous betrothed just died. I am a grieving widow after all."

Star snorts again before giving a strained smile to a passing pair of women. "You're not a widow. You didn't marry him. Royals have arranged marriages all the time, but the people can't resist true love."

I grit my teeth, giving him a murderous look.

"None of that, starlight. No one is going to believe us if you keep looking at me like that. But luckily for you, hate and love do often combine." He chuckles as his gaze rakes over me, from the silver clips in my hair to the boots hidden underneath the long skirt of my dress.

This time I'm the one to snort. "Good luck with that."

He leans close and his lips graze the shell of my ear. "You're more than welcome to threaten me with a dagger again. As long as it's not just to spill my blood."

It takes a moment to realize what he's talking about and I can't stop my lips from tugging when I do, the memories of his ridiculous reaction to waking up to an attempted murder resurfacing in my mind.

"I do remember you volunteering to be... *restricted* in bed."

"There she is," he says, his fingers tracing the binding mark on my neck. "Maybe we'll save it for our wedding night."

I'm about to retort something back when the triplets come running, almost crashing into the surrounding crowd of people, all wearing dresses in the usual shades of gold.

"There you are," Deya exclaims, her eyes darting between me and Star.

"Yes, you're both late," Delia says, her eyes flickering to our entwined hands.

"You can never be late to your own party, everyone else is simply early," Star drawls, the teasing smirk replaced by a bored expression.

"This party isn't only for you," Davina snaps, the tension in her features making worry and dread squeeze my heart.

As if he can sense my churning emotions, Star turns his head to look at me. "You're with me now. And if that sword even goes near you–"

The darkness in his eyes and growl in his voice startles me so much that for a second, I almost forget this is all an act to appease the people of our kingdoms.

"Well..." Davina touches my arm, startling my gaze away from Star's. "The people are starting to get impatient so we really should get going–"

"Fine." I suck in a few deep breaths before following my sisters to the center of the garden where the stone path ends in a large circle picturing the phases of the moon.

"You go ahead. I need a minute," I mumble, the triplets casting me angry looks as they step into the circle to join the others.

Star doesn't move from my side and a warm hand is pressed to my clammy forehead. "Having second thoughts, princess? Do I have to remind you of our deal?"

"No," I mutter through gritted teeth, carefully removing his hand from my face, resisting the urge to slap him away. There are too many eyes watching us.

Star's reply is lost to the Moon King's booming voice starting a speech about love and loss, his words aligning both with the Tournament and the fallen princes. "We will mourn but we will also celebrate. These past days we've mourned. Tonight is a night for celebration." The king holds out a hand, and Father surprises me by stepping forward.

Once again, he has the honor of giving me away to the enemy kingdom.

Star drags me through the crowd, placing us at the back of the stone circle next to my sisters.

"The Kingdoms of the Sky will continue to flourish through the Tournament of Day and Night." Father's thunderous voice reverberates through the crowd and a faint gilded light frames his body.

"A Victor is one of our most treasured and honorable titles, even more so than our nobility. And as a token and reminder of that honor–" He gestures at the Victor behind him and Elio steps forward to meet the king's outstretched hand.

My heartbeats quicken and a small spark of hope kindles to life in my chest.

Has he changed his mind? Is it finally happening?

I'm not the person the Sun King turns to.

Father gives me a cruel smile and reaches for my oldest sister.

A part of my heart cracks.

Solina steps forward, looking as much as the future Sun Queen as she possibly can. A small golden crown I've never seen before glitters in her hair, the gilded material reflected by the setting sun.

A perfect embodiment of the sun.

An invisible blade slams into my heart, twisting and poking the same way I used the Royal Sword on the dead prince's heart.

A golden ring with a large citrine rock glimmers from my sister's hand, and the blade cuts even deeper when I notice a golden band around Elio's finger.

The cracked part of my heart shatters.

Elio doesn't meet my searching gaze. The Victor looks straight ahead, a pleased smile breaking across his face.

Star's grip on my arm is as solid as the limestone statues in the garden.

"What is happening right now?" My voice is barely a whisper and my chest is constricted from the lack of air.

"I don't know," he says through gritted teeth. "Our engagement was supposed to distract the people from Castor's death. Not this."

The crowd around us is roaring and cheering as Father continues speaking about the importance of the Tournament and the Victors as if he didn't just implicitly announce the next king of Soria.

"Perhaps we'll need to cause some more trouble," Star continues, his eyes pure unyielding darkness. "It is a brilliant idea to strengthen the idea of the Tournament by basically crowning the last Victor as king. But a wedding between two royals of opposite kingdoms would've been even better."

"Not anymore." All traces of previous nervous energy have seeped out of me, only to be replaced by an aching heaviness. "Perhaps a royal wedding between someone else, but not me. Not the cursed princess who just lost her betrothed, only strengthening the rumors of me being a living curse," I whisper, eyes locked on the display in front of us.

Elio and Solina's hands are clasped together, the king holding them raised in the air for all to see. My sister is shining as bright as the sun, a beaming smile plastered on her sun-kissed face. The Victor beside her looks just as striking, his golden suit matching his victory mark.

"This changes nothing." Star's hand tries to tilt my gaze to his, but I shake him off. "Our bargain, the engagement, will still be the protection you need—"

I tune out his words, my eyes locked on the smile on Elio's face.

Another spark of pain shoots through my chest.

One after one, my dreams shatter like the ice coating the lake behind the Sun Palace during the harshest winters.

Ruling the kingdom with Elio at my side. Sneaking away from council meetings to steal a thousand kisses. Escaping to Helianthus to swim in the stream behind Vera's cottage. Training underneath the sun. Lounging in our bed—

It feels as if a lifetime has passed since our training sessions underneath the never-ending sun when my heart ached for my only friend to finally see me as something more than the cursed princess training for an impossible mission. The shy touches that ended in nights tangled in each other's arms.

The glimpses of what could've been a good life away from the nightmares of being the cursed princess doomed for misery, gone as if it never happened at all.

Our time together wasn't nearly enough, and now I will never get more of it.

I fight free from Star's arms, ignoring the shocked murmurs around me as I run through the shadows of the garden.

Away from the cheering crowd and newly promised couple.

Away from my shattered dreams and broken heart.

CHAPTER THIRTY-TWO

"We wouldn't have to act this quickly if you hadn't caused so much trouble, Asteria!" Solina is pacing in front of the sitting area of one of the libraries, her blonde hair breaking loose from her neat braid.

It's the morning after the celebration that altered my life and took away one of the few things I've dared dream of.

My sister barged into the room the moment the first sign from the sun appeared in the sky, ranting about security and how she was prevented from entering my room. I had just crawled back into the library from the hidden servants' halls, too restless to even attempt to get some sleep.

"It's not my fault the rebellion killed Castor." My voice is dull and hollow even to my own ears, just like the rest of me.

Solina stops pacing long enough to give me an indignant look. "I'm not in the mood for your lies, Asteria. And Castor's death is only a tiny part of the trouble you've caused."

Her lips pull into a sneer, and for a second, I see the Sun King's eyes glaring at me. "This doesn't only affect you. Of course, I've known about the upcoming engagement ever since Elio won the last Tournament but I didn't expect it to happen like this. We were supposed to do the announcement back home and—"

I don't hear the rest of her words. The betrayal stings so deeply that it takes my breath away. It clenches the rest of my fragile heart so tight I'm convinced it's going to fully crumble any second.

She has known since he won last year. And *he* probably knew too.

The last night we spent together was weeks after he was crowned Victor. Did he know then?

"You have known about it since last year." Fury slips into my voice and Solina stops pacing, the pity in her eyes only infuriating me even more.

"Asteria. I know you two have been...*friends* for a long time and you probably had something more in mind, but you need to understand he's a Victor with great influence and a high position in our kingdom. As the oldest of us, it's only fitting that—"

"Get out," I snarl, pressing my nails into the scars of my palms to resist the urge to strangle her.

"Asteria—"

"Fine. Then I'll go."

The door slams shut behind me, silencing her protests and condescending remarks.

The silent hallways are a relief compared to the room that quickly became too cramped with my sister's arrogance. Not even the shadows can scare me today.

Forcing myself to breathe in through my nose and out through my mouth, I push the anger away, willing ice into my veins.

But it's not long before I run into someone else who worsens the crack in my heart.

Elio holds out his arms to steady me as I practically crash into him, his touch no longer warm and soothing, but cold and unfamiliar.

His golden ring cuts into my skin.

"Asteria."

"Elio."

Hurt flickers in his hazel eyes when I pull away and his lips press into a thin line.

"Shouldn't you be busy with your new royal duties by now?"

His fingers wrap around my wrist as I turn to walk away, his touch still lacking its usual warmth. "Ria, please."

I narrow my eyes and he drops his hand, the nickname he appointed me when we were only children echoing deeper into the mountain.

"Please," he repeats, his voice slightly breaking, his eyes shiny with emotion.

The sight that normally would soften any emotion snaps the last string of restraint holding me back.

"Please what? You've lied to me this entire time! I thought you were my friend! I thought we shared something special! I thought that–" I swallow against the lump in my throat, forcing back the tears welling in my eyes.

"I am," Elio snaps, dragging a hand over his short-cropped hair. "I am your *best* friend, Asteria. Haven't I proven that enough? I thought I still had time. Time to find a way around the deal."

He takes a step forward, his hand twitching as if he is considering reaching for me again. "I thought *we* still had time. But then you bound yourself to the Tournament and then you were promised to Castor and–"

A humorless chuckle escapes me. "That doesn't change the fact that you lied to me. You should've told me!"

"I'm not the only one keeping secrets I shouldn't!" An angry line bulges across his forehead and I'm reminded of the last time we argued like this.

"That's different."

Elio makes an exasperated sound and pinches the bridge of his nose. "It's not. And you know that—"

"My secret didn't involve anyone else but myself." Fury sparks in my fingertips and I ball my hands at my side, pressing my nails into the scars so hard it's the only thing I feel.

"Was Solina your prize when you won the Tournament? Did you think of her when you brought me to your bed?"

He flinches and staggers a step back. "Of course not! There was only you—"

"But you knew."

He doesn't deny it.

The anger inside me roars but I push it all down.

He doesn't deserve it.

He is nothing to me now.

"I'm doing this for you! Don't you realize that?"

Another dark chuckle bursts from my lips. "For me? Well, that's nice."

Rage flickers across his features. "Have you forgotten all the times you told me your dreams of taking the throne and getting revenge on your father? Or do you remember what I told you?"

"A kingdom without a promised predecessor would be in chaos and easily conquered by the enemy kingdom," I say through gritted teeth, remembering all the times he stopped me from doing something very reckless by using his knowledge as a general's son.

"And I told you that wouldn't be a problem when I won the Tournament. The last Sun Queen won her throne that way, and so will I." My fingers find the birthmark behind my ear that seems to tingle in reminder.

"Exactly," Elio says with an indignant sigh. "But then you failed and got tangled with numerous princes–"

"I didn't fail–"

"You might as well have," he snaps, pain replacing the anger on his face.

"Well, I didn't. And there was only one prince, and he is no longer a problem."

His eyes widen in surprise and for a moment, all he does is stare at me like he's never seen me before, but then he takes a step forward with his arms extended as if he wants to catch me. "Asteria–"

"We're not talking about that." I take a step back, the distance between us seemingly endless.

I never told him about the first life I took, and perhaps that was when something started to change between us.

His face hardens and the anger is back in his eyes. "And what about the other one? You don't need to pretend with that bastard anymore. This will distract the people enough to forget about you."

"It's too late for that."

"It's not too late! You can still win the Tournament and take the throne when we go back home."

Home. The word sends a jolt through my chest. Is it really a home when the once cherished memories of it are no longer real?

I suck in a breath, trying to ignore the painful throbbing of my heart. "And what about Solina?"

"It doesn't matter." Elio takes another step forward, a muscle ticking in his cheek. "It wouldn't matter if you win."

"The Sun King will certainly care–"

"Not if he is no longer there," he says, his voice barely a whisper.

I'm so stunned by his suggestion I can't make my lips move to form an answer.

Elio lets out a heavy sigh that eases some of the tension in his shoulders before striding forward until he is standing so close I can feel his breath on my face.

"Everything I've done has been to protect you. Winning the Tournament, this–" he lifts his hand, gesturing at the golden ring glimmering on his finger. "Ria, please." His hands move to cup my face, his fingers stroking along my skin, and then he presses his lips to mine.

The kiss should be sparkling sunshine, fluttering butterflies, sweet berries, and everything I've ever wanted.

It's not.

The ice around my heart hardens.

I don't kiss him back, and I don't move to push him away. I stand completely still, my nails pressed into the scars of my palms, waiting to see if I'll feel *something*.

Elio breaks the kiss to lean his forehead against mine, his warm breath on my face doing nothing to melt the iciness within me. "Ria, please," he repeats, pleading and desperate. "I don't want to lose you."

My body is frozen and all I'm able to do is blink at him.

He whispers my name again, his lips grazing the skin on my temple.

For a brief moment, the once most treasured moments of my life flash in my mind.

His laughter against my skin.

His arms wrapped around me.

My nails scratching his back as his lips traveled paths on my bare skin.

But then I think of what he knew during those moments–

what he was hiding—and the warmth vanishes, leaving nothing but cold, empty darkness.

I step away from his touch, ignoring his pleading eyes and outstretched arms. "I'm starting to wonder if you ever had me at all."

And then I leave him and don't look back.

THE TAVERN IS SO overcrowded I'm debating finding another, but from the loud cheers and voices that greeted me the second I stepped into the royal city, it's safe to assume all other places are equally as crowded.

I find an available shadowed corner and a large glass of dull liquid is rushed to my hands. After pouring the liquid down my throat, I snort and make a mental reminder to tell Star he was wrong when he claimed the bad drinks came from Soria.

I don't bother hiding my face tonight, fulfilling the rumors of a cursed princess by having a permanent sneer on my face to keep away the other drunken guests.

A mourning bride flirting with her dead betrothed's brother only days after his death.

A princess in fighting leathers fit for the Tournament she so humiliatingly failed.

After I left Elio in the hallways this morning, the cold hollowness was instantly replaced by a burning anger so strong none of the weapons at the hidden training ring could tame it, the forgotten room carved into the mountain Auren showed me no longer the reprieve it usually is.

It quickly turns out that choosing a tavern to occupy my time is doing nothing to subdue the scorching anger raging inside of me.

A group of men roaring with laughter as one of them tumbles off a bar stool has me grinding my teeth in annoyance. The sound of glass shattering on the wooden floorboards pierces my skull. And the loud chatter and laughter give me the urge to scream.

I gulp down the rest of the pale brown liquid, throwing a golden coin onto the rotten table before hurrying out of the suffocating room, ignoring the questioning looks in my direction.

Outside, the fresh air is scented by blooming flowers and exquisite meals cooked underneath the stars. Laughter and music echo from every direction, merging with drunken toasts raised to the sky and screeches from children who should've been sound asleep hours ago if they lived in Soria.

I slip through the narrow alleys between the crowded buildings, focusing on each step instead of the burning anger.

"Our new sister out looking for trouble, is it?" A voice drawls from the darkness behind me, halting my steps.

"That's disgusting, brother. But yes, definitely hunting trouble from the looks of her. Care for a game, dear brother?" Another voice answers, so similar to the first that only a faint difference in tone separates them.

"Always."

Two men step out of the darkness and I resist the urge to scream when I realize who it is.

Two of the Moon Princes, twins and so alike I don't bother trying to discern them from each other. I can't even remember their names.

They're both wearing silk shirts in a pearly white fabric, and the open collars reveal a jagged scar in the shape of the crescent moon. Their dark blonde hair is twisted into low-hanging braids and binding marks are carved into their skin.

"Shouldn't you two be preparing to lose the next game? It seems to me that you're the ones out looking for trouble." I rest my hand on the hilt of the sword strapped to my side as my feet move into a fighting stance.

The twins' yellow eyes flicker to my hand and cruel smirks appear on their lips.

"Did you know Castor shared the same blood as us? Besides the king of course." They start pacing around me in a circle like predators circling their prey.

"No." I move the hand that's not holding the sword behind my back to where a dagger is hidden in the back pocket of my leathers.

"Do you know what the Lunans do to people who spill precious drops of their shared blood?" One of them sneers, teeth bared and fingers twitching as if he is itching to tear into me.

"I'm sure I can imagine." My gaze darts between them and I follow their movements, but one of them is always out of sight behind my back.

"Why don't you find out for yourself?"

They pounce from both sides and I roll away just in time, the dagger clasped in my hand.

"The little princess wants to play," one prince sneers and the other one finishes the rest of the sentence, "Sadly for her and luckily for us we very much enjoy playing with our victims."

The princes are quick on their feet and they move as if they're two halves of one person, as if they always know the other's next move and thought.

One of them reaches for me and the other throws a dagger that flies right past my ear as I jump back on my feet.

"Is this really necessary? I didn't do anything to your brother. He was my betrothed. Why would I harm him?"

"Don't think we don't know what you're up to, *Princess Asteria*."

One of the princes has disappeared from my sight, nowhere to be seen in the darkness surrounding us.

"I don't know what you're talking about." My back hits the wall of a nearby building as I frantically search the darkness, deeming it unwise to just run for it without knowing where the other one is hiding.

"We think you do."

It's impossible to tell where his voice is coming from. There are no skylights in the alley and the darkness is eagerly hiding its prince.

The other prince is prowling closer and he picks up the dagger from the ground, anticipation gleaming in his eyes.

"Scared, princess?"

"She should be."

Their voices are everywhere and nowhere, echoing all around me, and it feels as if the shadows are starting to reach for me.

If Star has figured out how to access the royal magic, so could the rest of the princes.

I need to do something.

Quick.

Before it's too late.

"You won't get away with this."

Their laughter snakes down my skin, and the sound echoes on the wind blowing through the alley.

The twin in front of me throws the dagger and I duck. The blade bores into the wall where my head was only seconds ago and blood trickles from a scrape on the top of my ear.

As I move to yank the dagger from the wall, something dark leaps from the roof above me. Hands as cold as ice wrap around my throat, the grip so strong it instantly makes my eyes water and my chest constrict from the lack of air.

I fumble for the dagger, kicking my legs out to hit my captor in the groin.

The prince mutters a curse, his grip loosening enough for me to pull the dagger from the wall and aim it at his throat.

"Let me go or I'll slit you open," I rasp, gulping down air to press the words out.

"I don't think so," he spits, tightening his grip around my throat again.

This time, he is not fast enough.

With a grunt, I push the dagger into his shoulder. He drops his hands with a small hiss, moving to reach for the dagger embedded in his skin.

At the next heartbeat, the other twin is upon me, another dagger barely missing my chest as I move away.

The smoldering embers of fury deep inside me erupt, the flames licking up my insides and fueling my body.

None of this would've happened if Father hadn't made a bargain with the enemy kingdom.

None of this would've happened if Elio hadn't betrayed me.

None of this would've happened if I wasn't doomed to be the cursed princess.

I will not take this one more time.

My body moves without thought. Sparks of anger explode from my fingertips, the small tingling pain bringing me forward as the sparks sizzle to the ground, the flickering lights lighting up the darkness.

The sword at my side is unsheathed before I even have the time to blink, the sharpened tip boring into the prince's skin and cutting a clean line across his throat.

His severed head hits the cobblestones with a thud. And when the rest of his body tumbles after and blood spills in a violent current, the flaming anger stills.

The sword clatters to the ground. I turn my head away and vomit all over the ground.

The other prince's devastated screams reverberate through my heart. He falls to his knees, one hand still clutching the dagger in his shoulder, the other reaching for his fallen brother.

A gust of dark wind sweeps through the alley, the black mist obscuring the sickening sight. A faint rustle sounds behind me and warm hands move my hair away from my face, tucking it down into the neck of my leathers.

"I thought we agreed to cause trouble together from now on."

I don't have the strength to answer him. I sink to the ground, my head hitting the cobblestones with a thud.

The remaining twin has stopped screaming. He yanks the dagger out of his shoulder and takes one last look at his brother before turning around and bolting into the darkness.

"I'll be right back," Star says with a heavy sigh as he leans down to remove one last strand of hair from my forehead before running after his brother who's no longer a twin.

A star shoots across the sky above and I think that the sky is too beautiful tonight. Too beautiful to witness something as horrible as this. Too beautiful for a cursed princess to look upon.

The fire has quieted when Star comes back and gathers me in his arms, only a faint sizzle remaining in my fingertips. He doesn't say anything, and I desperately hope he is unaware of the battle raging within me.

He carries me through the outskirts of the city, the only sounds the roaring in my ears and the steady rhythm of his heart against my cheek. His arms around me are solid and warm, so at odds with his usual dark and cold demeanor, and at that moment, it's strange to think that he is supposed to be my greatest enemy and competitor.

The outline of his face and the night sky blink in and out of existence. I feel so drained of life I wish the darkness would just claim me already, but it only catches me for moments at a time, forcing my eyes open with a jolt now and then.

"Wake up, princess."

The next time my eyes flutter, the sound of rushing water fills my ears, and then, slowly, a warmth spreads from my toes and up my body. Something cold is pressed against my forehead and I gasp, my body jerking away from the icy touch.

Star gives me a sly grin before pushing me back against the bathtub so the back of my neck rests on the edge, a white cloth dangling from his fingers. "Stay awake and I won't have to do that again."

I'm unable to speak or move away again, the sudden movements depleting the last bit of strength from my limbs.

Star dips the cloth into the warm water before continuing to clean my face, his fingertips featherlight on my skin as he brushes away strands of hair. "That wasn't your first time killing someone."

It's not a question so I don't answer.

"And you're in the middle of a deadly Tournament with countless casualties."

Another not-question.

"So why were you so bothered by the death before you?"

A question that shouldn't need an answer.

"After all you've seen in the games, a pesky prince shouldn't be the thing rattling you. Unless, of course, you were imagining me in his place, which we both know would never happen. Not after your last very weak attempt," he snorts and tosses the cloth onto the floor before starting to untangle the braid on my back.

My hair is splattered with blood–the white strands tangled and crusty. Star's fingers expertly extricate each strand of hair, his touch so gentle it feels like I'm an object made of glass that could shatter any moment.

After a few moments, he lowers my head into the water, one of his hands supporting my neck. My eyes land on the intricate patterns carved into the ceiling–the moon and its phases, Luna and its varying landscape, an ocean of glittering stars. The sounds of the room are distorted by the water, making it hard to discern if the low humming is coming from the prince or my imagination.

Star's fingers massage my scalp, the water around me now colored a pale pink from the blood of his deceased brothers. The movements combined with the muted sounds lull me into a sleep-like state, and once again I desperately wish I could just succumb to the darkness and shadows of the world.

Just when I'm about to let sleep drag me under, I'm wrenched away from the soothing water, the warmth replaced by ice-cold water poured over my head. Gasping, I fight against the strong arms holding me, my body shivering from the sudden cold.

"I warned you. Now answer my question."

I'm about to turn around and scream at him when another shower of cold water is poured over my head. My chest heaves from the shock, my heart beating so rapidly it hurts.

"He had someone who needed him, depended on him. And I took him away–"

"And I sent that person after him. Problem solved," Star snarls and moves to the side of the bathtub, his eyes pools of swirling silver when his gaze meets mine.

"You claim to have been training for the games for most of your life, but sometimes it seems as if you're not prepared at all." He grips my chin with his fingers, his touch no longer light and gentle. "Pull yourself together. We have work to do."

I open my mouth to protest, but his glare snaps my mouth shut.

"You're wondering why I care." He raises his eyebrows and the grip on my chin tightens. "I don't."

He releases me so abruptly I almost slip underneath the water. I grip the edges of the tub so hard my knuckles turn white. "All I care about is our bargain. I need you to stay focused. Death is inevitable. You can't forget that."

A gentle knock sounds in the distance, and as the prince disappears through the door, I stop fighting the exhaustion, allowing the darkness to finally claim me.

CHAPTER THIRTY-THREE

"Get up. We're going for a midnight stroll." Star is standing in front of the bed, arms crossed and teeth bared.

"Go away," I mutter, dragging a pillow over my face.

Everywhere in my body hurts, and a dark emptiness haunts my heart.

I don't want to get out of this bed ever again.

The pillow is wrenched away from my grip. It flies through the air and hits the floor underneath the large open window with a thump.

"I didn't see you mope like this when you were promised to Castor," he says, moving to drag away the silky covers. "I've let you sleep for an entire day. It's time to get up."

My fingers grab the end of the sheet to stop him. "It's barely even dark out, midnight is hours away. So go away."

No." His eyes narrow and he pulls harder until the sheet slips from my fingers and my body is bared to the breeze coming from the window.

I roll myself into a ball with a glare. "You can't just barge into rooms that aren't yours and strip away the bedding! What if I were naked?"

A suggestive smile spreads on his lips.

"Never mind," I grumble, scooting against the headboard. "Just go away."

"No." He plops down at the edge of the bed, crossing an ankle over the other. "You and I have things to do. Lives to take, bargains to fulfill. You know, that sort of thing." He gestures around us. "And this room is actually mine."

I blink at him before moving my gaze around the room–from the dark curtains hanging by the open window that reveals the ocean and not the usual view of the royal city, to the black walls and high ceiling picturing the starry sky, and finally to the bed that's definitely not mine.

"You brought me to your room?" I scramble out of the bed and notice I'm no longer wearing the bloody leathers from last night, all traces of the battle washed away and replaced with a satiny short nightgown. "And you changed my clothes while I slept?"

"Auren got the honor of that. Believe me when I say you're going to remember it when I take your clothes off." His gaze flickers to the bare skin on my thighs and I tug at the fabric as heat spreads across my skin.

And then memories from last night come crashing so fast I nearly fall to the floor. The sword in my hand, the burning anger, all the spilled blood, the brother no longer a twin, Elio–

Star jumps to his feet and grabs a light blue dress neatly folded at the end of the bed. "Let's get going then." He shoves the dress into my hands and turns me toward the adjacent bathroom.

"Have you forgotten what I did last night?"

"No." Silver flares in his eyes and a muscle ticks in his jaw. "It was not according to our plans, but it's an improvement nonetheless."

Made of obsidian stone with streaks of silver and dark blue, the bathroom is twice the size of the one in the blue room. The large tub sits in front of a large window that almost covers the entire wall, the silver details gleaming in the dim light of the darkening night. How I didn't notice all of this yesterday is beyond me.

Making sure I'm concealed behind the door, I remove the nightgown and step into the blue dress. "Did you...What happened to the other one?" A part of me is afraid to know the answer, while another is *relieved*.

"He's taken care of and won't bother you anymore."

I briefly close my eyes, willing away all thoughts of slaughter and scheming princes, focusing instead on the dress now covering my body. Gossamer silk and chiffon sleeves, light and easy to move in, the fabric is a beautiful combination of light blue tones that reminds me of the morning sky.

Star gives me an approving glance when I emerge from the bathroom. He strides across the floor and drags me through the room until the back of my legs hit the edge of the bed. He kneels on the floor and gathers the fabric of my skirt in his hands, tugging it upward until one of my thighs is bared.

"What are you–"

I suck in a breath when his fingers touch my skin. He gives me an arrogant smirk as he straps a scabbard around my thigh before fastening a silver dagger he retrieves from an inner pocket on his jacket. The silver dagger gifted by Auren I thought was lost to the darkness of the tunnels deep inside the palace mountain.

Star wraps his hands around my thigh, his fingers splayed on the sensitive skin. I have to force my gaze away from the intensity in his eyes, and I clear my throat before carefully nudging away from his grip.

"If the twins knew about Castor, some of your other brothers might know as well."

"Only time will tell," he says, removing his hands as he rises back to his feet. "Four down, eight to go."

"It's disturbing how unaffected you are by the possibility of killing all your brothers."

Star grabs my hand and slips a ring onto my finger—the ring I was sure I left in my room after the party that made a crack in my heart. "I told you they're not really my brothers. And who says we're going to kill all of them? Some of them might be useful."

He drops my hand and straightens the lapels of his black jacket. A blue shirt matching my dress peeks through the opening and the obsidian ring identical to my own rests on his finger. "Now, are you ready to get out of here?"

"I'm a little scared to ask what you have planned."

"Helping you survive the games, of course," he says, the corners of his lips tipping into a wicked smirk that sends a small shiver down my neck.

"Of course," I repeat slowly, raising my eyebrows.

"Or did the little incident last night make you forget about your lifelong goal? The seventh trial is barely a few days away and time is ticking. And if you want to survive it, we have a lot to do before then." He raises a dark eyebrow, his midnight eyes still devouring me.

"And dressing me up like this is going to help me how?" I gesture to the blue dress and ring on my finger.

"That reminds me." Star turns and reaches for something lying on the edge of the bed and something tightens in my chest when I see what it is.

A silver circlet made of glittering stars with a crescent moon in the middle–the symbol for Luna, the Kingdom of the Moon–sparkles in the dim light.

I frown as he carefully places the circlet on my head, his fingers pulling out a few strands of hair to frame my face. "You didn't answer my question."

"This–" he takes my hand, warmth spreading through my arm at the touch, "will help you survive the time leading up to the games. No one will dare touch you at my side. And it's time we show the people that."

We walk in silence through the darkness of the palace. I don't dare speak in fear of something or someone hiding in the shadows overhearing my words.

"For a distraction and part of a bigger scheme, you're taking this rather seriously," I mutter after we've moved long enough away from the guards at the palace gates.

He flashes me a wicked smile. "Of course. You heard the king. We have to appear madly in love. And what better way to do that than a midnight stroll through the royal city? Perhaps we'll even share a glass of wine and pastry."

I can't help snorting when he forces a dreamy expression onto his face and starts swinging our entwined hands back and forth.

"But that's not your only agenda tonight."

"Of course not. We're also preparing for the next game. It just so happens that the general honored to make the next trial is a drunken idiot on his nights off duty." Star leads us down the spiraling mountainside, the road lit up by occasional flickering skylights.

"How convenient," I mutter. "And you're allowed to just leave the palace like this without a horde of guards following us?"

Star gives me an indignant look. "We're not in Soria anymore, starlight. Being a prince comes with more freedom than you've ever seen, it seems. And for me–well," he shrugs, mischief glinting in his eyes, "let's just say the guards know not to follow me. Even the ones you can't see."

I'm about to question him further when we round a corner and the other silver gates come into view. The guards don't even glance at us when we pass.

"Smile for the crowd," Star whispers in my ear. He presses a soft kiss to my cheek before moving away, our hands still tightly clasped together.

The eyes of the people prickle my skin. Some glare while others gawk. A man crashes into the corner of a building and a woman crouches down behind a bench to hide. A child reaches for the skirt of my dress only to be yanked back by her mother, and a group of men step out of the shadows when they see me, halting when they notice the prince attached to my hand.

"Where's this general then?" I keep my voice low, ignoring the perplexed looks of the people around us when I attempt to give them a sweet smile.

"Patience, starlight. I told you we had two things to do tonight. First, it's time for our date." Star leads me toward the sparkling river that snakes through the city and all the way to the border where it cleaves the Kingdoms of the Sky into two separate lands.

"I thought you weren't serious about that. Isn't it enough to be seen together at the tavern?"

The prince gives me an incredulous look. "I would never take a woman to a tavern as our first date."

I snort in a very un princess–like way. "Theoretically, our first date was a sword fight in a crowded square in Moria."

"An honest mistake." His eyes twinkle as he gives me a suggestive smile.

We approach a restaurant with an outdoor seating area

underneath the darkening sky. A woman I presume to be the owner drops the wine in her hand when she notices us.

I brace against the panic that is sure to follow, but there's not a single trace of fear to be seen when she leads us to a table in the center of the restaurant, only adoration and excitement.

"I've prepared something very special for you tonight, Your Highnesses," the woman says with a wide grin, winking in my direction before she disappears inside the kitchen.

I raise an eyebrow at Star as he fills my glass with a sparkling silver liquid already present at our table. "You planned this?"

A knowing smirk is his only reply before he raises his glass. "A toast. To my dear betrothed, and–" he lowers his voice as he leans forward, "–my partner in trouble."

As the night darkens even further, and more stars twinkle to life, the royal city blooms with life. Music flows from every direction and people dance and laugh down the streets. The moonlight seems brighter, the shadows of the night parting to let it shine. Even the food and wine tastes brighter. The mix of spices and sauces is exquisite on my tongue and the silver drink soothes some of the pain in my chest.

The luminous river flows right past the restaurant and the crystal water shines as bright as the moonlight above.

The Tears of Elara, Star comments when he notices my longing looks, claiming the river to be the tears of a Moon Goddess named Elara, and promising he'll tell me her story someday.

More and more people seep into the restaurant, not only crowding the tables and chairs but hanging over the railings to catch a glimpse of the new royal couple. No one dares approach or ask about us, the shared meal and matching dark rings evidence enough.

I can't decide if Star savors the attention or if he would rather retreat into a shadowed corner of the world. He flashes delightful smiles in all directions and compliments the food to the owner as course after course is served along with more and more wine. But there's a tension to his shoulders and a hard edge in his features no amount of bright smiles and alluring words can conceal, and I think that maybe this is not easy for him either.

"Enjoying the view, starlight?"

His taunting tone snaps my attention, and I move my gaze from his exposed throat to the silver liquid in front of me.

"Are you finally going to tell me the reason for that nickname?"

He studies me as he swirls the wine around in his glass. "No. Not yet. You have to earn that right."

"Really?" The silver liquid that rushes down my throat is somehow both cold and warm. "And how am I going to do that?"

He bares his pearly white teeth with a wink. "You'll see. If not, I'll tell you the truth when I'm king."

He gulps down the rest of his wine, his obsidian ring visible for all to see. "Let's dance." He pulls a ridiculous amount of silver coins out of his pocket and drops them onto the table before getting to his feet and extending his hand.

We shouldn't. The last time we danced together was a big mistake—

"Remember the game."

He's right. This is just another game.

Gritting my teeth, I take his hand.

The crowd of people clears away to make a path to a small dance floor where a man is playing a violin. Sweat trickles down his forehead as he nervously looks at the approaching pair of royals.

Folding my hands around his neck, Star pulls me against his chest and wraps his hands around my waist.

"What do you know about forbidden dark magic?"

An emotion I can't place flickers across his face, momentarily breaking his mask of pretended adoration. "I know a lot of things, Asteria. Why do you ask?"

I shrug, trying to keep my face nonchalant. "I want to learn more about it."

He studies me for a moment, his dark eyes boring into me to strip away all my secrets. "Then I suggest visiting the library and not talking about it where anyone could overhear you."

"It's called forbidden magic for a reason. The library won't give me any answers," I mutter through clenched teeth. "And I thought this bargain was for my gain as well as yours,"

"It is." He swings us around, the hungry looks behind him making me very uncomfortable. "As I told you, be patient."

"I don't do patient. It makes me reckless." When he pulls me close again, I bite the bottom of his ear hard enough to taste the tangy taste of blood. The action only looks seductive and intriguing to the crowd around us, but he will get the warning.

"I'm well aware of that," he growls, his chest vibrating against mine. "This won't work if I always have to clean up your messes. We have to work together from now on."

"Then prove it," I growl back, grazing my teeth on his neck in another warning.

"Careful, starlight. Biting me only excites me."

I move my head away in disgust, hating that I have to conceal it from my face.

He chuckles against my cheek, the sound snaking down my body. "It amuses me how easy it is to rile you."

I bite the inside of my cheek to stop myself from doing something that would destroy our game of pretend. "You are the most insufferable person I've ever met. Just looking at you is enough to rile me."

"Yet you still find me irresistible." His breath is hot on my face, his lips close enough to graze mine.

"Irresistibly insufferable."

His eyes sparkle as bright as the stars above when he leans forward to press a light kiss to the corner of my mouth. "Oh, how sweet your lies taste."

"I'm not lying–"

Star places a finger on my lips to silence me, and it gives me the urge to bite it off. "Save your lies for someone else, it's time to get going."

His smirk widens at my glare, and a look that can mean nothing good flashes in his eyes. He steps away with a small bow before holding out his arm.

"Where are we going?"

"It's time for our next troublesome adventure."

STAR HAS HIDDEN a pair of dark cloaks behind a loose rock in the wall surrounding the outskirts of the royal city, the prince always prepared for a late-night walk to trouble.

"The tavern in question is no place for a princess of the enemy kingdom," he says, pulling the hood of his cloak over his head.

"And you?"

He waves a dismissive hand. "I have my ways. Warrior. Prince. Victor. The list is long and so are the favors owed to me."

I tighten the strings attached to the hood of the cape. "The dark marks and lines on your skin, don't tell me they're all bargains with other poor souls."

With the dark cloak hiding his blue shirt, the prince almost disappears in the darkness, only the silver in his eyes visible in the dim light. "I wouldn't exactly call you a poor soul. And I didn't expect you to memorize the look of my bare skin. Maybe I'll let you better your notes sometime," he purrs, dipping his head down to reveal a seductive smirk.

"I'm getting a little impatient over here," I snap, tapping my foot in emphasis.

"Fine," Star says with a huff of breath, gesturing for me to start walking. "I thought you enjoyed our little game as much as I do, but fine, let's get going."

I grind my teeth in frustration, my gaze moving to the lights of the city before snapping back to his face with a frustrated sigh. "You're going to have to lead the way, moon boy."

"That's what I thought. At least be patient enough to understand our plans and not ruin them." His lips curl into a sneer but he starts walking back toward the sounds of the bustling city without another word.

After a while, I can't take the silence any longer. "Will the princes be found?"

Star lingers on the corner of a building to send me a dark look. "Yes and no. Eventually perhaps."

"What's that supposed to mean?"

"You'll see." He disappears behind the corner, my exasperated sounds lost to the wind.

"This...*arrangement* is not going to work unless you start telling me things," I snarl when I catch up to him.

"What do you think we're doing right now?" He sends me another dark look as we approach a noisy tavern in the shape of a half-moon. "Follow my lead and stay out of trouble. You can manage that for a few minutes, can't you?"

Large rocks are placed against the silver doors to keep them from slamming shut on a gust of wind, and the large room within is brimming with soldiers and guards still wearing their uniforms. They are sprawled throughout the tavern, some with the jackets draped over their chairs, others barely having any pieces of the uniform left on their bodies, all acting in ways that are not appropriate for the Royal Guard.

It's not an unfamiliar sight. It is the same in Soria and no matter how much it infuriates the Sun King, he can't just get rid of all of them. He needs the numbers and so does the Moon King.

Star grabs my hand underneath the cloak, and to my surprise, he leads me toward a table in the center of the room and not a shadowed corner as I expected.

"Keep your hood up and ears open," he mutters, gesturing to a chair a little behind the crowded table.

"Fine," I say through gritted teeth, obediently sitting down in the chair despite all the protests itching to pass my lips.

Star removes his hood and bares his teeth at a half-dressed guard lounging in a chair. The guard scrambles away and the prince plops down in the empty chair with a pleased smirk.

I scan the rest of the guards at the table. One of them has several silver pins on his chest, discerning him from the others.

The man looks like a typical guard with short-cropped hair, but his hair is streaked with gray and there are lines etched onto his face. He's probably not fit to be on active guard duty anymore, but he is a general nonetheless. And just like Star claimed, he is a drunken idiot on the verge of tumbling to the ground or passing out any second.

"General Gavriel." Star has to repeat the name a couple of times before the general finally moves his drowsy eyes to the prince.

"Well, well, well, if it isn't the Victor Prince himself. Here to drown your sorrows? Just earlier tonight I heard a rumor about you and that cursed princess, and it was not a very nice one."

"No." Star waves a hand to an approaching server balancing a tray with glasses containing a dark liquid. "I came to have a drink with you, my favorite general."

The general barks out a laugh. "You always were the most flattering one out of you all. Tell me, young one, what secrets are you after tonight, huh?" The words are slurred and slow, accompanied by a drunken smile as he reaches for his new glass.

I shake my head when the server looks in my direction and she gives me a stern look. I won't be able to stay for long before being pestered to spend a few coins. No one would dare demand the same from the prince, and I wonder if the same would apply to me if I were to remove my hood.

Probably not.

"You know me, Gav," Star says, leaning back in his chair, "I'm always open for new information."

The general snorts and liquid shoots out of his nose and drips from his mouth. "You have something for me." He wipes his face with the sleeve of his jacket, adding new stains to the dirty uniform.

"Of course." Star fishes a pouch out of his cloak, dangling it in front of the general's greedy eyes.

I glance around the tavern, but the rest of the guests seem oblivious to the prince among them.

The general reaches for the pouch and Star snaps it away and hides it in his palm. "You know the rules, Gav. Information first, payment second."

The general snorts again before taking a large sip of his glass. "Fine. What do you want?"

"Tell me about the next game. I heard you were granted the honor of crafting it. Not surprisingly, of course. You are the only one fit for the job. And the Silver Court–" he whistles with a wink, "there are lots of opportunities there for someone as creative as you."

The general's cheeks flush with color. "You know I can't tell you about that. Anything else, my boy, but not that. If it were any other year and you weren't competing, I might have been persuaded to bend the rules a little, but not this time." He hiccups as he gulps down more of the dark liquid.

There are no rules during the Tournament Times.

Star's lips pull into a wide grin, his eyes glittering with the thrill of the challenge presented before him. And from the looks of the drunken general, it won't be a very difficult task.

"Of course. Being the honorable man that you are, it's no wonder the king personally picked you to be in charge of one of the most important games." Star leans back in his chair to cross his arms. "I'm sure it wasn't an easy job to decide how to torture those dreadful Sorians. Tell me, can I at least expect to outrun a few of them?"

"Outfly is more like it," The general slurs and dark liquid spills onto the stone table.

"Really?" Star puts his elbows on the table, his head resting in his palms. "That's very creative of you, Gav. Using the Tournament's magic to allow us to fly. I don't think that's been done for at least a few decades."

"It's even better than that. Think bigger. Like borrowing someone else's wings." The general gives the prince a wink. His eyelids are starting to droop and his eyes are unfocused.

"Surely you're not talking about bats or eagles," Star says, casting an awed look in Gavriel's direction.

"Absolutely not," Gavriel spits, drool and dark liquid spilling from his lips. "Think bigger." He extends his hands and almost causes his chair to topple over.

Star's foot shoots out to steady the chair and Gavriel's head rolls back and forth from the movement.

"Nothing can be bigger than the wings of a dragon."

Dragon.

The word sends a shiver down my back and my heartbeats stutter.

I've leafed through pages picturing the most vile beasts one can imagine, but always thought dragons were only the subjects of ancient myths and stories.

It shouldn't surprise me. The Tournament's magic seems to grow more and more each year, but dragons?

"Yes. The dragons will–" The general yawns, his head coming to rest on his chest.

"The dragons?" Star prods, his leg rocking the chair.

"The dragons will try to–"

The rest of the words are a mumbled ramble impossible to understand.

"Gavriel?" Star gives the chair a last tug, but the general is long gone. Loud snores resound from his body and his eyes are now fully closed.

With a heavy sigh, Star pushes to his feet. "Let's go."

"You didn't even give him the coins," I protest as he drags me out of the tavern.

He snorts before pulling his hood back on. "He will be lucky if he remembers his way home when he wakes up. He won't remember the prince asking questions he shouldn't know the answers to. And if he does, he won't tell a soul–living or dead–to risk the wrath of the king."

I struggle to keep up with his fast pace as we leave the city behind. When the prince starts to climb over the stone walls surrounding the city, I let out a frustrated sound.

"I'm getting really sick of you not telling me where we're going."

Star turns around long enough to give me an indignant look. "I just gave you very valuable information about the next trial, this time taking you directly to the source so you won't waste time debating whether to trust me or not. If I hear one more whiny word out of your mouth, I might decide to just leave to the beasts."

"We have a bargain," I snarl, almost crashing into his back when he abruptly stops walking.

"I'm well aware of that, princess" he snarls back, grabbing the collar of my cloak to prevent me from tumbling down the steep hill behind us.

Princess. Not starlight or Asteria, but princess. The word that seems like the worst possible insult he can think of from the venom lacing the word and the dark storm in his eyes.

"You were the one that insisted on the bargain–"

"Don't speak of things you know nothing about," he all but growls, holding my gaze for a moment longer before releasing the fabric of my cloak and continuing to walk forward.

"Then tell me about it!"

I run to catch up with him, momentarily startled when I notice him gently stroking the mane of a black horse lingering in the shadows of a large boulder.

I instantly recognize the beautiful horse as Esra, this time without the ornate harness and saddle she had on the last time I saw her.

"Where exactly are we going that is so far away from the city we need extra legs? And why didn't we just bring her to begin with?"

"Esra had her own things to take care of. And what did I say about your whining?" With a glare, he effortlessly heaves himself onto the horse's back.

"I'm not moving before you tell me what we're doing and where we're going," I say, crossing my arms.

"Fine. Stay. Don't survive the Tournament. I'm only trying to fulfill my end of the damn bargain!" He sighs heavily before pinching the bridge of his nose, his glowering eyes snapping shut.

I debate my lack of options for only a couple of seconds before moving forward. "Fine. But don't you dare touch me."

Star doesn't say anything as he scoots back to give me more room, his hands balled into fists in front of him.

"Let's get this over with," I say when I'm finally seated on the horse, my fingers curling in Esra's mane.

Star clicks his tongue and Esra darts forward, her feet moving quicker than what should be possible even for the strongest and fastest horse in the two kingdoms.

I'm thrown back against Star's chest, my fingers fumbling for anything to hold on to.

"You know," he breathes in my ear, one of his arms firmly wrapping around my stomach to keep me in place, "staying seated on a horse should be the easiest thing in the world for a warrior in the Tournament, and yet here we are."

I'm unable to answer him. The wind whips at our cloaks like we're in the midst of a storm as the horse practically flies forward. The landscape blurs and changes so fast it's impossible to make out anything other than swirling darkness, and by the time Esra slows to a trot, no more than a few minutes could've passed.

"I told you the next time would be better."

Heart in my throat and a string of curses erupting from my lips, I stumble off the horse, gaping at our surroundings.

The Diamond Mountains are roving in the distance, too close for us to be in the royal city. We're surrounded by nothing but rock and steep hills, the only light the moonlight above.

"How–"

Star gives Esra a pat on the side of her neck and the horse happily trots away to disappear in the night.

"What–"

He ignores me and turns around to walk toward a path in the rocky terrain.

"What the hell is going on? This isn't possible! We were just in the royal city and now we're all the way in–"

"The Court of Silver," Star shouts, not bothering to look back to see if I follow.

"If you don't give me an explanation right this second I will tackle you to the ground and–"

In a blink, he is standing in front of me, silencing me with the press of his finger against my lips. "And if you don't stop being so stubborn and demanding, I might just leave you here."

I slap his hand away, resisting the urge to just start screaming. "How did you do that? How can you move so fast? How did we end up here–"

"Esra, like me, is shadow born. There, an answer." His eyes flare with irritation before he turns around and continues walking up the hill.

The shadows betray you because they serve me.

I hurry after him, hundreds of more questions ready to leave my lips, all of them quieting when I reach the top of the hill.

The sight underneath is so breathtaking and magical I'm starting to think this is all just a dream.

An enormous pool is carved into the mountain, the water shining like thousands of blue crystals. The full moon illuminating the sky is reflected by the surface, and the combined lights are brighter than any skylight I've seen.

The water looks so inviting I'm tempted to just make a run for it, the radiant blue an unexpected source of light in all the darkness of my life.

"I don't see how a midnight swim is going to help me ride a creature that shouldn't even exist–" I snap my mouth shut when I notice Star has disappeared, the prince nowhere to be found in the shadows of the night.

"Star?" My voice echoes in the quiet night, the only sounds the wind ruffling my long cloak and the hammering of my heart.

A wave ripples across the water and a spurt of fire erupts from a rocky outcropping. The flames clear away to reveal an enormous dark figure and large wings tipped with gleaming silver talons spread against the night sky.

A dragon.

CHAPTER THIRTY-FOUR

The black scales of the dragon gleam in the moonlight as it lets out another burst of fire. Sharp silver horns and large violent eyes are the only traces of color on the majestic creature that is sculpted for darkness, and its body is so massive it's a wonder the stone underneath its feet is not crumbling to dust.

The dragon opens its mouth again, the jagged teeth snapping together with a loud clank as its shiny eyes narrow in my direction.

I stumble backward, the hem of my cloak catching on a rock.

"I wouldn't make any sudden movements if I were you, starlight." Star is leaning against the body of the dragon, a hand resting on one of the silver horns next to its ears.

Fear is squeezing every part of my body so hard that I can barely breathe.

Star let's put a dark chuckle and tugs at the silver horn. "This is not how you should greet a royal. Stop looking at her like that."

The dragon's narrowed eyes move sideways to glare at the prince.

"You can glare at me as much as you want, but stop scaring her."

The dragon puffs out a breath of gray smoke before thumping down on the ground, its large tail curling around its body, the spiked end barely missing Star's legs.

Star snorts. "We'll work on that." He moves his gaze to me, the corners of his lips tugging with amusement.

"Asteria, meet Alev."

The dragon's ear perk up at the sound of its name and the violet eyes snap back to me, no doubt debating if I would be a worthy meal. It may no longer be glaring, but that doesn't make it any less terrifying.

"I don't think I've ever seen you this quiet," Star says with another snort. "It would've been nice to see it a little more often."

I can't take my eyes off the dragon and I can't move.

This can't be real.

With a sigh, Star steps over the spiked tail, unafraid of the dragon he now has his back turned to—the dragon that could swallow him whole or burn him alive any second.

"Asteria." He strides across the rocky ground until he is close enough to tilt my face away from the creature that only moments ago was nothing but a myth.

"He is not going to harm you. Trust me." His midnight eyes bore into mine, and there is a look of sheer determination on his face. "Alev is harmless. Well...at least once in a while."

The dragon puffs out another breath that very much reminds me of a snort.

Star's finger strokes along my bottom lip and he angles his body until I can't see the dragon behind him. "I know countless questions are swirling in your mind right now. Go ahead, ask one."

Five heartbeats pass before I'm able to open my mouth to speak.

"You have your own dragon?"

"Of course not." He gives me an incredulous look. "Dragons are free beings. But it's not my first time in the Tournament."

"There's never been dragons–"

"I didn't say that. Not officially no, but here we are." He gestures behind him, allowing me to catch a glimpse of the dragon that makes dread coil in my chest.

"How–"

"You're asking the wrong questions, princess. We have limited time, remember? Obviously, the next game won't be a problem for me, but you need to make acquaintances beforehand." He drops his fingers from my face and crosses his arms over his chest.

"You can't expect me to not question how a large dragon is not attempting to eat you right now."

Star rolls his eyes. "I'm sure he has eaten dinner already." A faint black smoke rises behind his head and I hear the dragon shift on the rocks.

"He may not want to eat you but a cursed princess seems like a good meal for someone like him."

"Afraid, starlight?" He reaches forward to remove my hood. "And here I was thinking you might not be cursed after all."

"I'm definitely cursed now because of our bargain," I mutter, slapping his hand away with a glare.

He chuckles. "Alev only needs to get to know you. And with a little luck, he'll introduce you to his mate."

"Mate?"

Silver flares in his eyes.

"Don't tell me you're unaccustomed to the ways of nature. Do we need to move our lessons elsewhere? If you quit your whining, I might be inclined to give you a taste of our wedding night." His sensual smirk ignites an ember of heat deep in my stomach I choose to ignore.

I clear my throat, my gaze moving to the large beast behind him who is studying us with a tilted head.

"So, what's your brilliant plan? I don't particularly feel like going anywhere near the beast–Alev." I quickly correct myself at the small growl from the dragon. "And how do you even know his name?"

"Let's just say it took a couple of guesses." He turns to glare at the dragon who only puffs out a smoky breath in reply.

"How long have you known about him?"

Star taps his fingers on his chin, his gaze flickering to the sky above. "The dragons are not in Luna every year, but when they are they only seasonally reside in these mountains, leaving for unknown places during the harsh winters. Alev stays in the caves the entire year, living with his mate far away from the other packs." His gaze snaps back to mine and at my raised eyebrows, he gives me a small smirk.

"I met him during my first Tournament when I was thirteen."

My mouth falls open. "You participated that young? I didn't think that was allowed—"

Star gives me a bored look. "There are no rules, remember?"

"That's–" I search for an appropriate word, but none of them seem to fit. Sick. Brutal. Wrong—

He nods solemnly and a muscle ticks in his throat, but then the smirk is back on his lips along with a mischievous glimmer in his eyes. "You ready then?"

"For what?"

I don't like this and I hate that he knows so much more than me. Not just about the Tournament and its magic, but everything —everything from magical bargains to taming dragons to traveling in the shadows, and so much more about our world that I hadn't even considered to be possible.

"This," Star says, pointing to the glowing water, "is a sacred place. The water is directly blessed by moonlight. As I'm sure you can imagine, that means very much magic. Magic the dragons use to fuel their power, and magic that will transmit to a person going for a midnight swim, at least according to legends." His gaze rakes over me, from the dirt on the hem of my cloak to the silver circlet in my hair.

"What matters is that the dragons will recognize you as one worthy of them if you take a dip in the water." His smirk widens. "Naked, of course."

"Absolutely not." I cross my arms over my chest, suddenly feeling both very cold and very hot at the same time.

"It's important that the water directly touches the skin–"

"I don't see how taking a bath will help me with the dragons–"

"It will make them more willing to accept you if you smell of their magic–"

"I'm not doing it."

"Do you want to survive the next few weeks or not? This is the way to do it," he snaps, venom lacing every word, the teasing smirk replaced with an angry snarl that hints at the darkness lurking inside him.

A frustrated sound escapes me. "How do I know you're not just trying to trick and humiliate me?"

His eyebrows raise. "Haven't you already humiliated yourself enough? And what do you have to lose? Think about it." He shrugs. "I could always toss you in. It wouldn't be as effective, but–"

"Turn around and close your eyes," I snap with another frustrated sound.

He lets out a dramatic sigh but he slowly turns his back to me.

"You too." I glance at the dragon, ignoring the rising fear when he meets my gaze.

Alev moves his eyes in a manner that seems very much like the dragon equivalent of rolling his eyes before the large eyelids droop and finally snap shut.

The summer wind blows against my skin as I strip off the layers of clothing and place the silver circlet atop the pile, glancing at the shimmering blue water that is so clear I shouldn't have bothered to order the males to turn around if they're going to witness my swim anyway.

The water sloshes around me as I carefully maneuver over the rocks. The surprisingly warm water eases some of the built-up tension in my body and soothes away the pain and fear in my heart.

I duck underneath the water, relishing in the feeling of being submerged in its magic. It slithers across my skin, the light of the water making me glow more than I've ever done underneath the sunlight.

There is no pain or fear or darkness, only the light and magic that makes me feel so alive it nearly takes my breath away.

Star has turned around when I break through the surface. "Refreshing, isn't it?"

I roll my eyes, making sure to keep my body underneath the water, but judging from the way his eyes darken and the suggestive smirk playing on his lips, it doesn't do much good.

"Would you kill me if I joined you? It's been a while since I've been here and it's better to be on the safe side when it comes to dragons."

Alev puffs out a breath that again sounds very much like a snort. There's only curiosity in his violet eyes when he looks at me, and his posture seems more relaxed as if he's pleased with my decision to swim in the sacred water.

"I can't promise I won't try to drown you if I feel something slimy touch my leg," I say, crossing my arms in front of my bare chest.

Star's smirk widens. He removes his cloak, the suit jacket, and the pale blue shirt matching my dress.

It's not the first time I'm seeing his bare skin, but the sight makes my pulse quicken all the same.

His pale skin is illuminated by the moonlight, and the dark lines and marks covering his chiseled body snake all the way from his throat and down underneath his pants. Scars in all shapes and sizes peek out between the lines—all signs of a life honed to battle and games.

My gaze moves to the mark identical to my own, to the dark star resting in the crook of his elbow and a shiver rocks through my body.

"Enjoying the view?" His purring tone sends heat through my body and down to my toes. "Don't worry, starlight. I don't mind."

His fingers fumble with the buttons on his pants, and he raises his eyebrows when he notices I'm still looking. "I knew I wasn't the only one interested in my favorite body part."

Ignoring the fire igniting inside me, I turn around and duck back underneath the water.

The pool is deeper farther out from the rocks, and the darkness underneath should make me uncomfortable, but it doesn't. This is nothing like the vast ocean filled with beasts ready to kill me any moment.

There's a sense of serenity here I've never felt before.

I stay under a little too long to avoid the prince, and my lungs are aching for air when I break through the surface.

"Careful. The water may be filled with magic, but I wouldn't try breathing below." Star is standing waist-deep in the pool, the bright blue water sloshing around him.

I lift my chin, forcing my eyes not to linger lower than his throat.

The prince chuckles as if he knows exactly what I'm thinking before striding toward me and ducking his head underneath the water.

With a yelp, I turn around and do my best to cover myself with my hands, making sure my hair is covering my bare chest.

Star's deep laugh booms behind me before quickly fading away. "Gods, I hate that gilded sword."

Something tightens in my chest.

I turn around to see him clenching his jaw, his eyes swirling pools of shadow. His dark locks are dripping with water and hanging down to his forehead, and for a second, I'm tempted to sweep them away.

"He will never touch you again. Not as long as I'm with you. That much I can promise you."

A hollow laugh escapes me. "I'm well aware of your love for bargains, but even you shouldn't make promises you can't keep."

Star takes a step closer, his breath now caressing my face. "Let me make one thing clear, Asteria. The king will never touch you again. I don't need a bargain to prove that." His fingers grip my chin and he tilts my head up to make me look at him.

"Like I just said, you're too late. And you should consider switching out your guards when they allow the king of the enemy kingdom to just stride into your tower–"

His grip on my chin tightens, fury and rage evident in his features. "He isn't allowed anywhere near my tower."

I let out an indignant sound as I try to wriggle free from his grasp. "Then how did he manage to–"

"There are certain things I can't and won't reveal to you at this time, but I'll tell you one thing." He lowers his face until his eyes are aligned with mine, the intensity in his gaze giving me the urge to close my eyes.

"The second I knew what was happening, I did everything within my power to stop it and prevent it from ever happening again. I followed you as soon as it was acceptable for me to do so, and by then...well..." He trails off and drops his fingers from my chin.

"Don't think it didn't cost me. I'm sad to say I'm not invincible or out of reach for the king."

"Why would you even care?"

I'm taken aback by his words and I don't know why I bother asking, why I'm not running away.

Something is keeping me tethered to the water, to this moment with the prince that is revealing a side of him I never could have imagined.

He grabs my hand and places it on a large and ragged scar slashing across his chest, right over his heart. I trace the line with the tip of my finger carrying his ring, and his breath hitches when I reach his heart.

His eyes are a storm of silver stars when I look up at him.

No words are necessary.

For once, the truth is bared for me to see, and only me. And perhaps I'm the only one who can truly understand him, as he now understands me.

Two royals of opposite kingdoms, but both bound to the brutality of their kings and every scar that comes with.

"What about this?" I move my hand up to his shoulder, to a faint line I wouldn't have noticed if I weren't standing so close.

Star studies me for a moment, a hand sweeping away the locks on his face. "Each one has its own story. Some are short, others long. Some of them are well-earned, others reckless accidents and lucky strikes that should've claimed my life. I earned that one during one of my first rides with Esra."

I nod absentmindedly, my fingers trailing over the dark lines in the shape of clouds marking his collarbone.

He sucks in a breath, his hand grabbing my wrist and halting my movements. With my other hand, I tilt his hand to reveal the proof of his continuous participation in the Tournament—the seven scarred lines as dark as blood.

"Where are your victory marks?"

Star tilts his head to the side, displaying his present binding mark. "Here and there. I would be more than happy to give you a tour—"

I give him a stern look and he chuckles while moving my hand to a mark on his side. The dark lines bleed together in the shape of a tree with a snake coiled around the trunk.

"I don't know how it works, but they're not always black. Sometimes, they light up when I win a game, during a full moon, or other random times I can't find a pattern to." He shrugs. "If you didn't know where to look and the fact that they were there, you wouldn't even know I'm a Victor. My body is not only home to those marks."

I'm terrified to find out if the dark marks that are not from his victories are bargains or forbidden magic.

I study the rest of the marks, my cheeks heating when my gaze trails along a line going down the middle of his stomach before disappearing underneath the water.

When I force my eyes back to his, Star releases my hand and reaches forward to cradle my face. His fingers stroke my skin, rubbing away the droplets running down my face—the drops that either come from the water or my eyes. I'm not sure.

A white steam rises from the water around us, and my body vibrates from his touch, the fire within me roaring to life.

It has to be the magic between us.

Magic always comes with a price.

"Your eyes," he says, his voice husky and low.

"A blue too light to be of the sunny sky ringed with a blue too dark for the Sorian sky, too unnatural for this world. Cursed ice," I whisper, repeating the words Father screams at me when I dare look at him too long.

"No," he breathes, leaning closer to study me more intently. "They're not ice. They're...aloras."

He grabs my waist and pulls me forward so my chest is flush against his. "Moon crystals. Rumored to originate from the same magic as the skylights. Some believe they are made from moondust. They're only found deep in the mountains of the royal palace. A sacred and hidden treasure."

And then he whispers my name, his face so close that his lips graze mine as he speaks. He whispers it like a prayer, and I never thought my name could sound so...*unique* and *beautiful*.

The strings tied around my heart pull and desire and need grip my soul, tearing into my body with a force so strong it takes my breath away.

My fingers tangle in his hair and I marvel at the feel of his body against mine.

My lips meet his and I open my mouth—

And then Alev growls and the spell is broken.

I startle and stumble back, the water sloshing around me, and I feel its magic reach for me, trying to lull me back.

Star blinks at me, as if he too can't quite believe what just happened. I move to leave the water, but he grabs my hand, his fingers tracing the beginning of our matching mark–the lines carved with a dagger surrounded by smoke before I even knew he existed.

"Why did you do this?" There is an urgency in his voice I can't understand, my mind still muddled by the magic and the unexpected moment between us. He presses his lips into a thin line and his eyes are glowing as much as the water around us.

"I–"

For a second, I'm tempted to just tell him—to finally utter the words to someone and speak the truth I've hidden for what feels like an eternity. But then I notice the sky around us, the approaching sun, and reality comes crashing down.

"You have to earn that right," I snap, repeating his earlier words.

His eyes darken, a muscle ticking in his throat as he drops his hands from my arm. "Fair enough. Back to business then," he says through gritted teeth before turning around to walk out of the water.

"Where are you going?"

He turns his head enough to give me an impatient glare. "To keep us alive."

"How?"

"It's time you learn how to ride a dragon."

CHAPTER THIRTY-FIVE

In the Silver Court, where the jagged peaks of the mountains are blessed by the sky's tears, an unnaturally strong wind screams in the night.

The seventh trial is starting.

The blasting wind conjured by the Tournament's magic is a violent invisible opponent. It tears at my fighting leathers and ruffles my hood which is tied so tight it's almost suffocating. Its unseeable hands yank me sideways, eager to drag me down the steep valley.

I brace against the rising storm.

Star stands beside me, his presence now familiar and expected. We've spent almost all our time together, preparing for this game, and the rest I've spent sleeping so deep not even a beast could wake me.

"The seventh trial, the third Moon Trial, is this–" Elio's arms rise toward the sky, his magnified voice carried by the wind. The Royal Dais is standing on a flat expanse between the mountains, behind the warriors hungrily eying the horde of dragons scattered in the rocky valleys.

"On the back of a dragon, make it to the end of the race before the first trace of sunlight appears in the dark sky. As always, the rules are simple. There are no rules in the Tournament of Day and Night but one; survive. May the best Victor win."

As his starting clap thunders through the mountains, Star grabs my wrist and drags me in the opposite direction of the other warriors running down the mountainside to where the puffs of dragons can be heard between the screeching of the wind.

"Where are we going?"

"I already told you the plan," he snaps, pulling me along the side of the crowds of people, "multiple times."

"I'm a little sleep-deprived," I snap back, rolling my eyes at his hooded head.

A growl and a scream echo in the distance, followed by the crowd cheering and clapping.

"Alev won't be anywhere near the other dragons."

"Why?" He has probably already told me this too, but his irritated voice is a welcome distraction from the storm around us.

Star grabs my hand to help me down a large boulder, moving us in the direction of another mountain peak. "He's peculiar like that. He likes to keep to himself."

I ignore his hand and jump down on my own. "Like you?"

He gives me an indignant look, his hood blown away enough to reveal his darkening eyes. "Climbing to the top is a lonely place, starlight."

I roll my eyes as I walk past him, the wind so strong I have to concentrate to keep my balance. "I think I just found the real reason you insisted on the bargain." A smirk tugs at my lips at his answering snort and how I can practically feel him rolling his eyes.

We walk the rest of the way in silence, the sounds of battle and violent furious dragons echoing on the roaring wind as we maneuver through the narrow rocky paths.

Star has taken the lead again. I eventually had to admit not knowing the specifics of our plan. The prince only scoffed, his hand brushing against mine as he passed me to clear the path ahead.

Now, he stops in front of a mountain wall, turning his head to look at me. "I know climbing mountains isn't exactly your specialty–" he trails off, gesturing to a ledge in the mountain above us.

"As long as you don't stick a dagger in my shin, I'll be fine," I say through gritted teeth with a glare aimed at the back of his head.

He shrugs and reaches for the mountain. "Great. I won't wait for you. After all, it's not my first time beating you to the top."

We have a bargain. He is helping me.

I repeat the words like a prayer as I climb, ignoring the dread creeping into me at the memories of another mountain that should've claimed my life.

The mountain is steep and sharp, but it's nothing like Kylo– the holy mountain of the first game. The rock scrapes against my palms as the wind tries to blow me away, and I can almost hear the gods and magic rooting for my death. I focus on the dark figure above me, willing my eyes to adjust to the lack of light, ignoring the growing drop underneath me.

Star disappears from my sight and a warm hand wraps around my wrist and yanks me up the rest of the way. He catches me in his arms when I wobble both from surprise and the raging wind, and a low chuckle brushes against my ear.

"I thought you weren't going to help me," I snarl, pushing away from him.

"I got a little impatient. That's a very familiar feeling for you, isn't it, princess? I'm sure you can imagine how unpleasant it was to wait for you." He reaches out to brush a stray strand of hair behind my ear, tucking it into the hood of my leathers.

I roll my eyes, looking behind him to study the mountain. The ledge leads to a cave carved out of the mountain, and as I take a step forward to try and glimpse something in the darkness, a low growl reverberates through me.

"Patience, starlight." Star grabs my shoulders to stop me before reaching into a pocket on his chest to retrieve a small orb of glass where a tiny skylight flickers to life from his touch.

A pair of violet eyes blinks against the dim light and a large mouth bares long sharp teeth, a black smoke seeping out between them.

"Hello, old friend." Star's voice is calm as he extends a hand toward the enraged dragon, and he doesn't even flinch when a red ember barely misses his fingers.

Alev lowers his head after sniffing Star's outstretched hand, but his sizable body is still tense and alert, and smoke emanates from his mouth and nose.

"Something's not right," Star mutters as he scratches Alev's ear.

"What?" I walk forward, hesitantly holding out my hand for the dragon to sniff. Alev has reluctantly accepted me these past couple of days, but if something's wrong–

Alev pushes his nose into my palm and I let out a relieved breath, the steam puffing from his nostrils warning my hand.

There's a furrow between Star's eyebrows and he makes a contemplative sound before slowly moving past Alev.

The dragon lets out a warning growl, his eyes flickering to the prince, but when Star growls back, Alev nuzzles my hand, silently asking me to resume my petting. A content sound hums in his chest when I do, reminding me of a purring cat.

After a few moments, a string of curses resounds from the cave.

"What's wrong?"

Star is too deep in the cave to make out, the darkness in front of me unreachable by the skylight.

A scratching sound followed by a low grumble resounds from the darkness.

Alev puffs out a breath before turning around to walk into the cave, his spiked tail barely missing my head.

"I suggest you come see for yourself."

Heart hammering with fear, I walk further into the darkness, ignoring my screaming instincts warning me not to walk into the den of a dragon.

The tunnel in the cave opens to an enormous space where the high ceiling reaching for the sky is lit up by thousands of tiny skylights sticking to the stone. Hundreds of smaller paths are snaking out in all directions, connecting the cave to other tunnels deep within the mountain. Stalagmites and stalactites jut out of the ground, walls, and ceiling, the crystal rock glinting in the faint light.

Alev falls to the ground with a loud bang that rattles the stone underneath my feet, revealing another dragon behind him.

His mate.

The other dragon is a little smaller but just as majestic with white scales streaked with traces of a faint pink that reminds me of the sunset.

If Alev is darkness, his mate is light.

Large, glowing magenta eyes peek at me as I slowly walk closer and I will myself not to tremble.

"Is something wrong with...her? Him?" I whisper, careful not to startle the mighty creature.

"Her, definitely her. And no, not exactly," Star says, his hand beckoning me closer.

I don't notice it at first, but when I see it, my heart swells and all the fear dissipates.

A tiny dragon about the size of a very large cat is lying coiled in its mother's tail. Black spots dot the gleaming white scales on its body, the small tail a mix of silver and black.

"It's adorable," I croon, bending down to look at it more closely.

"It's a problem."

The small dragon looks up at its mother, the white dragon puffing out a small breath that causes the baby to jump out of the coiled tail and into my lap.

A surprised laugh bursts from my lips. The baby wags its tail and tilts its head to allow me to scratch its neck.

"You're so cute. Yes, you are." At any other moment, I would be embarrassed by the way I'm behaving, but not today, not when I'm meeting the child of creatures only believed to be real in ancient myths.

Star clears his throat. "However...nice...it might be to see you like this, we don't have a lot of time."

"Everything will be fine–"

"No," he snaps, sighing as he punches the bridge of his nose. "This wasn't part of the plan. I didn't know–I didn't know about–"

"About the baby?" I frown, looking at the black and white dragon.

It is maybe small for a dragon, but the size doesn't give any indication of when it could've been born. I don't think Alev would've let us train with him if he secretly had a baby in this cave. The birth must've happened very recently.

Something tightens in my chest as realization dawns on me.

"There's no way she's going to leave her child, let alone let me fly her. Her body is probably still healing–"

"I know!" Star drags a hand through his dark hair, the strands now disheveled and messy.

"What are we going to do?"

"Be quiet for a moment," he snaps, pacing back and forth, the eyes of all dragons following his movements.

"Don't tell me to be quiet—"

"I'll come back for you," he says, interrupting my snarled threat.

"Excuse me?"

"Yes," he says, tapping a finger on his chin. "That could work. I'll find the goal with Alev and then come back so you can ride him next. I'm sure he won't mind an extra trip. He loves flying. It's the only way. The rules don't say anything–" he chuckles, "there are no rules."

I cross my arms, glaring daggers at the prince, the baby dragon squirming in my lap at the loss of scratching. "No."

"Are my previous actions good for nothing?"

I raise my eyebrows. "You want to talk about your previous actions? Fine. How about the time you nearly took my head off with your dagger? Or when you tricked me into a bargain? Twice. Or how about the time you sabotaged me–

"Fine," he snaps, clenching his jaw. "If you won't trust me, trust the bargain. The magic is life-binding. I'll die if I don't fulfill my end."

"And what exactly is your end? You haven't been very specific, *Your Highness*," I snarl, causing the dragon to jump away from my lap and run back to its mother, the black wings scraping against the ground.

"Theoretically, you don't need me alive to crown me as

Victor. I'm sure that thought has occurred to you on more than one occasion—"

"We don't have time for this. You know the words of the bargain—

I jump to my feet, silencing him with a dark laugh. "It seems you never have time to answer any of my questions, *Prince Star*."

"What about our night in the pool? Or any of the other numerous times I've helped you live?" His chest is heaving and shadows are curling around his feet.

I can't deny it so I keep my mouth shut.

"Fine. Do whatever you want." He takes a few long steps so we're standing so close I can feel his breath on my face. "But right now—we need to make it through this game. And the only way to do that is for me to finish first and then come back for you–"

"No." I place a finger over his lips. "We'll go together. I won't take any chances in you leaving me behind. There's not enough time to find another pair of wings."

Star wraps his hand around my finger before moving it away. "I don't think that's wise. The Tournament has never been about working together. It's about bringing each other down."

"There are no rules, remember? And you've already broken that rule numerous times, your previous actions and all that."

"Oh, so now you admit I've been helping you." He makes an exasperated sound, his hands slapping against his thighs as he releases his hold on me.

"We're running out of time. Are you coming or not? I certainly won't hesitate to leave you behind. You can still help me win without participating," I say through gritted teeth, my shoulder bumping into his as I move past him to the opening of the cave where the largest dragon is already waiting.

"What do you say, Alev?" I stroke the dragon's face and his

violet eyes bore into mine. "Are you ready for a flight underneath the stars?"

Star scoffs and moves past me, effortlessly climbing onto Alev's back. He holds out his hand from atop the large dragon, his eyes glinting silver with challenge. "Scared, princess?"

I take his hand without answering. *Yes,* I want to scream, but there is no way I'm admitting that to him. My clammy palms and hammering heart are answers enough.

We couldn't actually fly during our training sessions. Star claimed it would be very dangerous for both of us if we were spotted by someone and that he simply wasn't in the mood for murder.

I'm not scared of being on the dragon safely on the ground. I'm terrified of being in the air.

Star chuckles as he pulls me up, positioning me in front of him and wrapping his arm around my waist.

One of the first questions I had about riding a dragon was whether we could make a saddle and harness large enough for Alev's body.

When I uttered the question a couple of days ago, Star only raised his eyebrows while Alev puffed out a breath that resulted in a sizzling flame, clearly insulted by the idea.

"I'm afraid not," he said, amusement tugging at his lips. "Although, I have to admit I did try something of the sort when I first met the beast. Didn't go over well though." He held up a hand to show me a scar that looked suspiciously like bite marks, Alev moving his eyes in a way that I've come to realize actually is the dragon equivalent to rolling his eyes.

Now, I'm once again tempted by the idea of something more secure than the prince's arms around me and my hands gripping the scales of the dragon's neck.

"Remember what I told you. Keep your hands steady and legs braced—"

"I remember," I snap, voice slightly shaking from the adrenaline coursing through my veins.

Star's breath tickles my ear as he pulls my hood back over my head, one hand coming to grab a scale next to mine.

He is not trusting me to keep us both seated on the dragon, and I can't blame him.

I don't trust him either.

It would be easy for me to shove him off, and it would also be easy for him to drag me down with him. We may have a life-binding bargain but if he accidentally dies—

"Don't even think about it," he warns, tightening his arm around me in emphasis.

"Likewise."

Alev huffs impatiently, his spiked tail banging against the rocky ground.

Rain is thundering down from the sky, soaking my leathers and making my teeth rattle. There's only a faint light coming from the sky, most of the stars washed away by the storm, the moon obscured by dark clouds.

Hopefully, we still have enough time to complete the trial, and hopefully, we don't combust by breaking the lack of rules by winning together.

"Okay," I breathe, clenching my thighs as much as possible against the large body underneath me.

Star told me not to treat Alev as a horse, especially not after the whole harness and saddle thing.

"He understands you. Much more than you would think. We have developed some codes over the years. But again, he's nothing like a horse even though some of the codes may remind you of that," he said, giving me a stern look, the corners of his lips tugging with amusement as Alev snorted a flame that barely missed the prince's legs.

I tap my feet against the dragon, signaling for him to take off, just as we've practiced numerous times before.

No amount of training could've prepared me for what happens next.

Alev stretches his wings wide, the silver talons glinting in the dim light, the mighty wings a wall of darkness as they vibrate in the wind. With a loud boom, he tucks them against his body, the movements rattling my bones. His claws scrape against the ground for a second before he darts forward and jumps off the mountain.

I swallow my screams as we fall through the air.

Mountains and grass and darkness swirl around us as we roll around in the air, Alev's sounds of delight drowned by the raging storm. The wind rips at my cloak, threatening to blow me away any second, and the rain beating a painful rhythm against us is so suffocating that it makes it hard to breathe.

My fingers tighten around the dark scales and I resist the urge to shut my eyes.

I'm about to start cursing the dragon when he finally spreads out his wings, pausing our plummeting descent.

The abrupt change of speed almost makes me topple off the dragon, Star's arm around me more helpful than I would've thought. Our training wasn't for two people riding at once, yet I'm not worried about Alev's ability to carry us both.

Alev soars higher and I notice other dragons with struggling warriors. Some of them are still battling on the ground, others are fighting in the air, and many are lost to the dragon's wrath.

It's hard to tell if anyone is close to finding the goal of the race, wherever it may be. It could be anywhere—deep in the ocean, high up in the air, in the middle of a deadly forest, or even in another world.

The mystery of the Tournament is part of the thrill.

It quickly turns out that trying to signal Alev is useless. The dragon maneuvers from side to side, making loops in the air and wagging his tail like a dog.

I wonder if he would be insulted by that comparison.

"No matter how much I train or prepare you, dragons have a mind of their own. Alev is not always willing to listen," Star had warned me during our late-night hours with the dragon. "But he's the best chance we've got."

What an understatement.

"What is the next step of the plan?" I turn my head a little to try and make my voice reach the prince behind me.

"Any plan we might've had is long gone now. We'll just have to make it up as we go. That's what you usually do, isn't it? Recklessly jump into things without a plan?"

My answering snort is lost to the wind. "Maybe you should try and take the lead. He doesn't follow my orders." I gesture to the large beast underneath us, spitting out the rainwater running down my face.

Star's arm tightens around me, the hand gripping a black scale reaching forward to pull one of Alev's horns.

The dragon slows down enough for some of the nausea to recede, my watering eyes now more accustomed to the harsh conditions.

"Let's circle the mountain ranges first," Star shouts, pressing his chest against my back to keep me steady.

"Fine." I give a curt nod, one that he probably can't see underneath my large hood. "And we should probably also look—"

My words are cut off by Alev growling and dropping in the air.

"What—"

"Duck."

Star presses my head down and something large flies right over us. I look up just in time to see a brown dragon with blood-red eyes diving for us, jaw snapping and nostrils steaming.

"Can all dragons breathe fire?" My shout is almost unintelligible in the storm as I rise back into an upright position.

"No." Star leans forward to talk in my ear. "But some have other *talents* that are just as bad. Like that one."

I don't get the chance to ask what he's talking about.

A black bubbling liquid erupts from the brown dragon, barely missing us as Alev swerves to the side.

The liquid fizzles past us, hitting the tree line far below. It eats the leaves and disintegrates the bark, leaving nothing but a steaming mess. Combined with the rain, the black liquid makes a sizzling sound that reminds me of burning flesh.

Star pats the side of Alev's neck and the dragon shoots forward so fast it takes my breath away.

The brown dragon hurries after us, dark liquid frequently erupting from its mouth.

Alev swerves back and forth, up and down and around to avoid the poisonous liquid that haunts us.

My fingers gripping the dragon's scales so hard I'm afraid it's hurting him, I try to ignore the building nausea and the way it feels as if my heart is going to burst from my chest any second.

"Why is he going after us?"

"Who knows? I don't see anyone else riding together—" Star trails off, adjusting his grip on me.

"I get it," I snap. "We can continue arguing about it after we've completed this game. Right now, we need to get rid of our competition."

Another dragon swoops from the air, this one with scales a

shiny green. A warrior is standing on its back, sword raised and ready.

Star mutters a string of curses and his grip on me tightens.

"I got it," I say through gritted teeth. "Move over."

He hesitates for only a second before scooting to the side, his hands braced on Alev's scaly neck.

"Keep him steady." With a silent prayer to the gods, I crawl behind Star before slowly rising to my feet.

The dark scales are slippery from the rain, the howling wind threatening to tear me away any second.

The green dragon is slowly moving closer, the male warrior shouting a battle cry.

I fumble for the dagger in my pocket, trying to divide my weight evenly and stand steady on my feet. The rain is beating down on my face so hard it's almost unbearable.

Alev makes a steep turn and my feet start sliding sideways toward his right wing.

The sword comes crashing down right above my head.

The muscles along my arm scream as I block the blow, my dagger a joke compared to the mighty sword.

"Shake him off," Star barks before snarling at Alev to keep steady and ignore the dragon beside him.

I let out a frustrated scream, my leg kicking out to hit the warrior's knees.

The man jumps away and I'm forced to move over to the green dragon, one of my feet now firmly planted on each of the dragons' backs. If one of them moves—

The warrior swings his sword again, and I duck just in time to avoid the blade cutting me in half.

After struggling for a few moments, I manage to grab the handle of the sword and I fight to shake off the persistent warrior.

Alev growls and moves slightly to the side, enough for my

stance to wobble and the warrior to nearly shove me off the moving bodies.

"Asteria!"

Star's warning shout fuels me enough to wrangle the sword out of the warrior's grip and toss it into the air where it tumbles to the ground below.

The man lets out a furious scream before leaning down to grip the green dragon's neck. And then he sends me a cruel smirk.

The green dragon darts forward and my foot slips.

I scream as my fingers grasp for anything to hold on to. The dragon's neck, scales, ears, horns, anything, but it's no use.

It's too late.

There will be no stolen life essence or magic to save me this time.

This time, my death will be final.

The reality of it comes crashing down so suddenly I'm unable to brace myself.

Whatever it takes, Asteria.

Never stop fighting, my light. And never give up.

It has been so long since the familiar voice said something else than the usual mantra that I almost don't recognize it. And by the time I do, a hand closes around mine, warm even in the ferocious storm.

Star hauls me back onto the dragon's back, placing me the other way around so I only see him in the darkness, his midnight eyes a comforting relief.

"I thought we trained for this. You should know how to keep seated or standing despite obstacles such as that," he growls, his face only inches from mine. His arms are a cage around me, his fingers curled around the dragon's horns behind me.

"Are you always this insufferable?" My heart is raging from the almost fall, my chest heaving with a panic that's slowly starting to take over, the adrenaline surging through me making my whole body shake.

"You know I'm not," he snaps, "but I am when you nearly kill us both."

Star's gaze flickers to me for a fraction of a second before returning to the horizon behind me. "You need to calm down. I can't risk you falling off again."

"I am calm." My trembling hands grab the leathery fabric on his chest, my breathing becoming more frantic and shallow.

He curses as dark liquid rains down beside us, barely missing the tip of Alev's wing.

"Asteria."

My vision is starting to blur, and my head is spinning from the shrieking storm.

Star sighs heavily before muttering another string of curses. "Hold on to me."

"What?"

"Put your arms around my neck and close your eyes."

"What?"

"Close your eyes, starlight. I got you."

I give him a confused look. The wind has torn my hood away from my head and my face is numb from the icy rain hammering down from the sky. It's as if the sky is weeping, screaming at the warriors daring to disturb its serenity.

"Just do it. Now!"

The pure command in his voice breaks through some of my panic, giving me something to hang onto. I rest my forehead against his chest, and as my eyes close, Alev drops from the sky.

Holding on to the prince with a painful grip, I bite my lip to suffocate a rising scream, instead trying to focus on getting some air into my lungs.

The wind screams around us, thrashing and pulling in protest of us getting away.

In.

Out.

In.

Out.

It doesn't do much. I'm barely able to get any air into my lungs.

The only thing keeping me from just letting go is the pain from pressing my nails into the scars of my palms and the warmth emanating from Star.

Just when I think I can't take it anymore, when I'm about to beg Star to just let me drop from the sky, Alev flaps his wings and the rapid speed transforms to a comfortable glide through the air.

"Open your eyes, Asteria."

A hand cups my face, tilting my chin up, another shielding my eyes from the rain. Fingers brush away the strands of hair sticking to my forehead, and I open my eyes to midnight eyes boring into my very soul.

"What are you doing? We need to finish the race—" I gulp down mouthfuls of air, my heart hammering so hard it's painful. Tears are streaming down my face, the salty taste coating my tongue.

"I need you to calm down before we continue," he murmurs, his fingers stroking down the sides of my cheek, his other hand still shielding me from the storm.

My shaky hands grasp his, readying to push him away if I only had a little more strength in me. "I am calm," I snap, followed by a wheezing sound that results in a cough.

Star gives me an indignant look before doing something so unexpected it clears away some of the rising panic.

He leans forward and licks a tear running down my cheek.

I'm so stunned it takes me a moment to find my voice, and when I do, I don't know whether to laugh or curse him. "What—"

He smirks before licking away another tear from the outer corner of my mouth, the action doing the opposite of calming me.

"We're losing valuable time—"

"Nothing matters if you get us killed."

I flinch at his harsh tone, and his gaze softens before he abruptly pulls me close to his chest, his strong arms wrapping around me.

"I'm sorry." The words are so low I'm not sure I heard him right. "That wasn't helpful. Just breathe, starlight. Let's take a couple of moments to just...be." His soft and gentle tone startles me even more than the harsh one, and if I didn't know better, I would've thought he just pressed a kiss to the top of my head.

"Remind me to show you some very useful mind stilling and breathing techniques when we're back at the palace."

My shaking recedes a little at his calming strokes over my head and down my back, and at the softness of the exposed skin between his throat and chest pressed against my lips. The storm around us quiets, the steady beating of his heart grounding me.

No one has ever held me like this.

No one has ever given me such a feeling of peace and warmth.

Safe. At this moment, wrapped in his arms, in the middle of a raging storm and battle, I feel safe.

It breaks my heart as much as it heals me, making me question every thought and emotion I've ever had.

And for once, I allow myself this moment. To savor the feel of his unexpected calming presence. To pretend for just a few moments that we're not destined enemies bound and marked by deadly magic.

And then I make a silent vow to the gods, and to the invisible presence whispering in the wind, promising them to never allow myself this freedom again.

I can't forget what I'm truly fighting for.

This is bigger than both of us.

When I'm finally able to breathe again and the trembling is reduced to only a slight vibration inside of me, I wriggle out of his grasp, ignoring the look on his face and the way my soul is screaming to be reunited with his.

"Okay," I breathe, "I'm ready to win this thing."

It quickly turns out we're too late to win.

The second we climb higher in the air, gilded light breaks through the storm, the color so bright it's almost as if the sun herself has decided to banish the darkness. The cascade of glittering gold falls from the sky, lingering for only a moment before the darkness sweeps it all away.

We both mutter a curse as Alev increases his speed, the air now a flurry of dragons in all shapes and sizes.

The brown dragon with the black liquid is nowhere to be seen, and neither is the green dragon and its warrior.

Star is quiet behind me as we keep to the bottom of the line of dragons searching for the goal of the seventh trial. One of his arms is still draped around me, but he has scooted as far away from me as possible.

The memories of the unexpected moment between us are already locked away, yet my hammering heart is refusing to steady.

Star was right when he said Alev likes to keep to himself. The dragon growls and snaps his teeth at every dragon flying a little too close, his spiked tail swinging out to hit them anywhere he can reach. After a particularly bad incident with a gray dragon getting a few of the scales on his tail scorched off, Star signals for Alev to fly on the other side of the mountain range away from the other dragons.

The sky is gradually growing lighter, streaks of light blue creeping through the blanket of darkness with little spots of color. Lightning flares and thunder crackles between the pounding rain, the land of Luna nothing but a furious storm around us.

It shouldn't be possible, but the wind grows stronger and stronger. By some miracle, Alev is able to fight through it, the dragon's mighty wings seemingly made for flying in harsh conditions.

After hours of flying without a single trace of the goal, we're all getting impatient and angry. I can't stop tapping my fingers on the slippery scales despite the prince sighing behind me every time I do so, and the dragon beneath us is growling and snapping his teeth, no doubt eager to get back to his family.

"We might need to give him a break soon," I shout over the storm, stroking Alev's neck in comfort.

"We don't have much time left," Star grumbles behind me, "but yes, maybe we should—"

"What?"

He reaches forward to pat Alev at the spot between his silver horns, causing the dragon to shoot up toward a bundle of dark clouds barely visible in the night sky, the intensity of the storm increasing the higher we get.

"I think I just found our goal."

Silver lightning is exploding from the dark clouds, and as we get closer, I notice a steep mountain thinner than all the others beside it, barely visible in the darkness, the top concealed by the storming clouds.

Alev spreads out his wings with a deafening flap when we reach the mountain, the tips of his claws skimming the rocky surface.

The mountain is so tall I don't know if I'm imagining the

thinning of the air, and I can't decide if my head is spinning from that or everything else.

The dark clouds block all traces of light, momentarily blinding us and giving me the urge to turn around–to flee far away and never be anywhere near this mountain ever again. The blaring sound of the lightning sends a sharp pain to my skull, my ears ringing and roaring from the sound.

Fight through it. It's all a part of the Tournament.

Whatever it takes, Asteria.

A savage growl erupts from Alev, and Star tightens his grip around me, his chest now firmly pressed against my back.

The slumbering panic is starting to awaken again. I can't take this anymore—

And then we're out.

The stormy dark clouds clear away to reveal a large flat expanse of rocky ground where numerous dragons and warriors are fighting in bloody and raging battles.

Alev's claws scrape against the ground and a tingle spreads from the side of my neck.

The seventh trial is complete.

CHAPTER THIRTY-SIX

Star slams his empty shot glass down on the table, his face contorted from the strong taste. I laugh and he gives me a sheepish grin, his eyes gleaming in the dim light.

We didn't linger long after completing the trial. Alev insisted on getting back to his waiting family, and the reunion with his mate and baby is something I'm going to remember in my next dark moment. Esra found us after and transported us back to the royal city so fast I barely had the time to catch my breath.

We quickly lost our disguises, trading the soaked fighting leathers for clothes hidden by Star in the same place as last time. A simple black dress and his usual dark shirt and pants. With the matching rings glimmering on our fingers, we look like a pair of royals fit for the night and its shadows.

The prince never misses a chance to scheme, but this time I'm a willing participant.

For the last hours, we've been lounging at an ornate tavern decorated with both silver and gold—a celebratory place for the winning warriors as much as a mourning place for the losers.

"What in the sky is this foul drink?" Star snaps his fingers for a server to refill his wine glass, scooting the small empty glass to the edge of our table.

I shrug before downing my own shot, the liquid sending a familiar burning sensation down my throat. "I could make up an elaborate story about it being a recipe from a deity blessed by the sun, but I'm sure that wouldn't fool you."

Star sends me a sly smirk before taking his refilled glass from the server. "I don't think you could ever fool me, starlight." His twinkling eyes send a flare of heat through me, my heart still fragile from our shared moments only hours ago.

"When are you going to tell me the reason for that nickname?" I swirl my finger on the rim of my glass with an alluring smile.

"Patience, starlight. You're going to spoil all our fun." His eyes flicker to my lips as he holds his glass out for me to toast.

"I wouldn't dream of that."

Our glasses clink together, our matching rings sparkling in the dim light.

"Speaking of fun–" he gulps down the rest of his wine before reaching into his pocket to retrieve a heap of silver coins that clatters onto the table. Then he pushes out of his chair and reaches for my hand.

I drink the rest of my glass before taking his outstretched hand. My head is fuzzy from the large amount of drinks we've consumed the last hours and I sway a little when I get to my feet.

Outside, the stormy night is only a distant memory. The sun has almost reached its peak in the sky, and there is only cloudless blue behind her. The late summer breeze ruffles my loose hair, enveloping me in its flowery aroma.

We waddle down the cobblestoned paths lit up by sunlight, oblivious to everyone but each other. Our entwined hands swing back and forth and our laughter echoes through the streets.

Star's midnight eyes are shining brighter than ever before and with his ruffled hair and drunken smile, he seems more *alive* and *free*. Joking and laughing beside me, so different from the dark warrior and scheming prince I've come to know.

It feels like he is letting me in on one of the world's biggest secrets by showing yet another side of him I never could have imagined.

And at the moment, I guess I'm far from the cursed princess too.

The thrill and relief of completing another game mixed with all the drinks are doing strange things to me. Something is rocking my entire existence, and I don't know when I started to question everything around me, even the supposed enemy beside me.

"Where are we going?"

"Anywhere!" Star gestures to the city around us as if it's only ours to take and live through. "A swim in the river? Breakfast in the park? Or I could show you a temple that's not ruined." He snorts at the last suggestion.

"Or maybe–" he yanks me in the direction of an abandoned dark alley, a secretive smirk on his lips.

"Where are we going?"

Star ignores my repeated question and the whine in my voice as he drags me behind him.

"Where are we going? Star—"

"One day I want you to call me by my true name, starlight." He turns his head enough to flash me a delighted smile.

"Let me guess, only after I've earned the right to know the reasons behind my nickname and only after—" a gleeful screech bursts from my lips when I realize where he's taking me.

The hiding place of the rebellion.

"I don't think they would want a prince among them when

they're plotting against the royals," I mutter before stifling a giggle with my hand.

"Don't worry. It's not my first time sneaking around." His wink earns another giggle and his smile widens at the sound.

We don't use the same entrance I walked through the last and only time I was here, the one that leads directly into the large cave used for the rebellion's meetings. Star moves us to the side of the ruined building where parts of the rotten wood are torn off.

"I don't like this," I say in a singsong voice, my hand still clasped in Star's.

He gives me a frustrated look. "If I wanted you dead, you would already be dead. Don't you trust me by now? At least just a little?"

A prickle of heat spreads across my cheeks. "Maybe a tiny bit. You did keep me from falling through the air last night."

"See?" His smile widens and an adorable dimple appears in his left cheek. "I told you I haven't just been bad." He ducks inside before I have the time to reply, his hand beckoning me to follow.

With a heavy sigh, I gather the hem of my dress into my hands and move through the opening.

A musty smell greets me and the sunlight seeping from the cracks in the walls and ceiling reveals the first floor of a house broken and rotten in so many places it really can't be considered a house anymore.

Star is already walking down a ragged stairway where the wooden floorboards are cracked and missing large pieces.

I hurry after him on unsteady feet, my muscles weighed down by the liquor.

"There's probably not a meeting right now. The game just ended, most of the people are probably still in—"

Star presses a finger to his lips. "Keep your voice down.

There's always someone around here. And we are not going to a meeting."

He halts in front of a crooked painting and pushes his hand to the wall underneath, revealing a narrow tunnel going into the mountain. "We're going somewhere else. Somewhere better."

With a grin that reveals his pearly white teeth, he retrieves a glass orb from the wall inside the tunnel, the skylight flickering to life from his touch.

The skylight casts an eerie light in the dark tunnel, and I'm reluctant to replace the morning sun with darkness.

"I don't want to go in there. Let's go dancing instead."

Star smooths the pout on my lip with his finger before grabbing my hand to drag me forward. "I promise you're not going to regret it, starlight."

I make an exasperated sound but allow him to pull me along.

"I need another promise from you," I say, leaning my head on his shoulder. "And not a bargain," I add quickly. "I need you to get rid of any spiders or–"

He tips his head back and laughs, the sound echoing down through the darkness. "You've survived beasts and deadly magic, and you're still scared of small insignificant pests?"

"Shut up." I shove his back, a smile playing on my lips.

The tunnel winds down in circles that makes me dizzier than I already am. Orbs of skylights flare to life when we pass, but despite the magical lights, the feeling of being so deep underground makes me highly uncomfortable and paranoid, the fear of being buried alive squeezing my heart.

As if he can sense my growing discomfort, Star's fingers squeeze mine, reminding me that I'm not alone. "Almost there."

I count each step, focusing on my breath and the firm pressure of his hand.

And just when I think we can't possibly go any deeper, the line of skylights reveals something else than stone and darkness.

A large door is gleaming in the light, its silver and gold surface carved with intricate pictures of the sky and the gods.

The door is fit for a royal palace. It shouldn't be hidden and forgotten deep within the mountain of an abandoned building housing the rebellion.

"What is this?"

My breath is stuck in my throat, a part of me terrified to find out what's on the other side of the door, another humming with anticipation.

Star places his fingers on two pictures on the door sticking out from the others. A crescent moon and a half sun click together into a circle when he pushes them together.

The door swings open on creaking hinges, the door moved by an invisible force that sends a shiver down my back.

"What is this place?"

Star turns around to look at me and silver flares in his eyes. "This is the truth."

A large fountain covers a large part of the massive cave. Heaps of coins in different shades of silver and gold are scattered on the bottom of the fountain, and in the middle of it, with pale blue water pooling around their feet, are two limestone statues dripping with gold and silver paint.

A man and woman are standing close together, their lifeless hands barely touching and their heads turned in different directions as if they couldn't bear to look at each other. There's a crown on each of their heads and the man is holding a sword that looks a lot like the Royal Sword too familiar with the skin on my back.

As I get closer, I notice the woman is crying. Tears of silver are dripping down her face, rolling down her neck and collarbone where they merge with the gold on her dress. Her lips are contorted into a silent scream, her eyes wide with some emotion I can't place, and her expressive features are so different from the impassive face of the man beside her.

"Elara and Helios," Star whispers in my ear, his breath tickling my skin.

"The first," he adds with a snort. "I can't believe your king took that name." He snorts again before taking a step away from me, his hand resting on my lower back.

Helios, the first and true Sun King, the God of the Sun, the one who lowered our kingdom from the sky, blessing the land with his magic. And when our enemies followed, tainting the world with their darkness, the king graciously agreed to an everlasting bargain instead of destroying them in a war they were destined to lose, and thus the Tournament of Day and Night was created to keep the balance between the opposing sides of the sky, only allowing the sides to meet during the Tournament Times. But the woman beside him–

"The Tears of Elara, the river?"

"That's the one." Star tucks a piece of hair behind my ear before dragging me away.

The room is a gallery of ancient artifacts—jewelry adorned with shiny gemstones in every shade possible, racks of unfamiliar weapons, magnificent gowns, and heaps of other treasures screaming to be explored. A rosette chipped with gold and silver is cresting the stone ceiling, like the moon or the sun is adorning the sky. Most of the items in this room are not separated into two opposite sides like things usually are in the two kingdoms— they're a mix of colors bleeding into each other as if there's a circle of life and not two sides.

"You said this was about the truth?" I ask as my gaze travels across the room, trying to take in as much as possible.

Star leads me to the edge of the fountain. "What do you see, starlight?"

I rub my arms, suddenly cold despite the fabric covering my arms. I'm still very affected by the drinks and wine, but there's a clarity starting to seep into my mind as if there is something urgent I need to figure out.

"Helios, the King of the Sun." My finger reaches forward to touch the ancient statue, but something makes me halt in front of the sword.

"And–" I turn my gaze to the woman. "Elara? The one to name the river in Nyx."

"Queen Elara, actually," Star corrects, making a mock bow to the statue. "The first and last Queen of Luna."

I blink at him, slowly. "That's why we left the city? For you to tell me there's only been one queen in your kingdom? I already told you I'm not actually going to marry you–"

"Let me finish." He takes a step forward, his eyes boring into mine.

"There has never been a queen after Elara, and without her crown and throne there never will be. Many have tried over the centuries, but any woman daring to sit on the throne of the king without the crown...well..." He trails off with a shudder.

"What happened to her crown and throne?"

Star shrugs. "Gone. Lost with her tears."

Before I have the time to ask one of my endless questions, he grabs my shoulders and turns me away from the ancient statues.

"Look at this." He points to a large map that covers almost the entirety of one of the walls lit up by tiny hovering skylights.

I let out a frustrated sound. The numbing effects of our adventures are starting to wear off and I'm getting more impatient by the second.

"I have seen a map of our kingdoms before. Believe it or not, I've had access to libraries despite being the cursed princess."

"Look again," Star insists.

The paper of the map is crinkled and fragile—some pieces are torn off and other places are scarred with burn marks. There's Soria with its varying land and lush vegetation, Luna with its mountainous landscape, and the ocean surrounding both kingdoms. But where the kingdoms should be divided by the Diamond Mountains, there is nothing but scattered trees.

"Notice anything different?"

"There is–that's not–what?"

Star traces a finger across the map, over the lack of names and symbols and borders. "There's not many people who know the truth. That our kingdoms haven't always been on the brink of war and that it doesn't necessarily have to be like that."

"That's not true." I walk back to the fountain and plop down on the edge. "The kingdoms are blessed by the two sides of the sky, light and darkness, destined to fight for space and resources in a Tournament crafted in an ancient bargain where the gods gift us their magic—"

"There it is. The fraction of a long story they've chosen to tell us. It's not the whole story. It's not the whole truth. This is the truth." The prince gestures to the room around us filled with forgotten treasures.

My head has started to ache, pain slowly spreading across my forehead and down the sides of my face. "I really need to get some sleep." I rub my aching temples before leaning my head in my hands.

"Focus, Asteria." Star is suddenly in front of me, kneeling to lift my head in his hands. "The truth is right in front of you."

"This is the work of the rebellion. It's what *they* chose to believe. It's not *my* truth. What's all this about?" I snap, the dreamy cloud of our day spent together slowly moving away on a cold breeze.

It feels as if it never happened at all.

And it looks like Star is starting to feel that too.

Some of the usual tension has crept back into his features and his eyes are darker and not as vibrant anymore. "You're proof of something different. Something more. And I guess I was wrong thinking you were ready to finally see that." His hands leave my face and he rises back to his feet, brushing the dust of his pants.

"What are you talking about?" A heavy tiredness has settled in my body and I stifle a yawn, my eyelids threatening to droop.

Star lets out a sound that reminds me of the growls of the dragons, his eyes a raging storm of darkness as he looks down at me. "You are a daughter of both sides of the sky. Blessed by the sun *and* the moon. There's not only royal magic coursing through your veins, but essence from light *and* darkness."

A dark laugh erupts from my lips as I jump to my feet, all signs of tiredness replaced by red-hot anger. "Well played, moon boy." I shake my head as I let out another dark chuckle. "You almost had me this time."

Star only blinks at me, his hands curling into fists at his sides. "This isn't a joke. This is not another game. Isn't this room proof enough?"

I ball my own hands into fists, nails boring into the scars in my palms. "What exactly are you trying to trick me into believing?"

"The Sun King is not your father. Well, not in blood anyway."

"That's ridiculous," I snap, ignoring the increased beating of my heart.

I'm not going to admit I used to dream about exactly that as a child. Every time he scolded me, with every harsh word and every cut of the royal blade, a part of me desperately wished I could've had someone else as a father.

That I didn't have to share the same blood as such a monster.

The look of pity on his face only fuels my burning anger. "Why do you think the king despises you so much? Why do you think you're so different from your perfect golden sisters? Why have you never truly belonged in your kingdom of sunshine and flowers—"

"Stop it." My arm swings out to stop the words pouring from his lips.

Star effortlessly steps away, baring his teeth before continuing to speak words that shouldn't be spoken. "I know there's a part of you eager to believe me. I told you I was going to show you the truth. This is it, and I think you know that too. This is why you've been so desperate all your life, yearning for a place and opportunity to prove yourself—"

A scream erupts from my lips and I retrieve the dagger hidden in the bodice of my dress, aiming straight for his mouth as I hurtle the weapon.

With a heavy sight, he catches the handle of the dagger before slipping it into the pocket of his pants. "You're angry. Fine. I get it. Even though I'm not the one to blame, I'll let you take it out on me this time. But you'll owe me one."

He crosses his arms across his chest. "Your real father is a warrior from Luna. Don't tell me you've never questioned where your white hair came from."

"My mother had blonde hair that was almost white in the sunlight—"

His mocking laugh drowns out the rest of my words.

A small knife hidden in my boot flies for his legs, clattering to the floor when he jumps away.

"I am a princess of the sun—"

"And the moon."

"Only through forced bonds and bargains," I snap as I pick up the first thing I can find—a silver rounded shield with golden stars.

Star raises a dark eyebrow in challenge before cracking his neck. "And through blood. Come on, let's see what else you've got."

"You think I'm weak? You're the one with these ridiculous stories. Is this really the best you've got?"

The shield flies through the air in a moving circle.

"Reckless and stubborn, yes, but never weak. And what could I possibly gain by lying to you at this point, princess?" His knuckles turn white as his fingers grab the moving shield, halting it in the air before tossing it to the side.

"You've refused to tell me what you're up to so I can only guess–"

The prince moves faster than ever before, appearing in front of me in a blink. His broad frame is a towering shadow above me, and power ripples of his body in the form of a faint black smoke.

"I brought you directly to the source of information regarding the last game before I helped you *survive* said game. And then I brought you here, to show you a truth you refuse to see. I'm only trying to fulfill my end of the bargain. I'm trying to *help* you. I'm trying to keep you *alive*."

My chest is heaving from the fury blazing inside me as I consider how to strike him next. "If what you claim is true and you are trying to help me, then why didn't you tell me sooner? And even if it was true, how would you even know–"

"I wasn't sure at first. Now I am, and I'm telling you." He grabs my arm and rips the fabric of my sleeve, revealing our bargain mark to the light. "I'm bound to you. I will die if I don't fulfill my end. Don't you dare forget that," he spits, a growl reverberating from deep within his chest.

Power vibrates in my blood and my body shakes from the fiery fury. "We may have a bargain, but that doesn't mean there aren't ways around it. You're obviously trying to trick me into believing something that could end my life so you can take the throne without fulfilling your end."

"But it's not going to work." I gesture to the room around us, to the statues, maps, and ancient weapons stacked against the walls. "Two gods supposedly ruling over a peaceful united kingdom has nothing to do with me—"

"Why don't you get it? King Helios betrayed Queen Elara, breaking her heart and pushing her into the darkness. His betrayal resulted in a bargain that would continue his destruction by forcing a natural circle into two opposing sides. Elara's anguish made mountains spurt from the ground and her tears carved into the land and cleaved it in two."

Star's fingers curl around the exposed skin on my forearm, breaking through the pattern of dark lines and swirls. "Much of the story was repeated with your mother. She found love with a Lunan warrior, so desperately in love that she ignored the decaying state of her body to give life to you. A product of magic both from the sun and the moon—"

"I don't want to hear another lie out of your mouth," I snarl through gritted teeth, trying to yank my arm free from his iron grip.

"It's almost funny when you think about it. The present Sun King with the name of the one to start all this trouble was betrayed in the same manner by his queen as the god betrayed his own."

"Stop—"

He releases me so abruptly I almost think the anger within me burns through my skin. "Ask the king. See for yourself. And don't come crying to me when you realize I was right all along."

"My mother loved the king—"

He lets out a hollow chuckle. "Perhaps. But not like she loved your true father. Not like she loved you."

I love you with all my heart, my light, more than anything in the world.

Promise me, Asteria. Promise me you'll do it.

I sacrificed my life for yours, and now I need you to promise me you will do what I promised them.

Her voice rings in my mind louder than ever before, reminding me of the first bargain I ever struck before I even knew what it would mean and how much it would alter my world and shatter my heart.

I trace my finger over the mark behind my ear, the mark hidden underneath long locks of white hair, the mark only I know about.

A faint line in a half circle, too faint to be a scar but too deep to be only a scrape—a birthmark and proof of my true purpose.

The last place she touched me before she left this world.

The last time I felt her warmth, but not the last time I felt her presence.

Is it true?

I want to scream the words.

I want to let my anger burn through the darkness until I find her.

I want to search through every part of every world so I can drag her back to this one and demand the truth.

Is it true, Mother?

Yes.

CHAPTER THIRTY-SEVEN

My dark heels click against the marble floor of the palace, my black dress dragging behind me like a river of shadows. The dark color matches my raging mood, and it's the only color suited for what I'm about to do.

I clench my trembling hands, the pain from my nails that usually grounds me doing absolutely nothing.

Just the thought of confronting the king sends sparks of pain through the scars on my back, and I can feel my awareness prepare to slip away like it always does during his punishments.

I can't face him like this.

I'm too filled with wrath and vengeance, too shaken and desperate. He will take me out in a second, even without using his magic.

I need more time.

When I reach a fork in the hallway, I choose another direction.

I don't bother knocking on the door with pale yellow stars—their dim color the closest I've seen to the Sorian shades in the palace.

Solina is seated on a white cushioned daybed in the sitting room, and a seamstress I recognize from Soria sitting opposite her with a sketchbook in her lap.

I catch a glimpse of a beautiful wedding dress drawn with golden ink and the sight of it sends a jolt of pain to my chest, reminding me of what I've been trying to forget the last two weeks.

Solina raises her golden eyebrows when she sees me. "We will continue this at a later time, Folina," she says to the woman in a too-polite tone that leaves no room for questions.

The seamstress quickly closes her book and rises to her feet. "Of course, Your Highness," she says, making a deep curtsey that gives me the urge to roll my eyes.

When the door clicks shut, my sister folds her hands in her lap and moves her honey eyes to me. "Asteria. I'm happy to see you've come to your senses. After our last conversation—well, I didn't expect to see you again this soon."

Her gaze trails across the black dress clinging to my body down to the ring on my finger, and disdain flickers in her eyes, there and gone so fast I'm not sure if I only imagined it. "I heard you've been...busy."

I cross my arms, hiding the ring behind my hand. "So have you." I nod my head to an assortment of gold jewelry lying on the table in front of her, brought for her to decide what to wear with her wedding dress.

"Asteria—" Solina sighs heavily. "I—"

"That's not why I'm here." I wave a hand to silence her before I have to endure anything else that will stoke my burning anger.

"It's not?" A furrow forms between her eyebrows, confusion written across her sun-kissed face.

"Nope." I plop down in a chair adjacent to the seating group, feeling the hilt of my hidden dagger press against my thigh. "I want to know what you know about our mother."

Her eyes widen and she purses her lips for a moment before the usual perfect polite mask is back on her face. "What about Mother?"

I shrug, willing my face to be neutral to not reveal anything that could cause her to lie or withhold information. "You were almost ten when she died. You must have a lot of memories."

"I do..."

I can practically hear the questions churning in her mind, and I resist a smirk when her fingers tighten around the fabric of her skirt.

She is nervous. And perhaps scared to figure out what I'm up to.

I raise my eyebrows and a muscle ticks in her jaw.

"You've heard them all numerous times."

"That was a long time ago, and I don't think that was *everything* you know."

Her composure is about to crumble. I can feel it.

"I can't be the only one who's questioned why I look so different from the rest of you."

Some of her perfect mask slips away. Her eyes narrow slightly and she lifts her chin. "It's not wise to talk about what you're hinting at–"

"And could that possibly be, dear sister? The whole kingdom knows there's something different about me. No, both kingdoms know that."

"I don't know what that prince has said or done to make you act like this," she says in a clipped voice, gesturing to my dark attire. "But consider this a warning. It would be better for all of us if you stayed away from trouble and stopped running around with warriors and–"

I lean my head in my hands, tilting my head to reveal the binding mark on my neck. "It's a little too late for that, don't you think?" I wiggle my hand in her direction, displaying the glimmering darkness on my finger.

"I took care of that for you," she snaps, the rest of her mask slipping away, a hint of golden anger flickering in her eyes. "And if you hadn't been sneaking around with him to cause indecent rumors you could have returned home after the games–"

A dark laugh slips out of me, interrupting her well-practiced words. "We both know *he* would never let me come back home again. Not after everything I've done. How easy it would be to banish me completely if he just told everyone the truth."

"The truth?" Wariness has crept into her voice and she studies me so intently it looks as if she is hoping to pull the words out of me.

That won't be necessary.

"The Sun King is not my father, not in blood."

Solina stiffens and she purses her lips together in a thin line as she searches for the right words.

They don't come.

"I'm not his daughter and you knew," I spit, accusation lacing every word, the anger inside me roaring. "I don't share a single drop of his blood. Is Mother even your mother or are we not sisters in any sense?"

Right now, I don't care how and why she knew. All that matters is that she robbed me of an opportunity I should've taken long ago.

"Did *Prince Star* tell you this?" The voice that comes out of my sister's mouth is so different from her usual confident tone. It's tense, angry, and...scared.

"You're not even going to deny it? It doesn't matter how I found out. All that matters is that I know the truth and that *you* didn't tell me," I snarl, my fingers itching to grab the hidden dagger and bury it in her skin.

"It's not the truth. You are a princess of the sun." Another flare of gold flickers in her eyes. "We are in enemy territory. All of them are scheming and trying to bring us down. I just didn't think you were stupid enough to be fooled by them."

Sparks of fury tingle at my fingertips and a ferocious scream is building in my throat.

"Then it's a good thing I'm partly one of them, and that I have scheming plans of my own."

THE KING NAMED after the God of the Sun is not in his quarters.

The guards outside the doors pale when I approach them like a dark brewing storm. After a scorching glare, one of them stutters out the king's whereabouts. It usually takes a little more persuading to get them to tell me anything useful, but nothing is stopping me today, especially not a stupid guard.

I find the king in one of the small gardens outside one of the guest wings, stifling a chuckle when I notice he has bothered to bring a little piece of Soria across the Diamond Mountains.

The Sun King always needs a trace of light in the darkness.

In the middle of the garden, there's a fountain displaying a limestone woman holding a small replica of the sun, her arms reaching for the sky. Bundles of pale yellow daffodils and marigolds cover the freshly cut grass, their petals scattered by the wind.

The king has his back to me, his gaze locked on the horizon where the sun is shining above his kingdom hiding in the faraway distance.

The Royal Sword is not present at his side.

It took a lot of scheming and sneaking around in the dark hours of the night, but I've made sure the sword is far away from the hands of the king.

It was hard to decide what to do with it. Despite the memories clinging to the gilded blade, I couldn't just destroy it or throw it in the ocean. My royal heritage is too important to cast aside.

It is, after all, a part of my mother too.

Perhaps one day I'll melt into a cage for the king and doom him to a destiny of rotting underneath the ground and not fly on the wind like his ancestors.

"I assume you are here to give me my sword back." His deep voice startles me, his words as cold as the ice coating the ocean during the harshest winter days.

The king doesn't turn around to look at me. It would be easy to sink a dagger into the golden fabric of his shirt if it weren't for the guards observing him from the windows and shadows, and the magic lurking underneath his skin. The magic, I realize, he never planned on teaching me as I do not share his blood.

"No." I lean against the shadowed stone of the palace, fingers resting on the hilt of my hidden dagger as I repeat the promise I recently made to the gods. "The Royal Sword will never spill my blood again."

When he turns around to look at me, his honey eyes are void of all emotion.

I can't help comparing him to the hidden statue of his namesake.

They share the same harsh expressions and regal postures. And it wouldn't surprise me if Helios the first was also touched by light as if the sun had gilded him—the honey eyes speckled with gold, the strands of golden blonde hair graying at the edges, the sun-kissed skin, and the traces of light always shining around him.

"I heard you have been causing trouble lately, daughter."

Daughter. The weight of the word is crushing and suffocating, and it stokes the fuming embers inside me.

"I don't understand why you've kept that lie all these years. Wouldn't it have been easier to just get rid of the child that stole the life from your queen, the result of your wife loving another man?" I tilt my head to the side, baring my teeth.

Bright golden light erupts in his eyes, but I don't stop.

"Tell me, *Father.* Was Mother planning to leave you before she died? Was she preparing to cross the border into the enemy kingdom to get as far away from *you* as possible—"

The Sun King darts forward so fast that I'm unable to stop his hands from wrapping around my throat.

"How dare you speak to me like that?" His fingers dig into my skin and he slams my head back against the wall.

My eyes bore into his. White-hot icy blue against bright gold.

I will never avert my eyes ever again.

And I will never let him harm me without fighting back.

I slam my knee into his groin as I twist his arm away, fury fueling every part of my body.

I've never laid a hand on him. Not once have I fought back, at least not with anything else than words and reckless actions. It can only be surprise and shock that allow me to slip away from him so easily.

A king he might be, but a skilled warrior is hiding underneath his golden exterior, and from the bright gold swirling in his gaze, I can only brace myself for the full effect of his power.

As I move away from him, putting much-needed distance between us, the king holds up a hand to stop the approaching guards, his eyes raging as he looks at me.

All it would take is one look from him and his magic could destroy me, the light coursing through him bright enough to blind an entire army.

Helios spits on the ground before smoothing the collar of his shirt and dragging his fingers through the unbound locks of his golden hair.

"I have warned you more times than I can count, Asteria. You do not want to get on my bad side."

"Haven't I always been on your bad side?" I cross my arms before stepping into a shadowed patch of the garden, away from the sunlight powering his magic.

"You're no longer in control of me. I am not of your blood. I never have been, and I will never pretend to be ever again." I give him a cruel smirk before delivering my next blow.

"Are you reminded of her betrayal and your loss every time you look at me? I can only assume that's the reason for all our... sessions...together. I have her eyes, don't I?"

I curl a strand of white around my finger, moving it toward the light until it glitters like snow underneath the winter sun. "And I guess this is from him, whoever he is."

"All I care about is that he isn't you," I spit, cursing the king like I've never even dared to do in my thoughts.

Helios studies me, his fingers twitching in the direction of where the Royal Sword should be. "This will not end well for you, Asteria. You are mistaken if you think this knowledge will be in your favor. A bastard-born princess is no better than a cursed one."

A dark chuckle escapes me. "Then it's a good thing I'm going to be the next Victor."

He lets out a mocking laugh. "Go ahead and try. A lot can happen in a year and *you* will not be able to bind yourself next year—"

"I'm not talking about next year," I say, a pleased smirk spreading on my lips.

"You are too late—"

"I'm not. I never quit."

"That is not possible." Understanding flashes across his features and light bursts from his palms.

I take a step deeper into the shadows of the palace. "Did she even die because of me? Or did you kill her when you found out I wasn't yours?"

The light flares brighter, the twining magic starting to reach forward.

"You deserve every scar on your back. And there are not nearly enough," he spits, his eyes a storm of gold.

Pure unyielding rage erupts through my veins like the brightest flames. And right now, it feels like I could burn down this entire world.

I look at the king who has been destroying me my entire life and fire explodes from my hands.

The flames licking up my arms are as bright as the sun in the sky. They light up the shadows around me as they burst toward the king.

Helios steps back in shock, the light in his hands flickering for a second before rising to meet my fire.

Our magic clashes in an inferno of power, the bright sun overhead witnessing it all.

My chest is heaving and there is a humming in my blood so strong it overpowers everything.

I have no idea what is happening.

I don't know how to control it.

I don't know how to stop it.

And I hate it. I hate that I share something with the man I was supposed to no longer have any ties to.

Helios lets out a roar, his magic forcing me to stumble back against the palace. The stone digs into my back and I feel the shadows seeping from the walls start to reach for me.

The sun disappears behind a cloud and the fire vanishes as suddenly and violently as it came, leaving me defenseless against the kinglight crashing toward me.

I duck right in time. The king's magic slams against the palace where my head was only seconds ago, rattling the earth underneath me.

I stumble away and into the darkness of the palace, Helios' thunderous roars reverberating behind me.

I run. Away from the sunshine of the garden and the king who is never going to rule me ever again.

CHAPTER THIRTY-EIGHT

Warm fingers are stroking my cheek, and the thundering sounds of countless people running through the palace get closer and closer as my eyes blink open.

Star is smirking down at me, his midnight eyes flickering to the sheer fabric of my nightgown. "How nice it is to see you not plotting my death. You almost look harmless asleep."

I yank the covers to my chin, glaring daggers at the prince. "Once again you're not where you're supposed to be and once again you're disturbing my sleep."

Star chuckles as he retracts his finger. "You were the one in a place you shouldn't be the last time I woke you. Although you're always welcome in my bed, starlight," he purrs, a suggestive smirk playing on his lips.

"And to what do I owe this displeasure? I thought I told you I needed sleep the last time I saw you."

His expression hardens, the smirk replaced by a thin line. "That wasn't the only thing you told me the last time we were together, but I'm glad to see you've finally accepted the truth and that I was simply trying to help you."

His eyebrows raise. "It would be a waste to use the dagger hidden underneath your pillow on me."

"If you don't tell me why you're here I might reconsider."

A shout reverberates from underneath us. Star straightens and moves to the armoire on the other side of the room, a muscle ticking in his jaw.

"You and I need to go on another adventure."

"I'm not in the mood."

A black dress with a bodice of burning red flies across his shoulder, hitting the mattress of my bed.

I repress the images crashing into me at the sight of the color, digging my nails into the scars in my hands.

I will not think about it.

"This isn't like last time. Let's just say the consequences of our troublesome actions are catching up to us." He sends me a glare as he firmly closes the doors of my closet.

He strides across the room, anger darkening his eyes. "Did you really think it wise to announce your participation in the games to the king? And, more importantly, that you now know one of the biggest secrets of his kingdom? Right at this moment?"

"I didn't plan to, I–" I snap my mouth shut with a glare. "I don't have to explain myself to you. That's none of your business."

Dread coils in my stomach and my heart beats a painful rhythm against my chest.

Does he know? Did he see it? If he did, he would've said something by now. Wouldn't he?

"We have a bargain." He pulls the covers away from the bed, leaving my body exposed to the cold of the night. "And it is my business when you're putting said bargain in danger by renouncing your royal status in Soria."

"I didn't–"

Star pulls at the hem of my nightdress. "It is only a matter of time—"

"Stop that," I hiss, trying to pry his fingers away.

"If you're not dressing yourself, I will. It's up to you, *princess*."

I glare at him until he rolls his eyes and turns around, his fingers impatiently tapping his thighs.

"I assume you're not going to tell me what this is about. As always, withholding information is your favorite thing to do—"

"The twins have been found."

I freeze at his words, my fingers halting the lacing of the dress. "Where?"

He turns around with an annoyed look, ignoring my protests at only being half dressed before quickly pulling down the skirt of my dress. "Trust me, you don't want to know."

I close my eyes against the images crashing into me. The blood, the devastated screams of the prince as his brother died, the severed head–

Warm fingers move strands of hair away from my face and my eyes snap open.

"If it makes you feel any better, Aro would have ended you in a much more brutal way than you did him, and he would have thoroughly enjoyed it."

"It doesn't." I move my face away from his fingers and take a step away to pull on my boots.

Star shrugs, his gaze flickering to the door of my bedroom. "We need to move. Now."

"What—"

He grabs my waist and practically carries me across the room to a tapestry on the wall where he reveals a hidden entrance to the servant's halls I didn't even know was in my room.

"Let me go—"

He puts a finger to my lips and pushes me against the wall, his lips brushing against my ear when he whispers. "We need to be quiet."

The space is so small every part of his body is pressed against mine, the narrow staircase not fit for more than one person.

Behind the tapestry picturing the starry sky, the door to the bedroom crashes open followed by running footsteps and shouting voices.

With a smirk that makes my blood boil, Star's finger on my lips moves to stroke the exposed skin above my collarbone.

I glare at him, pinching his finger as I move it away, an action that only widens his smirk. He rests his head back against the wall, his eyes roving over every inch of me.

There's no room to push him away unless I want to make him tumble down the steep stairway and make our presence known to the guards ransacking my room—a possibility that's getting more tempting by the second.

When the ruckus stills and the guards leave my room behind, Star grabs my hand and drags me down the stairs.

I plant my feet on the ground, halting our descent. "I'm not taking another step before you tell me what the hell is going on."

"The Sun King has sent out orders for your capture," he says through gritted teeth, tugging my hand.

"What?" I'm so stunned by his words I don't stop him the next time he pulls my hand.

"Orders of the Sun King. For your capture."

We move down the stairs, the only light coming from the small cracks in the walls, Star's hand dragging me down so fast I'm afraid I'm going to slip and tumble down any second.

"Orders for what? To send me to the gallows?"

"More like to rot in the dungeons until he decides to deal with you."

A jolt rocks my heart, the dread coiling inside me gripping my heart so hard I'm struggling to breathe.

The Sun King has finally had enough.

No more empty threats.

No more cruel punishments.

This time, it's for real.

"He can't do this. I'm a princess–"

"He's the king. He can do whatever he wants."

"And the Moon King?"

Star sends me a wary look. "He will do whatever he can to ensure the most spectacular Tournament and that means keeping Helios here long enough to see it through, even if he has to give up his current favorite warrior. Or perhaps he anticipates that your attempted escape will bring him even more entertainment."

It feels like an eternity has passed since I was trapped in a carriage with the Moon King's dark magic, but I remember how elated he was by my hidden participation in the games.

"I'm still a part of Soria's—"

"Do you think the people will protest? For all they know you're a cursed princess up to nothing but deadly trouble. And if he reveals your true nature–"

We've reached the end of the staircase and are now standing in front of numerous tunnels and paths, the routes as uncertain and unpredictable as my future.

I open my mouth to protest but quickly close it again and press my lips together.

I hate that he's right. I hate it with all my heart, with every cell and bone in my body, with all that's left of my soul, cursed or not.

The people of Soria would not care about me. They would savor my capture and punishment for what they deem the greatest crime in their lifetime—stealing their beloved queen.

Star reaches forward and tilts my chin up to look at him, his face swirling with shadows, his eyes a storm of silver lightning. "Luckily for you, starlight, the Sun King can't touch you once you're officially a princess of the moon. It would be an outright act of war against Luna. He won't do that. Not in the middle of the Tournament."

"But I'm not a princess of the moon—"

My mind is a raging chaos and I can barely think over the heavy beating of my heart.

I might have to actually leave this time. To set sail for a continent far far away from the two kingdoms.

But I can't.

I have to win the Tournament.

I have to become the next Victor.

"Unless my real father is a king?" A snort escapes me before I press my eyes shut, not bothering to shove the prince away.

"Unfortunately not, but it's something I can take care of nonetheless." His hand leaves my face, sliding down my side to grasp my hand. His fingers turn the ring on my finger—the ring I keep forgetting to take off.

My eyes snap open and I stumble away until my back hits the stone of the palace. "I'm not marrying you."

"All we need is a priestess to bless our union before he can catch you," Star mutters, seemingly unaware of my protests.

"I'm not marrying you!"

My chest is heaving from both fear and fury, and I curl my hands into fists when I feel a small spark in my fingertips.

"The whole point of our *union* was to distract the people. We were never supposed to actually go through with it. By the sky, we were never supposed to be engaged in the first place but you just had to make plans on your own-"

"Times have changed," Star snaps before disappearing into one of the tunnels.

A frustrated scream that echoes through the mountain bursts from my lips as I hurry after him.

I need more information.

I need more time.

Winning the Tournament won't solve all my problems, but it will solve a lot of them. The Sun King won't dare imprison a Victor without a very good reason. And even if I lose my title as princess, being a Victor is just as important, the title carrying all the glory I need.

"How do I know you're not trying to trick me? Maybe you sent the guards to make all this more believable—"

His answering snort echoes of the tunnel walls. "Sometimes I wonder what you truly think of me. I want to take the throne, tying myself to you is not the best way to do that, is it? But alas, we have a bargain I need to fulfill before anything else."

He sighs heavily before continuing to speak, his voice ringing in the eerie silence. "If you thought the king would just allow you to continue as always after your little show-off in the garden, you're more reckless than I thought. But I can't deny that going for his favorite body part wasn't very entertaining to watch."

"You were there?" My breath hitches and my heartbeats stutter.

Star turns around to look at me and silver flashes in his eyes. "Yes. And then I kept an eye on the king, which is how I know about his plans for you."

If he didn't see it, maybe it didn't happen at all.

"And why would you do that?"

We round another corner, the tunnel longer and steeper than I would've expected. Does it lead all the way down to the royal city?

"As I've said before, your death would be an inconvenience for me, especially considering our bargain."

Another frustrated scream escapes me as Star chooses the left option of three paths branching out from the tunnel.

"I told you making a bargain with me would be in your best favor, starlight. After all, you would be rotting next to the Royal Sword if it wasn't for me."

"What did you do to the sword?"

"Don't worry. I took care of it, but you will get the pleasure of deciding its fate."

Large boulders placed to make an improvised stairwell that has partly merged into the mountain greet us at the end of the tunnel. The stones reach for the sky, and the sight of how far up they go fills me with fear as I realize how deep underground we must be.

Star doesn't hesitate as he steps onto the first boulder. He bends down to hold out a hand—an offer for more than just help up the large stone.

I gather the skirt of my dress in my hands, ignoring his outstretched hand as I climb onto the stone.

"I'll get you another dress if that helps you make up your mind," Star says as he continues to walk up the stairs in front of me.

"It won't."

"My mistake. What about a new dagger? A sword? An arrow? Or maybe even one of those nailed clubs–"

"Can you shut up for one moment so I can hear myself think?"

"I'll leave you in silence after we've made our promises to the gods. Like I've tried to tell you numerous times, we don't have a lot of time."

"And I've told you, *numerous times*, that I won't marry you–"

"

"What other choice do you have?"

I focus on climbing the stairs, my mind desperately searching for a solution to my growing list of problems.

At the top of the stairs, a door has been carved into the stone and as Star yanks it open, silvery white light breaks through the darkness of the mountain.

I step through the door and my heart skips a beat before a humorless chuckle breaks through my pursed lips.

The scheming prince has brought me to a temple.

The ocean roars underneath us, the crashing waves lit up by the moonlight. Carved into and out of the mountain, the temple's pillars rise toward the sky, and there's an opening in the high ceiling perfect for the moon and stars to shine through. The temple is open to the elements, and in the center, right underneath the opening in the ceiling, a statue of gleaming silver reaches for the sky—Elara, the Goddess and Queen of Darkness.

"I should've guessed you two would be in on this," I say with another dark chuckle, gesturing to Skye and Thunder standing next to a cowering priestess in long black robes.

"We wouldn't want to miss a royal wedding," Skye says with a sly smile, her eyes twinkling in the moonlight. Thunder only grunts in reply, his eyes not moving from the priestess.

I turn to the prince leaning against one of the pillars, his gaze locked on the palace towering over the city in the distance.

The loud sounds of searching guards echo through the city, their approaching presence a painful reminder of my dark predicament.

"What will it take for you to understand the meaning of the word no?"

Star raises an eyebrow. "We don't have time for this," he says before moving to close the distance between us. "Don't tell me you would rather die than marry me."

"I would, actually."

Thunder coughs behind us in a very bad attempt to mask his chuckle.

Star sends a glare in his direction before tucking a strand of hair behind my ear. "And the Tournament? Your goals of conquest and—"

"Goals I can accomplish without a marriage—"

"No," Star all but growls. "Not when you're being hunted by the kings. You'll be dead before the next trial even begins."

"I'm capable of finding a hiding place on my own," I snarl back, giving him my best glare.

The prince barks out a laugh. "In an unknown kingdom with nearly every guard and soldier in both armies searching for you? That is, in addition to all the people wanting to claim the prize of bringing you forward."

"So what? I marry you and you stow me away in a dark corner?"

"No." Silver lightning cracks across the midnight sky followed by a thunderous boom that rattles the temple. The prince takes a step forward, the same silver light flashing in his eyes.

"You marry me and you will never have to hide again. You marry me and no one will touch or harm you ever again. You marry me and I'll make you Victor. You marry me and we can fulfill our bargain once and for all."

"I don't need your protection." Dread fills me at the thought of making another stupid promise. It wouldn't just be a promise to him, but a bargain to the gods.

Star bares his teeth, an impatient sound escaping his throat. "Right now you do. You can't run, and you can't hide. Not unless you want us both to leave this world and I'm not letting you do that. Not yet."

Another flare of lightning cracks across the sky.

More and more guards are spilling out of the palace, their

armored uniforms gleaming in the moonlight. Some of them have reached the end of the city.

They will be reaching the temple any minute now.

I will not let them bring me to the king but—

I can't fight them all.

I can't hide in the city.

The mountain underneath me is a labyrinth of dark tunnels and I have no idea what could be down there, and the ocean is so far below there is no way I'll survive the fall.

There is no way out—

Whatever it takes, Asteria.

Promise me.

Promise me you will do whatever it takes.

Her voice is a painful throb in my mind—loud and unyielding.

Remember the cost.

Remember what will happen if you fail.

Promise me, Asteria.

Promise me you will do whatever it takes.

"Fine," I scream, willing the voice to quiet.

I *will* do whatever it takes. I have to.

"This is only a part of our bargain, nothing more. And once the Tournament is over–"

"When our bargain is done, so are we," Star says simply, grabbing my hand and placing it in his.

It is a ridiculous vow. Our marriage will be blessed by the gods, unbreakable until darkness claims us.

From this moment, we will never truly be done.

"You know what to do," Thunder growls, nudging the priestess with his boot.

The priestess scrambles forward while muttering low prayers to the gods. She raises one of her hands to the sky, the other hand touching the joined hands of the prince and the princess of enemy kingdoms.

The lightning flaring across the sky brightens, the booming thunder closer than before.

The priestess closes her eyes, her lips starting to form a series of chanted words reserved for the blessing of lifelong unions.

After a few seconds, her eyes snap open, her irises a swirl of dark colors as she seeks permission from the gods to tie us together. A deep furrow forms between the aging lines on her forehead and her hand falls away. "There's already a bond between you—"

"Just bless our union, priestess," Star growls impatiently, his eyes flickering to the approaching army behind us.

The battalion of soldiers is almost within shooting distance, their swords raised and ready to fight if necessary.

"Do it," I say through gritted teeth.

The next flash of lightning is so close I'm afraid it's going to strike us down, the following thunder rattling my bones.

The priestess swallows before bowing her head. The ceremonial words continue, her cold hand back on our skin.

With every passing word, the sounds of the soldiers grow louder, their shouts ringing off the cliffs and mountains and echoing back to the palace where the kings are awaiting our capture.

Magic is shimmering in the air, the moonlight streaming through the temple illuminating our hands, the matching rings glowing in the night.

Star's midnight eyes are looking at me with an intensity that makes it hard to breathe.

Whatever it takes.

A prickling sensation spreads from the ring on my finger and all the way to my heart. The heart that is beating so hard it feels as if it's fighting to break through my skin. The heart that is being pulled toward the prince holding my hand.

The priestess' chanted words halt and the magic around us starts to hum. The power vibrates through my blood, gripping my soul and tearing out a part that will forever belong to another person, filling the empty space with essence from the person that is now a part of me.

"It's time to seal the marriage. A kiss or–"

Star's lips are on mine before the priestess can finish her sentence. The kiss is desperate and possessive, branding and final. His tongue pries my mouth open before colliding with mine, and his hands snake around my waist, his fingers digging into my skin.

The humming magic reaches its crescendo. Flares of bright light and shadowy darkness erupt around us, the magic of two royal bloodlines clashing together in a way that has never happened before.

This is it.

This is the moment everything changes.

Forever.

"Step away from the princess, Your Highness," a loud voice shouts, accompanied by the sound of hundreds of arrows being nocked. "We have orders to escort her–"

A low growl reverberates from the prince's chest. His lips leave mine, his eyes nothing but unrelenting darkness as they move to glare at the general next to me and the sword only inches from my side.

"No one touches my wife."

CHAPTER THIRTY-NINE

Star's grip on my hand is as solid as the mountains around us. Powerful and unbreakable–like the bond now surging between us, the bond that merges with the bargain and ties us together in every way possible.

The prince is growling and snapping threats at the guards around us, demanding them to keep a distance from me.

His wife.

Out of all the things I could be thinking about right now, only one thought stands out.

I don't even know my husband's real name.

"Leave us. We'll walk the rest of the way alone," Star tries to order the guards when we reach the gates at the bottom of the palace mountain.

"I'm afraid not, Your Highness. Orders from the kings are to escort the both of you to the throne room," the general says, the silver pins on his uniform gleaming in the night.

A heavy sigh mixed with a growl reverberates from Star's chest as he starts dragging me up the steep hill, trying to escape the guards hurrying after us.

"A couple of guards ruining your plans, *husband*?"

The word is strange in my mouth—unfamiliar and a little...*intriguing*.

He flashes me a sly smile. "Absolutely not, *wife*." A muscle ticks in his jaw and the smile disappears. "But you should prepare yourself for what we're about to endure. It won't be pretty."

"I know."

We walk in silence, the guards' heavy bootsteps following behind us, their swords raised and ready to strike at a moment's notice.

Lightning crackles between dark clouds gliding across the sky and a dark mist is creeping up from the mountain. Thousands of glittering stars paint the night sky, each one a reminder of who I'm now bound to.

The closer we get to the towering palace, the heavier my heart beats.

Star's hard grip on my hand is the only thing keeping me from tumbling off the mountain.

Too soon, the gates of the palace grind open to reveal another troop of soldiers armed for battle.

With a roll of his eyes, Star saunters forward until they clear a path between them, leading me to the main entrance of the palace.

My body is visibly shaking as we walk through the dark hallways of the palace, both fear and anticipation coursing through me.

I can't wait to see the look on Helios' face when he realizes he can no longer *punish* me, not unless he wants to take his precious kingdom with him.

When Star leads me to a large mountain wall, I give him a confused look.

"I thought we were going to the throne room—"

"We are."

There are no doors or other signs of a throne room, only a smooth part of the mountain swirling with tendrils of shadow. The power seeps out of the stone, reaching in our direction, halting right in front of the prince.

"Time to put on your mask, starlight. Preferably one of your more threatening ones," Star mutters beside me.

With a loud crack and gust of black wind, the stone crumbles to reveal the massive room within.

I straighten my posture and will ice into my bones as we walk through the cracking stone—together, hands firmly clasped, rings clanking against each other.

A throne of obsidian stone rests against the far wall, the stone taken out of the darkest parts of the night. A black carpet lines the middle of the stone floor, leading the way to the kings waiting in the middle of the room.

There is no light in the room, only the night's magic and a faint gilded light on the Sun King's hands.

Helios' harsh features are contorted into a mask of so much hatred and fury it makes the scars on my back throb with pain.

There's a part of me that's pleased by his fury, a deeply buried part that screams to conjure up a rage of my own that will bring nothing but destruction, but there's also a part of me that is nothing but a terrified child in front of an unrelenting king.

"Star," the Moon King growls, the dark king also a raging storm of fury. "A word." He snaps his fingers, and dark tendrils of magic swirl around them.

"Anything you have to say can be said in front of my wife," Star says, baring his teeth in an equally menacing manner.

"Excuse me?" Helios' snarl shoots through the large room and straight through my heart.

"You heard me," Star snarls back even louder, the prince a beast ready to pounce.

Footsteps sound behind us and Thunder steps around us, his hand curled around the long fabric of the priestess' robes. "It's true."

The priestess scurries forward and lands on her knees in a deep bow, her forehead pressed to the stone in front of the Moon King's feet.

"Speak," Helios spits, ignoring the glowering looks from the Moon King at uttering orders in front of a throne that's not his.

"Their Highnesses' union is blessed by the gods, Your Majesty," the priestess says, her voice shaky and so unlike the steady chanting barely an hour ago.

The gilded light in Helio's palms flares brighter and he takes a step toward the priestess. "You had no right–"

The Moon King holds out a hand, the shadowy tendrils moving dangerously close to Helios' face, stopping him from smothering the poor priestess. "I am sure the priestess was only following orders. Who is she to deny a prince?"

With another wave of the king's hand, Thunder grabs the priestess to escort her away and I can't help wondering how the general managed to hide the fact that he was present for the ceremony and did nothing to stop it.

Helios makes a frustrated sound. "This is unacceptable! She is mine to rule–"

"No," Star snaps as he takes a step in front of me. "The latest rumor is that you are going to banish her from your kingdom and forsake your blood claim on her. So since you're no longer claiming to share her blood and she is currently living here at the palace, she is no longer yours to rule." Silver lightning sparks in his eyes and the shadows of the throne room curl around his feet.

"She is mine. And no one touches her but me."

His growled words echo through the room, his raging eyes daring anyone to lift a finger or even glance in my direction. It's as if the darkness sings in his presence. The throne room steadily grows darker, the magic clinging to the high ceiling and seeping out of the walls eagerly greeting the prince's wrath.

"Well, this is certainly an interesting development," Moon chuckles and Helios stomps his feet against the ground, sparks of gold sizzling to the stone underneath him.

"Whether I share her blood or not does not change the fact that she is the child of my deceased queen, and therefore a part of the royal family. *I* will decide her fate," Helios all but screams, his honey eyes now liquid gold as he readies his magic to strike.

Star opens his mouth, no doubt to say or do something to infuriate the Sun King even further, and I take a step forward.

"No one decides my fate but me," I say, willing my heart to steady as I challenge all the men around me.

"Shut your mouth, Asteria," Helios snaps, his fingers twitching to his empty side, and the action makes me give him a cruel smirk.

"No," I snarl, taking another step forward. "You're not my king anymore."

The Moon King lets out a delighted laugh as he claps his hands together. "It has been a long time since Luna had a princess. All that remains is to see how long it will last." His black eyes gleam with anticipation and a sinister smile plays at his lips at the possibility of another deadly game in his kingdom.

"It will not be long."

Light explodes from the Sun King's hands, the magic so bright that even though I snap my eyes shut, I can still see it.

Only a heartbeat passes before the light is gone, and when I open my eyes, there is only the Moon King's darkness.

The Sun King is trapped in smoky darkness.

"I would not do that if I were you," the Moon King snarls. " Asteria is now an official part of Luna's royalty, however it came to be. Any act against her is an act against me and my kingdom. Do you really want a war right now?"

Helio's eyes are blazing with gold, his jaw clenched so tight it looks painful.

"I would be more than happy to remind you of where you are currently standing, Helios, and which part of the sky is blessing us," Moon croons, and a mist of darkness seeps out of the floor, rising to reach our knees and increasing the darkness around the king that's usually always surrounded by light.

I can tell it takes every bit of the Sun King's willpower to collect himself and repress the urge and need to unleash his power —the power that would've killed me by now if it weren't for my new connections.

Helios straightens the lapels of his golden jacket before smoothing down his disarranged long locks, the last flickers of his magic smothered by the darkness. "For now, the Kingdoms of the Sky will settle this in the Tournament, as always," he says, his voice calm despite his raging eyes.

"Indeed," the Moon King says with a cruel smirk, the darkness around Helios vanishing as fast as it came.

Some of the tension in my body slips away and I repress the urge to suck in a relieved breath.

The gods know how much destruction and chaos will come if the full force of the kings' power is unleashed on our world.

But today, we won't get to see it.

The world is safe.

For now.

Helios stalks past me and Star moves to intercept him from striking me.

He may have agreed not to use his magic, but there are other ways he could harm me.

The king chuckles, his eyes still flashing with gold. "You

always were one to hide, *Asteria*," he spits, once again using my name as the worst insult he can think of.

The king who's been ruling me all my life turns his head when he reaches the opening wall, casting one last glare in my direction. "I look forward to the rest of the Tournament. I hear there is another prize to win," he sneers before disappearing out of the throne room.

"Well–" The Moon King rubs his hands together, a delighted smile breaking across his face. "Let us discuss these new arrangements."

The crumbled stone of the mountain solidifies, caging me in with my new family.

An hour later, we finally emerge from the throne room, the stone behind us closing on a phantom wind of shadows, leaving no trace of the room within.

The second the last stone slips into place, I whirl around to look at Star. He lets out a heavy sigh that removes some of the tension in his body. "Well," he says, raking a hand through his hair, "that went better than expected."

I give him an incredulous look, allowing my mask of indifference and confidence to slip away.

"It did." Star raises his eyebrows, his eyes now back to their usual midnight blue. "I half expected war to break out in that room, but fortunately, we've been given more time to accomplish our goals."

I force myself to take a few steadying breaths.

For once, he is right.

It could've gone a lot worse.

"What now?"

Star shrugs, absentmindedly twirling the ring on his finger. "I have a few ideas, but I'll let you decide for now. Consider it a wedding gift." He gives me a wink, the corners of his lips tugging.

"Anything?"

"Anything," he purrs with another wink, and a sultry smirk breaks across his face.

I snort and I'm about to retort something back when the last person I expected to see rounds the corner.

Elio.

He's wearing his golden uniform, looking like he's just come from battle.

"Elio–"

A guard catches up to him, his hand braced on the sword at his side. "You're not allowed here, Victor."

Elio ignores him, his gaze locked on me, at the ring resting on my finger. "Tell me it's not true." His voice is hollow and furious, and he sounds nothing like the friend I've grown up with.

"What–"

The guard bows his head when he sees us, and Star dismisses him with a lazy wave of his hand. The guard shoots one last look at Elio before moving against the wall where he disappears in the darkness.

"Tell me it's not true," Elio repeats, hazel eyes wide as he steps closer.

"I'm not sure what you're talking about," I say, stepping in front of the fuming prince.

"What have you done, Asteria?" Elio's voice breaks at my name and anguish flickers across his features.

"Elio–"

His arms are suddenly around me, his lips pressed to my forehead. "I'm so sorry, Ria. About everything. None of this would've happened if we had just left Soria like we always talked about. We could've been far away on a ship sailing for the horizon by now if only I hadn't been so caught up in the glory of winning and–"

"Step away from my wife, Victor," Star growls, his hand grazing the small of my back causing a shiver to run down my spine, "or I will remove you."

Elio tightens his hold on me so much that it hurts. "This doesn't concern you, *prince*."

"When someone has their hands on my wife, it does."

A gust of black wind rushes forward so fast I don't realize what's happening until Elio is slammed against the wall, the force of the movements sending me back into the awaiting arms of my husband.

Elio's eyes are wide, his face contorted by rage as he struggles against the darkness pinning him to the wall.

I'm so stunned it takes a moment to get my body to work. I blink at the dark magic swirling through the air before tilting my head back to look at Star.

"You–"

"I told you, we're in this together now. Didn't I promise that no one would ever touch you in my kingdom?" His heart beats heavily against my back, the silver stars in his eyes so bright it takes my breath away.

The dark magic reminds me of the Moon King's power strangling me in the carriage, but—

I'm not afraid.

There is not a single trace of fear inside me and perhaps that is what should scare me.

"Asteria," Elio croaks, snapping my attention back to the Victor trapped by darkness. "It's not too late. We can still leave before war breaks out over this nonsense–"

"How can you even say that? You know I can't just leave. The Tournament–"

"There are ways–"

"Don't you dare interrupt me ever again," I snarl, glaring at him like I've never done before.

Star chuckles in amusement and Elio flinches when the darkness holding him intensifies, the dark smoke rising to his throat.

"I'm–"

I snap my mouth shut against the words threatening to spill from my lips.

I'm not sorry. I shouldn't be.

"After everything, I can't believe you're still asking me to leave, to give up. I will do whatever it takes to win the Tournament, and if war comes–" I shrug, willing away the memories and emotions coursing through me as I look into his familiar hazel eyes.

"And besides, you have your own duties now, remember?" I glare at the golden band around his finger and the royal pin on his chest.

"Ria, please–" he struggles against the magic, but the darkness doesn't budge.

"It's too late, Elio," I say, ignoring the hurt flickering in his eyes as I turn around and step away from what I once considered a bright future.

Star has an expression on his face I can't place, and in the middle of the dark hall, he looks so regal and powerful it's a wonder the throne isn't his yet.

"About that wedding gift," I say, ignoring the pleading Victor behind me as I start to walk away.

"Yes?" Star follows me, his fingers grazing mine.

"Does the offer for anything still stand?"

"It does. Do you want another taste of–"

I stop him before he can distract me, the meeting with Elio only making me more determined to follow through on my plans.

"I want the truth." I suck in a breath and my heart thunders in response.

"I want you to tell me everything you know about my father."

Star halts in the middle of the hallway, the moonlight seeping in from the windows casting his frame in a silvery light. "That wasn't exactly what I had in mind when I offered you anything and everything."

"Well," I say, crossing my arms and lifting my chin, "that is what I want."

He studies me for a moment, his silver eyes boring into mine.

I don't know if his magic is still keeping Elio trapped at this distance or whether he has relinquished his hold, and I don't plan on asking.

"Are you sure that is what you want—"

"Yes," I say before he is finished speaking, before he can change my mind.

The prince tilts his head to the side, his binding mark a stark contrast to his skin. "The truth is not going to be what you expect, starlight. I'm warning you now."

"I'm ready."

I'm not.

I've barely had time to think about *him* since I learned the truth, and now, with the rest of the truth right in front of me, I'm terrified to find out that I'm part of someone even worse than the Sun King.

But I have to know.

I just have to.

Star sucks in a breath. "If that's what you want, then fine, I'll take you to...see...him."

My mind goes blank and stars dance in front of my vision. "What?"

Star flinches, his hand reaching out as if he is afraid I'm going to break apart at his next words. "I'm sorry, starlight. I shouldn't have said it like that. I just–" he drags a hand through his hair before pinching the bridge of his nose, and seeing him so troubled almost makes me forget what we're talking about.

Almost.

"Your father is no longer in this world."

Something shatters deep in my chest.

My knees buckle and Star is there in an instant, one arm around my waist, the other brushing hair away from my face.

It was foolish to even for a second dare to hope for something else.

Of course he is not alive.

The Sun King knew about him and my mother, and there is no doubt in my mind that he was the reason for my true father's death.

"It's fine," I say, swallowing against the current of emotions crashing through me and the tears threatening to spill from my eyes.

I didn't know him.

I didn't even know about him until very recently. So why do I mourn him?

"Asteria—"

"Is that all?" I ask, forcing myself to step away from his arms. "You said you would take me to see him. How?"

Gods, please don't let him be buried somewhere, his life essence prevented from returning to the sky.

Silver flares in Star's eyes and a shudder rocks through him. He closes his eyes for a moment, and when he opens them, they are back to midnight blue. "I think it's best I just show you before I say anything else."

"But–"

"Asteria, please. If you were ever going to trust me, now would be that time," he says, his hand reaching forward, silently offering me the choice to back down and just forget about all of this.

I take his hand.

Entwining my finger with his, I swallow down my endless list of questions.

Star leads me down a dark corridor where we step into a tunnel hidden behind a large painting of Nyx, the royal city magnificent underneath the starry sky.

The Moon Palace never runs out of secrets.

We walk in silence, the only sounds the thumping of our feet and the roaring of my heart. At times, the halls are so dark it's a wonder the prince is able to find the way.

My hand firmly clasped in Star's is the only thing tethering me to the present and keeping me from completely unraveling.

When we reach steep stairs descending into even deeper darkness, I'm half tempted to beg him to return me to the moonlight and fresh air.

Whatever it takes.

My legs are shaking by the time we reach the end, my grip on Star's hand so hard it's a wonder I'm not crushing his bones.

I instantly recognize the musty smell and molding walls around us, and images of a fallen prince and the Royal Sword flicker in my mind.

"Why did you bring me here?" My voice is barely a whisper and the hand that is not holding Star curls together, my nails pressing into the scars in my palm.

I never wanted to be back in this place. The last time I was here didn't result in anything good—the dark mark on my arm is proof of that.

"We are not staying here," Star says and reaches for a glass orb hanging on the wall, the inside lighting up by his touch. "We are just passing through."

He leads me in the opposite direction of the dungeons until we pass through another entrance concealed in the dark.

I repress a groan when the skylight falls on another set of stairs.

"I would offer to carry you," Star says, a weak attempt at lightening the mood but one I appreciate all the same, "if I didn't think you would aim your dagger at my favorite body part at the suggestion."

I don't answer him as I carefully start to walk down the stairs, focusing on the warmth of his hand instead of my growing dread.

"What is this place?" There's a prickling sensation at the back of my neck that gives me the feeling of being watched despite the empty darkness.

"A forgotten place," Star says, his voice sending a haunting echo in the quiet darkness. "Just like the rumors of Elara's lost crown being drowned by her tears, this place is also born of legend and myth."

The sound of rushing water fills my ears, and as we round a corner, a raging river greets us.

The Tears of Elara. The river that divides the kingdoms runs through the palace mountain.

Star leads me farther into the darkness, to where the river ends in a violent waterfall.

For a second I'm tempted to just fall into the water and let the currents wash away all that has happened since I bound myself to the Tournament, but then Star gives my hand a firm squeeze and guides me behind the waterfall so only its mist hits my face.

There is a room hidden behind the rushing water.

"It's rumored to be the resting place of the god of war and some other minor deities I can't bother remembering." Star shrugs as he fastens the flickering orb in a holder on the wall. "I've tried opening the caskets a couple of times but it's not possible."

My breath catches in my throat when I notice the line of stone caskets in the middle of the room, so dusty only a hint of silver is visible on the cracked surface.

"Who in their right mind would try to open the sleeping places of gods? And we aren't supposed to be restricted to the earth—"

"I'm not going to question the ways of the gods at the moment," he says with a stern look, "and neither should you."

"But to answer your other question—" he sends me one of his usual smirks, "a young prince bored of his royal duties. A prince ashamed of falling off the back of a dragon countless times. A prince waiting for the next Tournament to start—"

"Okay, I get it," I say with a heavy sigh. "And this has something to do with my real father because—"

"Because this is where I first learned of him," he says before crossing the room and reaching for something I can't make out in the dark.

With my heart in my throat, I slowly walk through the room, doing my best not to brush up against the caskets.

There's a box in the prince's hands. Open, with a sheet of dark crimson covering the contents.

"I'm warning you again, Asteria. Are you absolutely sure—"

"Of course I am," I snarl, ignoring the raging of my heart and the shaking of my hands as I reach for the sheet, the gray dust covering my fingertips.

I yank the fabric away and wish I wasn't so stubborn, impatient, and reckless.

This moment will forever be burned into my mind.

Nothing can make me forget this.

There is a hand in the box. Chopped off right above the elbow, the skin graying white and cracked like a statue. A sapphire ring with carved pictures of the sun and the moon rests on one of the fingers, and the sight of it sends a jolt through my heart.

"What–"

Something else catches my attention. A dark mark is carved onto the skin beneath the wrist, the lines as dark as the shadows around us. But where the magical marks of the Tournament are more alive, this mark is just…dead.

I fall back and my hip hits the sharp end of a casket.

Star mutters a low curse and takes the box from my hands, carefully placing it back onto the shelf carved into the mountain.

My whole body is shaking, even more so than after the Sun King's favored punishments. A sharp pain stabs at my heart and Star catches me in his arms when I start to sway, gently lowering us to the floor.

"Is that—how?" A violent wave of nausea surges through me as a memory rises to the surface of my mind—a young princess sneaking into the queen's quarters to play among her things.

"That ring—my mother had one just like it. I–I found it one day and put it on my finger." A shudder rocks through me. "I'm lucky he didn't chop the finger off." Another shudder rattles my bones and Star wraps his arms more tightly around me.

"Just tell me," I breathe, clinging to his strong arms that are keeping me from falling apart.

"It's him."

Another part of my heart cracks.

"How?"

"The mark—" Star sucks in a breath as if it pains him to speak.

"What about the mark?" I turn around in his arms to look at him. There's a pained expression on his face and his lips are slightly trembling. "Was he a Victor?"

Star shakes his head. "No, but it was a magical mark, one of the most powerful and binding—" he sucks in another breath followed by a low hiss of pain.

"What is wrong with you—"

"That's not important," he snaps before quickly lowering his voice back into a gentle tone. "There are things I can't directly tell you—"

"Because of your other bargains?" A flicker of anger flares inside me at the thought of magical bargains.

"I can't tell you–"

"You promised me the truth," I snarl, moving to wriggle free from his grasp.

"I know," he snarls back, tightening his hold on me. "And I'm doing my very best–"

"Then tell me about him!"

"Your father's life was bound to the queen's," he says in a rush, the words coming so fast it's almost impossible to discern them from each other.

"What?"

"Please don't make me say it again," he says through clenched teeth, his chest heaving from something I can't understand.

"Your father was lucky if anything can be considered luck in those circumstances," he continues, silver flaring in his eyes. "Just imagine what could've happened if the Sun King got to him. You should take consolation in knowing that his death was swift.

Star's gaze flickers to the box in the wall. "Unfortunately for him, the Moon King had to preserve some proof of the poor man's undoing in case Helios would come snooping, or perhaps he just wanted something to gloat about."

"How do you know this?"

He sends me a pained look and I sigh. "Right, you can't tell me. Was it the Moon King who–" I trail off, unable to utter the words.

"No, and you should thank the gods for that too. Your father died when he tried to cross the border. He was on his way to get your mother out of Soria before she gave birth to you, but he was never able to leave Luna in time."

It feels as if there is something more I should know, something just out of reach. It's like trying to look through murky water, and it's hard to think over the pain crushing my heart.

"But mother died giving birth to me," I say, my thoughts a muddled mess as I try to fit the pieces together. "She already had six daughters. Her body couldn't take another birth–"

"No," he says, his fingers tilting my chin up to look at him. "The queen died because your father did, because her life was bound to his."

"So it wasn't because of *me*?"

My heart is beating too heavy to stay in my body. I'm terrified to hope for another answer than the one that has been screamed at me all my life.

I stole the life of my mother, cursing the kingdom to live without a queen.

"No."

A relief so strong it takes my breath away crashes into me and I'm unable to stop the heaving sobs breaking out of me and the rivers of tears streaming down my face.

I can't even remember the last time I cried.

Star pulls me close and I bury my face in his chest, inhaling his now-familiar scent. I cling to him, allowing him to hold me through the shattering of my world.

I don't know how much time passes before I'm able to

breathe more calmly. I rub my wet face, not daring to look at the prince still holding me—the one who held me steady through the storm.

"Are you sure?" My voice is barely a whisper.

I brace against his next words, half convinced that he will tell me it was all a joke and that it was foolish to trust him enough to tell me the truth.

"I'm sure." With gentle fingers, he tilts my head up so I can't escape his eyes where there is nothing but honesty and pain. "I'm so sure I would bargain my soul to the gods."

"Haven't you already done that?"

He snorts and brushes his knuckles across my cheek. "Fine, give up my royal title then, or even my favorite body part."

I relax against him, a strangled sound somewhere between a sob and a laugh escaping my throat. "All this time, that was why I never went against him and now to find out he lied–"

A single tear runs down my face only to be swept away by Star —the only one brave enough to tell me the truth.

"Why doesn't anybody know this?"

"Think about it," Star says with a sigh. "What would be better for the king's reputation? To reveal that his queen found love in the enemy kingdom and was planning to leave him pregnant with her lover's child, but then she died because she used ancient and forbidden magic to bind herself to him, or that she simply died of childbirth?"

He would never tell the people that.

He put the blame on me.

Did he even love her?

"Why? Why would they do something so stupid? My mother was the queen. How could she ever think she would be safe?"

Star doesn't need to answer, because *she* does.

It was the only way I could ensure his safety, the only way Helios wouldn't touch him.

And yet it still failed.

"How does the magic work? You said it was ancient and forbidden."

Star is silent for a long moment before he answers, his voice quiet and clipped when he does. "Just think about the Tournament. Warriors bind their lives every year—" he trails off with a shrug.

And I bound the last of someone's life to mine, ensuring my continued survival after what should've killed me in the first game. The suitor was already dead, I only borrowed his essence, but it was the same forbidden magic, the magic only reserved for the Tournament. It has to be. Mother was a Victor and queen. She would have had access to all sorts of knowledge and power.

I glance at the box in the wall, shuddering as I think of the contents within.

"I didn't want you to see this," Star murmurs against my hair.

A dark chuckle escapes my lips. "If only I wasn't so stubborn and impatient."

"If only."

"Please just get me out of here," I mumble against his chest, my hands on his back fisting the fabric of his shirt.

Star lifts me from the ground and gathers my legs in his arms. I close my eyes and listen to the steady rhythm of his heart as he carries me away from forgotten war gods and the only memory I will ever have of my father.

When we finally reach his tower, he breaks the silence. "Tell me what you're thinking."

"I'm thinking that you told me the truth when no one else would, and for that, I will be forever grateful."

He stiffens, his heartbeat quickening against my cheek. He is silent as he moves toward the door of my room, the moonlight seeping in from the windows casting magnificent shadows across the planes of his face.

"No, please. I can't stand the thought of being alone right now," I whisper, tightening my grasp around his neck.

Star's midnight eyes study me for only a second before he continues walking, their silver stars drawing me in as he walks down the hall and into his room where he gently lays me down on his bed, never breaking eye contact.

"It seems you finally got me into your bed," I croon as he attempts to untangle my hands from his neck.

He sends me an amused look, the corners of his lips tugging upward. "It's not the first time."

"I guess not," I say, dragging the skirt of my dress up to unsheathe the dagger strapped around my thigh.

"What are you doing, starlight?" His hands are braced above my head, his lips only inches from mine.

"It is our wedding night, after all." I smirk as I drag the tip of the dagger in a straight line down his shirt. I tear at it with my hands, the fabric easily parting to reveal his chiseled chest marked in more ways than one.

"Asteria—"

His eyes darken when I turn the dagger to my chest, the silky fabric of my dress gliding away with barely any resistance.

A groan mixed with a growl reverberates from his throat as his eyes rake over my partly naked skin, and liquid heat surges through me.

"Is this your wedding gift to me? Torturing me until I beg you to let me worship every inch of your body?"

His breath is hot on my face, his words igniting a desire so strong I don't need any begging or pleading at all.

I might be the one doing that.

I lean forward to bite his bottom lip, earning another groan.

"Tell me, Asteria, what exactly is it that you want?" His lips graze my jaw, one of his hands moving to tangle in my hair.

"I need to feel something," I breathe against his neck, my lips nibbling on his skin, on the part where his binding mark starts, "something other than pain and despair and anger."

Star hums a contemplative sound against my collarbone. "My wicked wife. You want to use me as a distraction."

His words send a prickle heat to my cheeks and I'm about to apologize and scramble off the bed when he presses a kiss to my heart, the touch igniting an inferno of flames inside me.

"I've never denied wanting you in my bed. You may use me as a distraction any time you want." His lips trail a path from my chest up to my neck, each scorching kiss sending a pleasant tingle down my spine.

"But there is something else I need to tell you–"

"I can't take any more. Not tonight. I just need to forget, please, if only just for one night." I take his face in my hands, pressing my lips against his and silencing whatever he was going to say that would shatter this fragile moment.

I reach for his hand and press it to my heart, his fingers splaying across my chest.

Star releases another groan and finally lowers his body to mine. He rips the rest of the dress off my body, the ruined bodice fully disintegrating at his touch.

"I actually liked this dress," he breathes against my skin, his hands landing on my hips. "And it was your wedding dress–"

"I'll get you a new one if it helps," I say, gasping as he places another kiss on my heart.

"It does." He chuckles against my skin, his lips closing around the sensitive peak of my breast.

"Don't you think this is rather unfair?" I reach for his shirt, determined to yank it off and toss it to the floor when suddenly my hands are pinned to the mattress above my head, tendrils of shadowy magic caging them in place.

"Patience, starlight. I've dreamed of this moment for many nights now and I plan to take my sweet time. Just let me—I want to look at you." His lips leave my skin and he rises onto his knees.

His eyes are pure darkness when he looks down at me. His gaze starts at my fingertips before moving across my face, down my neck, over my chest, and then lower and lower until he is hungrily gazing at the very center of me.

"You are absolutely divine, starlight," he says with a groan, his eyes trailing all the way down to my toes before very slowly moving back to my face.

"Tell me the reason for that name, tell me now," I breathe, swallowing a moan as he leans down to trail his fingers along the same path his eyes just traveled.

Star's finger halts at the apex of my thighs, and I'm about to beg him to continue when he finally speaks, his voice only a whisper. "Because when I'm with you, *Asteria*, I no longer feel only empty darkness. My people channel their magic from the shadows and light of the moon, but the starlight–the starlight is there to light the path when the moon is hiding, the starlight is just pure bliss and hope and so much *life*."

He reaches up to pluck at a strand of my hair. "And then there's your hair, so white it's almost silver, woven starlight in the darkness."

And then he leans down to press a kiss to the inside of my thigh, and at the first lick of his tongue, I'm on fire.

Pleasure ripples up my body in violent waves.

This is everything I need.

This is everything I've ever wanted.

At this moment, I feel *free*. I feel *alive*.

His lips and tongue are everywhere, bringing me pleasure I've never felt before, coaxing me close to the edge before starting all over again.

The magic holding me doesn't budge against my movements. His shadows slither against my skin, the feel of them only bringing me more delight.

"I thought you were the one who wanted to be restricted in bed," I gasp between the moans escaping my throat as I writhe on the mattress, "and not the one doing the restricting."

Star lifts his head to give me a feline smirk, the silver stars winking to life in his eyes so bright that I think he is the one who should be called starlight.

"I told you I wanted to take my time and we have all night. Did I not promise to worship every inch of your body?"

The magic releases its hold on me and I instantly pounce on him, dragging his face up to mine and slamming my lips to his.

And then there is nothing else than our shared breaths and the tandem beating of our hearts.

There is no war, no bargains or wretched kings, no magic and no Tournament, only our souls clashing together as our bodies tangle, as I bind myself to him in another way, perhaps the most magical and powerful of them all.

CHAPTER FORTY

The moon is vibrant the night everything changes. Its light illuminates the royal city, the gray roofs of the buildings reflecting the bright stars scattered across the darkening sky.

The late summer breeze ruffles my hair, causing strands of white to slip free from the braid at my back, the hood of my fighting leathers not firmly tucked over my head as usual.

I'm done hiding.

The Moon King publicly announced the new union between the two kingdoms this morning, blaming two young people eager and in love for the sudden ceremony.

But that wasn't the only secret he revealed.

The king finished his speech from outside the palace gates with a promise of a grand celebration and renewed ceremony after the Tournament. "Of course, only should both of them manage to survive the rest of the games," he said with a cruel smirk.

I don't know if announcing my participation was Star's punishment from his king for doing something so reckless without his permission, or if it was one of Helios' demands when he decided to hold back war until the Tournament is over.

No matter the reason, his speech will make it even more difficult to survive the eighth trial of the Tournament—the last game before the finale.

An alarming dread hangs over me—the feeling that something terrible is about to happen very soon.

I slipped out of Star's bed in the early hours of the morning, untangling myself from his arms, the prince still peacefully asleep next to me.

The memory of him still lingers on my skin, his vow to worship every inch of my body proven true again and again in the dark hours of the night.

I refuse to think of what it could mean.

I have more important things to think about.

Whatever it takes, Asteria.

I've never been able to summon Mother's presence when I truly need her. Other than her revealing herself to me years ago, I've only sporadically heard her voice, usually reminding me of the bargain I've promised her.

I hang onto it now, allowing it to fuel my strength and prepare me for the dangers before me, willing some of the magic around me to seep into my bones.

With a sigh, I strap my silver dagger and an array of other weapons to my new fighting leathers. Another wedding present from my husband–the black clothing lined with faint stars both silver and gold–was lying in my room when I returned from witnessing the Moon King's speech. The fabric is perfectly sculpted to my body, a dream to move quietly and efficiently in, with a lot more hidden secrets than my old ones.

I fidget with the ring on my finger, ignoring the swelling of my heart when I look at the pale stone carved into the middle, the crystal I've come to realize is alora—the moon crystal that is the exact same shade as my eyes.

The Moon King's threats to make our union seem real are suddenly not so difficult and far-fetched anymore.

"It's time." Star emerges from the shadows of the palace, the prince also strapped with weapons and ready for battle. He seems unfazed by our previous encounter, the only indication that he is not a slight tug of his lips and darkening of his eyes when he looks at me.

It was just a distraction, nothing less and nothing more.

At least, that was my plan but—

I'm not so sure anymore.

Taking a deep breath, I steal a last glance at the royal city resting beneath the mountain. The city is bustling with life in the early evening, the sounds of excited people echoed by the wind.

How simple it would've been to just be an observer of the deadly games instead of a bound warrior.

To see and experience the entirety of the Tournament is a right I've been denied all my life. I've only gotten stolen glimpses and snippets of the speeches, never daring to dream that one day I would be able to leave the kingdom and see it all.

My life has changed so drastically in the last months that I barely even recognize myself.

The alora eyes and snowy hair are still the same, but there's a gleam to my eyes and a sharpness to my features that wasn't there before. It is the look of someone in the middle of battle, destruction, and war—a war that has both only just begun and been going on for centuries, started by the gods and handed over to the mortals.

And then there's the magic coursing through me, the cracks in my heart, and the moments I'll never forget.

"Asteria." Star's deep voice snakes down my spine, tearing me away from my raging thoughts and filling me with memories I shove away.

"I'm ready," I say, closing the front of my leathers as I slip one last dagger underneath the fabric.

I am ready.

Ready to face the next trial.

Ready to finally prove myself.

No longer a princess of the sun, but borrowed by the moon, ready to finally step forward as a queen.

THE EIGHTH TRIAL takes place in the Night Court—the court located next to the Moon Court where most of the land is as an extension of the royal court reserved for nobility and generals.

Close to the royal court's border, an ancient arena rises amid the mountains and thick forest, its true purpose in the age of the gods unknown.

Tonight, it will be used for a purpose perhaps not so different, the marked warriors proving as the entertainment.

And the targets.

At least that's my guess based on the closed-off space brimming with bloodthirsty warriors.

According to Star, the arena is frequently used throughout the year by warriors waiting to bind themselves, soldiers battling for a place in the Royal Guard, and other darker purposes and I only imagine the cruelty of from the serious expression on his face.

Shaped like the moon, the arena's large circular space is lined by stairs and benches that make up the high walls reaching for the sky. Tonight, the seating areas are filled with cheering people from both kingdoms, banners and flags in silver and gold raised from their hands.

The arena is so large I can barely glimpse the other side, the cracked stone haunting in the pale light emanating from the sky, but in the middle of the space, with the best view of the entire arena, is the Royal Dais. The silver and gold-flecked columns gleam in the moonlight, and a dark smoke is seeping from the ground underneath it.

In magnificent gowns of gilded yellow, all of my sisters are standing in a perfect line at one edge of the dais. It's impossible to see that there should be a seventh sister among them, and from the well-practiced smiles on their faces, it doesn't look like they're missing me much.

Elio is standing at the front of the dais, well-rehearsed words pouring from his lips. He's wearing the same golden uniform he did when he confronted me outside of the throne room, his golden ring shining on his finger.

When the Victor finishes reciting the story of how the Tournament came to be, he steps aside to give room to the Moon King.

Dread coils in my stomach as the king raises his hands to the sky.

It's not often that the kings speak before the games. That honor is reserved to the most recent Victor, or the one before that if the first one has mysteriously stopped breathing or vanished—something that happens quite often.

"This trial has specifically been crafted for both of our kingdoms," the Moon King's voice rings out, his arms stretched wide as a delighted smile spreads on his lips. "As always, there are no rules in the Tournament of Day and Night but one; survive. Stay alive until the sun rises. But tonight–"

As the king raises his arms even higher, magic crackles in the air and darkness erupts from his fingertips, the tendrils of his power seeping out into the arena.

When the darkness retreats into his hands, countless bows and quivers filled with gleaming arrows are scattered throughout the ruins.

"There is an infinite prize if you manage to hit a glowing target. And if you do not, it will be the end of your participation in the Tournament."

The second the last word is out of the Moon King's mouth, the warriors around us prepare to scramble forward to capture a weapon.

But the king is not done.

Dark tendrils emerge from the smoke rising underneath the dais, curling around the Moon King's body like hundreds of tiny snakes, and his delighted smile turns cruel.

"And what a sight the glowing targets are."

A spark of pain bursts through the binding mark on my neck and then bright light erupts around me.

I was right. The warriors are the targets.

And the light coming from my binding mark—

Silver. Silver for Luna, the Kingdom of the Moon.

The gods' magic doesn't mark me as Sorian anymore.

The light is brighter than the sky above where the moon and stars are obscured by dark clouds that only allow a sliver of light into the arena, and the beams of light reach all the way to the sky.

It will be impossible to hide. The light will give us away.

This is just another elimination round, but more creative than the one in the Shadow Court.

This will be more entertaining for the people.

Star's fingers tighten around mine, and then I glance around me and realize I was wrong.

There are only two silver binding marks lighting up the darkness.

The warriors are not the targets.

The newlywed royal couple is.

Star mutters a string of curses as he touches my glowing neck before quickly shoving my hood over my head.

My hands are shaking as I trace my fingers over the silver lines on his neck, the feel of the magic making my skin tingle.

Star moves my hand away and yanks the hood of his leathers onto his head, only dimming a fraction of the light.

But it's too late and it won't stop anyone from finding us.

Everyone has seen us and the warriors around us are like vultures, the hungry looks in their eyes making fear grip my heart.

How can we survive this?

"So," the Moon King says, clapping his hands together, "hit a glowing target and make it to the finale. And here is a little help," he winks at the crowd, "they usually wear crowns and gowns but today they have traded all the splendor with dark leathers and even darker fear. What a thrilling honeymoon that must be." Another wink and a mocking laugh follow his words.

"And if you do not hit a target—" he breaks off with a shrug, gesturing for Elio to step forward again. "May the best Victor win."

I'm dreading the moment Elio will clap his hands together and every arrow will fly in search of the royals with targets on their necks, and from Elio's stiff posture and the way he has to force himself to move forward—he's perfectly aware of what this means.

This is not another trial in the Tournament.

This is a game of revenge and assassination.

It all makes sense now.

The silence. Helios' lack of pursuit against me. The Moon King's suspiciously good mood at dinner. And Thunder's warning as we walked behind the royal procession toward the arena.

"This is a very bad idea. Every warrior in that arena will be hunting you and many of them won't even care about the game. You two will be the real prize. Maybe you should just leave and forget about this."

Star didn't reply, only tilted his head in my direction with a silent question on his lips.

"Never."

Now, standing in the middle of an army of bloodthirsty warriors ready to kill me, I'm struck by a fear so crippling I'm half regretting not heeding his warning.

The Tournament has turned out to be nothing like I expected, the stakes higher and the loss greater with each new trial.

Perhaps this one will finally be my last.

As Elio nears the end of the usual speech about the Tournament, his voice now clipped and hard, Star pulls me to the back of the crowd, ignoring every harsh shove and growling word.

"I can't deny this being a very creative punishment," he says with a humorless chuckle.

"Who ordered this?" My hands are clammy and I can barely breathe around the fear curling around my heart.

"Your guess is as good as mine. Either king would have the means and motive to arrange this. Don't tell me you expected this bargain to be easy." The hand that's not pulling mine fidgets with the hood on his head and I notice that the beam of light around him is getting fainter and that his body is starting to blend into the darkness of the night.

"I'm waiting to hear your brilliant plan," I say through gritted teeth, my hand firmly pressed over the glowing binding mark in a desperate attempt to make it less bright.

Star sends me an exasperated look. "I know I've swooped in to save you numerous times now, but that doesn't mean I'm invincible."

"You could've fooled me," I mutter, resisting the urge to roll my eyes. "Use your magic then. I know you have access to the royal magic in your blood and that you're refusing to share the knowledge with me but—"

A thunderous boom interrupts me. The clap from the Victor that signals the start of the trial echoes through the arena and rattles the ruins around us, causing a smoke of dust to seep from the ground that only increases when the warriors dart forward to catch the scattered weapons.

Something urges me to grab the bow and quiver in front of my feet and I quickly strap the weapons across my back.

"Don't tell me you're considering shooting yourself," Star snarls as he grabs my arm again to drag me into the shadowed ruins of massive pillars where there's a hole barely big enough for the both of us.

The darkness might conceal our bodies, but it won't hide the beams of light reaching for the sky.

"No, but I might shoot *you* if you don't come up with a better plan than this," I hiss, trying to angle myself as far away from him as possible—an action that is pointless in the small space, resulting in me practically sitting across his lap. "Anyone walking by could see us—"

Star snorts, turning an arrow away from his face. "Perhaps I should've taken a bow of my own then."

"Yes, you should have, but we can't stay like this. Anyone could see us—"

"Be quiet for a moment," he snaps as he squeezes his eyes shut.

I open my mouth to curse him, but what happens when his eyes snap open has me biting my lip to keep quiet.

For a moment, there is nothing but darkness in his eyes, and it's almost as if the soulless eyes of the Moon King are staring back at me, but then the darkness in his eyes vanishes as fast as it came only to erupt from his lips.

I swallow a scream as the smoky darkness moves toward me and I brace myself for the shadowy hands that strangled me the last time I saw them.

They don't come.

The magic is featherlight against my skin, caressing my cheek before moving to the side of my neck where it feels as if an icy kiss is pressed to the heated skin of my glowing binding mark.

The light disappears.

I look back at the prince with magic he shouldn't possess and see that all that remains of the light marking him as a target is a silver gleam so faint no one will see it unless they're as close as I am.

Star sucks in a breath as silver flares in his eyes. More darkness bursts from his hands and seeps out around us, closing the hole at our side that is exposing us to the night.

The magic is like a thin glittering veil that moves as if it's alive, translucent enough to see the ruins on the other side.

It won't be enough to hide us—

A man halts in front of our hiding spot, close enough to see us, but there is not a single trace on his face that he does.

Another warrior emerges behind him and the man runs away.

Another warrior runs by, then another, and the third is shot down by an arrow hitting his back.

They can't see us—

I turn my gaze to Star. There's a faint furrow behind his eyebrows and a strain to his features, and I can't help wondering how much this is costing him.

"How is that for a better plan?"

The arrogant smirk on his lips erases every trace of compassion inside me.

Again, his power should terrify me.

It doesn't.

"It might allow us more time, but it doesn't change the fact that we're doomed—"

"Keep your voice down. The magic isn't able to block our voices," he whispers with a glare.

I don't believe him, not when I've witnessed the great power lurking within him.

But just in case, I obey his order, whispering the next time I open my mouth. "How are we going to win the trial if we are the goals? We can't hide here forever. And we have a bargain to fulfill—"

Star leans forward to whisper in my ear, his lips grazing my skin. "We'll have the whole night to come up with a solution—"

"You heard the king," I say through gritted teeth, "if we don't hit a glowing target, we don't make it to the finale."

He moves away from my neck and leans his head back against the ruin wall. "Let's worry about that in a couple of hours. For now, just be patient and quiet. Two things I know are very hard for you but—"

I silence him with a shove of my elbow before trying to make myself more comfortable.

It's going to be a very long night.

As the night moves on, the warriors in the arena are getting more impatient and desperate, and arrows are not the only weapons flying through the air.

We might be the true targets, but that doesn't mean anyone is going to pass up a chance to slay each other. And even if they did, the Tournament's magic is making it very hard to resist the urge.

My body is aching from staying still for so long, and I'm so restless I can't stop my fingers from tapping the stone of the ruins, an action that only infuriates the prince in front of me. Every time a warrior gets a little too close, he pulls me to his chest with a hand over my mouth, ordering me to be quiet and not risk the dark magic concealing us from the searching eyes.

Apparently, his shadowy magic isn't at its best tonight. The tension in his body increases with his rising fury, and at times, the fathomless black is back in his eyes.

"It takes a little more effort to conceal the both of us and for this long–" a heavy sigh escapes him as he drags a hand through his dark locks that are already disheveled.

"If only I had some time to prepare myself for this. But someone just had to go against the Sun King and alter our plans so we had to go into this completely blind." His glare challenges my own as we continue to stare each other down.

It feels like there's something else he isn't saying. Another reason why his magic is faltering, but I keep quiet in fear of asking him something I shouldn't, something that is not important at the moment, and something that would be much easier to ignore if only I didn't have to be so close to him.

Every time he shifts and another part of him brushes up against me, a memory rises to the surface.

His lips trailing a path from my chest down my stomach.

The muscles on his back flexing as my nails dig into his skin.

The lust clouding his gaze as he looks up at me, his tongue halting on my skin.

His lips kissing every inch of my scarred back until the hatred and shame is barely anything at all—his lips making new memories to overshadow the terrible ones.

The feel of our bodies as one—

"We can't stay like this. I can't do it anymore," I snap after a few more hours pressed up against him, desperately trying to ignore my screaming growing urges.

"We don't have much choice, princess. There's no way to leave the arena before sunrise—"

"I don't care! I can't stay like this a minute longer—"

His hands wrap around my hips, turning me around on his lap so we're facing each other again. "I'm really not in the mood for another of your panicky moments, starlight."

Starlight.

The sound of his nickname for me on his lips sends an involuntary shudder through me, a spark of heat igniting low in my stomach.

And from the way his hands tighten around my hips and the silver flaring in his eyes, I know he is thinking of the same moment.

Because when I'm with you, Asteria, I no longer feel only empty darkness.

"I'm not panicking," I say, my voice breathless. I'm too aware of the lack of space between us and the intensity of his gaze.

"Really? Then why is your heart racing so fast?"

"Because we're in the middle of an arena with warriors hunting us," I snap, leaning my face as far as possible away from his, "and we have no plan out of this."

Star snorts before he leans forward to whisper in my ear. "My wicked wife, the sweet little liar."

Another shudder rocks through me and I repress a gasp when his lips nibble at the bottom of my ear.

That's it.

I can't take this anymore.

"Maybe I'll just try to get out of here on my own—"

"No," he hisses, moving his face from my neck to glare at me. "We're not dying tonight." His arms tighten around me, caging me closer to him.

I narrow my eyes. "You can't keep me here forever. Maybe I'll just shoot you now and be done with it."

Star chuckles before his face suddenly turns serious. "Actually, that might be it."

This time I'm the one to chuckle. "I didn't expect you to volunteer but by all means."

The glittering veil of magic thickens as a group of warriors circle the ruins, their angry shouts sending a wave of fear through me.

"We have a bargain, remember? We might actually have to shoot each other." Star's gaze flickers to my lips, the lips that are only inches from his.

Another snort leaves me. "*That* is never going to work. There's no way I'm taking an arrow for you. That's not what I signed up for."

The silver that sparks in his eyes is like lightning ready to strike. "You shouldn't be so quick to use the word *never*, but like I've said before, times have changed."

"Your end of the bargain is to help me win the Tournament and become the next Victor. You're a Victor of multiple games, you don't need this. I do." I shift in his lap and yank my arms free from his.

And then something occurs to me, the thought making a kernel of hope bloom in my chest.

"If my arrow pierces your skin, I've practically already won. That only leaves the finale—"

"No," Star says through gritted teeth, shadows rippling off his sharp features. "The bargain was that we work together. I'm not letting you out this easily. If we're going down, we're going together." He shoves me off his lap so I'm pressed against one side of the pillar while he leans against the other, leaving more space between us than we've had the entire night.

"So what? You would shoot your wife?" I cross my arms against the air of the night that is suddenly too cold now that he is no longer close to warm me.

Amusement tugs at his lips and mischief glints in his eyes. "Don't look so offended. You're the one eager to shoot your husband. And besides, if I won't, who will?"

Fine. Let's play another game.

He is bound to help me win. He won't shoot me.

He will let *me* shoot him and his end of the bargain will be fulfilled.

"Only if you catch me first."

I retrieve an arrow from my back, aiming it at his thigh.

Star's smirk widens. "Bring it on, starlight."

The glittering veil moves from the opening in the pillar, separating us from each other. It thickens until it evaporates into black smoke, and when the smoke clears away, the prince is gone.

And so is the magic that hid me from the bloodthirsty warriors hunting in the arena.

The shadows caressing my binding mark are gone, the silvery beam of light back and reaching for the sky.

I can't believe he just left me like this. He has a funny way of helping me.

His magic is an unfair advantage, but two can play this game.

A woman in white fighting leathers streaked with blood is the first to find me. She utters a battle cry before aiming an arrow at my head, another scream leaving her mouth when I duck and scramble out of the pillar.

A shower of sharp arrows and other weapons follows her attempt, whooshing after me as I dart away from the ruins.

Warriors rush toward me from all sides, their number increasing everywhere I turn.

I don't stop running.

I can't hide. The light from my neck is getting brighter with each step I take and no amount of darkness can hide it.

Unless the prince changes his mind.

My hood is blown away by a gust of wind and an arrow grazes the top of my ear, a few drops of blood running down my neck.

I duck behind a large boulder as another arrow whizzes right above my head.

I can't outrun them all.

My gaze darts around the arena as I move from ruin to ruin, each attempt to strike me closer than the last.

The prince is nowhere in sight.

There is only the army of warriors and the storm of weapons, the dark fog seeping from the ground, the magic crackling in the air, and—

The Royal Dais.

The limestone crafted from the gods' magic is still in the middle of the arena, abandoned by the royals hours ago. The kings got tired of waiting for the hiding targets to emerge and planned to return closer to sunrise, but word has no doubt already been sent back to the palace about the new developments.

The dais is empty and inviting, its pale gleam haunting in the darkness of the night.

The warriors steer away from it, and no one ventures close enough to climb up the steps. The magic of the Tournament will eliminate anyone who touches it without royal blood running in their veins, the wrath of the gods powerful enough to scare anyone from even breathing too close to the mighty dais.

It's a good thing I don't care about the gods at the moment.

And it's a good thing I'm of royal blood descendant from the gods themselves.

I run forward, past the weapons flying through the air,

crashing into the warriors blocking my path, and leap onto the first step of the dais.

The second I tumble onto the stone, the arrows and weapons chasing after me hit an invisible wall. The sound of the countless weapons clattering to the ground echoes through the arena and the crowd of people and warriors roar in protest.

But there are no rules in the Tournament but one. All I'm doing is surviving.

I let out a humorless laugh.

Oh, how I wish I could see the look on the kings' faces when they realize their scheming plans didn't work out. The sky and gods have a twisted sense of humor.

The warriors roar louder. Some of them try to follow me but the Royal Dais makes them crumble into nothing but dust before they even get close enough to step onto the stairs.

They don't stop screaming as they start taking their anger and frustration out on each other instead of the real targets.

I suck in a breath as I climb the rest of the stairs until I'm standing on the flat rock of the dais.

This is good.

I'm safe.

For now.

"Come out and play, *husband*," I croon as I nock an arrow in my bow, my eyes scanning the arena around me.

The silvery beam from my binding mark makes up most of the light in the arena. There are no skylights with the crowd of cheering people, and only a bleak light is coming from the sky above. Dark clouds glide across the sky, hiding the moon and stars in their darkness, and the dark smoke rising from the ground makes it hard to see every part of the arena.

It's the perfect arena for a prince with dark magic.

There are no signs of his glowing binding mark, but I know he's here somewhere.

He can't hide forever.

We have a bargain to fulfill.

He has to let me shoot him.

A faint breeze ruffles my hair and I startle when invisible fingers move my braid away from the side of my neck. A light kiss is pressed to the glowing mark, the familiar feel of his lips sending a spark through me.

"That's not fair," I curse and jump away, the arrow still ready in my hands.

"Since when have either of us ever played fair, starlight?" His voice is everywhere and nowhere, carried by the wind and echoed by the darkness.

"Stop hiding in the shadows," I say through clenched teeth, startling again when an invisible hand brushes over my raised arm.

"But it's so fun," Star purrs from nowhere, his voice snaking down my neck.

Crowds of people are starting to seep back into the benches surrounding the arena, all eyes on the crazy cursed princess talking to herself.

"Just let me shoot you and this will all be over," I snarl, turning around in a circle, searching for signs in the darkness of where the prince may be hiding.

I'm getting sick of this game.

"Not before I shoot you first. This is going to hurt a little, but I promise to kiss it better tonight, my wicked wife."

A sharp pain erupts in my thigh before I even have time to register his words, a black arrow with silver fletching protruding from my skin.

A string of curses dishonoring the gods and totally inappropriate for a princess bursts from my lips.

"I guess I earned those names," he says with a low chuckle, his form emerging from the darkness.

The prince leans against the railing of the dais on the opposite side of me, only a faint glow emanating from his mark, the shadows of the night still clinging to him.

And then the sky above flares with color. A storm of lightning cracks across the sky—all of the light silver, the same bright color that is now twinkling in Star's eyes.

My fingers wrap around the shaft of the arrow and I grind my teeth together as I yank it out. "Fuck you," I spit, muttering a few other curses as I press a hand to my bleeding thigh.

Star rolls his eyes before sauntering across the dais. He halts right in front of me, kneeling to wrap a strip of dark fabric around my bleeding wound, his fingers briefly lingering on the exposed skin. The pressure of the fabric is tight and uncomfortable, but will it stop me from bleeding out before I can find a healer to stitch me back together.

For a second, the sight of him kneeling in front of me blocks out everything else, but then he gives me a wink, silently telling me he knows, and fury roars inside of me.

"You better hurry in getting your revenge, starlight. We're running out of time." He rises to his feet and walks back to lean against the railing, his arms and legs spread wide as if offering me a hug.

Spots of light blue have started to break through the darkness of the night and the dark smoke is starting to retreat into the earth it came from.

He is right, we're running out of time.

I am running out of time.

Trying to ignore the stinging pain in my thigh, I pick up the quiver and nock another arrow.

I aim the arrow straight at his face, gritting my teeth when the action only causes him to give me one of his arrogant smirks.

"I wouldn't do that if I were you, starlight. I know you love my pretty face."

"You shot me," I spit, my hands slightly shaking from the shock of it.

"I know." His smirk falters. "I wouldn't have done that if we had another choice, but we don't."

"You didn't need to. The bargain–"

"The bargain means that we're in this together–"

The rest of his words are drowned out by another voice, the voice of another Victor—a Victor who became the Queen of the Sun.

End him now and you have won the Tournament.

I blink through the fog of anger and adrenaline and catch a glimpse of the Moon King behind him. He is standing with his arms crossed on the lowest bench, his eyes locked on a small group of warriors running through the arena toward the dais in the middle.

The other princes.

The gods' magic won't stop them from killing us.

I vaguely recognize the two running together as Celix and Coly, and Cyan—the prince I danced with who warned me to work with Star—is just behind them.

As they get closer to the dais, Celix and Coly ready arrows in their bows and fear grips my heart.

I have no idea if their arrows will be stopped by the dais' magic.

As if the gods can sense the growing excitement, the darkness of the night starts slipping away faster than before. The few stars visible disappear one after one, and the light blue spots expand into streaks that shove the darkness with a violent force.

The princes free their arrows and the silver tips fly through the air as if there is no magic at all.

I duck just in time.

The princes don't stop running.

Celix is the first to start climbing the stairs to the dais. Coly tackles him to the ground, their limbs entangling in a brutal battle between them.

Cyan halts behind them. He looks up at me with a roll of his eyes, and I notice that, unlike the other princes, he doesn't have a bow and quiver.

The dais rattles underneath me as the two princes battle their way up, blood dripping from their faces.

When Coly manages to raise his bow and aim an arrow at my heart, another arrow whooshes past my head. It flies through the air and bores into the skin right between Coly's eyebrows.

The prince's eyes widen and he falls back, his body hitting the ground below the dais with a thud.

Dead.

My mouth falls open as I turn around to look at Star.

The warrior prince seems unfazed by the death he just inflicted, only a slight irritation slipping into his features. "Time is running out, Asteria."

The Victor's voice in my mind is screaming now.

Whatever it takes, Asteria. Delay the inevitable and he will only end you in the same way.

I study the prince in front of me. My enemy, ally, husband. The other part of a life-binding bargain.

I will help you win the Tournament and become the next Victor, and you will help me get what I want.

And then I realize he just broke that bargain.

I could've been a Victor. Right now.

Whatever it takes, Asteria. Whatever it takes!

You made an unbreakable vow.

He tricked you—

I don't have a choice. I have to do whatever it takes to win.

Even if that means killing the prince who has stolen a piece of my heart.

I aim the arrow straight at his heart.

Star goes completely still. Surprise and fury flicker across his beautiful face before his silver eyes transform into the deepest and darkest black I've ever seen.

"What, exactly, do you think you're doing?" His growl reverberates through me and shadows ripple off his body.

"Becoming the next Victor," I say through gritted teeth, ignoring the painful throbbing of my heart as it shatters.

"And what about our bargain?" His eyes glare at the tip of my arrow.

"You will fulfill it right now by helping me win and we will be done, just like we vowed."

"We are not done until the bargain is," he growls, taking a step forward. "You have your own part to fulfill. Need I remind you of how bargains work?"

"My end won't matter when your soul is in the Shadow Realm, perhaps you can find a throne there," I say, my hands shaking as I move to pull the arrow. "After all, a grieving widow is a role I've played before."

"You've never been a widow. Castor didn't make it long enough to become your husband. I am, and I'm telling you to shoot me somewhere safe before it's too late and you lose your spot in the finale."

"I don't take orders from anyone, especially not you," I mutter, looking at him from the tip of the arrow still aimed at his heart.

"And here I was, thinking I had finally earned your trust," he spits.

"You have," I breathe, biting my lip against the tears blurring my vision. "But I have to win, no matter what it takes."

"Asteria, starlight–"

The sound of my name on his lips makes waves of emotions and memories crash through me so viciously it nearly makes me topple over.

I can't do this—

Whatever it takes, Asteria. Whatever it takes!

His life is nothing compared to the Crown of Victory.

Nothing.

"Asteria. This changes nothing. I'm still bound to help you win."

He is standing in the way of your crown. A crown that already could've been yours—

I don't know which voice I should listen to. My soul is torn between two opposing forces and the pain exploding from my heart is making it hard to think.

"Asteria."

I'm about to beg him to just be quiet to make this easier, when an arrow sizzles past my head, the sound snapping my attention back to the other princes.

Celix utters a battle cry, his body halfway up the second stair to the dais, a hand pressed to a bleeding wound on his neck, the other fumbling to nock another arrow.

Cyan wrenches the bow away from Celix's hands before kicking the other prince off the side of the dais, the bow thrown away after him.

The prince with the kind eyes doesn't make a move to come after either of us. He only crosses his arms as he leans against the stairs, a secretive smile on his lips as he raises his eyebrows in challenge.

"Asteria."

My eyes dart back to the prince who still hasn't made a move to stop me. The arrow is still ready in my bow, and my arms strain from holding the position for so long.

Whatever it takes, Asteria.

Do it.

Do it now!

Victory is only moments away.

"I have to do whatever it takes to win," I whisper, a sob working its way up my throat as tears start streaming down my face.

I force myself not to look into his eyes.

Star mutters a low curse. "Look at me, Asteria."

I shake my head, my fingers straining as my heart and mind fight two different battles.

Whatever it takes.

"Look at me!"

I wish I didn't, but there is a part of me that can't resist him. Ever since I first met him, ancient unyielding magic has drawn us together.

The sight of the silver stars twinkling in his eyes nearly brings me to my knees.

"You are not doing it," he says as if it's that simple.

"I have to—"

Star utters a low growl. "Bring me down and you will go down with me. Without getting the honor of becoming a Victor."

He is lying.

"I won't. You can't kill me without killing yourself. The bargain—"

Another growl reverberates from the prince as his gaze flickers to the lightening sky.

The sun will appear any second now.

"And neither can you," he snarls. "If I die, you die."

Everything that comes out of his mouth is a lie.

"You're wrong—"

Star bares his teeth and silver lightning sparks in his eyes. "There is more to our bargain than you think. We are bound–" he sucks in a sharp breath and mutters a string of curses aimed at the sky.

He unsheathes a dagger and cuts a line in the leathery fabric on his thigh. He tears at the fabric with his hands until he reveals a wound similar to my wound from his arrow.

"Like I said, if I die, you die, no matter if you're the one to make the blow," Star says before bracing against something I can't see or understand.

"You're lying. That doesn't prove anything—"

He digs a finger into his bloody wound and I swallow a scream as pain explodes through my leg.

"You feel that? That is nothing compared to what you'll feel if you try to kill me."

He is lying. You've seen what he can do. It's only a trick of his magic—

"No amount of royal magic can accomplish this," Star snarls as if he can hear the screaming voice in my mind. He digs his finger deeper, the pain so blinding I'm afraid of passing out.

I gasp as I force my shaking arms to keep the arrow aimed at his heart. "You're lying," I say through clenched teeth. "What you claim is not possible, and I don't have your wounds—"

"It is only a matter of time," he snaps as a violent shudder rocks through him, forcing him to stop poking the wound.

Whatever it takes, Asteria.

Don't listen to him.

Do it! Do it now!

"No," I snarl, lifting my chin and readjusting the arrow. "Don't say anything else. You're only trying to distract me–"

"You and I are bound together. For life. And maybe even death too. Forever." he says it all in a rush, the words almost unintelligible. He staggers a step backward, his face contorted with pain.

"I'm perfectly aware of our marriage but it won't change anything–"

Star utters a ferocious growl unlike anything I've ever heard before. "I'm talking about our bargain, and not the one we only recently made."

An anguished breath escapes his lips and my heart screams. "Why do you think we had the same marks on our skin before we even made the bargain?"

"What–" I blink at him, the voice in my mind roaring louder than ever before. "What did you do—"

"I didn't do anything," Star snaps as he takes a step forward, only one step away from his chest touching the tip of the arrow. "You did. When you carved forbidden magic into your skin and uttered words you didn't understand the meaning of–"

I don't hear the rest of his words over the roaring in my mind and the flickering images and ferocious emotions crashing through me.

My blood dripping onto the face of the dead suitor as his glassy eyes stared up at the sky. The memorized words pouring from my lips in the middle of rising smoke.

The truth of my parents. The mark on the hand of my deceased father.

The unexplainable pains and aches in my body.

The unrelenting magic urging me toward the prince in more ways than one.

The silver eyes peering at me from the darkness of my mind as the forbidden magic tore through my soul—

My hands fumble with the bow, and as it slips from my hands, the arrow flies.

Star doesn't even flinch as the arrow bores into his side.

The mark on my neck tingles just as the first ray of sunlight hits my face.

And the side of my body, on the exact spot where my arrow hit Star, screams from pain.

CHAPTER FORTY-ONE

The raging warriors gathered around the Royal Dais move to clear a path for the Moon King. A cruel smirk is plastered on his face as he walks forward, the only sound in the arena the slow clapping of his hands.

I don't know if he hoped one of us would kill the other or if his grand plan was exactly this.

Helios comes running through one of the now open entrances of the arena, parts of his Royal Guard clambering in behind him. The king's golden hair is blowing in the wind, his eyes nothing but pure gold as his gaze locks on me.

Star yanks the arrow out of his side, his fighting leathers soaked from his blood. The sound of the arrow clattering to the ground snaps my attention and my gaze moves to the bleeding wound.

As I watch, the skin stitches itself back together, leaving only smooth unharmed skin. And with the vanishing wound, the aching in my side disappears.

Who is this man I've bound myself to in more ways than one, and how can he have so much power?

Did he lie when he said he wasn't invincible?

The wound on my thigh is still hurting, but the pain is nothing compared to the one in my heart.

I glance at the exposed skin on Star's thigh, where his skin is still bleeding, and the prince quickly binds the wound with another strip of fabric retrieved from his pocket.

His eyes snap to mine and there is no midnight blue or silver in his gaze, only black fury. "We better get out of here."

"Why?" I raise my eyebrows before spitting on the dais with a cruel smirk at the kings. "We might as well continue our conversation here in front of everyone–"

A low growl interrupts my words, and Star grabs my arm, his grip like iron—like the shackles chaining our lives together.

How did I not notice them before?

"We are far from done and *you* are not doing anything to improve our chances. We still have a bargain, remember?"

"A bargain you failed to tell me all the details about," I snarl, trying to yank my arm away from his iron grip. "A bargain that could've been over if only you weren't a lying conniving–"

"If I had let you kill me," he says, silver flashing in his eyes, "both of us would've been dead along with the bargain."

I feel the burning anger rise inside of me, and I'm terrified the flames will reveal themselves right here and now to the whole world.

I push it all away as I purse my lips and plant my feet on the stone of the dais, halting our movements.

"Do I need to carry you?"

"I'm not leaving until you tell me *everything*." The flames of fury flare and I grind my teeth together.

"Not here," he snarls, reaching forward to pull the dark hood over my head. "Right now we need to get out of here."

I'm about to scream that I don't care who might hear us when the silence of the arena vanishes as fast as it came.

The crowd on the benches roars along with the warriors still in the arena, and the chaos of sounds is so loud I can barely hear myself think.

"The Tournament is not for the royals!"

"Newlyweds in the finale? What a joke."

"The Tournament is not for royals but for the people!"

"She will curse us all!"

"Kill them!"

"May the gods strike from the sky and disintegrate every royal into nothing but ash!"

The Royal Dais is shaking from all the movement and the ancient stone is suddenly feeling too fragile.

Realization hits me like a slap to my face.

The finale.

Only two people will compete for the Crown of Victory.

The title of Victor has never been closer but—

Star is also in the finale. The enemy who has always been my biggest competition who turned into the best ally I could ever get is now back to being nothing but an enemy.

Magic always comes with a price. Especially for someone like you.

A strangled laugh bursts from my lips, the witch's warning ringing in my head.

"This is not the time for jokes," Star growls as he pulls his hood on before pulling my back against his chest.

"Get away from me—"

His hand wraps around my throat and he lowers his lips to my ear, his voice a growled warning. "Be quiet."

And then we disappear in the shadows of his magic.

Star practically carries me down the stairs, blending into the shadows that are quickly disappearing as the sun rises in the sky. His grip around me tightens when we leave the protective magic of the dais and I hold my breath as we carefully move through the crowd of warriors.

An army of soldiers sweeps into the arena with a violent force, swords and arrows clanking against their shields as they push the battling warriors off each other and away from the dais where the Moon King has stepped onto the stairs.

The searching eyes prickle my skin, their shouts boring into my skull.

What will be the consequences of Star revealing his magic to the world? Or does everyone already know? Maybe that's how he won seven Tournaments.

For all I know, all the princes possess the knowledge of how to access the royal magic.

More and more openings reveal themselves as we maneuver through the crowd, the arena ready to free the warriors and let their wrath and vengeance into the world.

Star rushes us to a door at the far side of the arena where the morning sky is barely visible between the thick forest, and as we get closer, I notice the general standing right outside with his arms crossed and a glare on his face.

When we emerge from the arena out into the early morning, Star reluctantly releases me from his arms.

"I told you this was a bad idea," Thunder says as I take a long step away from the prince.

Star doesn't reply. His dark gaze is locked on me and my moving feet. "And where do you think you're going?"

"As far away from you as possible. Our bargain is done. I've practically already won the Tournament so I don't really need you anymore."

"Not this again," Star growls, striding forward until he catches up with me. "You know the consequences of breaking a magical bargain—"

"Then we will both die," I growl back, slamming my knee into his favorite body part.

Whatever it takes.

He grabs my knee with a low grunt, his fingers digging into the leather. "My end of the bargain may be coming to an end, but yours is not. Break it and you'll not only face my wrath, but the wrath of the gods that created the magic of this world." He towers over me, darkness still clinging to him despite the light of the early morning.

"This is not the time for flirtation," Thunder cuts in through clenched teeth, eyes flickering to the arena behind us. "Esra is waiting."

People are seeping out of the arena, startling the birds hidden in the trees of the forest. They scatter to the sky, dark flecks blocking out the rising sun.

There is so much sound and movement that for a second I'm convinced the ancient ruins are going to crumble into nothing but dust in the wind.

The last trial of the Tournament might be over, but the war has only just begun.

THE PALACE MOUNTAIN is a raging battleground. Not only the warriors who lost their spot in the finale are fighting their way to the palace, but people from all over the two kingdoms. Some of them try to climb up the mountain, others try to push past the guards at the gates to access the steep mountain road.

They are shot down one after one, only a few of them gifted

another chance in the palace dungeons or other places I'm scared to know the details about.

Esra was waiting in the forest behind the arena when the trial ended, and with a low command to Thunder I was unable to hear, Star plucked me from the ground and placed me atop the horse, ignoring every curse and insult from my lips.

The journey back to the palace was so quick I barely had time to catch my breath, and when we arrived at the palace, Star handed Esra over to a frightened stable boy, dragged me to his tower without answering any of my angry questions, and dropped me, leathers and weapons and all, into a bath that was somehow already waiting for me.

"Stay here until I'm back and we'll continue our conversation," he said, ignoring my furious sounds and curses as the warm water hit my aching thigh. "I have some things I need to take care of first. Can you manage to stay out of trouble until I'm back?"

And then, without waiting for my reply, he strode out of the room, the door slamming shut behind him, and only minutes later, Auren was there to tend to my wound.

When the day starts bleeding into evening and there is still no sign of the prince and I've paced through his room more times than I can count, the burning anger inside me is almost impossible to hold back.

A flame flares inside me every time I catch a glimpse of the dark mark on my bare skin.

Every time the shiny crystal on the obsidian ring on my finger gleams in the sunlight, I bite down on my lip to not scream until there is nothing left of me.

And when my eyes land on the rumpled silky sheets in his bed —invisible daggers poke the cracks in my heart.

There's no way I'm the one who bound us together.

The dead lord's life essence saved my life when I fell from the holy mountain and went through the temple roof. That was it, that was what I bargained for.

The prince was the one to initiate the other bargains.

He is the one with magic.

He has lied and schemed since the second I met him.

But he has also been the only one to tell me the truth.

None of this makes any sense.

I need more answers.

A wicked smile spreads across my lips as an idea forms in my mind.

Reckless and dangerous, definitely, but something that might reveal the whole truth once and for all.

Hastily pulling on my old fighting leathers, I run out of the palace before I have the time to change my mind.

The stable boy gawks at me when I give him a handful of silver coins and order him not to reveal to anyone that I've left the palace.

"But, Your Highness, it's impossible. You can't leave the palace now—"

My answering glare makes him snap his mouth shut and disappear from my sight.

I may not be able to leave the palace unnoticed, but Esra can.

The shadow-born horse is not inside the stables. She is outside staring at the moon when I approach her, her dark eyes snapping to mine before I've even made a sound.

Her keen eyes remind me of Alev, and I can't help wondering how different she actually is from the other horses.

She puffs when she notices the apple in my hand and trots forward until she is close enough to yank it out of my hand with her mouth and drop it to the ground.

"I promise to bring you something better if you bring me to the witches in this kingdom, wherever they may be."

Esra kicks the apple away but lowers her head to my outstretched hand. "And I won't force you into a bridle and saddle."

She puffs again, her eyes blinking as if offended by the suggestion, but then her head swings in the direction of her back in what I can only assume is a silent yes.

The second I'm seated on Esra's back and my fingers are gripping her mane, the lingering sunset is whisked away by a black smoke that blocks out everything around me.

The horse of shadow darts forward, and for a few moments, all I see is darkness, but then I catch snippets of Nyx's roaring sounds and light before the night turns quiet and the city is replaced with dark forests and mountains.

The landscape bleeds in and out of focus as Esra travels on the wind and through the shadows, the world around us nothing but darkness occasionally broken apart by streaks of pale moonlight or glittering stars.

A cold breeze ruffles my hair and I relish in feeling the fresh air against my skin.

It has been a long time since I've felt so *free*.

Free underneath the open sky, free to roam as I wish without the fear of being discovered.

Pain jolts my heart when I realize the other moments I've felt this free are with *him*.

I brace myself against the memories crashing into me.

Sneaking into the royal city. Dancing underneath the stars. Swimming in a moonlit pool. An embrace on the back of a dragon gliding through the air. Stolen kisses in the darkness—

The only times I've felt a sliver of freedom have been in his company, and I can't help but wonder if that is only just a coincidence.

I'm not the only one happy to be away from everyone else.

Esra happily races forward, snorting occasional sounds of ecstasy. Whether the horse chose to obey my request due to its master or its own free will doesn't matter, not at this moment underneath the open sky.

And then suddenly, the night changes and I know without a doubt that we've crossed the border to the Shadow Court.

The night darkens. A colder wind blows through my leathers. The sound of birds chirping and chattering vanishes. A dark smoke rises from the ground and the moonlight is overshadowed by the thick fog that seems to permanently reside in this court.

I shiver as we near a mountain where gray smoke is seeping from a cave dimly lit by a burning fire.

The smell of herbs and something unfamiliar envelops me as the tangy taste of magic fills my mouth.

"It has been a while since a princess of the moon has given us the pleasure of a visit," a voice croaks from the darkness and a shudder rocks through me.

"I'm a princess of the sun," I say as I jump off the horse. Esra huffs out a breath before stalking off to grass nearby, unbothered by the eerie place.

"Are you sure about that?" Another voice croons and a woman steps out of the darkness of the cave.

A witch.

Her skin is as dark as the night, her bare arms covered with marks drawn by something that looks a lot like blood. A sapphire pendant hangs from her nose, matching the sapphire ringlets in her ears.

"I guess I'm kind of both at the moment," I say, staggering back a step.

There's something vaguely familiar about the witch, something I can't place with the dread roaring in my ears.

"Have we met before?"

"Perhaps in another life."

I toss an overfilled pouch of coins next to the fire, repressing a frustrated sigh at her ambiguous answer.

The witch snorts. "I have no use for your mortal artifacts."

"Then what do you want?" I cross my arms against the cold wind, trying to block the coldness that seeps into my bones and the fear gripping my heart.

"For what you are asking? A drop of your blood and a strand of your hair will have to do."

Magic always comes with a price. Especially for someone like you.

Ignoring my better judgment, I pull away my hood and untangle the knot at the back of my neck.

As my hair falls loose, the witch darts forward. Her long fingers glide through my hair, twisting and curling the strands. A hungry gleam appears in her white eyes as she leans forward to sniff my hair.

"Take your strand and get away from me," I say, willing my voice to be steady, ignoring the heavy beating of my heart.

The witch rolls her eyes before yanking loose a strand of white. She curls her hand and when she opens it, the hair is gone.

"And now for your blood—"

I retrieve the silver dagger strapped to my thigh and slice a line in my palm before she can suggest something grotesque.

I might have bargained with a few witches in Soria, but I'm in enemy territory now, and in the middle of nowhere. The witches in the royal court have long lost their true traditions, greedily bargaining only for riches and power. These witches are something else—primal and dangerous.

The witch holds out a small glassy container and I squeeze my hand, allowing a single drop of blood to drip before quickly moving away to wipe my hand on the fabric of my cloak.

The witch chuckles before tucking the container in the pocket of her ragged pants—stolen or bargained from a soldier a *very* long time ago.

"Ask your question, Princess of the Sky." The witch bares her sharp teeth and her eyes swirl with ancient magic.

"Is it true that my life is bound to Prince Star and his to mine?"

She tilts her head to the side and it feels as if her eyes can see right to my soul. "Have a seat, princess. And you may call me Nim," the witch—Nim—says before stoking the fire with a long bone, the sight of it sending a shiver down my back.

With a heavy sigh, I sink into the black fur lying on the rocky ground next to the fire, trying not to think about where it might come from.

"Show me your mark," Nim says, the bone in her hand clattering to the ground.

The dark mark bleeds into the night as I remove the sleeve of my leathers. As the witch takes my arm in her hands, the lines pulse and throb underneath the moonlight, emanating a faint silver glow.

I flinch when her cold finger traces the lines, her nails boring into the skin on my wrist when I move to yank my arm away from her grasp.

"Patience, princess," she snarls, the words reminding me too much of the familiar words of another.

"Answer my question, witch," I say through clenched teeth, ignoring every screaming instinct to run far away.

This was a mistake.

She could kill me in a second. And even if I managed to run away, who knows how many witches are hiding in the shadows?

"Tell me the exact words of the spell you used, in the exact order."

Nim tilts her head back to look at the sky as I describe the spell I used in what feels like another life. Her unnaturally cold fingers stroke over the pulsing lines of the mark while I speak, the lines glowing brighter at her touch.

"So?" My heart is beating so hard I'm convinced she can hear it, and with every second that passes, the fear around my heart squeezes harder. "Is it true?"

"Yes."

I startle at her sudden honesty and lack of ambiguous answers. The pain that is now permanently living in my heart intensifies and all the magic in the air is making it hard to breathe.

"So if he dies...I'll die too?"

"Yes, although I nor the gods think you wish to see him dead."

I yank my arm away from her grip, ignoring her low growl.

"How can I know you're telling the truth?"

The witch studies me for a moment, the pendant in her nose swaying in the wind, her eyes reflecting the rising flames of the fire.

"Tell me, *Asteria*, have you not felt something different about the prince? Strings pulling you together, urging you to go to him? The bond works in mysterious ways. The gods know if it was destined without your tampering."

She flutters her fingers and I notice my strand of hair between her fingers. "And now that you are aware of it, I am sure the gods will move more quickly."

"That's not an answer. And what does that even mean?" I roll my sleeve back to cover the mark, its silver gleam glowing through the fabric.

Nim chuckles as she studies my hair between her fingers. "A bond between two souls will continue to develop over time. A wound for a wound, a thought for a thought, a life for a life, a soul for a soul." Her voice echoes off the mountains, reverberating through my very bones.

I should leave.

"Why did the magic connect me to him and not someone else?"

I was only trying to get an advantage in the first game. I didn't intend to bind my life to anyone, and especially not *him*.

The witch tilts her head to the other side, eyes unseeing and omniscient at the same time. "Faith is a strange thing indeed. Your destinies have been carefully threaded and woven over millennia, two souls destined to be entangled one way or another. And blood magic certainly has an expensive price."

The truth seems more difficult to find than I expected.

I can't trust anyone.

Death is the only final answer and by then, it will be too late.

"How do I end it?"

"Do you want to end it?"

"Of course I do–"

"That is not for you to decide."

"I made it so I should be able to undo it–"

"The gods work in mysterious ways, princess," Nim interrupts, tying the strand of hair around a braided bracelet on her wrist. "Ways you mortals have been trying to understand for centuries. I am sure you have been warned before that it is not wise to mess with the true nature of things. Using magic so carelessly–"

She moves her gaze to the sky above where only a single silver star is visible in the darkness. "Too many witches have forgotten our ways. As have you. Allowing such atrocities as those wretched games–" she clicks her tongue in disappointment.

"The Tournament is the way of the gods."

At least that's what I've been told my whole life.

What I've *believed* all my life.

But I've seen things that are starting to make me uncertain, things that are untangling the stories I've been told all my life, resulting in forbidden thoughts that are making my heart race.

"It is not." Nim's eyes snap back to mine and it's almost as if I can see the ancient gods displayed in their glassy surface. "It is the way of a deep love destroyed and betrayed. Another sign you should not try to meddle with your destiny, child."

"My destiny is not Star," I say through gritted teeth, nails digging into the scars of my palms.

"Flame and shadow. One cannot exist without the other."

A frustrated scream bursts from my lips and I jump to my feet. "I don't believe you, *witch*. I'm not accepting this. I'm not bound to him. I'm not his, and he certainly isn't mine."

A cackling laugh resounds from the witch as I start to move toward the horse emerging from the darkness. "Deny it all you want, princess. But do not say I did not warn you when more signs start appearing. It is only a matter of time. Now—" she claps her hands together. "Was that all?"

I halt, feeling the string tied around my heart starting to pull me back to the Moon Court. "Actually, there is one more thing."

Magic sparks in the witch's eyes as a sinister grin widens her lips.

"Will two strands of my hair be enough or do you require more of my blood?"

Whatever it takes, Asteria. Whatever it takes.

CHAPTER FORTY-TWO

A raging storm is tearing through the streets of Nyx and the sky is angry.

Lightning cracks across the night sky, thunder rattles the earth, and a roaring wind blasts the hammering rain sideways. The sounds of countless battles ring throughout the city. The cobblestoned streets are stained with blood and scattered weapons. Uniformed guards patrol the streets, shields and swords raised and ready. The usual cozy restaurants and crowded taverns are closed, the doors and windows sealed shut.

The magnificent city royal city is now a place bursting with uprisings and the beginnings of a war that may obliterate both kingdoms.

The finale is only days away.

The princess of the moon is being hunted tonight and there is only one place she might be welcomed.

Hidden underneath my dark cloak, I dart through the shadows, past deserted bloody streets and ongoing battles, aiming for the house tucked into a mountain with more secrets than I can count.

A group of people are gathered around the ruined building—warriors, guards, servants, and other people wearing various colored clothing.

As always, it is impossible to tell who is a part of the rebellion.

I hesitate in the shadows of a narrow alley, my heart hammering as hard as the rain beating the ground around me.

I don't know if it was luck that got me unnoticed into the ancient room hidden deep in the mountain the last time I was here or if a certain prince used his magic without my knowledge. And the first time I was here for the meeting, I was able to blend in with the rest of the crowd.

Now, with the rumblings of war within the kingdom and the infinite prize on my head, I doubt I'd be able to pass without being checked.

I'm so wrapped up in my thoughts that I don't notice the approaching warrior before it's too late. She pins me to the wall, the tip of a dagger pressing against my throat.

"It's not a good time for a princess to be out in the darkness. Tell me, how many golden coins would I get for your head?"

I curse every god and deity I can think of, adding myself to the bottom of the list.

"I'm not the one you're looking for," I say, my fingers curling around the hilt of the dagger hidden underneath my long cloak.

The woman snorts before reaching forward to yank my hood off, her face sneering right in front of mine. "I would recognize that hair and eyes anywhere. You look even more cursed up close than you did on your precious dais." She spits on the ground, barely missing the tip of my boots.

"Let me go and I won't kill you for insulting me," I snarl, tightening my grip on the dagger.

"What will happen if I kill you now? Will your prince win the games at once or will the magic resurrect you long enough for him to kill you himself? Or maybe–" the warrior tilts her head to the side to display the binding mark on her neck, "–maybe they will allow someone else to take your place. Someone who didn't cheat her way to the finale."

"There are no rules in the Tournament of Day and Night," I snarl, pushing her hand away until the tip of the dagger leaves my throat before I slam my head against hers.

The woman shouts a curse as she stumbles away and one of the guards lingering next to the ruins turns his head in our direction. "Hey, you two over there! Stop it or you'll be dragged to the dungeons!"

The woman hurtles the dagger and the blade sinks into the wall next to my head. "The traitor princess is over here!"

The rest of the people react immediately, shouting and shoving each other as they run forward. Their weapons gleam in the night and an arrow whooshes right above my head.

With another string of muttered curses, I turn around and run in the opposite direction.

The army of angry people chases me through the darkened streets of the city, the storm around us increasing in intensity.

I trample through crimson puddles, jump over discarded shields and ruined swords, and change directions every time another group of people joins the angry mob and more and more arrows try to strike me down.

The trial might be over, but I'm still a target.

And then suddenly, I'm yanked into the darkness of a narrow alley.

"Hello, Asteria," Skye croons, grinning at my raised dagger. "It's been too long. We need to catch up more often."

The mob runs past the alley and I press myself against the wall, Skye leaning against the other. The warrior has replaced her blue fighting leathers with a dark cloak, her striped hair hidden underneath her hood.

"Did Star send you out to spy on me?"

Skye rolls her eyes. "He might like to act like it, but he is not my boss."

"Then who is?"

She shrugs. "No one. Or the highest bidder. That might've been the prince for a while, but—" she raises her eyebrows, a sly smirk tugging her lips, "—it seems *you* could use some help right now."

"I can take care of myself."

"Maybe." Skye shrugs again. "But it would be easier to return to the palace with my help. What are you even doing out of it?"

"The finale is approaching," I say and sheath the dagger back on my thigh.

"Ah, yes." She taps a finger on her chin. "And you were hoping the rebellion might help a banished princess in trouble."

"You were pleased enough when I ended my betrothal to Castor," I say with a shrug.

Her eyes twinkle in the dim light and droplets stick to her eyelashes. "So you want in? It would be *interesting* with a royal among us."

"Maybe. That would depend on what's in it for me."

Her smirk widens into a grin. "And what do you want? Protection? A new crown?"

"At the moment—information."

"Are you sure about that? I think you need a distraction to help you get back to the palace before your dear husband realizes you're missing."

"He is not the boss of me either," I mutter through gritted teeth, ignoring the way the mention of *him* stokes the embers of fury inside me.

"Maybe not, but I have a feeling he's going to be looking for you very soon."

"I'm not some perfect bride to warm his bed," I snarl, my fingers itching to reach for the dagger again.

"That's exactly what the latest rumors say," Skye mutters with a knowing smirk.

At my answering glare, she waves a dismissive hand and rolls her eyes. "Luckily for you, I don't believe everything I hear. If I did, my soul would've been gone years ago."

"Do you know where I can get information about the finale or not?"

"There's not much to say. The Moon King has dismissed all generals in charge of planning the previous games. He wants this one all to himself." She snorts. "And we all saw how well that turned out the last time."

An exasperated sigh bursts from my lips. "Tell me something useful or leave before I cut you down myself."

Skye rolls her eyes with a low chuckle. "You might be my favorite royal out of all the ones I've been unlucky enough to meet. And here I was thinking I had already been useful to you a time or two."

I can't deny that she's been helpful throughout the Tournament, in her own way at least.

"So that's a no? You don't have any information about the finale and you don't know where I can find some?"

"I'll give you something useful, princess." She takes a step away from the wall, seemingly unbothered by the shouting army still running past our hiding place, screaming for the cursed traitor princess to come out and play.

If it were any other day, I might've been tempted to join them.

"You better hurry before the prince hunts you down. He might be insufferable and arrogant but I'm sure he's aware that the monthly bleeding isn't from the throat." Skye says, nodding toward my throat.

I press my fingers to my skin and curse when they come away bloody. The rain has numbed my skin so much I didn't realize I was bleeding.

I could really use some of *his* magical healing abilities right now.

My gaze snaps back to the smirking warrior.

At least now I know that *she* knows enough to be a threat.

"Don't worry, princess. I won't tell if you won't," Skye says with a wink. "You being a part of the rebellion would benefit both of us."

"Why does the rebellion even want a cursed princess?"

"We have our reasons, let's just leave it at that. Do you want our help or not?"

I'm about to say something more when furious screams reach our ally.

Skye places a finger to her lips as she moves to lean against my wall and whisper in my ear. "I strongly advise that you agree so I can create said distraction and we can get you out of here without the prince destroying the entire kingdom to find you."

I glance to each side of the alley where the paths are blocked by vindictive people, their weapons glinting in the dim light.

There is no way *he* is going to save me from this. I would rather hand myself over to the warriors.

I've already made a lot of stupid promises, so why not make another one? Bargains on the other hand—

"Fine."

A wicked grin spreads across Skye's face. "Give me your cloak."

"It looks just the same as yours—" I purse my lips when she gestures to the ripped hem I vaguely remember getting caught in

Alev's spiked tail when I tried climbing onto his back during one of our long training sessions.

"What exactly does the rebellion want from me–"

"We'll get to that later. I'll add this to the list of favors you now owe me." She winks at me before pulling the hood of my cloak over her head.

"Count to twenty-three before leaving the alley," she says as she hauls herself up on the wall of one of the ruined buildings, her feet resting on a broken wallboard.

"And please don't get yourself killed. We have work to do now." The warrior climbs the wall like a spider climbing its net, a dark figure in the thundering rain.

When she reaches the roof, she waves at the angry mob with a loud whistle. And then she starts running, effortlessly jumping onto a nearby roof as the crowd starts to chase her.

"The Moon King planned this all along. To destroy the Tournament–our most sacred and ancient tradition–is a disgrace to the gods and the very foundation of the Kingdoms of the Sky. The Tournament is not for the royals, but for the people. The rulers of the sun have always made sure to keep it that way, never stealing the title of Victor for ourselves. As we've all seen, Luna does not share those values. I hereby revoke Soria's peaceful visitation and support of the Tournament in Luna."

Auren hesitates, twisting her hands together in her lap. The servant is seated on the bench underneath the large window in my room with a grim expression on her face.

"Tell me the rest. I need to hear all of it."

"Princess Asteria no longer has any ties to Soria and is not welcome within our borders."

I halt pacing and blink in confusion. "That's what he said? Those words seem rather...*nice* for the king."

Auren flinches. "It's what he meant. Let's just say he has basically declared war on Luna and that he wants nothing more to do with you."

"Fair enough," I mutter before plopping down on my bed. "I promise to pay you as much as possible as soon as I can get my hands on something from the moon–"

"Don't worry about that," she says, waving a dismissive hand and giving me a weak smile. "I'm confident in our deal. And besides, you have other things to worry about right now."

"Unfortunately yes." I press my nails into the scars of my palms, but instantly let go when I remember *he* may feel it. "Is there something else?"

Auren studies me for a moment, an emotion I can't place flickering across her features. "The Victor is still here."

My eyes widen. "Elio? He didn't leave with the king? What about my sister?"

"He's the only one left."

Jumping out of the bed, I drape a robe over my nightgown.

"You really should get dressed no matter where you're going, Asteria," Auren shouts after me as I run down the hallway.

If anyone knows anything about the finale, Elio is going to be my best chance.

Groups of servants are carrying suitcases and bags from the guest wing, frightened expressions on their faces as they rush through the halls.

The Sun King left in a hurry.

I find Elio standing in front of a window in what appears to be an office. On the table behind him, between scattered books and papers, there is a large map of the two kingdoms, pinned with different colored needles and threads.

"I thought you weren't allowed out of your tower," he says without turning around.

"And I thought you knew I didn't take orders from anyone."

"You've changed so much I barely recognize you anymore."

Walking to him, I try to see what is so interesting outside of the window that he refuses to meet my eyes. The day outside is bleak, the sun hidden behind gray clouds and the thick fog surrounding the mountains.

"Are you feeling homesick?"

Elio finally turns to meet my gaze, his hazel eyes lined with fatigue. "Aren't you? Everything was so much better back home."

"Maybe for you," I say through gritted teeth, wondering if *he* will feel it if I squeeze hard enough. "It was better for a Victor praised with glory, but not for the cursed princess. My life may not be any better or easier here, but at least I'm no longer only a cursed princess."

Pity flickers across his features. "You know that's not what I meant. Things were better between us and that is what I miss." He reaches forward to grab my hand but I step out of his reach, ignoring the way he flinches from my rejection.

"This is not why I came here."

Elio lets out a heavy sigh. "I guess it was too good to be true." His eyes flicker to my open robe and I quickly tie the strands around my waist, regretting the rushed departure from my room. "Let me guess, the prince has turned his back on you and you want my advice on how to finally kill the bastard and win the Tournament?"

"You once promised to help me. Before you practically begged me to drop out." I don't care about the blood trickling from my scars as I glare at the Victor–my former lover and best friend.

"Of course I'll help you," he snaps before pinching the bridge of his nose as if *I* am the one causing *him* pain. "Contrary to what you might believe, I still care about you and whether you live through the next few days. The Tournament is going to be the least of your problems–"

"I'm perfectly aware of that," I snap, still glaring at him.

Where there used to be warmth and sunlight between us, there's now only cold, empty darkness. If my heart weren't already so shattered and broken, I might've felt something, but I don't feel anything at all.

"Do you know anything that might help me or not?"

"I was supposed to leave with the king," Elio says, dragging a hand over his short-cropped hair.

"And what about the finale and final ball? The Victor is usually the one to move the Crown of Victory."

He lets out a low chuckle. "Who knows? The king won't come back for the finale. He has basically declared war on Luna." Elio gives me an expectant look as if he wants me to need him.

"Tell me something I don't know." I wave a dismissive hand, ignoring the urge to smirk at his disappointed look.

Elio narrows his eyes and crosses his arms. "The latest rumor was that the final ball was supposed to be your wedding celebrations, but now it's more likely to be a life-ending ceremony. And you need to make sure it isn't yours."

"What is that supposed to mean?"

"What do you think?" He takes a step forward, his hands once again reaching for me.

"For the first time in perhaps forever, if not at least centuries, there are only two people in the finale. And to top it all off, two royals. Two royals who just got married and are supposed to be madly in love. You're more naive than I thought if you think the Moon King isn't going to use that chance to humiliate his enemies even more than he already has. The last game was proof enough of their intentions."

"*Their* intentions?"

"Your prince has secrets of his own," Elio spits. "He is very close with his king."

I roll my eyes. "I'm not worried about the prince."

I am. And I am not.

I plan to deal with *him* later.

Elio narrows his eyes again. "You saw how the last game played out. It's only fair to believe the king will order the finale to be a battle to the death."

"That's not going to happen. It can't happen."

"And how can you be so sure of that?"

"Because we have a bargain," I snap, regretting the words the moment they leave my mouth.

Elio's eyes widen and he staggers back a step. "Please tell me you're joking, Asteria. Please tell me you weren't stupid enough to make a magical life-binding bargain with the enemy–"

"You have no idea of the sacrifices I've had to make these last months," I snarl, fury sparking at my fingertips, the rage trying to break free of the ice that's pushing it all away.

"You keep forgetting I've been in the games too," Elio snarls back. "Don't you dare say I don't understand."

"That's different–"

"No, it's not. I might not be a prince, but I've been a warrior in the Tournament and I'm well familiar with the sacrifices. You were barely present for my participation! You know nothing–" He clenches his jaw so tight I'm afraid his teeth are going to break.

"I did everything I could to be there. You know why I couldn't–"

The Sun King made sure I wouldn't be able to leave the palace, let alone move from the ground of the dungeons.

Elio flinches.

"And you know this Tournament is different," I continue,

trying to suppress the dark memories. "It's not just games this time. It's not only for entertainment. This is war."

"It's always been war—"

"No," I say, my mind a swirling mess I'm unable to grasp. "There is something else this time."

Elio steps forward and takes me in his arms before I can protest, his arms trapping me against his chest. "We can still leave. Get out of here and leave everything behind. You no longer have any obligations to Soria. You're finally free of him. Just leave with me."

Pressed against him, my body is so tense it hurts, but still, I let him hold me, knowing this will be the final time I see him.

"And what about your duties to Soria?"

Elio sighs as he tightens his grip around me so much it hurts. "I'm no longer bound to the Tournament. My duties are done. I'm free again too."

"And what about Solina?"

He doesn't answer for a while, his breath brushing the top of my head. "I told you I was supposed to leave with the others, but I stayed for you, Ria."

I let him hold me for a little while longer, waiting to see if the familiar feeling of warmth will resurface, if there's still something left between us. When I feel nothing but the same numbing cold, I break free of his hold.

"There may not be much left for me in Soria, but the games are far from over and I have to win. Whatever it takes."

"Asteria—"

"You should leave while you still have the chance."

One last look at my past and once promising bright future, and then I leave it behind for the final time.

CHAPTER FORTY-THREE

With the tip of my silver dagger, I carve a star into the skin on my arm.

A message to the prince and an extension of our mark.

An icy stillness has seeped into me after I visited the witches and royal city, the burning fury hidden deep behind the cold fortress of my heart.

I study the crimson star, my fingers absentmindedly stroking the jagged lines.

Maybe this isn't such a bad thing.

I won't be forced to kill him now.

The star lingers for a couple of minutes before the skin stitches itself back together, just as Star's arrow wound.

Maybe the witch was right when she said more signs would start appearing now that I'm aware of the bond between us.

I'm lounging in his bed when he barges through the door.

"What–" he snaps his mouth shut when he notices me, the silver in his eyes blazing like the brightest flames.

Putting the now empty wine glass on the bedside table, I

stretch my legs on the mattress, allowing the sheer black nightgown to rise higher on my thighs.

A muscle ticks in his throat and the silver in his eyes flare brighter. I give him a devious smirk. "I got a little impatient."

Star's gaze lingers on my skin for a heartbeat longer before he strides into his seating room without a word. Moments later, he comes back with a glass of black liquid and takes a seat in a chair on the opposite side of the room, as far away from me as possible.

He sips the drink in silence, his gaze locked on the painting on the wall where a mountainous landscape is shrouded by darkness.

There's something different about him. Something I can't quite put my finger on.

"Did you enjoy your journey to The Shadow Court? And what about your little adventure in the city?"

I startle at the sound of his voice and feel my carefully perfected plans already start to disintegrate.

He lets out a low chuckle. "You took my horse. Did you really think I wouldn't find out?"

I shrug and lean back against the headboard, brushing my hair to the side to reveal my neck and collarbone.

Another flare of silver and he tightens his grip on the glass, the pressure coloring his knuckles white.

"Yes, I did enjoy the journey. The witches in this kingdom are certainly something else."

Shadows explode from his fingertips and the glass shatters in his hand.

Invisible glass cuts through my hand and blood trickles from my skin.

Star mutters a string of curses before quickly retrieving a washcloth from the bathroom, the blood on his hands already gone when he comes back.

"Give me your hand," he says through gritted teeth.

I obey, allowing him to clean the blood from my hand.

The cuts from the shattered glass are already gone.

"And was your journey a success?" Star finishes cleaning my hand and tosses the cloth back into the bathroom before sitting down at the edge of the bed, his fingers absentmindedly twirling the ring on my finger.

I repress a shiver. At his touch, cracks are starting to form in the frozen walls shielding my heart.

This reaction to him—It has to be because of the bargain and bond. Just like the witch said.

"Maybe."

"But you're not going to tell me."

"That depends." I raise my eyebrows in challenge, patting the empty spot next to me on the bed.

The corners of his lips tug a little, a small trace of amusement slipping through his rage. "You want to consummate our marriage right this second? Oh wait, we already did that."

He chuckles at my glare before raising a perfectly sculpted dark eyebrow. "Or is this your master plan—seduce me into spilling all my secrets? You seem rather...*calm* for someone who just learned we are bound for all eternity."

"And you seem rather calm for someone who just nearly died."

Star narrows his eyes. "Don't forget you almost did too," he snarls, his fingers moving to grab my arm and reveal it to the morning sun seeping in from the window, the lines of the mark throbbing at his touch.

"Something you failed to tell me," I snarl back, trying to wriggle free from his grasp. "You lied to me. After everything, you still lied to me. I trusted you—"

He flinches and drops my arm. "I told you there were things I couldn't tell you and there still are—"

"And yet you found the perfect time to tell me."

"You were about to get us both killed," he snaps, his chest heaving. "Don't think it didn't cost me."

"You still could have told me—"

"And what about you? Only hours ago you tried to *kill* me. I only withheld something I was prevented from telling you."

"I didn't have a choice—"

"Neither did I. And why, exactly, didn't *you* have a choice?"

I purse my lips, the birthmark behind my ear stinging in warning.

Star lets out a humorless laugh. "Ah, let me guess, you can't tell me."

I open my mouth to say something, anything, but he beats me to it. "Don't worry. *I* won't kill you for not telling me every single detail of your life. And even if I wanted to, I *can't*."

I jump out of the bed, anger sparking at my fingertips. "Tell me how you know. I want the truth. *Now*."

"Fine," he snaps, leaping from the bed to tower over me. "You already know how."

He grabs my wrist and trails his fingers over the lines on my arm, the mark glowing brighter at his touch than the witch's. "You know what you did," he snarls, dropping my hand as if he is burned by my touch.

As if I'm cursing him.

There it is. Another sign that *something* is different. That *something* has changed.

I look into his eyes and see nothing but darkness and no signs of the person I've come to know.

His next words tear through the ice around my heart, carving a crack so deep no amount of magic can repair it.

"You have no idea how hard it has been to look at you, knowing you've stolen parts of my soul, without being able to do anything about it." His voice is lethally calm as shadows rise behind him.

And then the dark tendrils of his power shoot forward with a violent force, halting right in front of my throat and heart.

"You had no right!"

Darkness explodes around us.

This darkness is not calm and soothing, it is terrifying.

It blocks out everything.

It fills every part of me, searching through me for every speck of light so it can destroy it.

"Star–"

"This is nothing compared to what I would've done if my life wasn't tied to yours."

I can't breathe.

I can't think.

I can't feel anything else than the power pressing against me and the knowledge that this will destroy us both if he doesn't stop.

The darkness vanishes as fast as it came, the only sign it was there the blackness now swirling in his eyes.

I heave for breath, my heart struggling to get back to its rhythm.

Star is glaring at me like he never has before, all his rage and resentment and fury directed at me. His dark gaze flickers to the mark on my arm and shadows rise from him again. He balls his hands into fists at his side and the shadows retreat, only a faint smoke clinging to his form, as if it takes everything in him to hold back and not unleash himself fully.

I don't recognize this man.

"I didn't–"

"You did. You tampered with ancient forbidden magic you had no right to, not knowing the price and consequences, just like your mother."

I take a step back, sucking in a sharp breath. "You don't know it's my fault. The witch said it probably would have happened anyway–"

He lets out a humorless laugh. "I don't care about the witches right now. Our bond happened because of *you*."

I open my mouth to protest but he cuts me off. "The mark appeared when you used forbidden magic and the bond fully snapped into place when I tried to kill you the first time I saw you, showing me the truth and preventing me from giving our souls to the Shadow Realm."

"The first time I saw you was at the bindings and you barely even touched me–"

"That was the first time you saw me, but it wasn't the first time I saw you. I knew you had stolen something. I just assumed it was part of my magic, but for once I was wrong. Magic always comes with a price, and you made *me* pay it," he says through gritted teeth, his chest heaving with anger or perhaps unspent magic.

Magic always comes with a price. Especially for someone like you.

I didn't know the price would be someone else's life.

"When I fell from Kylo, the dead suitor helped me survive–"

"No," he snarls. "I saw my life flash before my eyes and pulled as much of my magic I could into you." His eyes are pure silver when he blinks–proof of the magic running in his veins.

"You are alive because of *me*. No one else."

"Your magic–" I snap my mouth shut at the vicious look on his face and choose another question instead. "Why did you insist on a bargain if we already shared a bond– another bargain?"

"To make sure you didn't take my life with you when you stupidly got yourself killed in the games. I needed time to find a way to break the bond. I still do. Sometimes another bargain can overshadow the first one." He rakes a hand through his hair, disheveling the dark locks.

"But it didn't."

"No, but I'm hoping this one will. The Tournament has the most powerful magic in the two kingdoms—"

"I used magic from the gods—"

"I'm perfectly aware of that," he snaps, adding a string of curses. "But right now, that's the only plan I've got."

"You can't know for sure that we are bound together."

Star lets out a low growl and retrieves the silver dagger from the floor. With quick movements, he cuts a shallow line across his throat. Drops of blood pour out of his skin, and as the blood touches the blade of the dagger, pain and blood trickle from my own throat.

The dagger clatters back onto the floor.

He doesn't offer to clean the blood this time.

"I won't deny that our bargain means that there's a bond between us, but it still doesn't prove that our lives are connected and bound," I say, shaking my head. "Maybe to a certain point, but we can't know for sure that ending your life would also mean my end."

An infuriated sound works its way up his throat. "Are you willing to take that chance?"

I might have to.

Star curses as if he can hear the unspoken words in my mind.

"You said my death would only be a small inconvenience to you—"

"It would."

I blink at him, ignoring the parts of me that want to reach for him. "You–you want to die?"

"Not particularly no, but if it happens then it happens."

"That's–"

He shrugs and straightens the lapels of his jacket, still looking nothing like the man I thought I could trust.

"You don't really care about the Tournament, do you? You've won numerous times. You're already a Victor. You don't need to prove yourself. Not like I do."

"No, I don't." Silver lightning flares in his eyes and I can't look away.

"You called me to Soria with your fucking *curse*."

The ice around my heart disintegrates and the sharpest sword in the world digs into my heart.

No–

I did curse him, didn't I?

When I finally thought I was free, I'm still nothing but the cursed princess.

Star takes a step forward, shadows once again starting to reach for me. "You are a curse, Asteria. You cursed me into those fucking games I swore to never again be a part of. You cursed me to be a part of you. Forever."

My fragile heart shatters.

Pain unlike anything I've ever felt before tears through my soul.

I can't survive this–

"Everything I've done has been to keep myself alive. *Everything.*"

A storm of memories crashes into me so fast I'm unable to brace myself.

Every time he saved me–the labyrinth, the ocean, the cages, the dragon race, the elimination round, the target game.

When I fell from the holy mountain.

The way he held me in his arms on the back of a dragon.

How he told me the truth when no one else did and how he held me together when my world fell apart.

His vow that no one would hurt me in his kingdom.

Our wedding night–

Every taunting word, every touch, every kiss–it was all a lie.

Everything.

I can't breathe.

I don't know when a part of me started hoping, when a part of me started to feel something more than just the pretended feelings.

And I don't know if the things I've felt are because of some destined bond or cursed bargain or if they come from the stolen moments I never even dared to dream of.

Between all the fury, resentment, and hatred that came with the realization that he had kept the most important secret from me, a part of me started hoping we might conquer this together, and what a foolish thing hope is.

It takes everything in me to pull myself together, to not reveal the battle raging inside of me. I push it all away, willing the walls of ice to rebuild themselves back around my heart.

It's not enough.

"And let me guess, your best tactic was luring me into your bed?"

"That was all you, Asteria."

My heart screams at the sound of my name on his lips. The lips that are too familiar with the most intimate parts of me, the lips that spoke the truth when no one else did.

And the lips that lied to me over and over again, and are now breaking my heart with the words pouring out of them.

"Not all of it." I cross my arms, suddenly feeling very

ridiculous with my lack of clothing.

"No, I guess not," he says with a shrug as if we're just discussing something trivial and meaningless. And to him—our time together meant nothing at all.

This was just another game to win.

"Don't look so surprised." A cruel smirk pulls at his lips, every last trace of the prince I've gotten to know these last months replaced by the enemy he was supposed to be all along.

The enemy he was all along.

I just didn't see it.

His silver eyes look at me too intently for my liking, giving me the urge to just forget about all of this and continue what we started on our wedding night. "What about your own scheming plans? Play along and then kill me in the end? Only you didn't consider what it might do to your own life, *starlight*."

"Don't call me that." My nails break through the scars in my palms and Star opens his palm, glaring at the blood now gathered there.

To a certain point, yes, that was my plan, but then things changed between us, and I—

I was just as willing to give everything up for the chance to win the Tournament and become the next Victor.

"So what do you suggest we do next?" I ask, willing the rising inferno inside me to calm, extinguishing the flames with cool indifferent fury, ignoring the blinding pain in my heart.

"We still have a bargain to fulfill and a bond to break."

"How? If what you claim is true, and you have been trying to do that ever since we met, how will we accomplish that? How can I possibly win the games if we are bound together—"

"I will end the bond between us. Even if it's the last thing I do in this life. I will never stop trying to tear your soul away from mine, not until the stars stop shining."

CHAPTER FORTY-FOUR

The sapphire ring, forgotten and dusty until moments ago, clanks against the large paintings on the walls of the palace hallways, the symbols of both sides of the sky casting shaped lights onto the stone floor.

The ring is the only piece of my father I will ever have, and the truth of who I truly am.

I don't know what urged me down to the hidden room I swore I would never step back into, much less what possessed me to reach forward and remove the ring from the stony hand bearing a dark mark similar to mine.

Mother was quiet when I retrieved the ring, a faint warmth brushing against the birthmark behind my ear the only sign she was aware of what I was doing.

As I mourned the loss of what could've been, I made a vow to the unknown warrior that I would do whatever it took to avoid the same fate he suffered. I've already gotten too close, but the marks on my skin won't be eternal like his.

There's still hope.

As long as I'm still breathing, there is hope.

Whatever it takes.

The stone covering the entrance to the throne room is already cracked open along with other openings throughout the massive room that allows slivers of moonlight to seep into the darkness.

The throne room is quiet and empty except for a silver crown that rests on the obsidian throne, its spiked tips casting eerie shadows across the room.

My boots thud against the black carpet on the stone floor as I move toward a jagged opening in the mountain wall that reveals the night outside.

Almost there.

The garden outside of the throne room is not empty. It is crowded with people and night-blooming flowers illuminated by the moonlight, but as always, h*e* is the first one I notice.

The prince.

The warrior.

My husband.

The other part of my life–binding bargain and–

Curse.

Star's eyes snap to mine as I emerge through the mountain, and when his gaze moves to the new ring gleaming on my finger, silver flares in his eyes.

He is wearing his usual dark fighting leathers, but his chest is pinned with numerous silver crescent moons intertwined with golden suns–victory pins. The dark ring glimmers on his finger, the pale stone the only trace of color on the prince of shadows.

The sight of him stokes the fire that threatens to melt the icy fortress within me and consume my soul until there is nothing left. Invisible strings yank at my heart and soul, the magic I always thought to be the Tournament's magic urging me to destroy my enemy.

I'm not so sure anymore.

You are a curse, Asteria.
Everything I've done has been to keep myself alive.
Everything.

My nails bore into the scars of my palms so hard I feel the skin break.

Star discreetly wipes his hands on his thighs and I resist the urge to give him a cruel smirk.

It is only when I look away from his eyes that I notice the crowd around us.

Nobles, generals, and a handful of lucky warriors and people are all eagerly awaiting the finale. An army of soldiers are patrolling the edge of the garden and all the way around the palace, scouting for bloodthirsty warriors and rebellious forces.

In the middle of the garden, there is a circle picturing the moon and its different phases, the dark stones glittering in the moonlight. And in the middle of the circle, in the very center of a full moon, is the Moon King.

A vicious smile pulls at the king's lips when he sees me and the crowd around him falls silent. "The princess has finally graced us with her presence," he says, slowly clapping his hands together.

Star grabs my arm and starts leading me toward the ring, sparks shooting through me at the feel of his skin.

"Don't touch me," I say through gritted teeth, willing my face to stay impassive.

"The game isn't over," he grits back, his eyes a dark storm.

"Neither is our bargain. Don't forget this is *my* win."

"Afraid you're going to lose?" His grip on my arm tightens. "Is that why you were out stirring trouble last night? You've certainly been busy in the days since our last conversation. The court was brimming with talk of a princess on the run. They thought she was trying to escape the games, but we both know that's impossible."

"Only as impossible as escaping our bargain. My end of the bargain might not have been specific, but yours was. Help me win the Tournament." I dig my nails into his skin, instantly regretting it when his pain appears on my arm.

"And what exactly do you think I've been doing all this time?" A growl so low only I can hear it reverberates from his throat.

We halt in front of the Moon King who looks between us with a cruel smirk. "What a tragic way to spend your newlywed days," he says, earning a laugh from the crowd around him. "But the terms of the Tournament cannot be broken."

As if he hasn't broken those terms multiple times already.

The dark king extends his arms, his hands reaching for the sky where lightning erupts in rapid intervals. The silver light flares through the garden, lighting up the darkness of the night.

A dark smoke seeps from the king's raised arms and then a sword appears in each of his hands.

One silver and one gold.

The Royal Swords of the Kingdoms of the Sky.

My heart stops beating and the scars on my back throb with pain.

The betrayal cuts so deep it takes my breath away, and I clench my hands together so hard the prince beside me sucks in a breath.

Fury licks up my insides, the ice inside me vibrating and on the brink of shattering into thousands of tiny shards that will only fuel the uncontrollable power that is screaming to be unleashed on the world.

I let every trace of the rage and hatred seep into my gaze as I turn to look at the last person standing in the way of my crown.

Shocked murmurings break out around us, all eyes on the sacred swords that glimmer in the night.

The flaring lightning disappears as thunder rumbles above. Dark clouds glide across the sky, obscuring the moon and stars in its mist so only the light of the swords is visible in the darkness.

The Sorian sword is too gold, too bright, the color indistinguishable from the gold in Helios' eyes when his magic is raging.

I've always hated how beautiful the brutal sword is. From the golden handle to the intricate carvings telling a story I've been dying to figure out.

The most sacred artifact in Soria's history and he just left it behind. A gift from the gods passed on for generations and centuries, left behind for the enemy to take and dishonor.

In a way, the Moon King has already won the war by having the symbol of Soria's strength and glory in his possession.

The Moon King lowers his arms, holding out a sword to each of us—silver to Star and gold to me.

I only allow myself to hesitate for a second before tightly gripping the handle of the sword. The carvings bore into the tender skin of my palms and it feels so wrong it's hard to hold on.

I'll never forget the last and only other time I had it in my hands.

"This finale is nothing like we have ever seen before," the king says, his booming voice echoing off the mountains, reaching all the way across the two kingdoms and to the golden king left with no choice but to listen.

And all the way to the gods and the sky witnessing the ruination of their sacred legacy.

"Two royals of opposite kingdoms–" A cruel smirk in my direction earns a few snickers from the people gathered around the stone circle before he continues speaking. "Although she may have stepped into her new role as a princess of the moon, Asteria will always have the blood of the sun. Thus, the symbol of the golden Royal Sword."

This finale is not only the end of the Tournament—the ancient trials created to keep the balance and hold back the war. This is a power play between the kingdoms, a way for the Moon King to display the winner of the war.

His kingdom.

It's too bad that I have a bargain that ensures my win and that I can't die without taking his precious prince with me.

"The prince and princess may have an understanding between them, but as we all know—there can only be one Victor. To honor the gods, I have decided this finale to be one of the ancient ones. And we all know how the gods settled things between them." His smirk widens into a grin as he once again raises his hands to the sky, another thundering crack sounding overhead.

The king claps his hands together, the sound even louder than the thunder above. "As always, the rules of the Tournament are simple. There are no rules but one; survive. The finale is a battle to the death. The one left standing is the winner, it's as simple as that. There can only be one winner, there can only be one Victor. And may the best Victor win."

"No–"

A crack. And then another. The walls of ice around my heart are not strong enough. My heart is too large for my chest, its beating rhythm a painful reminder of the little time left.

No.

This is impossible.

If this is the finale, I can't become the next Victor if we're bound together.

I can't.

If he dies—I die.

Whatever it takes, Asteria.

Even if I have to give up my life?

And his?

Whatever it takes, Asteria!

"I am sorry, Princess Asteria," the Moon King spits, "but you do not get to decide the rules of the finale. That right is reserved for the king of the currently hosting kingdom."

His hands fall to rest at his sides and he steps out of the ring. "Now, I would urge you to get on with it before the sun rises and you both travel to the Shadow Realm."

Whatever it takes, Asteria. Whatever it takes!

I'll do it.

I have to.

Whatever it takes.

Even if I have to bring the Crown of Victory into the Shadow Realm.

Stair raises his sword toward me, the silver blade glinting in the dim light.

I don't want to look at him, it will make this too hard, but I'm unable to stop the pull of the strings tying us together and I look into his eyes for what might be the final time.

There is a silent message in his eyes, the usual silver stars overshadowed by the darkness of the night.

Play along.

Maybe the message isn't silent at all, maybe I've gained the ability to actually hear his unspoken words, or maybe our time together—lies or no—has taught me to read him like no one else. It's hard to tell over the roaring in my ears and the thundering beat of my heart challenging the thunder bellowing in the sky.

Whatever it takes, Asteria.

Gold meets silver in a mighty clank as I swing my blade toward the prince, my feet stepping into a well-practiced rhythm as we start to dance around each other.

Our first meeting was with swords between us, and now our final meeting will be too.

Star meets every blow as effortlessly as he did the first time in Soria during the bindings, his dark eyes never leaving mine.

I try to ignore the screaming voice inside my head that refuses to quiet, focusing on each move of my body.

The crowd is muttering and cursing around us, the warriors greedily staring us down, and I can't help wondering if someone is suddenly going to barge between us and end us both.

"You went back for the ring," Star mutters, swinging his sword in a wide arc.

"Yes." My sword clangs against his, the force of it making my teeth rattle as the sound rings in my ears.

"Tell me why."

"You lost the right to ask me questions."

"You've asked me an endless list of questions since the first time we met." He snorts, his sword just missing my shoulder.

"I assume you haven't found a way out of our bond," I say, ignoring the ticking clock of my heart.

"No."

"Then I hope you have another brilliant plan. We both know either both of us or none of us are leaving this ring alive." I step away from his blow, swinging my sword of gold low. "And there can only be one winner, one Victor," I say, repeating the Moon King's smug words.

"There will be." Star moves forward, pushing me toward the end of the circle.

If this were any other fight I could've just stepped out of the circle and that would've been it, but this is not an ordinary sword fight.

Nothing about the Tournament is ordinary.

The golden sword reflects my alora eyes, and I can't hold back the words any longer.

"You gave him the sword," I spit, and Star falters for a

moment, the blade of my sword slicing across his shoulder, the pain instantly bursting from my own skin.

"I didn't have a choice." A muscle ticks in his jaw, his eyes a dark storm of shadows as he moves away from my next strike. "Don't give me that look. That's the exact same words you used the last time you tried to kill me."

I purse my lips and his eyes flare with silver.

I didn't have a choice then and I don't have a choice now. If this has to end with both of us dead for me to become a Victor, then that is the way it has to be.

I don't have a choice.

I have to do this.

Whatever it takes.

No matter how much it threatens to break the rest of my fractured heart.

"Stop playing with each other," the Moon King croons through gritted teeth, his voice snaking down my back.

What if I turned the sword around and aimed it at my own heart?

If we are truly bound together, it doesn't matter which heart I strike.

"Asteria!" Star swings his sword out, trapping mine to the ground, the gilded tip boring into the stones beneath our feet.

"I have to do it this time," I say, willing the icy fortress around my heart to solidify. "No matter what it takes."

Whatever it takes.

"Asteria," Star snaps again, shadows rising from his back, the silver flashing in his eyes as bright as the lightning above us.

Grunting with effort, every muscle in my body screaming, I struggle against his sword. He doesn't budge, and for a second I'm terrified I will have to fight him for real.

I won't stand a chance.

"Look at me, Asteria."

Invisible hands yank my soul, the strand wrapped around my heart pulled taut. My whole essence is at war with itself, the Tournament tugging me one way and the bargain another. And then there is the voice of the late queen screaming so loud I can barely hear anything else.

A part of me wants to kill him. And right now, I'm not sure if that is because of the roaring magic of the Tournament or if it's my broken heart screaming to banish his soul to the Shadow Realm so I never have to look into his eyes and feel his betrayal ever again.

Another part wants to run into his arms and never let go, to pry and scream until he admits that not all of it was a game of lies.

"Asteria!"

My eyes snap to his, the unseeable strings pulling so hard it hurts and I'm left with no choice but to obey.

Star is breathtaking in the night. Each flare of silver lightning across the sky lights up his mighty frame, the shadows clinging to him rippling off his body. His eyes are pure black, all traces of midnight blue and silver stars gone in the night.

An involuntary shudder runs down my back, and I'm so captivated by him that I barely notice he has finally released my sword.

"Asteria," he breathes, my name on his lips conjuring all sorts of memories I'm desperately trying to forget.

"Focus. Just a little longer." He raises his sword, only striking when I'm jolted back to the present moment by another flare of lightning and a loud rumble of thunder.

We continue our dance of swords, silver and gold clanking as my mind races to find a solution. Everything is so loud, so dark, and yet so bright.

I don't know how much longer I can go on.

What will happen if the sun rises and we're still fighting?"

"We can't keep this up forever—"

"We could," Star says, gritting his teeth. "But we won't." His sword slams against mine so hard I have to bite my lip to not let out a scream.

"Smile, princess. You're about to become the next Victor of Day and Night."

"What—"

Star's sword swipes for my feet and I stumble, my back slamming against the stones of the moon circle.

A mocking laugh echoes behind me as I stagger to my feet, and I just know the Moon King is rubbing his hands together in anticipation behind my back.

Star's eyes flash with silver stars as he swings his sword again, this time silver meeting gold high up in the air.

Swerve to the right.

I startle at the words—somehow both a silent message conveyed by his eyes and a command shouted in my mind. I search his features, our swords still pressed together in the air.

A faint black smoke is seeping from his skin, and the silver stars in his eyes are now replaced by nothing but darkness. Power ripples of his body, the feel of it making my heartbeats stutter.

He nods.

We have a bargain. He is helping me.

There once was a time when I would've trusted him and our bargain, but I can no longer discern the truth from his lies.

Star's eyes narrow and he increases his pressure on my sword until the gilded blade is grazing my forehead.

I glance at the sharpened tip of the Royal Sword, remembering the time it cut through a prince's heart and wondering what it will take for it to do so again.

A low growl reverberates from Star's chest, and the black

smoke rising from his skin thickens until a tendril curls around my hand—the hand that is holding the gilded sword, and I know that I can't win without his help.

I have to give him a last chance, and if he cheats his way out of our bargain—I'll slam the sword into my own heart until the both of us are nothing but shadows.

Swerve to the right.

As the Moon King makes an impatient sound behind me, I retract my sword and move to the right, my boots landing on the grassy ground beyond the circle.

With a roar that rattles my heart, the silver sword cuts through the air where I was only seconds ago, its bearer's face contorted with so much wrath and vengeance it makes me terrified.

A storm of lightning lights up the darkness, thunderous booms following each flare as screams erupt around us.

A raspy breath and a low growl resound behind me, and with my heart in my throat, I turn around.

The sight behind me can't be real.

Luna's silver Royal Sword is protruding from the Moon King's chest. The handle is illuminated by the moonlight, the dark clouds blocking the sky long gone as if even the gods want to witness this.

The king's eyes are glassy as he staggers back. The darkness in them evaporates, leaving only a white blankness where the soulless black was only moments ago.

And then dark magic erupts from the king.

Shadows seep out from his eyes, his mouth, his chest, everywhere. Dark tendrils of magic shoot from his hands, his fingertips stained black from the magic, and his chest is heaving as darkness bursts from his heart in violent waves.

The storm of power rushes through the air, the magic

crackling across the sky in a cascade of silver lightning and thickening smoke.

And then, for a few moments, everything is black and quiet.

The magic slows to a faint smoke, and when the king is once again visible, he raises a hand for the last time, his finger pointing straight at my heart before his eyes roll back in his head and he falls to the ground where his body dissolves into nothing but black smoke.

The sword clatters to the ground and the magic roars.

The shadows twist and bend into a violent wind with silver sparks that crackle as loud as the thunder above. The power rushes forward, through me, slowing my heart and rapidly speeding it up, before hitting the warrior next to me.

Star welcomes the power with open arms.

The violent power rushes through him with powerful gusts of wind that threaten to topple the palace from its mountain and rattle the entire world, and at this moment, I believe the myths of a queen carving the land with her tears.

The prince of shadows is magnificent in the storm. The magic is an extension of his being, and he greedily absorbs the power.

Star's eyes are pure silver as he plucks the silver sword from the ground, the smoke of the dead king seeping into his arms. He raises the Royal Sword toward the sky, the blood of its last king dripping to the ground where it's soaked up by the palace mountain.

When the tip of the Royal Sword reaches the sky, silver light flares from an endless sea of glittering stars so bright it's a wonder we're not all going blind.

And then the shadows of a crown appear on the head of the new king of Luna.

CHAPTER FORTY-FIVE

"What have you done?" The words are so faint and quiet that I'm unsure if I've uttered them or if they got stuck in my throat.

The new King of Luna's gaze flickers to mine as he wipes the bloody blade of the sword on his leathers before sheathing it at his side.

Star's eyes are pools of liquid silver in the darkness of the night and dark tendrils of magic ripple off his towering form.

The magic that has always clung to him seems much stronger now, and it is.

He now holds the power of Luna, the Kingdom of the Moon, and tonight he truly looks like a god–and king–of shadows and destruction.

"It's done. It's over." His dark voice sends a shiver down my back and his eyes leave mine to glare at the crowd around us.

Thunder elbows his way through the crowd to kneel in front of his king.

When no one else follows, the general lifts his head to glare at the people behind him. "You will bow before your king or bleed before him!"

A cruel smirk tugs at Star's lips. He snaps his fingers and a few of the gathered people fall to the ground, clutching their chests as they heave for breath.

Another storm of lightning cracks across the sky and the tangy taste of magic fills my mouth.

The screaming crowd falls silent as they drop down on their knees, faces lowered to the ground, some of them muttering low prayers to the gods.

Even the Moon Princes lower themselves to the ground, glares on their faces and curses pouring from their lips.

Only Axton remains standing, the oldest of the princes, the one who was expected to inherit the throne up until only moments ago. "You can't do this."

Star narrows his eyes, and as he tilts his head, Axton's legs crack and the prince collapses on the ground.

"I am the king. I can do whatever I want," he snarls and a gust of black wind blows through the crowd.

The king glares at his half-brother for a moment longer before the cruel smirk is back on his lips. "Now, as is the tradition, you all have the right to challenge me in a battle to the death, but only after the final ball. Any attempt before that will result in your death, thanks to the Tournament's magic."

Axton struggles to get back on his feet, but the magic seizing his body makes it impossible. The prince is forced to stay on the ground, his glare matching the rest of his brothers. When Axton tries to protest again, Star only needs to look at him for his lips to stop moving.

"There can't be a final ball without a Victor," one of the other princes says. "The finale isn't even completed–"

"Oh, but it is," Star says as he walks forward to grab my hand, his usually warm skin cold in the night. "There can only be one winner, one Victor. And there can only be one king."

My arm is raised in the air, the first ray of sunlight lighting up our entwined hands as the dark magic of the king reluctantly moves aside to make room for the sun.

"Asteria of the sun and the moon, the Victor of Day and Night!"

As Star's voice echoes throughout the garden, the sound bearing all the way across the Diamond Mountains to Soria, silver erupts in the sky, the color mingling with the rapidly rising sun and creating a luminous cascade of silver and gold.

Victor.

The word rocks through me, my heart jolting as ancient magic slams into me. Pain erupts in the binding mark on my neck, and the bright light in the sky makes it impossible to discern which color it transforms to, although the sinking feeling in my stomach leaves little doubt in my mind.

No–

This is not how I was supposed to win the Tournament.

Royal power plays and schemes have replaced the warrior games and the title is now practically shoved upon me.

Whatever it takes, Asteria. Whatever it takes.

This shouldn't be possible.

How? How did he manage this? The Moon King had immense power and Star just killed him as if it was nothing.

I didn't even win our fight.

I don't deserve to be a Victor.

Not like this.

Whatever it takes, Asteria. Whatever it takes.

But–

Whatever. It. Takes.

I shake my head, trying to quiet the victorious shrieks in my mind.

This can't be right.

This *isn't* right.

I'm not a Victor, am I?

With a slight tilt of Star's chin, Thunder rises to his feet and moves to retrieve an embellished box that has magically appeared between the dark flowers in the garden.

I'm still numb when the king places a victory pin on my chest, the silver crescent moon and the golden sun reflecting shapes onto the ground.

A Victory Dagger is shoved into my hand, its handle digging into my skin.

The Crown of Victory comes next. Made of gold and silver threads picturing every aspect of the sky, the ancient crown is crafted for and from the gods.

When Elio wore the crown last year, I thought he looked like a god of the sun. Now, that same ceremonial crown sits heavy on my head, a weight threatening to push me deep into the ground, and I feel nothing like a goddess.

Star's cool fingers touch the skin on my forehead as he crowns me Victor of Day and Night, and the feel of his newly gained power makes dread coil in my stomach.

"You can't be serious," I say through gritted teeth, shivering when his fingers move to the back of my neck.

"Of course I am." He untangles my braid and drags his fingers through the white strands, letting them fall to my waist.

"I'm king and you're Victor. Take the title before I throw you in the dungeons," he mutters before taking a step back.

"And our bargain?"

"Our bargain is done. I helped you win the Tournament and you helped me get what I wanted. You're free to leave my palace," he says with a slight shrug, as if we haven't just changed the very foundation of the two kingdoms.

A choked chuckle bursts from my mouth. "But it's not over. You said our life-binding bargain was independent of our other bargains. We're still bound together. And not only like this—" I hold up my hand with the alora ring identical to the one on his finger.

"Not for long. I'll announce our separation plea to the gods at the final ball."

"And the bond?"

"Hopefully it will dissolve with the remains of our marriage now that our bargain is over."

"And if not?"

An icy glare is his only reply before he turns around to greet his new kingdom.

I'M at the top of the tower when she comes.

The sun is magnificent in the sky, her golden light shining down on the kingdom that will soon miss her until the next Tournament arrives and she will grant the people with her temporary presence.

The wind carries the musky and crisp smell of autumn, and in the midst of the Tournament's chaos, I haven't even noticed the changing colors of the leaves.

I look down at the tower basking in the sun and notice something else I haven't had the time to see.

In the middle of the darkness, dark blue flowers grow in between the cracks in the stone, the vibrant petals a piece of light in the dark. And the smell emanating from them–musky and sweet with a hint of citrus–sends a shiver all over my body.

They smell like *him*.

It has been almost a day since I was crowned Victor. The new King of Luna left the garden in a hurry. I was in no rush to follow him, and somehow the roof of his tower is where I ended up.

Now I know why.

Queen Oria is as radiant as she was the last and only time I saw her. Her existence is an extension of the sun, her form a shimmering golden near translucent veil unreachable by my touch, her presence only a ghost of what she once was.

"Hello, Asteria." Her voice is a whisper in the wind as much as a bell ringing in my mind, the sound of it all too familiar.

She leans over the stone railing and makes a wistful sound as she gazes down on Nyx gilded by the sunlight. "It has been a long time since I've had the pleasure of being here."

I'm so shocked by her appearance that it takes me a moment to find my voice.

"I–I didn't expect to see you. You told me it couldn't happen again–"

I refuse to let on that a part of me started hoping when her voice started reappearing in my mind when the games started, and especially when she answered one of my questions deep underneath the royal city.

Oria turns around to look at me. "I couldn't resist congratulating you in person." Her gaze moves to the sapphire ring on my finger and a pleased smile crosses her face.

"What was his name?"

Her smile turns sad. "Orion. His name is Orion. Oh, how I wish you could meet him and how I yearn for the life we could have had together."

Queen Oria and the warrior Orion.

I fidget with the dark blue ring, trying to imagine a warrior who might look like me and how different he must've been from the king ruling me.

"Even though *he* is not my father, I still share something with him," I whisper, not wanting to even utter his name in her presence. As if it knows I'm finally acknowledging it, the dormant power sends a spark to the finger carrying the deceased warrior's ring.

"I'm aware."

"And?"

"The power of the sun does not come from him. He may borrow it, just like you, but it is not his," she says, her voice suddenly sharp.

"Is it yours too?" I ask, studying the way her shimmering form sways with the wind, the golden light different from the kinglights gilding the Sun Palace.

"The sky belongs to everyone and we all belong to it," she says with a shrug as if it is that simple.

"Why didn't you tell me? About Orion—about *everything*!"

Oria looks back to the sun, her long wavy hair fluttering in the breeze. "There are a lot of things I wish I could have told you, my sweet light, but the one thing we did not get was time."

"My entire life, I thought I was the reason you died. I thought I was *cursed*—" My voice breaks at the last word and I desperately ignore the aching of my heart.

"Now I know that I was not the reason you died, but I am cursed. Cursed by you and the gods." Anger blazes inside of me and I press my nails into the scars of my palms to keep myself from reaching for the power screaming to be let out.

Oria purses her lips for a moment, her golden eyes boring into mine. "I know you think this is unfair. So did I, when I became queen and found out the truth. Our lives were decided by the ones before us, and I was unable to break out of it. I did everything I could to forge another path for you, another life, but I failed. I tried, and my life is gone because of it. I blame no other than myself for my death."

She continues before I'm able to say something, her voice slicing new scars—not on my back, but on my soul, on my heart. "Now that burden is yours to bear, and if you don't find a way out, it might be placed upon another until the end of our world. Or—the end will come when you fail."

Oria shrugs, her hair fluttering in the breeze like gilded waves from a faraway ocean I will never get to see. "You are not the chosen one, Asteria. It could be anyone, and know that many people have tried. It is your turn now. This is your burden to carry, your *curse*, if you want to call it that. There is nothing you can do about it other than find a way. I will not apologize for that."

"You could have told me—"

"No," she snaps, fire flaring in her eyes. "You were not ready for the truth. Your pain and fury is what kept you alive. I will not apologize for that either."

"You are no better than *him*," I spit, cursing the world and everything in it.

"Maybe not," she says, the fire in her eyes vanishing as fast as it came. "But *you* will be."

"Why are you still here? You could've just said your congratulations and left," I snarl, crossing my arms to shield myself against the growing wind.

"Because we are not done yet."

"You told me I had to win the Tournament and now I have—"

"It is not enough, Asteria. You know what you need to do now." She takes a step forward and reaches out a hand for my face, and when she touches my cheek, I feel nothing at all.

"Your oldest daughter will be the next Sun Queen and you

will have your queen for the stupid prophecy!" I move away from her light, shielding my heart as much as my body.

"It has to be you, Asteria. You know that."

"Why? What about the others?"

"I love all my daughters," she says simply, "but you, Asteria, you are special."

"Because I'm a part of him?" I fidget with the ring, the blue surface casting shadowed shapes onto the stone of the tower.

"Yes, and no. This is bigger than all of us." Oria reaches for me again, and this time when she lays her hand on my cheek, I feel a faint warmth. And at that moment, I feel like the eight-year-old girl seeing the ghost of her mother for the first time.

"Will you tell me why?"

"I already told you why, when you promised me you would do whatever it takes to win." Her hand moves to stroke my hair, and I'm filled with a deep sorrow for what could've been if only she hadn't bound her life to someone else.

"How could that possibly be my responsibility?"

"As I've already told you, it is not only your burden to bear, but change has to start somewhere. I sacrificed my life so you could live, Asteria. I need you to finish what I started. No matter what it takes."

We stare at each other, two royals of the sun forced to fight for the same cause–one of us long gone, the other in the middle of a raging storm.

"You vowed to do whatever it takes, Asteria. Don't go back on that promise now." She beckons a hand. I ignore it.

"I'm banished from Soria. I may be a Victor, but I'm in no position to take on an entire kingdom to get to the throne, and besides, no one is going to listen to the cursed princess, or queen, for that matter."

"Then make them listen."

I lean over the railing, longingly gazing at the city I've yet to explore further. The sun has started to make her descend in the sky, and it is now only hours until the final ball where Star is going to announce my banishment from this kingdom too.

"It's not as easy as you make it sound," I say, letting out a heavy sigh.

Oria laughs, the sound musical and light. "If it was easy, I wouldn't have picked you to do it. And who said you had to become the next Queen of the Sun? After all, Luna also needs a queen, and who better for the job than a Victor already bound to its king?"

I'm about to deny it, but snap my mouth shut at her knowing look. And who is she to scold me when she made that mistake herself?

"That's impossible. He would never let me do that. There hasn't been a Queen of Luna since Elara, and without her crown there never will be."

"Is it really? Impossible?" She clicks her tongue disapprovingly, giving me a glimpse of the mother she could have been. "And nothing is ever truly lost. You just have to know where to look. And you, my light, can accomplish everything as long as you're willing to do whatever it takes."

I look down at the river coursing through the city before disappearing underneath the mountain carrying the palace, thinking of another queen losing her true love. The water sparkles in the sunlight, the blue as clear as the brightest crystals.

And then, suddenly, I know where to look.

"There you go," Oria says with a beaming smile, placing her gilded hand over mine, her finger briefly stroking over the sapphire ring.

"Will you stay with me?"

I don't know what makes me ask.

Maybe it's the eight-year-old child in me, maybe it's the baby cradled by her dying mother's arms, or maybe it's me right now—one Victor to another, a future queen to a lost one.

Or maybe it's just a daughter with one last wish to her mother.

"I can only stay for a little while longer. As I said, time is the one gift we were never given, and I'm afraid this will be the last time I'm able to speak to you, but yes, let's share one last moment together underneath the sun. And, Asteria, you know I never truly leave you. I'll always be with you. As long as there is light left in this world."

We stay like that for a few more moments, the time ticking away too fast.

When she turns to look at me, her shimmering form grows more and more faint until I can barely glimpse any of her light.

"Whatever it takes?"

"Whatever it takes."

CHAPTER FORTY-SIX

The Victory Crown glimmers in the light of the night, my starlight hair iridescent and curling down to my waist. A shimmering veil of black and silver drapes the ground behind me, the swooshing sound of the fabric on the stone floor grounding my steps.

Elaborately decorated with silver, black, and deep blues, the palace is ready for a celebration of the kingdom crafted from the night and its shadows, but also its light.

The largest ballroom has been reserved for the final ball, if it can even be called a ballroom. The room is carved into the palace mountain with a magnificent view of the royal city, massive ancient pillars that bleed into the mountain the only walls.

Last year's final ball was a celebration of Soria and its new Victor, this one is only for Luna. Not only has the kingdom gained a new Victor, but a new king.

The mountain room is more crowded than I would have expected. I don't see anyone from Soria, but I'm sure the Sun King has at least a handful of spies hidden among the guests.

I haven't seen Elio since our last conversation when he

claimed he stayed for me and promised to help me, and I can't help wondering if he saw the humiliating way I was crowned Victor or if he left after I turned him down for the last time.

There is a low dais in the middle of the room with a throne made from heaps of silver stars stacked on top of each other. Two crescent moons rest at the top of the stars, one serving as the back, the other as the seat where the new king is lounging.

The silver crown with spiked tips adorns his head, his body clad in one of his usual dark suits despite his new status and title. A cruel smirk pulls at his lips when he sees me approaching, his dark eyes devouring me with a hungry gleam.

"Your Majesty."

"Victor," he croons, rising from his throne to hold out a hand for me.

Our rings clang together as our hands meet, the bond between us crushing my heart, the wall of ice encasing it too fragile.

"May I have this dance?" He raises a dark eyebrow as he dips his head toward me.

"Since you're actually asking me this time, how could I possibly say no?"

He leads me onto the dance floor, a snap of his fingers making the orchestra play a slow seductive tune. The king's arms snake around my waist and I fold my hands around his neck, ignoring the invisible bond trying to draw us closer together.

"Don't look at me like that, starlight. I told you it would all work out in the end."

I don't realize I'm scowling until he reaches forward and smooths the frown between my eyebrows with his thumb, his touch sending a pulse of heat through my body.

"But everything didn't work out, did it? The bargain may be over but our bond is not, or has your mark disappeared? Mine certainly hasn't." As if in answer, the mark on my arm throbs, and for a second it feels like the black lines are alive—like snakes coiling and twisting underneath my skin.

Star twirls me around, the silver skirt of my dress gliding across the floor. "The final ball isn't over until the sun wakes up. There's still time left."

"If there's one thing we're lacking, it's time," I mutter, ignoring all the eyes upon us.

He snorts. In the dim light of the ballroom combined with the moonlight seeping in from the open walls, he looks so much like a king it's heartbreaking.

"Will you just tell me one thing?" I erase all anger from my face, replacing it with my best look of innocence.

Amusement glimmers in his eyes, the dark storm retreating just enough to let some of the midnight blue shine through. "Ask away. As king, how could I not grant the latest Victor a favor?"

I repress the urge to give him a cruel smirk. "Starlight. Tell me why. You said you would tell me the truth when you became king."

His body tenses underneath my hands, the muscles on his back shifting underneath the fabric of his jacket. His eyes bore into me, his head tilted to the side to reveal the binding mark that is still lingering even though he just replaced his title of warrior prince with king.

There's a gleam in his eyes when he finally opens his mouth to answer, a mirror image of the glittering stars above. But then his gaze flickers to something or someone behind me and his striking features are overshadowed by anger. "I'm afraid you'll have to wait for that answer just a little while longer, starlight," he says, ending our dance and grabbing my hand to lead me back to the dais.

The crowd of people parts to let us through, the music halting as the entire room falls silent.

"If I may have your attention," Star says as he steps onto the dais. "Because of the unfortunate circumstances of the finale–" the corners of his lips tug as silver flares in his eyes, "–the crowning of the new Victor was rushed and not as grand as it should be."

He reaches forward to adjust the crown on my head, his fingers tucking a loose curl behind my ear. "I'm sure you're all curious about what these new circumstances will mean for me and my wife." He holds up a hand, a secretive smile on his face. "Don't worry, we will address such matters in a moment, but for now–"

Star steps away so I'm the one standing at the front of the dais, the long skirt of my dress draped down the stairs. "It's time for the words of victory." He gives me a wink before leaning his hip on the armrest of his silver throne.

I glare at him before turning around to greet the crowd of people in front of me, the eyes of the ones behind me boring into my back.

I've only seen one victory speech. I didn't make it to the finale, but I made it just in time to see Elio's crowning.

Elio was so shaken and bruised he barely got any words out, and the moment of his crowning will be forever seared into my mind. "This–This is–Winning the honor of becoming a Victor has been a lifelong dream," he said, his lip bloody and bruised and one eye black from taking a blow to his face. "This year's Tournament has as always been filled with magic and magnificent games challenging every aspect of what it means to be a true warrior. Such a warrior as I am honored to represent for the next year."

The Sun King placed the Crown of Victory on Elio's head in the middle of a battleground with dead warriors lying at their feet. The burning of the bodies had just started, and black smoke rose behind the new Victor of Soria.

The scene was an entirely different one than this, the following ball a grand celebration and beautiful ceremony filled with so much light even the sun struggled to outshine it.

It is clear that neither my words nor my presence is welcome tonight. The people send me displeased looks as low murmurings pass between them, none of them at all interested in the supposed Victor before them.

I do my best to ignore the growing need to just vanish in all the darkness of this kingdom as I start speaking. "As the king said, the finale was under unfortunate circumstances," I say, my voice not as high and confident as I would like it to be.

A woman standing at the front of the crowd rolls her eyes before muttering something to another woman beside her.

I press my nails into the scars of my palms so hard I break the skin and an exasperated sigh sounds behind me.

"I'm sure we can all agree that a Victor shouldn't be crowned under such circumstances–"

A man standing at the side of the dais yawns before sending a scowl in my direction.

I turn my head enough to look at the king behind me. He raises an eyebrow in challenge, one of his usual smirks on his lips. I suck in a sharp breath before turning back to the crowd that's only looking more bored and displeased.

Make them listen.

The words echo in my mind, the loss of her presence squeezing my heart, but the words linger, allowing me to clear my throat and raise my voice.

"I'm not here speaking as your Victor."

I remove the Victory Crown from my head, holding it up for all to see and shocked voices break out around me.

No one has ever removed the Victory Crown before absolutely necessary and especially not on the day of the crowning. It is a symbol of an ancient bargain, a glorious victory, and a prize for the Victor's kingdom.

The entwined strands of silver and gold glow in the moonlight as I carefully place it in Skye's awaiting hands at the side of the dais, the warrior giving me a pleased grin when her fingers close around it.

The Crown of Victory in the hands of the rebellion.

And then I gather the fabric of my dress in my hands and reach underneath my skirt.

The shocked murmurs change to scornful words and mocking laughter.

And as I uncover another crown from the thick folds of my dress—shouts and screams erupt throughout the large room.

The crown of Elara shines in the night—so bright that even the sun would be envious.

A large crescent moon gleams at its center, the other phases of the moon shining underneath, and silver stars make up the rest of the crown. Crystal pearls hang between the symbols of the night sky, the crown brighter than the stars above and the throne behind it.

A crown displaying the great power coursing through the veins of the one bearing it, the power of the Goddess of the Night and the Queen of the Moon.

A crown lost no longer.

"I am here speaking as your queen."

I place the crown on my head.

Finally.

A violent pulse rocks through me and silver light erupts from the mark on my neck.

Ferocious waves of magic blast through the room, darkness and silver blending into a raging inferno. Dark tendrils of power claw on the pillars holding the room together, the force of the magic rattling the entire mountain.

It's as if a door has been unlocked, the room within crammed with so much power–too much power–that has been growing and screaming for a release for centuries.

The magic is crafted from the darkest night, but most apparent is the silver light so different from the gilded light of the sun. The light of the moon, yes, but also the light of the countless stars around it.

Starlight.

The magic reaches for me and strikes my heart with a forceful shove that makes me stagger back, my heartbeat slowing before rapidly speeding up again.

The feel of the magic pouring into me is strangely pleasant, and it feels as if a last missing piece is finally being put together and making me complete.

In the reflection of the dark pillars, I see that the now silver lines of the binding mark have expanded, now reaching up to my jawline and down to my collarbone and shoulder. And as I lift my hand to the moonlight seeping into the room, I see that the hand bearing the alora ring is marked too.

It's as if the veins on the left side of my body have replaced the crimson blood with pure silver, the magic of Elara filling me so much that my body has no choice but to change.

Or maybe this is my victory mark?

I don't know how much time passes before the bright light dims and the magic retreats back into my soul and heart. The lines don't vanish, they only recede a little, still displaying the ancient magic I've claimed.

"This is the destiny between me and your king, as he promised would be addressed tonight," I say, my voice clear and loud as it echoes through the mountain and reaches far away from the palace. "Luna finally has a queen."

I can feel Star's dark presence behind me, the bond between us stronger than ever before. I can almost see it, and if I were to focus on it, I'm certain I could grasp it and bend it to my will.

Skye is the first to kneel. Auren follows quickly after, her servant's uniform replaced by a simple blue dress I found in my wardrobe. A few other people I don't recognize fall to their knees, likely from the rebellion.

The rest of the crowd is a chaos of loud voices and screams. Some of the people are clambering to escape the ballroom, others are frozen with shock, and most of the guards stationed around the room are looking at the king who is still deathly quiet behind me.

No one dares reach for me, and if they did–

I'm confident I'd be able to stop them.

Glaring at each person daring to look at me, I wait for the inevitable wrath that is sure to follow, and when a hand lands on my shoulder and the king finally moves to stand beside me, I don't even flinch.

"You heard her. Bow before your queen or bleed before her!" His voice reverberates over the chaos, a few of the people closest to us trembling as they fall to their knees.

And then I see that I'm not the only one marked by ancient magic.

The silver lines marking half of Star's body only make him more striking. The lines are pulsing and alive underneath the moonlight, lighting him up in a way I never could have imagined.

The light of the magic seems to fuel his power to a tangible darkness in the air, his power only a soft caress against my skin. His eyes are pure silver when he looks at me, his essence drawing me toward him, my soul yearning to be reunited with his.

I have no idea what this means.

There hasn't been a Lunan Queen since Elara and the consequences of a new one are unknown to the entire world, but I feel a storm brewing, the promise of lightning and darkness only a breath away.

"What are you up to, starlight?" Star mutters in my ear as he glides a finger over the crown on my head. His breath is hot against my skin, and every nerve in my body responds to his closeness.

"You're not the only one capable of playing games, Your Majesty," I mutter back, keeping my head high as I look down on the kneeling crowd.

"I guess not. I must say you are full of surprises lately." His finger trails down the side of my neck, over the silver lines, and I repress a shudder.

"The same could be said for you."

"How did you even find it?" There is a faint trace of curiosity and something that sounds a little like pride mixed with the anger in his voice. His eyes are back to their usual midnight blue flecked with silver stars, and the familiarity makes me grind my teeth together.

This is just another game.

"I've learned from the best schemer in the kingdom not to reveal my secrets."

Every trace of light disappears from his face as darkness erupts around us.

This time–I'm not afraid.

Star moves to stand in front of me, a towering figure of shadow. He leans forward so close his lips graze mine, and a pulse of fire surges through me. "Welcome to the darkness, Asteria."

The darkness disappears as quickly as it came.

Star moves back to his throne and pulls me with him, seating me on his lap and draping an arm around my waist to keep me in place. "I thought you were praying for freedom. Now our bond will never fade, not when you've declared yourself my queen."

I drape my legs over his thigh and look him straight in his dark eyes. "You were the one insistent on our marriage, and as your wife, it is my right. I refuse to be your consort."

A low chuckle mixed with a growl reverberates from his throat. "I should've guessed as much when you agreed to marry me. And what about your freedom? What about breaking our bond?"

"I will never be free as long as I'm bound to you. If I had left I would've been forced to feel every injury and attempt on the new king's life, only waiting for the day you would lose your throne and take my life with you," I snarl, leaning back to get as far away from him as possible–which is not far considering our compromising position.

"After everything, you have so little confidence in me." He bares his teeth, the silver lines on his neck blazing. "You could've been free. Now we'll never know if my plans to end our bargain would have worked. Congratulations, starlight, there is no escaping each other now."

"You owe me an answer," I say, narrowing my eyes and ignoring his fuming anger.

"Fine," he snaps. "You really want to know?"

"Yes–"

"Isn't it obvious? You're a part of the kingdom of night, of darkness. You always have and always will be, even though you just became aware of it. You are a part of the night, yet you're filled with light. The night is not only darkness. It also has the brightest light, and you have light from both sides of the sky."

"You knew from the start."

It's not a question but he answers anyway. "Yes. I didn't fully understand why. Now I do."

I bite my lip to keep from revealing my rising anger, only giving him a strained smile instead. "And the nickname has nothing to do with your nickname, Star?"

"Of course not," he snarls, his eyes once again nothing but pure darkness.

This time, I'm unable to stop a cruel smirk from crossing my lips. Star's grip around my waist tightens, and I relish in knowing that I seem to be the only one able to break through his carefully polished demeanor.

"I'll tell you another truth, *starlight*." His lips trace the curve of my neck, his breath tickling my ear. "You have the light to fully bring out my darkness. You have the light to fuel my dark. My magic. My power. And you just made a grave mistake in declaring yourself my queen and giving me very easy access to that power."

My body is nothing but heat as flames blaze inside me, my heart beating so hard I'm confident he can feel it, perhaps even hear it—who knows what the royal magic does to mortal senses.

"This changes nothing between us," Star growls in my ear. "My goal is still the same. No matter how much you try to stop me, I will end this. Once and for all. I will never stop trying, not until the stars stop shining."

Invisible shackles snap shut around my wrists, trapping my magic and seizing control of my movements, and with no training of my powers, I have no way to break out of it.

The king snaps his fingers, nodding at two guards emerging from the shadows. "Take her to the dungeons."

"But, Your Majesty—"

"Now," he snaps, pushing me off his lap. "And be discreet about it." His black eyes rake over me, from the crown adorning my head to the hem of my dress, before boring into my eyes.

"This isn't over," I sneer as I glare at him, willing my eyes to be a fiery storm of alora—the very essence in the mountain underneath us.

"Oh, definitely not." He snaps his fingers again and the guards step onto the dais.

"You're wrong," I say as one of the guards places a hand on my arm to escort me away. "I don't have the light to fuel your darkness. I have the light to destroy your darkness. To outshine it once and for all, with light from both sides of the sky. And what are you if not shadows and darkness, *King* Star?"

EPILOGUE

The wall of the dungeon is cold against my back, the musty smell of wet stone filling my nostrils. A lonely silvery flame flickers in the skylight on the wall outside of my reach, licking up the wall like the fury fuming inside of me.

Gods, I hate this place.

There are guards stationed outside of my cell. They think I don't see them, and perhaps I wouldn't if it weren't for the darkness now living inside me.

The guards don't even glance at me as I rip the sleeve of my dress to reveal the throbbing silver lines on my arm. In the light of the skylight, the lines sparkle with unspent magic, and a primal part of me is screaming to let it all out.

Not yet.

I unclasp one of my earrings, the silver star luminescent in the palm of my hand. A sigh of relief leaves my lips as I press the pointed end of the earring into the skin above the dark mark that is now entwined with the silver lines.

The blood pouring from the wound is not red. It is pure silver.

A name is a very powerful thing. Make sure you just don't give yours away to anyone.

Star isn't your real name?

Of course not.

And what if someone knew your true name?

They would have a whole lot of power.

The silver lines are curious at the new addition–they glow brighter, the pulse within them beating harder.

The bleeding lines linger for only a second before the skin stitches itself back together, and when it does, I repeat the message over and over again.

The message is not a star this time, but letters.

A single word.

A name.

Caelus.

The name of a destined enemy and an unexpected ally.

The name of a warrior. A Victor. A prince. A king.

The name of my husband. The name of the new Moon King. Star's name–his true name.

Caelus.

The magic inside me is thrashing and roaring as I lean my head back against the wall, not bothering to prevent the drops of silver from seeping into the fabric of my dress.

I'll drown the entire mountain in my blood if I have to.

The magic is singing louder now, urging me to let it out, screaming to light up the darkness within me.

No one ever believed I could be queen.

My life was doomed from the start, cursed by the actions of those before me. I was forced into a deadly bargain shoved upon me by another queen, forcing my destiny to the enemy kingdom where my light would be diminished forever, replaced by a never-ending darkness.

No one ever believed I could be queen.

But look at me now.

My fingers trace the bleeding letters on my arm, pressing them deeper into my skin, the pain soothing and welcome.

Caelus.

The silver blood is clear evidence of the royal magic of a queen now flowing in my veins, the lines marking half of my body daring anyone to question me.

No one ever believed I could be queen.

But look at me now.

I am *the* queen.

A dark presence seeps into me as the true name of the king throbs on my arm. It's as if my mind and soul have finally been connected to his, my heart no longer only beating for me, but for the both of us.

CAELUS.

I scream the name in my mind, over and over as more of his darkness creeps inside of me like a dark mist trying to shroud the light.

The flame in the skylight explodes into an inferno of flames that licks up the walls and ignites the guards before they're smothered by a gust of dark wind that leaves everything in darkness.

Caelus.

Asteria.

A cruel smirk pulls at my lips as his voice echoes in my mind, blocking out the screams of the dying guards in the darkness.

The Tournament might be over, but the war between our kingdoms has only just begun. Just like the war between the King of the Moon and the queen with light from both sides of the sky.

Let the real games begin.

TO BE CONTINUED...

Printed in Poland
by Amazon Fulfillment
Poland Sp. z o.o., Wrocław

36578081R10363